P9-APN-343

the

WHISPERS
of WAR

ALSO BY JULIA KELLY

The Light Over London

the WHISPERS *of* WAR

JULIA KELLY

GALLERY BOOKS

NEW YORK LONDON TORONTO SYDNEY NEW DELHI

Gallery Books
An Imprint of Simon & Schuster, Inc.
1230 Avenue of the Americas
New York, NY 10020

This book is a work of fiction. Any references to historical events, real people, or real places are used fictitiously. Other names, characters, places, and events are products of the author's imagination, and any resemblance to actual events or places or persons, living or dead, is entirely coincidental.

Copyright © 2020 by Julia Kelly

All rights reserved, including the right to reproduce this book or portions thereof in any form whatsoever. For information, address Gallery Books Subsidiary Rights Department, 1230 Avenue of the Americas, New York, NY 10020.

This Gallery Books Canadian export edition January 2020

GALLERY BOOKS and colophon are registered trademarks of Simon & Schuster, Inc.

For information about special discounts for bulk purchases, please contact Simon & Schuster Special Sales at 1-866-506-1949 or business@simonandschuster.com.

The Simon & Schuster Speakers Bureau can bring authors to your live event. For more information or to book an event, contact the Simon & Schuster Speakers Bureau at 1-866-248-3049 or visit our website at www.simonspeakers.com.

Interior design by Michelle Marchese

Manufactured in the United States of America

10 9 8 7 6 5 4 3 2 1

The Library of Congress has cataloged the hardcover edition as follows:

Names: Kelly, Julia, 1986– author.
Title: The whispers of war / Julia Kelly.
Description: First Gallery Books hardcover edition. | New York : Gallery Books, 2020.
Identifiers: LCCN 2019027311 (print) | LCCN 2019027312 (ebook) | ISBN 9781982107796 (hardcover) | ISBN 9781982107802 (trade paperback) | ISBN 9781982107819 (ebook)
Subjects: LCSH: World War, 1939–1945—England—London—Fiction. | GSAFD: Historical fiction.
Classification: LCC PS3611.E449245 W48 2020 (print) | LCC PS3611.E449245 (ebook) | DDC 813/.6—dc23
LC record available at https://lccn.loc.gov/2019027311
LC ebook record available at https://lccn.loc.gov/2019027312

ISBN 978-1-9821-4332-9
ISBN 978-1-9821-0781-9 (ebook)

For my family

the
WHISPERS
of WAR

prologue

How quickly Marie had become used to her new routine. Breakfast for two in the morning—porridge cooked on the hob with water since milk was already becoming scarce. On days when she wasn't working, she would tidy up and do any necessary food shopping before a small lunch. And, without fail, just around two o'clock, she'd listen for the brass flap of the letter box to squeak open and the second post to drop with a satisfying thunk *onto the polished entryway floor.*

Now she sat wrapped in a blanket in the corner of the big rose-patterned sofa that faced the mews she'd come to think of as home. She'd somehow managed to forget everything—the war, her worries, her fears—and relax into the pages of her book, a Rosamond Lehmann novel she'd borrowed from the built-in shelf next to the fireplace. Forbidden at her aunt and uncle's flat, it seemed less daring here, as though she were the sort of woman who read about divorce and affairs every day.

Marie was so caught up that it was only when the letter box flap rattled back into place that she realized the post had arrived. Setting her book and blanket aside, she slipped her stockinged feet into a well-loved pair of slippers and rose.

Shivering, she pulled her light blue cardigan tighter as she stepped into the corridor and crouched to scoop up the scattered letters. She began flip-

ping through them, looking for her name. She may technically have been a guest in this house, but she still received a letter or two a day.

Marie set aside two brown envelopes on the little sideboard. Three large square envelopes followed those. Then she saw her neatly typed name on a slim white envelope. She ripped it open.

Her hand began to tremble even as she stared down at the cheap paper, willing the sentences to rearrange themselves. Desperate for them to say something else. But there was no denying the typed words.

Her legs buckled under her, and she crumpled to the floor.

SAMANTHA

Now

one

Samantha clutched her passport, shifting from foot to foot as the line inched forward. All around her, her fellow passengers from the red-eye to London yawned, stretched, and blinked against the fluorescent light of the immigration hall. She hardly noticed the jostle of bodies, her attention fully fixed on the weight of the package and the half-scribbled notes in her brown leather shoulder bag.

She should have made this trip earlier. "Never put off for tomorrow what you can do today," one of the posters in her third-grade classroom read. It was stuck above the dry-erase board so her students couldn't miss the warning against procrastination. But teaching that lesson and actually living it were two very different things.

A series of dings sent her digging into her purse to retrieve her phone. She'd connected to Heathrow's Wi-Fi as soon as she was off the plane, but her messages had only just come through. There were six: one from her best friend in Chicago, Marisol, and five from Dad.

She read Marisol's first:

Saw U landed on flight tracker. U okay? How was the flight?

She fired back a quick message:

Long trip but I'm feeling okay. Just need to get my bag and
figure out the Tube. I'll let you know when I meet her.

Then she clicked over to Dad's messages. Rather than send one
long message, he always wrote a text a sentence, leaving a string of
stream-of-consciousness messages in his wake:

Hope you aren't too tired, sweet pea.
Your mother and I are waiting up to hear from you so let us
know when you land.
Your mother says she's proud of you for doing this for her mother.
I am, too.
Love you.

She smiled and shook her head, sending him a quick message:

Just landed. The flight wasn't too bad. Will you and Mom go
to bed? I don't want to throw off your doubles game for your
tennis tournament tomorrow. Love you both.

She slipped her phone back into her purse and pulled out her passport as she approached the front of the line. A guard behind a high desk
checked it without comment, and she couldn't help but be grateful she
didn't have to explain why she was in the country. If she had, what would
she say? This trip wasn't business, but it certainly wasn't bringing her any
pleasure either.

After collecting her small suitcase, she navigated through the cus-
toms gate past immigration and out into the bustle of Heathrow's Ter-
minal 5. Even after the crowded passport line, the shock of all of those
people almost knocked her back. Loved ones hung over the sturdy silver
barrier separating the arrivals space from the restricted area. Clusters of
drivers in crumpled white shirts and slim black ties looked bored as they
held up names on iPads or hastily scribbled on pieces of paper. Everyone

here seemed to know who they were waiting for. They had a reason to be there.

You have a reason to be here, too, and there's no more ignoring it.

She shook her head to throw off the thought and focused on her first challenge: getting to West London. It shouldn't be too difficult. She took the El from her Lincoln Square apartment to school every weekday. She could navigate the Tube. And then it was just a matter of finding the right combination of streets that would lead her to the house.

Maybe it had been a mistake to accept Nora's invitation to stay with her. The woman was 103 years old—it was incredible she was still living at home—but Nora had been insistent from the moment Samantha called the number her grandmother's lawyer had provided. Every email exchange between Samantha and Nora contained some variation of the phrase *I won't hear of my dearest friend's granddaughter coming all the way from America and staying at a hotel. You'll stay with me. And you must meet David, too.*

Samantha tilted her head back to read the signs overhead. Trains to her right. She settled her carry-on higher on her shoulder and adjusted her grip on her suitcase handle, but then she spotted a tall, dark-haired man holding a sign that read Samantha Morris, Chicago. Her name. Her city. But she didn't have anyone here to pick her up from the airport.

Unless . . .

"Excuse me, are you David?" she asked, stopping in front of the man.

"Samantha?"

She swallowed. "Yes."

David will meet you at Heathrow, one of Nora's emails had read. But she'd batted away the offer. Being collected by her grandmother's best friend's grandson was a step too far. She wasn't helpless. Except now that he was here, she couldn't help but feel the tiniest bit of relief.

"I thought that might be you. You look like your photograph." His hand dove into the pocket of his jacket and out came a photograph, a little bent at one corner. He handed it to her. "My grandmother gave me this to make sure I'd be able to spot you."

She stared at the photo. "This was taken when I was eighteen, just before I left for college."

"I did point out that it might be a little out of date, but she insisted. She said that your grandmother hardly aged from eighteen to forty, and you wouldn't either."

"I had no idea Grandma had sent this to her," she said, toying with a crease at the corner.

The left side of his mouth tipped up, showing the hint of a dimple in his cheek. "You should prepare yourself for Gran to know quite a bit about you."

She pressed a hand to the center of her chest and the guilt that had lodged itself there. She should know more about this woman who had clearly been dear to her mother's mother, but Samantha had learned of Nora less than a year ago. There was so much of her grandmother's life that remained a mystery, and it was her own fault.

"We should hop on the Tube. Gran has been tracking your flight since it was over Ireland and calling me every ten minutes to make sure I haven't forgotten that I'm to pick you up," David said, taking her suitcase so gently she hardly noticed he'd done it.

"She sounds like quite the woman," she said as they fell into step.

David's eyes slid over to hers, and the corner of his mouth kicked up again as though he were enjoying a joke that only he knew the punch line to. "Oh, she is."

❧

Throughout the entire trip into London on the Piccadilly line, David carried the burden of the conversation as Samantha's foggy brain tried to contend with being rocketed six hours into the future. He was just telling her about his work as a strategy consultant for a digital marketing firm when he paused.

"Let me know if you'd like me to stop talking. It's just that I always struggle to stay awake on the train back after flying in from the States and find distraction helps," he said.

"Do you work in the US often?" she asked.

"From time to time. It depends on the client and the project."

"Well, please don't feel as though you need to stop talking. If I don't have something to focus on, I think I'll fall fast asleep," she said.

"Gran will help, too. She's thrilled you're visiting and will want to hear all about your family."

She shifted in her seat, acutely aware of the notebook filled with half-started ideas and crossed-out lines that was wedged in her purse. "I don't know what I'll be able to tell her that she doesn't already know. Nora said she wrote Grandma Marie letters right up until she died."

He nodded. "Your grandmother was one of the few people she would still write to with pen and paper. She has arthritis in some of her fingers, and holding a pen can be uncomfortable. She mostly emails now, although she is a demon with texting, too. I taught her how to use dictation software about six months ago, and she's better at it than I am."

Samantha found that she liked the idea of a 103-year-old woman so effortlessly adapting to technology that stumped people fifty years her junior.

After they transferred at South Kensington and rode the District line three stops to West Kensington, David led her up the stairs and out of the train station to a large street he told her was North End Road. Black cabs, red buses, motorcyclists, and cars streamed by on the wrong side of the road. People lined up outside of a minuscule boutique coffee shop. A couple of schoolgirls in matching blazers and pleated skirts shrieked and ran, pursued by a pair of boys in maroon sweaters and navy trousers.

"They're still in classes?" she mused out loud.

David glanced over. "What was that?"

"I'm just surprised. I'm an elementary school teacher, so my life has always been dictated by academic year. It's actually the reason I'm here now. We let out the third week of June, but I gave myself a week off before traveling," she said, trying not to think about how she'd also let the academic year serve as a convenient excuse to put off her trip until now.

"Then you have good timing. Schools don't let out here until closer to the end of July, which is when most people with kids go on holiday. It can become a little hectic traveling," he said.

They turned off the main road, and David led her down a couple of side streets before stopping in front of a three-story white Victorian terraced house. He pulled out a key, opened the door, and stepped back to let Samantha pass him.

"David, is that you?" called a voice through an open door off the hallway on her right. The voice was aged, but unmistakably strong. "Is Samantha with you?"

"In you go," he said, nodding to the door with a smile of encouragement.

Keeping her left hand wrapped around her purse strap to hide its tremble, Samantha edged through the doorway and into a wide room painted in a soft white with two bay windows that looked out over the street. Generous deep blue curtains fell in graceful folds to the floor, and a black iron fireplace topped with an elaborately carved mantel on one end of the room emitted a sense of grandeur and comfort all at once. And sitting near that fireplace in a high-backed wing chair was an old woman who sported a carefully combed snow-white bob and cherry-red lips. Nora Fowler.

Nora, who Samantha could see was tall even sitting down, was swathed in a gray cardigan with a colorful silk scarf tied at her throat. Near at hand on a side table rested a late-model iPhone and a slim computer.

"You must be Marie's granddaughter," said Nora, nudging her glasses up her nose to study Samantha with sharp pale blue eyes.

"Hello," said Samantha, the leather of her purse strap cutting into her hand as she gripped it even tighter.

"My word, you look like her. You have the same hair." Samantha had to resist the urge to fuss with her shoulder-length blond hair.

"I'm glad David found you," Nora continued. "I should've known when he didn't text me."

David, who'd just rounded the door, swooped in to give his grandmother a kiss on the cheek. "I should've texted you."

"Yes, you should have. Come, sit with me, Samantha," said Nora, gesturing to the sofa across from her.

Samantha sank down into the spot. "Thank you for sending David. He has been a great help."

"I didn't want you lost and wandering around London, although he very rightly pointed out that it's difficult to become lost these days with mobile phones. Still, I couldn't take the risk. Not when you said you have something for me."

Samantha sucked in a breath. She had expected to have a little more time to . . . she didn't know. Make small talk and drink tea? Wasn't that how her grandmother had said Brits started every visit? But somehow Samantha doubted that small talk had ever interested the woman in front of her.

"When Grandma died, I found out that she'd made me the executor of her will," said Samantha, pulling out the packet she'd carried with her from Chicago.

"Not your mother or your aunt or uncle?" asked Nora.

She hesitated. "I was surprised, too. If there was a motivation behind the decision, Grandma never shared it with anyone. She laid out her wishes, and she had three very specific instructions. She wanted a memorial service, not a funeral, and she was very clear that it should be celebratory, not sad."

A soft smile touched Nora's lips. "What's left of my generation has seen too much sadness to want to invite any more somberness into the world."

"She liked summer best, so the ceremony will be next month." A sudden wave of longing for her grandmother's soft accented words, brilliantly colored dresses, and orange blossom perfume came over her. She wanted to hear Grandma Marie call her *mein Liebling* again. Samantha cleared her throat around a lump of emotion. "The next request was that she wanted me to deliver this to you. In her will, Grandma said it had to be delivered by hand. She wanted to make sure that you received it."

"What is it?" asked Nora, eyeing the parcel in Samantha's lap.

"I don't know, actually. All the instructions said was that it's meant for you. I'm sorry that it's taken me until now to bring it to you."

"She died last October," said Nora.

"I'm a teacher. I couldn't—" She stopped herself. "I could have asked for a leave of absence from my school. I could've made arrangements to come sooner, but I didn't."

"Why did you wait? I'm one hundred and three years old. Time isn't something I have a great deal of," said Nora, managing to sound teasing rather than sharp.

"It hasn't been easy losing her. We were very close when I was a girl, but then I went to college," she said.

"And life got in the way?" Nora finished for her.

Samantha nodded, the shame coursing through her.

"What was the third request?" asked David.

She started, realizing she'd forgotten he was there. "Oh, I'm supposed to give her eulogy at the ceremony."

"Not an easy thing," said Nora.

"No. I have a whole notebook of ideas in my purse, but nothing sticks. How do you eulogize a woman when all you really know about her is that she was a sweet grandmother who drank coffee all day and hummed Nina Simone songs while she mopped the kitchen floors? Her life was more than that."

Nora smiled. "Much more. Remember, I knew her before any of us knew who Nina Simone was."

Tell me! It was on the tip of Samantha's tongue. Most of her memories of her grandmother were from her childhood. She remembered snowy winter afternoons hunched over a puzzle together at the dining room table. She recalled how Grandma Marie would sneak more marshmallows into her hot chocolate than her parents would allow. She could almost feel the heavy clack of the old antique typewriter as she pretended to interview Grandma Marie and write up little stories to proudly hand out to her family members, her own little newsletter.

Then the memories became more vivid but somehow less personal. Samantha breezing by her grandmother in the living room on her way to go out with friends. Begging off the early start to cooking Christmas lunch because she was in college and she was going to use every extra moment to catch up on the sleep she hadn't gotten during the semester. Samantha had started to grow up, and her relationship with her grandmother had slipped to the background of her life.

Now, sitting in a living room more than three thousand miles away from home, Samantha lifted up the package her grandmother had entrusted her with. "So here it is."

"Bring it here," said Nora.

Carefully, she placed it in the old woman's lap and watched Nora's fingers glide over the thick manila envelope. They lingered on the address written in faded ink. "David, be a darling and help me with this."

He stood and leaned down to peel back the flap of the envelope. "Would you like me to take the things out of it?" he asked.

"I'm not helpless, David," Nora chided him.

Samantha watched as Nora began to draw out bundles of paper tied with string—six in total—and a velvet bag.

"What are they?" asked David, peering over his grandmother's shoulder.

Nora let out a long sigh. "My letters from the war. I sent them from all over, but you'll be able to tell the ones I wrote when I was on leave because I always marked that I wrote them from Cranley Mews. I was so proud of that house. I bought it before the war when young women did not own their own homes. David's uncle Colin lives there now with his partner, Greg. And I had a job, too—quite modern, really."

Nora picked up the velvet bag, undid the drawstrings, and tipped it onto its side. Out into her wrinkled hand fell a thin gold chain and pendant set with a deep blue stone.

"That looks like yours," said David.

"David, will you go fetch my jewelry box?" his grandmother asked, her eyes still fixed on the pendant.

"Are you okay?" Samantha asked Nora as David slipped out of the room.

The old woman looked up, as though just remembering that Samantha was there, too. "Yes. Nostalgia has a way of creeping up on me these days."

Samantha watched as she set the necklace aside, undid the ribbon on one of the bundles, and pulled the top letter out of its envelope.

"'The twenty-sixth of February, forty-four,'" Nora read. "'Dear Marie, I know if I tell you where I am the censor will only black it out, so all I will say is that I've never experienced a February day like this one.'" Nora glanced at her. "I had been dispatched to Afghanistan. I don't think I've ever been hotter in my life."

David came back, a black leather box fashioned in the style of a small steamer trunk in his hands. He set it down next to his grandmother's laptop and waited as she opened the box and pulled out the stacked trays. Rings studded with gems of all colors caught the light, and rows of earrings sat like bonbons in a chocolate box. Nora lifted the lid of a little built-in box and drew out a necklace on a gold chain from which hung the pendant's twin.

"I gave this to your grandmother, Samantha," she said, gesturing to the necklace from the velvet pouch. Then she ran her thumb over the necklace she'd just retrieved. "This one was our friend Hazel's. And this"—she reached into the neckline of her sweater—"is mine. It's lapis lazuli. I had them made for us out of a bracelet I used to wear. I wanted to make sure that no matter what happened during the war, we would always have a piece of each other with us."

"Did you say Hazel?" asked Samantha.

"Yes. Why?" asked Nora.

Samantha rummaged around in her purse until she found her passport. She flipped to the identification page and then held it out for the older woman to see.

"My middle name is Hazel. Samantha Hazel Morris. But all I know about her is that she's a family friend I've never met. Who is she?"

"Was. She died about twenty years ago. You probably were too young to remember your grandmother coming over to visit Hazel and me every five years or so," said Nora. For a long moment, she sat silent, but then she nodded, as though making up her mind. "David, will you go put the kettle on? I think we're going to need fortifications for this, and I'm sure Samantha is tired from her trip. A cup of tea will perk us all up."

"Now." Nora turned her attention back to Samantha. "I met your grandmother in 1928, when she and Hazel and I were all put in a dormitory together. The Ethelbrook Misfits, we called ourselves that first term, although the name never stuck."

MARIE

August 1939 to October 1939

two

AUGUST 25, 1939

The threat of war hung heavy in the air, refusing to dissipate with the fog each late summer morning. It was impossible to ignore as Marie shuffled around a newspaperman who stood outside the Hyde Park Corner tube station shouting, "Britain signs on to help Poland! Mutual assistance treaty!" as he hawked the evening edition.

Marie ducked her head and hurried on, knowing that buying an evening edition of the paper would only delay her more. She'd stopped at the shop around the corner from work to pick up two extra batteries after seeing the queue at lunch, and it had taken her twice as long as she'd thought it would to hand over her shillings. Still, her handbag was heavy with the batteries now, and she knew she'd made the right choice, because if war came there was sure to be a run on them.

If? When. She gritted her teeth and shoved the thought back as though that would somehow keep Hitler from grasping for any more of Europe.

She was nearly panting by the time the Harlan Club came into view, its proud redbrick face embellished with a cornice of white stone—a gem even on stately Mount Street. Wallace, the doorman, stood tall in his oxblood uniform coat, ready and waiting for the arrival of any of the Harlan's ladies as they popped in for cocktails or a bit of supper before a Friday night at the theater. She may not have been a member, but she liked to think that she might one day be mistaken for the sort of woman who could walk up to this building knowing she belonged.

Wallace opened the door and, with a tug on the brim of his black top hat, folded into a half bow. "Good evening, Miss Bohn."

"Good evening, Wallace. Has Miss Walcott arrived?" she asked.

"I'm afraid not, Miss Bohn, but I'm sure Mrs. Harper will make you comfortable while you wait."

Drat. Mrs. Harper, the club's receptionist, always glared at her as though Marie intended to filch the club's silverware when her back was turned.

"Marie!" called Hazel from the club's lobby with a cheerful wave that sent her strawberry-blond pageboy sweeping her shoulders. "I was just wondering where you'd gotten to."

"Batteries," she said, leaning over to brush her friend's cheek with a kiss light enough that her cherry-red Tangee lipstick didn't transfer.

"That was me last Saturday. Forty minutes to buy two tins of potatoes, one of peas, and six boxes of matches. None of the government's warnings against hoarding seem to be making a bit of difference."

"I suppose everyone's afraid there might be rationing again." The Harlan's grandfather clock chimed the quarter hour. "Is that really the time?"

"At least you're not as late as Nora. I feel as though we've been waiting for her to show up whenever we meet ever since we were at school."

"Because we have," said Marie.

"Well, Mrs. Harper and I have spent the last quarter hour becoming quite fast friends," said Hazel with a grin.

The receptionist glared over the edge of the desk she sat behind. If the Harlan were a medieval castle, Wallace merely operated the drawbridge. Mrs. Harper was the true gatekeeper, always watching at her perch. The stout, sour-faced woman, who knew every club member on sight, had never really approved of their band of three's habit of meeting at the Harlan on the last Friday of every month. Luckily, there was little she could do. Marie and Hazel were Nora's friends, and while she may not have been able to guarantee them membership to the exclusive—and expensive—club, Nora had enough clout to make sure they would always be welcome as guests.

Wallace swung the door open again, and Nora rushed in, her color high and her black handbag slapping against her side.

"Is Scotland Yard after you? You're practically running," said Hazel.

"I know, I know. I'm late," said Nora, her gasps of breath making her cut-glass accent even more pronounced as she stooped to kiss each of them on the cheek. "I'm sorry."

"Marie was late, too," said Hazel.

"No one likes a tattletale," said Marie.

"Like the time you told Miss Burford that I was sneaking sweets in the back of math class?" Nora asked.

Hazel shrugged as Marie and Nora handed off their coats to Mrs. Harper. "In my defense, I was thirteen, and it was only because you never shared your sweets—a character flaw, I will point out, that has not improved with age."

"If we're going to start the evening by pointing out all of my bad qualities, can I at least be armed with a drink?" asked Nora.

The Harlan's bar shared much of its design with the rest of London's much older Clubland properties, most haunted by gentlemen whose father's fathers had put their names down on the register the day they were born. The chandeliers were heavy brass and crystal, and gilt-edged mirrors lined three of the four walls. The pitch emanating from the room, however, was higher and altogether more distinctive, because the Harlan was entirely a woman's domain. The Founding Few, including Nora's grandmother, had started it in the waning years of the last century. Marie knew Nora relished telling the story of the ladies all sitting together in a Belgravia drawing room after a dinner party, talking about what an injustice it was that their husbands could swan off to their clubs whenever they felt like escaping the country or their families. Then one enterprising lady asked, "Why can't we do the same?"

Determined and well funded, the ladies had drummed up a membership, secured dues, and signed a lease on a property in the space of three months. From its opening, the Harlan offered respectable rooms to distinguished ladies for whom staying in a hotel without a chaperone was simply too scandalous. By all accounts, it had been a little bit home, a little bit meeting place, but mostly it had been a sanctuary.

Now, decades later, the three friends claimed the small cluster of armchairs closest to the Harlan bar's large iron-fronted fireplace. It would be some weeks before the weather turned cold enough for the staff to stack the grate with heavy logs and light a roaring fire, but Marie had always liked this spot, even in the warmer months.

"I swear the Underground is worse every day. I was stuck on a train that wouldn't move for ten minutes," said Nora, explaining away her tardiness.

"It's only going to be worse if they decide to institute the blackout. Just think of it, not a single light allowed on the trains aboveground at night or in the stations," said Hazel.

"We'll be living by torchlight," said Marie, increasingly glad for the batteries in her handbag.

"What does Nathaniel think of all this?" Nora asked.

Hazel rolled her eyes at the mention of her husband. "He thinks the whole world has gone barmy. That all of this is just Hitler grandstanding, and that the Munich Agreement will be enough to keep him at bay."

The prime minister, Neville Chamberlain, had held off Hitler with the Munich Agreement almost a year ago, and much of Britain had breathed a collective sigh of relief. There would not be another war, they'd assured themselves. Now it looked less and less like a guarantee of "peace in our time," even if many people, like Hazel's husband, clung to it with all their might.

"But what of the Germans and the USSR signing a pact?" Marie asked, remembering a rather spirited debate a set of undergraduates were having earlier that week when she walked by them on her way to the German Department. "And the evening editions all have our treaty with Poland on the front page."

Hazel sighed. "Nathaniel refuses to speak to me about any of it. He thinks I'm warmongering."

"The thing that all of the girls in the Home Office can't stop talking about is this new program out of Hamburg. The host claims to be a former British diplomat who's seen the light and gone over to support Hitler," said Nora.

"Henrik insists on playing that," said Marie, her lips curling in disgust at the mention of her cousin's favorite program.

"I've never heard of it," Hazel said.

Nora leaned in, lowering her voice. "No one is supposed to be listening to it because it's pure propaganda, so of course everyone is. I'm sure it sends the BBC into fits that it can even get through."

"The man who hosts it is awful. He says the worst things about the British. Naturally, Henrik finds it hilarious," said Marie.

"The host sounds like one of us," said Nora.

"He sounds like you. Not me," Marie pointed out. When she'd arrived in this country from Munich, she'd tried to lose her accent, but no matter what she did it lingered. Most days it was soft—but recognizable nonetheless—but if she was ever angry or drank one glass of wine too many, it came out in full force. Which is why she never let herself lose her temper or indulge in "just one more drink." She'd learned over the years that it was best to make everyone around her more comfortable by being just that little bit less. Less German, less aggressive, less objectionable.

"Marie, have you had any word from your mother?" Hazel asked.

She dipped her chin, wishing her friends didn't know her so well that they'd spot a lie from one hundred paces. "Yes."

"But surely that's a good thing," said Hazel, always optimistic.

"What did her letter say?" Nora asked.

She unsnapped the top of her handbag and pulled out the letter, now soft from being read over and over. "Here. It's in French." All of her letters over the years had been in French. Hannah Bohn acted more like a nineteenth-century Russian princess than a German businessman's wife, forsaking her native language for the elegance of French.

"You read it," said Hazel, nodding to Nora. "Your French always was better than mine."

"'Dear daughter,'" Nora read, translating as she went. "'We are well. The Schmieds asked after you yesterday evening as they always do, and Horst in particular was interested to hear that you had not been back to Munich in so many years. He says he misses you.'" Nora glanced up at her. "Who is Horst?"

Marie blushed and waved away the question. "Just a boy I used to play with. Skip down to the middle of the page."

"Spoilsport," said Hazel.

Nora skimmed down and resumed reading. "Here we are. 'You know that nothing bores me more than these questions you ask about politics. We did not send you away to school for you to cultivate an interest in things that are no business of a young lady.' Well, that is rich."

"Keep reading," said Marie.

"'It's fortunate for you that your father is more amused than insulted by all of this,'" Nora read. "'He tells me to write that he would never do anything to sacrifice the health of the business or our life here in Munich. He doubts there will be any war at all, and that the very best thing for him to do is to remain a friend to everyone.' So they're taking a stance of neutrality?"

Marie leaned over and plucked the letter out of Nora's grasp. "So it would seem." *Mutter acts as though the threat of war is a mild irritation, while it is all I can think about.*

"What does the rest of the letter say?" Hazel asked.

"One of their neighbors' daughters had her fourth child, and that same woman's youngest has joined the League of German Girls and already has a half dozen boyfriends. She also asks when I'll stop wasting my time in England and come home to marry. Of course, it would be a man carefully selected from an appropriate family—probably one in metal or who makes a part that Vatter could use in his engines."

"And you still don't think they would ever join the Nazi Party?" Nora asked. "There are all sorts of stories . . ."

"No," said Marie firmly. "Vatter has too many foreign contracts at the factory to want Germany at war, cut off from the rest of Europe. It almost killed the business during the last war when my grandfather was still alive. He will not want that again. Honestly, can't we talk about something else?" she asked.

Nora's eyes darted over to Hazel. "Can I ask how you're doing?"

The gentleness of Nora's voice—usually so direct and forceful—belied the importance of the question. Marie could see Hazel digging her fingers into her thigh, grounding herself.

"I'm as well as can be expected," said Hazel.

Marie glanced around to make sure no one was listening and lowered her voice. "Did you go to the doctor?"

Hazel bit her lip and nodded. "He says there's nothing more that can be done. We just need to keep trying, but we've been trying for six years. Ever since . . ."

Moving in tandem, Marie and Nora each picked up Hazel's hands.

"I'm sorry, I shouldn't have asked," said Nora.

Hazel shook her head. "I want you to ask. It's just difficult. I should know by now not to become excited, but this one was almost three months along. I thought we might finally have a chance."

The yearning in Hazel's voice tore at Marie's heart. She knew how badly her friend wanted a baby. How every month Hazel would tense with anticipation. How often she'd been disappointed. How elated she'd been the three times she'd realized she was pregnant. How each of the miscarriages had knocked Hazel back, threatening to plunge her into the darkness that had swallowed her when she'd lost her first baby, just weeks after marrying Nathaniel.

"Enough," said Hazel, tipping her head back and blinking rapidly as though fighting tears. "There's too much depressing talk in the world right now. It's our Friday together. Let's enjoy it."

Pierre, the Harlan's long-standing bartender, set down their usual drinks in front of them, and each of the women took a moment to sip from hers.

"Tell us what happened at the agency this week," said Nora, leaning her chin in her hand so that her bangles—all gifts from her grandmother—clinked as they settled halfway down her arm.

A little glint lit up Hazel's eyes, and Marie couldn't have been more thankful for Nora's ability to pull Hazel back into the light.

"You won't believe me when I tell you," said Hazel.

"This is promising," said Marie, smiling gamely.

"The Repeater is back."

Nora snorted as Marie groaned, "Doesn't that man have any pride?"

"Clearly not, and this time he's grown a mustache and dyed his hair raven's-wing black," said Hazel.

Tales of the Repeater had been a staple of their monthly suppers since the man had first shown up at the door of the Mayfair Matrimonial Agency, where Hazel worked as a matchmaker. The third son of a baronet with impeccable breeding but a serious deficiency of funds, the Repeater at first had seemed promising enough that Hazel suggested Nora might give him a go. Nora had laughed it off—just as she did all of Hazel's matchmaking suggestions—and a good thing, too. Hazel soon learned that no matter whom she matched him with, the woman would never be good enough. The lady would be too talkative, too tall, too rosy-cheeked, too blond, too made-up, too stupid, too well read. The Repeater was impossible to please.

"If you tell me that you've set him up again, I'll walk straight out of this bar," said Nora.

"Then it's been lovely seeing you, because I'm determined to find him a Mrs. Repeater," said Hazel, her eyes narrowing at the thought of solving the puzzle of her troublesome client. "Although at this point

I'm suspicious that he's mostly interested in watching me jump through hoops like a trained circus poodle."

"Perhaps he keeps coming back because of you," suggested Marie.

Her friend scowled. "You say that every time I mention a difficult client."

"And yet you still don't believe us," said Marie.

"Even after that grocer with two stores in Fulham who proposed with a cut-glass sapphire ring," said Nora. "You said he wouldn't stop telling you about his plans to expand his empire with you by his side."

"Oh, stop teasing me. I have Nathaniel. I'm happy," said Hazel with a sniff.

Marie caught Nora's eye, but neither said a word.

"Well, God help the poor girl who ends up with the Repeater, whomever she is," muttered Nora, adjusting her steel-rimmed glasses before taking a sip of her gimlet.

"Do you know, it's funny, with all of this talk of war you would think that business would be slowing down. Instead, it's never been better. I had three new clients at the agency today," said Hazel.

"Anyone interesting?" asked Marie.

Hazel scrunched up her nose in thought. "One. A widower. Actually, Nora, you might know him. His late wife's family runs with your mother's set."

"That is not necessarily a recommendation. What is his name?" asked Nora.

"You know I don't share names," said Hazel.

"What are Marie and I going to do with his name?" Nora argued back. "Plus, if I do know him, I might be able to help."

Hazel sighed. "Mr. Richard Calloway."

Nora cocked her head in thought. "It doesn't ring any bells."

"What happened to Mr. Calloway's wife?" asked Marie.

"Cancer. He didn't go into too much detail, but it all sounds very tragic," said Hazel.

"Poor man," said Marie.

"He's good-looking in a quiet, elegant sort of way. Smart, too. A civil engineer," said Hazel.

"Like Onkel Albrecht," said Marie.

"Precisely," said Hazel. "I think he's going to be one of the considered ones. Hard to place, but when he knows, he'll know."

"That's better than jumping into things feetfirst, I suppose," said Nora. "If you're interested . . ."

Nora scowled at Hazel. "Don't you dare."

Hazel sighed. "I wish you would let me match you up. Either of you."

"Not a chance," said Nora with a firm shake of her head.

"Marie?" Hazel asked hopefully. "You know, I won't simply pair you up with just anyone. I am actually quite good at my job."

"You know we think you're a smashing matchmaker," said Nora. "It's my skills as a prospective wife you should worry about. I'm hardly at home because I'm usually at the Home Office—"

"Working too hard for a boss who doesn't really appreciate you?" Hazel filled in sweetly.

Now it was Nora's turn to scowl. "All I'm saying is that I'm hardly domesticated myself. How could I possibly be expected to keep a husband?"

"A husband is not a dog. It isn't as though you'd need to walk him every day," said Hazel.

Nora shrugged. "Still."

"Marie?" asked Hazel.

"Oh, no, thank you," she said in a rush.

"Why not?" Hazel pushed.

"I—"

"Maybe she already has a man in mind," Nora teased.

Marie's mouth opened then shut again. Was she that transparent? She couldn't lie to her friends, but there were things she kept from them—little bits of herself she wasn't yet ready to share—and Neil was one of them.

"Don't worry, Marie. You needn't tell a soul until you're ready," said Hazel, leaning over to pat her arm.

"There's no one," Marie insisted before realizing she was fussing with the hem of her skirt for no good reason.

"Mm-hmm. Marie's the kind of dark horse who won't tell us that she's seeing a fellow until two weeks before there's a ring on her finger," said Nora.

"And you're the kind who would telephone the day before her wedding and invite everyone around without letting them know what the celebration is for," Marie shot back.

Nora pointed to herself. "I'm not planning a trip to the altar, remember."

Hazel slumped dramatically into her chair. "I don't know why I bother."

"Frankly, darling," said Nora, "neither do we."

three

The mornings were Marie's favorite time of day. Rising an hour earlier than anyone else in the family, she could pretend that she had the flat to herself, except for Frau Hafner, who came before any of them awoke. Her aunt and uncle's housekeeper would set out toast and pale yellow butter for Marie along with the tall, chipped stoneware coffeepot that radiated comforting heat. Even after years of school breakfasts and teas while boarding at Ethelbrook, Marie couldn't understand the British devotion to the insipid brown water that was tea.

Steam curled up off the coffee as she poured it into her cup. A twinge of guilt gripped her, as it did every morning. Her aunt and uncle lived a comfortable life, although it didn't touch the grandeur that Nora had given up when she'd left the family home after her father's death. Still, Marie knew that if Neil ever found out that the Müllers employed a housekeeper to cook and clean five days a week, he'd disapprove.

So when Marie left her aunt and uncle's home every day, she became a different woman. No longer was she the devoted niece who had spent months helping Tante Matilda work intricate lace for the antimacassars that covered the sofa and armchairs in the sitting room of their Bloomsbury flat. She became Marie the university secretary, and every other Monday, she would take the bus to Tottenham and become Marie the comrade. That version of herself could walk into a party meeting next to Neil, shoulders back and head held high. That Marie felt special.

Neil had asked her twice before she'd agreed to attend her first meeting of the Communist Party of Great Britain. Even then she wouldn't have said yes if it hadn't been for Anna, the secretary to the Russian Department. Her offices were just two doors down from the German Department, which Marie kept running in perfect order. Anna often came along for a chat at midmorning, cigarette hanging from her long fingers and cup of coffee in her other hand. But for all that Marie liked Anna, her friend enjoyed stirring the pot just because she could.

Anna had been leaning against Marie's desk, speaking with great authority on the "reducing" effect of cigarettes, when Neil walked out of Herr Gunter's office. As the graduate student who showed the most promise and seemed most likely to obtain the one vacant role in the department after completing his dissertation, Neil had the run of the place. The way he swaggered into the offices might've repelled Marie, except that she found herself drawn to the sheer charisma of him. At some point, she finally admitted to Anna that he was handsome. Anna had teased her but agreed, and Marie had felt a squeeze of jealousy in her chest.

On that day, he stopped in front of Marie's desk, his hip leaning against the edge of the pressed wood. "Do you want to come see me speak tonight?"

"Speak?" Anna asked.

"At a meeting of the CPGB—sorry, the Communist Party of Great Britain," said Neil.

"I know what the CPGB is," said Anna, flicking a bit of ash into the tray Marie kept on the far corner of her desk.

"It's just a party meeting, not a rally, but I could use the moral support all the same." Neil grinned down at her. "I've been asking Marie to come with me for months, but she always says no."

"Is that right?" Anna asked, casting her a sly look.

"It isn't the easiest thing to get away on a Monday night," Marie protested.

"I think what's really the matter is that her aunt and uncle disapprove of radical politics," Neil told Anna.

He was right, but that didn't make Marie any less annoyed when Anna's eyes narrowed—a sure sign she was about to do something mortifying.

"I'm sure Mr. and Mrs. Müller wouldn't mind if you were to attend meetings of the Women's Institute. Such a good Christian organization," said Anna.

Marie stared at her. "You want me to lie to my aunt and uncle?"

Anna shrugged. "People do it all the time."

That might be the case, but Marie didn't. Not to Tante Matilda and Onkel Albrecht. How could she risk their disappointment, when they had done so much for her? They'd given her a home, a family, a life here in London. They'd welcomed her to stay when nothing waited for her back in Germany but empty days and hollow disappointment.

"I couldn't lie to them," said Marie.

Neil laughed. "You sound horrified, *kleine Maus*."

Little mouse. It was the sort of endearment a man might bestow on his girlfriend—or a parent on a child. But there was something about hearing *him* say it that made her believe that maybe one day he, Neil Havitt, prodigy of Herr Gunter and one of Royal Imperial University's bright stars, might see her as something other than the department's diminutive secretary.

"I'll go."

Neil and Anna looked at her. "What will you tell your aunt and uncle?" he asked.

She pressed her lips together, unsure of whether he was teasing her or not. "I will think of something."

"What about you, Anna?" he asked.

Anna's glaze flicked between Marie and Neil, and then she blew a stream of smoke out of the corner of her mouth. "Another time, maybe. I'm engaged this Monday."

"Then it will just be Marie watching, and I'll consider myself a lucky man," he said with a wink for Marie. He'd strolled off to the office he shared with another graduate student, leaving Anna holding back her laughter.

Faced with her commitment to Neil, Marie had, in fact, told her aunt and uncle the fib about the Women's Institute. It was so little a lie that it wouldn't hurt them, she'd rationalized. Tante Matilda had been delighted Marie had decided to join the thoroughly respectable group of do-gooder women, which had made Marie's stomach clench, but she smiled through the discomfort. On the following Monday evening, she'd met Neil for the bus to Tottenham.

The party meeting had been a crush of people, all greeting each other and chatting. He seemed to know everyone and introduced her around as she hung close to his side until it was time for the speeches.

Neil had spoken fourth out of a lineup of six and had come off the stage wearing a light sheen of sweat on his brow and a triumphant glow.

"How was it?" he asked, dabbing at his forehead with a handkerchief.

"You were brilliant," she said, although in truth his speech had been shorter than she'd expected. She was so used to Neil, the apple of the German Department's eye, that she'd been a little disappointed when he hadn't been the main speaker.

But before she could examine that thought any further, he'd leaned down and kissed her on the cheek, pausing long enough to say quietly, "Thank you, *kleine Maus*."

She'd let him persuade her to come to the next meeting two weeks later, and then the next. That had been four months ago.

A door creaked open somewhere in the flat as Marie spread butter on a roll. She sat up a little straighter. Then the dining room door swung open and she relaxed again. It was only Henrik.

"Why do you always wake up so early?" her cousin asked in German, squinting in the glare of the overhead lights that lit the room.

"Good morning to you, too," she said, watching him drop into his chair with a wince. "Do you have a hangover?" She clacked her cup hard on its saucer.

Sure enough, he winced again and rubbed his forehead. "Not so loud."

Marie rolled her eyes but said, "Here," and lifted the heavy coffeepot, pulled his cup closer, and poured. "Drink this."

He gripped his cup so tightly it was a wonder the handle didn't snap off, and drained it. Then he extended it expectantly. With a sigh, she refilled it.

"Where is Frau Hafner?" Henrik asked, slumping back in his chair.

"Probably in the kitchen, where she usually is at this time of day."

He waved a hand before him. "And where's my breakfast? What's the use of a housekeeper if she doesn't do her job?"

"Frau Hafner isn't a mind reader, Henrik. She likely didn't know that you would be up this early."

"This is breakfast time, isn't it?" he asked.

"It is for most people." This was the first time she'd seen Henrik at breakfast in weeks.

As though summoned by his surliness, Frau Hafner pushed through the door, holding a plate in one hand and a pot of jam in another. The housekeeper's eyes fell on him, and she stopped short. "Herr Henrik, good morning."

"I want breakfast," he said.

Frau Hafner's nod was wooden as she set down the plate in front of Marie. "I will bring you something now."

"Thank you," Marie murmured, and the housekeeper laid a gentle hand on her shoulder that seemed to say, *He is a burden we all must carry.*

Marie turned her attention back to Henrik. He had stolen a slice of toast off of her plate and was crunching on it.

"Are you going to work today?" she asked.

"It's Monday, isn't it?" he shot back.

She leaned on the table. "It really is fortunate that you work under your father, Henrik. Who else would tolerate you showing up late on a Monday morning stinking of schnapps?"

"I don't stink of schnapps," he said. But then he gave the air a sniff. "I will bathe before I go."

"What exactly were you doing yesterday evening?"

"I was out with like-minded men," he muttered.

Drunken fools who like the sound of their own voices is more like it, she thought, but kept her opinion to herself. They'd had this quarrel before, and it wouldn't be very long until Henrik would snarl and remind her that she was his cousin, not his sister, and therefore a guest in this house no matter how long she'd been living there.

She sighed and pulled the folded newspaper set at her uncle's place toward her. All she could see of the main headline was "Britain to—"

"Should you be touching that?" he asked.

"Why not?"

"It's my father's."

Her gaze flicked up, but Henrik's head was turned, making his expression difficult to read.

"Onkel Albrecht encourages me to read the paper. He says it's best that we all know what is happening in the world. He doesn't trust Hitler," she said.

That earned her a grunt and nothing else.

An only child, she'd wished for a sibling, and she'd briefly hoped Henrik might fill that role. Instead, her cousin mostly treated her with contempt or simply ignored her. Once, when he was twelve and she was fourteen, he'd stolen Frau Hafner's tin of cooking oil and dumped the entire thing over Marie's bed while she was shopping with her aunt for Christmas presents. The oil had destroyed the mattress, bedding, and Marie's suitcase that had been sitting next to the bed. That had been the one time Marie had ever heard Onkel Albrecht yell at the boy, and Henrik had spent all of the holiday sulking in his room.

Accepting that she would never have an easy way with her cousin, she'd instead clung to her sisterhood with Nora and Hazel.

She folded her napkin and pushed back from the table. "I should finish getting ready." She left, but not before unfolding her uncle's paper so she could see the full headline: "Britain to Germany: We Stand by Poland."

"Our cause is the cause of the people. We must do everything we can to quell the spread of fascism across Europe. It is time for the people to rise up—rise up against the fascist state that has infected Germany!"

The hall exploded into applause as the barrel-chested man who had barked his speech for the last hour brought his remarks to a thunderous close. Marie watched him clutch the podium and look out over the crowd before him with the satisfied expression of a man who knew his command over the public.

The woman sitting next to Marie nudged her and shouted over the applause, "You'll write to your friends and family in Germany, won't you? Tell them that we are with them."

Marie started, but Neil leaned over her, his hands still clapping. "Of course she will. Marie is as dedicated to the cause as any of us."

The woman gave a satisfied nod and returned to her adulation of the speaker.

"Neil," Marie whispered to him.

He shrugged. "We all have to do what we can, Marie. I've told you, it isn't just about attending meetings."

She bit her lip. She was doing more than attending meetings. He, more than anyone else, should know that.

After her first two visits to CPGB meetings, Neil had asked her to look over one of his speeches before he delivered it the following week. He'd probably thought she would just read it and hand it back to him with morale-boosting praise, but as she'd been sitting at her desk it had seemed natural to reach for a pencil. She'd marked up the text, scribbling suggestions in the margins and swapping out phrases with ones she thought would have more impact. He had the ideas, but the execution had been . . . well, she had been sure he'd simply had an off day.

The next time he'd stopped by her desk, she'd handed the papers back to him, a little sheepish even though she knew her suggestions were good. He'd glanced at them, thanked her, and walked away. For a week, she'd been crawling with nerves, but when he took the stage she heard her words coming out of his mouth. The next time he had a speech, he appeared again, set the typewritten sheets on her desk, and walked off. She'd edited him again, and again his speech had shone. Every time someone had walked up to him to praise his words, she'd felt a little of that shine rub off on her—even if she was the only one who knew it.

"Come on," Neil said as the applause around them died down. He grabbed her and tugged her along the row of seats as people began to stream out of the hall. Clear of the seats, he looped her hand through the crook of his arm.

"Did you enjoy the speech, *kleine Maus*?" he asked.

"It was . . . illuminating," she said softly. She still lost her tongue a little when he called her *kleine Maus*. Nora would've burst out laughing, but it wasn't Nora's teasing she was most wary of. It was Hazel, who would smile and then launch into a thousand and one questions about who Neil was, what she liked about him, how he made her feel. Marie couldn't answer those questions. Not yet. She knew that Neil wasn't perfect. He could be a bit pompous, marching into Herr Gunter's office within days of beginning his graduate work and demanding to meet the cantankerous academic with an air that made it sound as though Herr Gunter should be honored to work with *him*. And Neil had a habit of speaking about his work on Goethe and the Sturm und Drang movement a little too long. And there were moments when Marie thought that he wielded *kleine Maus* as a reminder of her place rather than the endearment she hoped for.

Still, Neil was human—complicated and fascinating—and most importantly he seemed to like her. He wasn't perfect, but neither was she. She kept her worlds apart—her home, her friends, and dinners at the Harlan were so different from the infectious excitement of the CPGB meetings and Neil.

"The pub?" Neil asked.

"Yes," said Marie, still a little tickled by the mere idea of going to a pub. Even ones that allowed ladies in the lounge seemed slightly daring to her, for she was sure that Tante Matilda had never stepped foot into a British drinking establishment.

Neil glanced around. "Let's go a different way this time."

Breaking off from the crowd, they walked in silence. Marie relished the heat emanating from Neil's body and how it warmed her gloveless hands. He steered them down Scales Road, the lights in a few windows of the short, squat row houses diffused by cheap curtains.

"My friend works in the Air Raid Precautions Department. She says that the entire city will be under blackout orders if we end up at war," she said, remembering seeing the marked-up prices for black cloth at the shop near her aunt and uncle's flat the previous weekend.

"My mum remembers the blackout from the Great War . . . and the zeppelin raids." He fell silent for a moment before saying, "The speaker tonight was right. Hitler won't be kept back with diplomacy."

Marie swallowed. "We don't know that."

"I do," Neil insisted. "I can see it everywhere, but no one wants to come right out and say it. We're going to be at war again sooner rather than later, and the more we deny it, the more ill prepared we'll be."

"I don't think the government will let us be unprepared," she said, thinking back to all Nora had confided about her work.

"The Home Office is gearing up as though we're going to meet the end of days," Nora would say. "Air raid shelters, gas masks, volunteer air raid wardens. We don't know what Hitler will hit us with—if he hits us at all—but we'll be ready for him."

Every time, without fail, Marie had the same thought: *How wonderful it must be to feel so confident. So British.*

Yet Marie was glad for it. She wanted to think that people like Nora would be behind the great men of government if they found themselves at war.

"Don't make the mistake of trusting the politicians to take care of this." Neil snorted. "What will they do except send off a lot of men to be slaughtered, just like in the last war?"

She blushed. "I was just saying—"

But he cut Marie off with a decisive swipe of his hand through the air. "It's coming. The Germans want nothing more than to knock us back, and the people need to be prepared for it."

Marie stopped abruptly, and Neil's heel ground against the road as he swung around so they were facing one another.

"What?" he asked.

"Can't we talk about something else? It seems as though all anyone can do is mention the war and we aren't even in it," she said. "I'm tired of it."

He laughed. "What else are we supposed to talk about, silly girl?"

"Do not call me a silly girl," she bit out, surprised at her own intensity.

In the streetlight, she saw Neil's mouth open as though he could hardly believe that the woman he called *kleine Maus* had snapped at him. After a moment he said, "I'm sorry. I shouldn't have called you that."

"It's just that, well, you know I wasn't born here," she started to say.

His concern softened into a smile. "Is that all?"

She searched his face. "Do you know what happened during the last war? Thousands of Germans living here were forced to leave their homes. Put in camps. They lost their freedom. It ruined people's lives."

"That won't happen to you. You were practically born here," said Neil.

"Practically born here" was not "born here," but how did she explain that to a man who had never been taken by his uncle at the age of twelve to the local police station to register himself as an alien resident? He might be a student of German, loving the language and the culture and the people, but Neil wasn't actually *German*. He had the undeniable right to live in this country, while she was here because of the goodwill of the government. Marie suspected goodwill wouldn't go far during wartime.

Neil reached out a hand and tucked a wisp of her stick-straight hair behind her ear. Her lips parted, shocked at the achingly intimate gesture.

"You worry too much," he said.

"I don't," she whispered.

"I think perhaps . . ." But instead of finishing the thought, he kissed her. Their first kiss—soft, careful, and measured. It was a dreamy kiss, but the center of it held a question of more. She leaned into him in answer, gripping at the lapels of his jacket. He clasped her tighter to him as his lips pressed harder against hers, moving to suck on her bottom lip. She whimpered, her knees going weak, but she didn't pull back. She'd waited so long for this, hiding smiles as he walked into the offices, thinking about him when she looked over his speeches at the little desk in her bedroom.

Finally, Neil pulled back, his breath coming a little fast as he paused, their lips a mere inch apart. "Well, that was unexpected."

She flushed, flustered as her mind whirred back into gear. Unexpectedly good? Unexpectedly bad? What if she'd done something wrong?

As though reading her mind, he leaned in again and kissed her swiftly and softly.

Good enough. It must have been good enough.

Her fingers unlocked, and she slowly let her hands fall to her sides.

Neil scooped up her hand, tucked it back onto his arm, and gave her a small smile. "Come on, *kleine Maus*. There's a glass of sherry waiting for you and a pint of ale for me at the Stag and Hound."

four

The scrape of metal chairs against the cheap laminate floor of one of the Royal Imperial University's many teaching rooms pierced Marie's ears as she flipped her notepad closed and stuck her Biro through the metal coils at the top. She rocked her head side to side, seeking relief for the tired muscles in her neck and the headache that throbbed against her right temple. She'd been sitting in this room for nearly six hours now—lunch had been brought in by a pair of women pushing metal trollies laden with sandwiches—but Herr Gunter was bound to march her back to the department offices and plant her in one of the chairs across from his desk to take dictation.

With a sigh, she hauled herself to her feet, centering the cloth-covered belt of her light blue cotton dress. Without a glance back at her, Herr Gunter began to make his way out of the symposium room.

In the corridor, the stale scent of captive cigarette smoke dissipated and her headache eased a bit. Tante Matilda would probably take one look at her and send her to her room, a cold compress on her forehead and the lights dimmed low. It would be good to be mothered a bit after the long week.

It was nearly six o'clock, and the courtyard around which Royal Imperial's main campus was built was nearly empty save for a few undergraduates hurrying through the lightly misting rain with their books tucked under their arms. Most professors and lecturers were already on their way back to their country homes by train or by car. It was not, Marie had learned, fashionable to remain in London for the weekend if one were a serious academic. Far better to sequester oneself in the dimly lit study of a cottage, scribbling away at one's next article for publication.

Herr Gunter, however, was a different sort of breed. He *liked* the bustle of London, he'd told Marie when he'd arrived at the university just over a year ago. Therefore her boss was wholly unconcerned about keeping her past the hour that most commuters left for Paddington, Marylebone, and Waterloo.

"Fräulein Bohn, I wish to dictate my notes from the symposium," Herr Gunter threw over his shoulder as they approached the department offices.

"Of course, Herr Gunter."

"And I should like the notes to be typed and on my desk by Monday morning," he said.

From inside the department office, a telephone began to ring. Herr Gunter opened the door, and Marie saw that it was the phone on her desk. "I'll just be one moment," she said, hurrying around to pick up the receiver.

"German Department."

"Marie! Finally!" Hazel's voice came out sharp across the line.

"Hazel, what's the matter?" she asked as Herr Gunter unlocked his office and disappeared inside.

"You don't know?"

"Don't know what?" she asked with a frown.

"I've been trying to ring you for hours. It's happened. Germany marched on Poland."

Marie's notepad and pen slipped from her hands. "What? When?"

"Early this morning. The news broke a few hours ago. It's all over the evening newspapers and the radio bulletins. You really didn't know?" Hazel asked.

"I've been locked in a room with ten professors of German language and their graduate students all afternoon," she said, gripping the phone in both her hands. "I haven't been outside."

"Turn the radio on. The prime minister is due to speak any moment now."

"Maybe it isn't an invasion. Maybe it was just—"

"The Germans are bombing Polish cities. Troops are marching. There are tanks. Nora says there can be no doubt that this is the beginning." Hazel paused, and when she spoke next, her voice cracked. "I'm so sorry."

Marie sank onto the edge of her desk. It was happening. It was actually happening. A part of her had wanted to believe that Hitler wouldn't be so rash as to start another war, but it was impossible to deny what she could see all around her. People had begun fashioning crude carriers for their gas masks, looping string around the cardboard box they came in. Across the street from her building, workmen had taped long Xs on the windows in hope that it would minimize damage in case of explosion. All around her, Britain was preparing.

"Nora and I have been calling you all day," Hazel was saying on the other end.

Herr Gunter stuck his head out of his office door. "Fräulein Bohn."

"Hazel, I need to go," she said.

"No, you need your friends. Meet us at the Harlan as soon as you can."

"It's not our usual Friday," she said, numb.

"Take a cab, take the bus, walk. Just get to the Harlan," said Hazel.

Herr Gunter was glaring at her, so she agreed and carefully set the phone down in its cradle.

"I thought I made it clear that there are to be no personal calls in this office, Fräulein Bohn," he said.

Marie pushed by him.

"Fräulein!"

He could chastise her. She didn't care. She made straight for the small radio sitting on a card table to the right of his desk and switched it on. The radio gave a crackle and then came to life.

"This is the BBC World Service. The time is six o'clock," a presenter intoned.

"What is the meaning of this?" Herr Gunter raged behind her.

The presenter continued. *"Prime Minister Neville Chamberlain is due to speak to Parliament after reports of the German invasion of Poland before dawn this morning."*

Marie turned to see the blood drain from Herr Gunter's face. He knew just as well as she did what this all meant. Britain had signed a treaty with Poland. Any act of aggression against that country would mean war for Britain.

"German airplanes have begun to bomb Polish cities, including Warsaw," the presenter said in clipped, restrained consonants.

"That was my friend calling to tell me. We're at war," she said.

"Not yet," he said, edging away with his eyes locked on the radio as though it was the cause of all of this chaos. "Not yet. The British will give Hitler a chance to withdraw."

"Hitler won't withdraw."

"You don't know that," Herr Gunter barked so sharply she started. "I am sorry, Fräulein. Please turn that off."

She switched the dial off and hovered, not knowing what to do. Herr Gunter, however, began muttering to himself. He pulled his battered leather briefcase up onto the desk and began to open his drawers. In went a few papers and a leather-bound notebook.

"Is there something I can do, Herr Gunter?" she asked.

Not looking up, he said, "Call Emily. Tell her I must cancel dinner."

Marie frowned. "I'm sorry, sir, I don't know who Emily is."

Herr Gunter froze for a second, his eyes wide, but then he again dropped his attention to his bag. "Never mind, never mind." He shut the briefcase then and snapped the locks closed. "You may go, Fräulein. I will see you on Monday."

Marie walked quickly to her own desk, tossed her notepad into the top drawer, and pulled on her coat. Herr Gunter was still clattering around in his office, but she didn't want to stay to see if he would change his mind. She jammed her hat on and left.

Outside on the street, Marie thought about hailing a cab, but when she turned to stick out her hand, she caught a glimpse of a headline under the arm of a man waiting to cross the street: "Germany Invades Poland." Even after so many years, her accent was still unmistakable, and she didn't know what would happen if she approached a cab and asked to be taken to Mayfair.

Halfway down the block, a bus pulled up to the stop. Marie clamped her hand on her hat and sprinted for it as fast as she could in her heeled shoes. The mist made the pavement slick, but she managed to make it just in time. Handing her fare over to the man collecting it, she stopped herself before thanking him.

The bus was nearly empty, and she huddled in the back left corner for the entire trip until her stop on Park Lane. The rain had begun to pick up, and her hat and coat were soaked through by the time she made it to the club's front door.

"Miss Bohn," said Wallace, springing forward to put an umbrella over her even though the rain had already done its damage.

"Are they here, Wallace?" she asked.

"Miss Walcott and Mrs. Carey are just inside, miss."

Wallace held the door open for her and hurried her inside like a mother hen. Just inside the doorway stood Nora and Hazel. They both rushed to envelop her in a hug.

"You're here," said Hazel at the same time Nora asked, "Marie, how are you?"

She shook her head, her wet hair sticking to her forehead. "I don't know."

"Come," said Hazel, catching her by the elbow. "Sit down right here."

Her friends maneuvered her onto a red velvet sofa. "Let's get this off of you," said Hazel, lifting Marie's hat from her head. Without a word, Nora unbuttoned Marie's coat and helped her ease out of the clinging, wet fabric.

Marie watched as both of her friends fussed over her. Neither of them met her eyes, and her heart pinched. They didn't know what to say to her. These were her best friends in the world, and they didn't know what to do because everything had changed.

"When did you find out?" asked Marie quietly.

"I came to work, and the office was already in chaos. The journalists hadn't gotten hold of it yet and nothing official had been announced, but details were coming in over the secure channels. Sir Gerald was called into an emergency meeting to assess our preparedness, and I sat in to assist him. I rang you and then Hazel as soon as I could catch a moment," said Nora.

"Nora asked me to keep trying you because she wasn't sure that she would be able to stay by her phone," said Hazel.

"I see," said Marie.

Hazel covered Marie's hand with one of her own. "It could still be stopped. The prime minister has given Hitler until Sunday to withdraw his troops from Poland."

She shook her head. "He won't withdraw. We're going to be at war again soon, and I don't know . . . I don't know what that means for me or my family."

"Miss Bohn." They all looked up to see Pierre standing before them, a neat row of crystal glasses of two fingers of whisky each balanced on a silver tray. "If I might be so bold as to suggest that a little refreshment might be welcome."

"Thank you, Pierre. That's very kind of you," said Nora.

Marie was just reaching for a glass when Mrs. Harper swept around her battlements and descended on them. "No drinks in the foyer. Club rules."

Pierre straightened. "Given the circumstances, I thought an exception might be made."

"No exceptions," said Mrs. Harper.

"If any club member complains, I will be happy to speak to Lady Dora myself," said Pierre, invoking the name of the club's chairwoman.

With Pierre assuming the responsibility for any blame to be handed out that evening, Mrs. Harper turned, but not before muttering, "No need for any bowing and scraping to her kind either."

Nora shot to her feet, towering over the woman. "I beg your pardon, Mrs. Harper? Perhaps you would like to repeat what you just said."

Mrs. Harper stilled, and Marie died a little. Her hands clasped together tightly in her lap, and she prayed that Mrs. Harper would mutter an apology and this would all be over. Instead, the woman rolled her shoulders back and stared straight down her nose at Marie.

"I said that her kind should never've been welcome in a place like the Harlan. Now more than ever," said Mrs. Harper.

Marie grabbed at Nora's hand. "It doesn't matter."

"It does," said Nora, not looking at Marie. "Miss Bohn is my guest. Where she was born shouldn't matter to anyone, but within these walls it is completely inconsequential. I expect her to be treated with the same sort of courtesy that you would extend to any other guest of this club. Am I understood?"

"Young lady—"

"That is Miss Walcott to you," said Nora sharply. Marie could count on one hand the number of times she'd seen her friend unleash the full imperious nature that so many of her class wore proudly. She'd always loved Nora for her restraint, but in this moment she couldn't deny that her friend's fury was glorious.

However, Mrs. Harper still set her jaw and said, "I don't care if you're a Founding Few's granddaughter. I won't be told what to do by some jumped-up deb thirty years my junior." Mrs. Harper's voice broke, but she held her head up nonetheless. "It's the Germans that killed my Johnny."

Marie wished the floorboards would crack open and swallow her whole. The widow's grief was so acute it didn't matter that everyone had lost someone during the last war. And now to see it happening all over again . . .

"Nora." Marie tugged on her friend's hand. Nora looked down at her, some of the fire gone out of her eyes, but still she could feel her friend's body primed for a fight.

"We're very sorry about the loss of your husband, Mrs. Harper," offered Hazel.

"But that doesn't change the fact that Marie had nothing to do with it. You have no right to treat her that way," said Nora.

"You may put on airs, but that doesn't change anything. You're still a bloody kraut, and they should lock you up," Mrs. Harper hissed at Marie.

"What is the meaning of this?" The commanding voice of an older woman froze the foyer. At the head of the club's stairs stood Lady Dora, Countess of Dartman and Harlan Club chairwoman. Pierre wrung his hands next to her.

"Lady Dora, I must insist on making a complaint about the treatment of my friend. Miss Bohn came to the club at my invitation because she is understandably in some distress over the invasion of Poland and Mrs. Harper verbally attacked her. Completely unprovoked!" Nora exclaimed.

"And I say that her kind shouldn't be allowed past these doors. There is a war on, and we know what the Huns did the last time," said Mrs. Harper, the vehemence and vitriol back in full force.

Lady Dora arched a snow-white brow. "Mrs. Harper, unless you know more than the prime minister, I believe you will find that we are not yet at war. I would also remind you that you are not employed to impose your opinions upon the Harlan. You greet members and make a record of their guests."

"But—"

"Miss Bohn is German?" Lady Dora preempted as she began to descend the stairs, elegantly austere in a prim olive suit. "Of that I'm quite aware, as are the rest of the members of the club and its staff. You will also remember that Miss Bohn is the very good friend of Miss Walcott, which means that she is welcome at this club as long as Miss Walcott is."

When the countess reached the bottom, she turned to Marie. "I have no doubt that you will encounter your fair share of ugliness if this nonsense with Germany is not called off. However, I hope that you will find the Harlan always to be a place of comfort, good manners, and rationality in what will no doubt be irrational times."

"Thank you, Lady Dora," said Marie, rising from the sofa on shaky legs.

"Good, now I expect you ladies may need something fortifying given the day's events. Pierre will escort you to the bar." Lady Dora looked over her shoulder. "I will find someone to relieve you of your duties at the desk tonight, Mrs. Harper. Then you will come see me in my office."

As they followed Pierre up the stairs, Hazel let out a long, slow breath. "I don't think I've ever been so in awe of someone in my life as I am of Lady Dora right now."

"I should've just left," Marie murmured.

"No, you shouldn't have," said Nora firmly. "You have every right to be here."

"But I don't really, do I? And if something like that can happen at the Harlan . . ."

"You're almost as British as British can be. You've been here since we were girls," said Hazel.

"That doesn't matter," said Marie. "Everyone knows I'm foreign. I still have to register at the police station if I move. And—"

"It does matter. This is Britain. We're nothing if not logical. You've nothing to worry about," said Hazel.

But, although Nora nodded along, Marie couldn't miss the wariness in her friend's eyes.

five

CHURCHES EXPECT RECORD NUMBERS
AS CHAMBERLAIN'S DEADLINE APPROACHES
—*London Sunday Chronicle*, September 3, 1939

The waiting was the hardest part. All weekend, Marie pored over the morning newspapers that Onkel Albrecht discarded after his breakfast. On Saturday evening, even Henrik had lingered to sit around the radio in the flat's front room, listening to the news bulletin at half past seven.

"The British don't want another war," Onkel Albrecht had said after the bulletin had ended, looking to each of them. Tante Matilda had smiled tightly, Henrik had snorted and left the flat without a word, and Marie slipped off to her room, because if she had to pretend she wasn't frightened any longer she might scream.

Now, on Sunday morning, with the deadline for Germany's withdrawal inching ever closer, Marie and her aunt and uncle sat in the front room, the only sound Tante Matilda's knitting needles as she worked on the pale yellow cardigan for Marie. Finally, Tante Matilda clucked her tongue and muttered to herself in German, "It cannot be. It won't be."

"Chamberlain promised that appeasing Hitler and the Munich Agreement would work. It *must* work." Onkel Albrecht put a hand on his wife's shoulder, but Tante Matilda's mouth stayed a rigid line.

"All that we've done. Everything we gave up to come here. It could all be gone in a moment," said Tante Matilda.

"We left for Henrik," said Onkel Albrecht. "That was reason enough."

Marie had heard the stories in bits and pieces. Her aunt and uncle had lived through the Great War only to face hyperinflation as Germany tried to pay off its crippling war debt. While Tante Matilda's sister, Marie's mother, had married a man wealthy enough to survive on their foreign investments, the Müllers didn't have that luxury. Seeking stability and a better life, they'd moved in November 1923—just a few days before Hitler's failed Bier Hall Putsch.

Marie's aunt and uncle couldn't have known that Hitler's attempt to seize control of Bavaria, which landed him in jail, would be a sign of something much more sinister on the horizon. Instead, they continued to send Henrik back for the summers to stay with Onkel Albrecht's family. That is until August 1933, when over breakfast with her aunt and uncle in their flat, Marie had watched Onkel Albrecht open a letter from his brother.

"Henrik is at a Hitlerjugend camp?" Onkel Albrecht had asked, stunned.

Tante Matilda snatched up the letter. "But we told your brother—"

"He sent Dieter and Willi and he writes that he couldn't see us having an objection to sending Henrik, too."

Marie watched as her aunt lurched to standing, leaning heavily on the table with both her hands to brace herself. "Telephone your brother right now."

"But, Matilda, the cost of calling Germany—"

"I want him out, Albrecht! I read the papers just like you do. I know Hitler's consolidating power. And then there are other stories. Marta Bleiberg wrote me last month. She said it's not a good time to be Jewish back at home. They're thinking about trying to immigrate to New

York, but they're worried about interrupting the boys' schooling. Adele Tager said that people are being very careful who and what they speak about. I don't want our son anywhere near any of this. Bring him home, Albrecht," Tante Matilda finished in a whisper, but there had been no mistaking the force there.

Henrik had arrived on their doorstep a week later, sour-faced and sullen, and Marie had watched for the next six years as Hitler grasped for more power, more glory for Germany. All of the speeches Marie had listened to at her last CPGB meeting had left her with no illusions about the willingness of a man in power to cut a path of destruction in order to satisfy his own vanity. After Chamberlain's deadline passed at eleven o'clock, there would be no turning back.

She cleared her throat. "May I put the radio on?"

"Where is Henrik?" asked his father, folding the edge of his paper down to peer over the top of his spectacles.

Tante Matilda's lips thinned again, so Marie knew her aunt had also heard her cousin fumble with the lock and stumble into the flat around two that morning.

Onkel Albrecht sighed. "I'll wake our son. I cannot imagine anyone sleeping through this morning."

Marie turned the dial of the large radio inside the polished walnut cabinet that stood in the corner of the room.

"Not too loud," said her aunt immediately, as though that would somehow make the next few minutes better.

Dutifully, Marie turned the volume dial down just as the doorbell rang. She jumped, but Tante Matilda put her hand up. "Calm, calm, *mein Liebchen*. I will answer it."

Marie sank down into a seat, her hands folded in her lap to keep them from trembling as the last prayers of the church service being broadcast finished. Just two minutes until the deadline.

The drawing room door swung open and a rumpled Henrik shuffled in.

"You look terrible," said Marie automatically.

He scowled at her. "Where's Mutter?"

"She just went to answer the door," said Marie, peering closer at him. "You almost slept through a war."

"I wasn't sleeping, I was just resting my eyes," said Henrik, dramatically dropping onto the end of the sofa not occupied by his mother's abandoned knitting.

"Marie," called Tante Matilda, "your friends are here."

Nora and Hazel burst into the room, their hats still perched on their heads although they'd shed their coats between the front door and the sitting room. Her aunt followed them, a pleasant smile fixed on her face.

Marie shot up out of her chair and hugged them each. "Oh, I'm so glad you're here."

"Miss Walcott, Mrs. Carey, it is always a pleasure to see you," said Onkel Albrecht, switching to English out of courtesy to their guests.

"And you, Mr. Müller. I hope you don't think us rude to come crashing in like this," said Nora.

"Not at all," said Onkel Albrecht. "We're grateful you took care of Marie on Friday."

"Nathaniel is with his mother this weekend, so I rang Nora up and told her that if there was one place we should be this morning, it's with you," said Hazel. "Luckily she was already halfway out the door to a cab, ready to come collect me and loop back around to Bloomsbury. I hope you don't mind."

"What happened on Friday?" asked Henrik.

"Nothing," said Marie.

Her cousin narrowed his eyes, but Marie ignored him, not wanting to revisit the humiliation. It had not been the first time she'd felt anger directed at her because of her nationality. It was simply the first time her friends had seen it.

"Are you sure that—"

But Tante Matilda was cut off by Prime Minister Chamberlain's voice crackling over the radio.

"I am speaking to you from the Cabinet Room of 10 Downing Street. This morning the British ambassador in Berlin handed the German govern-

ment a final note, stating that unless we heard from them by eleven o'clock that they were prepared at once to withdraw their troops from Poland, a state of war would exist between us."

Marie's gaze swept around the room. Tante Matilda and Onkel Albrecht gripped each other's hands, eyes fixed on the radio as though praying Chamberlain would take it all back. Nora wore a grim look of resignation, and Hazel—Hazel was actually tearing up. Only Henrik seemed to be unaffected by the prime minister's words, which held all their lives in the balance. He sat with a leg hitched up over the arm of the sofa, as rumpled and unimpressed as a nineteenth-century fop.

"I have to tell you now," the prime minister's broadcast continued, *"that no such undertaking has been received and that, consequently, this country is at war with Germany."*

A presenter came on then, but slowly Onkel Albrecht rose to switch off the radio, his hand hesitating over the dial before turning back around to face his wife.

"Mein Liebchen," he started as tears began to roll down her face.

"You said it would not happen again," Marie's aunt said in German. "You said that if we moved here we would have a new life and no more war."

"I don't know. I don't know what to say," Onkel Albrecht murmured.

"Twenty-six years, Albrecht!" Tante Matilda's voice rose. "Twenty-six! Now you know what's going to happen to us. We're enemies. They'll send us away to those horrid camps they put people in like during the last war."

Marie's gaze cut over to her friends, both of whom stared dutifully at their hands, knowing they were witnessing a fight between husband and wife even if they couldn't understand the language. She knew she should herd them off to her room or out of the house entirely, but she was rooted to the spot.

What will happen to me? Will I be allowed to stay? I don't even know if I would recognize the house in Leopoldstrasse after all these years. What are we going to do?

Her breath came short and fast, and she pressed a hand to her chest over her frantically beating heart. This was Britain, a people of manners and honors and codes, yet the scars of the last war were deep. Everyone had sent their sons and brothers, husbands and cousins to fight, and so few of them returned. Marie saw the reminders every day. Veterans begging on the streets, some missing limbs or wearing half masks to hide the scars on their faces. The men who dropped their regiment casually into conversation to show they'd done their part for king and country. The furrowed brows as people calculated her age and realized that while she couldn't possibly have been born before the last war, they still didn't trust her.

"This wasn't supposed to happen," her uncle muttered again.

Henrik slammed his fist down on the rolled arm of the sofa with a thud. "Who cares if Hitler runs the entire German army over Poland's borders?"

"Henrik," his father said sharply.

"I'm going to my club," Henrik spat in German.

"To do what?" Marie asked.

"What do you think?"

Her aunt and uncle fighting. Henrik determined to get blotto. It was as though the declaration of war had ripped open a seam, and her family was coming undone.

The unmistakable, high-pitched wail of an air raid siren cut across London.

"Oh God," Hazel murmured, wide-eyed.

"Is it real?" Tante Matilda asked through her tears. But it was very real. They were at war.

Nora snapped into action, whipping around to face Marie. "Do you have an air raid shelter in the building?"

"The basement."

All at once, everyone was hurrying out of the flat, snatching up their gas masks as they went. The stairwell was filled with the muffled fall of footsteps against the carpet as the entire building wound their way down.

"Everyone in!" Mr. Thompson from the third floor was shouting at the basement door, waving people through as he leaned on his cane. "Hurry up! That's the ticket. Find a seat."

The basement was lit with a line of bare bulbs that hung on thick wires from the ceiling. Wood benches, constructed in June by a father and son who lived on the first floor, lined three walls. A small door next to the stairs led to what the neatly typed letter slipped under each flat's door had called "the facilities."

Nora and Hazel grabbed space on the far left wall, while Tante Matilda and Onkel Albrecht huddled in the corner a few people down. Henrik made a point of skulking near the stairs, arms crossed and frowning.

Marie could just hear Tante Matilda ask in German, "What is going to become of us all?"

The adults Marie had relied on her entire life were falling apart, and she didn't know what to do.

Seeing Marie's hesitation as she looked between her aunt and her friends, Onkel Albrecht nodded to her friends. "Go with them."

Marie tucked into the space Nora and Hazel made for her between them as the now-faint wail of the air raid siren continued.

"We've been swamped at work with requests from local councils for air raid shelters. I imagine there will be more call for them now," said Nora.

"Perhaps it will just be a brief conflict," said Hazel hopefully. "Germany was crippled by the reparations. How much money can they really have to spend on an army?"

But Nora shook her head. "I haven't seen any of the reports—they're considered top secret—but everyone at the Home Office says that Germany will be a tougher fight than the press is making it out."

"What about your parents?" Hazel asked Marie. "Have you heard from them?"

The question knocked her back. What about her parents? She'd hardly thought of them at all. Which made her wonder: Did they have a thought for her? Her last letter had been the one she'd shown the girls in the Harlan the previous week—hardly a surprise, since Mutter wrote once a month and never more—but maybe there would be a letter on its way. What parent wouldn't write to her daughter when war broke out between their two countries?

"I'll try writing, too, although I don't know if the letter will make it through," said Marie. "They live far away from any borders, so at least I know they will see very little of the fighting in Poland."

Hazel and Nora exchanged a glance. "You don't think they'll want you to come home?"

She huffed a laugh. "I expect Vatter will be too busy trying to figure out how to make sure the factories aren't requisitioned by the government, and Mutter will be strategizing how best to appear neutral in case popular opinion turns against the Nazi Party. That's the most important thing. Being smart and choosing the winning side by choosing no side."

"Marie, I heard something at work I think you should know. It's about registered aliens," said Nora.

Marie's chest squeezed so tight she could hardly breathe, but before Nora could say more, a soft voice asked, "Where do you work?" It came from a sweet older woman Marie recognized as Mrs. Scherer, one of her aunt's friends from the third floor. She sat next to her husband, a book in her hand as though she was just off to find a bench in a park to sit and read awhile.

"I'm at the Home Office. Air Raid Precautions Department, but I sit in meetings with the man who leads the Aliens Department," said Nora.

Marie knew in an instant what Nora's news was. "We're being classed as enemy aliens now, aren't we?"

"Yes," said Nora.

"It's what they did last time," said Mrs. Scherer with a sigh.

"What does that mean?" Hazel asked.

"It means any of us who are German could be arrested and interned," said Marie.

"Austrians, too," said Nora.

From her spot, Tante Matilda said, "I'm sorry, Mr. and Mrs. Scherer. You shouldn't have to go through that again."

Marie sent the older couple a questioning look.

"They interned Harald in one of the camps in the last war," said Mrs. Scherer, looking at her husband. "We spent so long apart."

"At first it was just people they thought might be dangerous," said Mr. Scherer, "but then more arrests started. You would see a friend at the market, and the next week you might find that they had been detained and sent away. After the *Lusitania* sank, people began to protest. They wanted all of the men locked up."

"I still remember when the police came to take Harald away while we were eating dinner," said Mrs. Scherer, touching her husband on the arm. "It was the worst night of my life."

"Sophie," he said softly before turning back to Marie and her friends. "It was chaos. No one knew what to do with us. I spent my first night in a jail cell, and then they sent me to Knockaloe on the Isle of Man. There were thousands of us all crammed together. The conditions were terrible."

"I managed to avoid being deported, but many of my friends and their children were," said Mrs. Scherer. "I knew families who lost their businesses, their homes, everything."

"But you stayed," Marie blurted out. "After, I mean."

Mr. Scherer patted his wife's hand. "This is our home."

"Harald was released when the war ended, and we did what we could to put our lives back together," said Mrs. Scherer. "The things we hear from our family back in Düsseldorf . . . We're happy we stayed. We're Jewish, you see."

"It won't be like last time," said Nora. "It can't be. There are many people in the Home Office who don't want to see mass internment again. If people are found to be sympathizers, they'll be locked up, of course—"

"And good riddance," said Mrs. Scherer.

"Everyone with an ounce of sense seems to admit that the mass internments in the last war were a mistake. Too many innocent people were locked up. People who hadn't done anything wrong," said Nora.

"And you really think that they won't do the same thing this time?" Marie asked.

"No, they're planning to do things differently," said Nora. "They're setting up tribunals. All of the Germans and Austrians in Britain who are registered aliens will have to be processed. There will be hearings before the tribunals, and they'll categorize people based on how much of a threat they might be. Category C will be people who are no threat and free to go about their business. Category B will have some restrictions placed on them. Category A will be considered a threat to security and detained."

"But they are still going to use the camps?" Mr. Scherer asked.

Nora hesitated. "Yes. The Home Office has already identified locations for some."

"Just like in the last war," Mrs. Scherer muttered.

"Will men and women both be interviewed?" Marie asked.

"Yes," Nora admitted.

She gulped a breath, trying to calm herself, but it was impossible. Months of fears she'd kept bottled up now had nowhere else to go. She'd been spiraling with anxiousness since the Munich Agreement, not believing Chamberlain one bit, and she'd been *right*.

"What's going to happen to me? What's going to happen to my family and Mr. and Mrs. Scherer and our friends?" asked Marie.

"I don't know," said Nora softly.

"Nothing is going to happen, because we won't let it," said Hazel.

"How can you say that?" Marie asked, her voice rising.

"I'm trying to be optimistic," said Hazel.

"But you don't know!" she cried, cutting through the murmurs in the basement. "We could all be taken away tomorrow. Or maybe it won't be that sudden. Maybe Onkel Albrecht loses his job. Then he cannot pay the mortgage on this flat because no one will hire him. Then what happens? What happens to all of us then?"

"Marie," said Tante Matilda from her spot down the bench.

Everyone was staring at her. She'd snapped. At her best friends. In front of all of these people.

Marie clapped a shaking hand to her mouth. "I'm so sorry. I'm—"

"Miss Bohn," said Mr. Thompson, using his cane as leverage to push himself out of his seat. "I hope that you know that, at least in this building, you and your family will always have friends."

Tears pricked her eyes as most of the people lining the benches nodded. "Thank you," she whispered.

Nora leaned in to her to whisper, "We'll always be."

"Just us three," Hazel finished the silly phrase they'd started saying to one another their first term of school at Ethelbrook.

Marie nodded weakly. She was still terrified, but she did appreciate the show of solidarity—from her neighbors, from her friends—even if it couldn't stop what was happening.

Through the silence came the faint wail of the all clear. Mr. Thompson nudged Henrik, who was still leaning against the wall next to the stairs, with the tip of his cane. "Come on, then. Up you go, young man, and open the door for the rest of us."

Henrik retreated up the stairs, and a moment later the basement filled with light. People began to stand cautiously and file out.

"I'm sorry if it seems as though I didn't understand why you're worried. I just don't want you to lose heart," said Hazel.

"I know," said Marie.

"But Hazel was right. No matter what happens, we will do everything we can to make sure that nothing happens to you," said Nora.

Hazel looped an arm through Marie's, and Nora did the same on her other side. She squeezed her eyes shut as her friends pulled her close to them. She wanted to believe her friends—she was desperate to—but she knew in her heart of hearts that there was nothing any of them could do if she came up category A.

six

Marie swayed as the bus swung out to take a lazy corner. It was the same bus she always took to work, but for the last few weeks she'd found herself surreptitiously eyeing her fellow passengers.

It was her voice that was still the problem. A dead giveaway. She could look every inch the young British woman, going to work just like so many other unmarried women living in London, but if she were to speak, this entire bus would know.

Still, she would rather take her chances here than cower at home. Tante Matilda spent too much of the day wringing her hands for her relatives who remained in Germany. Onkel Albrecht came home from work every night, his face drawn. He was, Tante Matilda confessed to Marie, afraid for his job and had pored over the family's bank accounts again and again, trying to predict whether they would be able to hold on to the flat if he lost his job in a wave of anti-German sentiment.

The government had offered all Germans and Austrians a solution to these pesky problems: go home. They had called it "Z plus 7" day—for seven days from the declaration of war, anyone who wished to return to Germany would be able to if they chose. Nora had told Marie that the Home Office suspected few would take the British up on this offer because many of them felt the way the Müllers did. Britain was their home now.

Even Henrik hadn't mentioned "Z plus 7" day. Instead, he seemed content to waste his hours away in his club. She truly didn't know why. From what she could tell, it had none of the grandeur or comfort of a place like the Harlan. Instead, it occupied a single floor of a building in Pimlico and seemed to attract a membership of young men who enjoyed drinking themselves silly on beer.

Twice she'd found Henrik in the early morning, facedown on the sofa in the living room with his shoes still on, sleeping off his drink. The first time she'd woken him up and then walked straight to the dining room, having no interest in or sympathy for his behavior. When it happened again last week, however, she'd stayed rooted in the spot.

"Your mother is worried sick over the war. I would think the last thing you'd want to do is add to her misery," she said, staring down at him with her hands braced on either hip.

Her cousin groaned and threw an arm over his face. Several papers covered in German scribbling came loose and floated to the floor when he moved his arm. The tangy scent of stale beer wafted up to her nose.

With a sigh of disgust, she turned to leave, but he said, "You act as though you're a part of this family."

A sour taste rose up in her throat. "I am a part of this family. I have been for years."

His scoff sounded like sandpaper, but that didn't dull the derision behind it. "You're not a Müller."

"My mother is your mother's sister. That makes us blood." But even she couldn't deny that those words rang hollow. Her mother had foisted Marie on her sister. Tante Matilda and Onkel Albrecht were compassionate and caring, but Marie had always wondered if some part of them couldn't help but resent her a little bit for that.

Taking perfect aim for the heart of her vulnerability, Henrik said, "You've been living off of my parents' charity for too long, pretending to be a lost little girl whose family doesn't love her. What did you do that your own parents sent you away, anyway?"

Slash after slash after slash. They were shallow cuts, but together they wounded deep.

The bus doors opened, and Marie readjusted the black leather hand-bag that hung on her wrist. She opened her mouth to ask the large gen-tleman wearing a brown suit to move but stopped herself. Instead, she put one hand to her hat, angled her shoulder, and pushed through to the crowd.

"I beg your pardon," said a short, red-faced man with an umbrella hooked over his arm that threatened to poke anyone who came too near.

She gave him a small smile but still pushed through until she stepped down onto solid pavement.

The rush of air after the stuffy bus felt good against her skin. She resettled her handbag on her arm and hurried through the tall iron and redbrick gates of Royal Imperial University's south entrance.

Students scurried around her, including two men with small cases on long leather straps that bounced against their hips as they walked. Their gas masks. Everyone was supposed to carry them or risk being fined by one of the volunteer air raid wardens who now patrolled London's streets. Normally Marie dutifully toted hers around, but that morning she'd heard stirrings from inside Henrik's room. In her hurry to leave the flat and avoid her cousin, she'd forgotten to pull her mask out of the coat closet near the front door.

Marie tucked her chin down and sped up her steps as she made her way down the eastern corridor of the main campus courtyard, right through the door to the humanities building, up two flights of stairs. There was no light on under the door of the Russian Department offices. No Anna yet.

The door to the German Department offices was unlocked, but that was hardly a surprise. Herr Gunter kept unpredictable morning hours. Sometimes he would come in for afternoon classes only, choosing to write his articles at his house in Wimbledon in the mornings. But then there were days when Marie would come in and find the office already hazy with cigarette smoke. Sometimes Herr Gunter even made his own coffee in the little kitchenette to the right of her desk, something he would never do if she was at work.

She put her handbag into her desk drawer and took off her hat and the cropped light brown and white checked jacket that topped her dress. Then she removed the dust cover protecting her typewriter. Before sitting down, she knocked on Herr Gunter's door. A pause. No sound. She checked her watch and frowned. That was odd. He must be in because she was certain she'd turned off the lights when she'd left the evening before—last one out, as happened so often these days as she tried to avoid Henrik's nights at home.

Deciding that Herr Gunter must've gone in search of something to eat, Marie set about pulling things down from the cheap laminate kitchenette cabinets to make fresh coffee while water boiled in the kettle. The professor was particular about his coffee, demanding a freshly made pot next to his hand whether he chose to drink it or not. It was one of the first things she'd learned when he'd taken over the German Department.

When the kettle had boiled, Marie poured the water over the grounds, replaced the lid on the Arzberg china coffeepot, and hefted the tray set with all of the accessories. She made her way back to the professor's door, setting the tray down to knock again. When there was no answer, she twisted the doorknob, picked up the tray again, edged the door open with her hip, and stopped in her tracks.

Herr Gunter's usually impeccable office was an absolute mess. Desk drawers were pulled half open, and the large leather office chair sat askew. Papers were strewn everywhere, as though someone had sifted through them at a manic pace, not caring that they were all over the floor. Half the books were missing, leaving those that remained leaning drunkenly on their shelves. The prints that lined his walls were all still there, but the oil painting of a ship canting dangerously in a storm by a minor nineteenth-century artist was gone.

"What on earth . . ."

Neil stood a few feet behind her, peering over her shoulder at the ransacked office.

"The door was unlocked when I came in, and when I opened it . . ." Marie looked in dismay at the office.

"Was he robbed?" Neil asked.

"I don't know." Marie looked around for a place to set the tray but every surface was covered. If this had been a robbery, the police wouldn't want her disturbing anything.

"Here, let me," said Neil. His fingers brushed over hers as he took the tray from her and set it down on her neat desk.

"Thank you."

She snuck a glance at Neil from under her lashes as he came back to join her just inside the door. She'd hardly seen him since the night he'd kissed her. After war had been declared, Tante Matilda had been nervous about Marie going anywhere in the evenings.

Still, she'd missed him. Seeing him in the department was always so different. Here they were on uneven ground, and she could feel it even more acutely since their kiss.

"What if he was taken?" Neil asked, breaking the silence. The letters ordering Germans and Austrians living in Britain to attend tribunals had starting coming out of the Home Office, just as Nora had warned her they would. Every resident alien now lived in fear of the postman, knowing that soon an envelope with their name on it would appear in their letter box.

Still, something nagged at Marie.

"Half of his things are missing. Far too many to fit into a simple briefcase. And the painting that hung over there was too large to pack away easily. I think he left it because he had to," she said.

"Very astute, Miss Bohn." A deep voice made both Marie and Neil jump. Behind them, a man in a nondescript gray suit came through to the main office trailing Dr. Bertram Hughes, the dean of humanities at Royal Imperial University. The two men stopped, their eyes fixed on Marie and Neil as though trying to read straight into their souls.

Marie folded her hands behind her back. "Dr. Hughes, good morning."

"Good morning, Miss Bohn. Is that coffee you've made?" he asked, staring down at the service on her desk. She nodded. "It's a shame it's not tea, but never mind. This is Thomas Dennison, from the Home Office."

Marie's hand flew up to the base of her throat. The Home Office didn't come out to German professors' offices for no reason.

"Miss Bohn. And you are?" Dennison asked, looking straight at Neil.

"Neil Havitt." He stuck out his hand, and Dennison examined it a moment before gingerly shaking Neil's hand.

"Are you a professor?" Dennison asked.

"One day," said Neil with a grin.

"Herr Gunter was Neil's adviser," said Dr. Hughes quickly.

Neil's smile fell at the mention of the connection between himself and Herr Gunter, but Dennison didn't look at him. Instead, he pulled a handkerchief out of his pocket and began to methodically wipe the hand he'd used to shake Neil's. "I see."

"Miss Bohn is Herr Gunter's secretary, as I mentioned," said Dr. Hughes.

"Yes. Miss Bohn, I'd like to speak with you," Dennison said. It was not, Marie noticed, a request.

"Of course," she said.

"Here is fine. And we'll have coffee, since you've made it," said Dennison.

Marie's spine stiffened. She wanted to tell the man that she wasn't his secretary—he could pour his own coffee if he wanted it so badly—but he was from the Home Office, and something about him made even Dr. Hughes nervous. Reluctantly, she set about pouring.

Neil stepped back toward the main door as Dennison and Dr. Hughes rearranged chairs in front of Nora's desk. She looked up and sent him a silent plea not to leave her, but he must not have registered it because he quietly opened the door and slid out.

Dennison gestured to Marie's desk chair as she tried her best to set down his cup without letting it rattle against its saucer. "Please sit, Miss Bohn."

She sat and smoothed her skirt.

It was Dr. Hughes who started the conversation. "As you'll have deduced, Herr Gunter is no longer with the German Department of Royal Imperial University."

"What happened, if I might ask, sir?"

"I received a phone call very early this morning from the professor. He told me that he was leaving the country. He doesn't believe that Britain will be safe for Germans now that there is a war on, and he has chosen to go to live with his sister in America," the dean said.

She frowned. "It doesn't seem like Herr Gunter to leave without word. And without all of his things—some of his papers and books. He is very particular about them," she said.

"That, Miss Bohn, is why the Home Office is interested in him," said Dennison. "The Home Office has reason to believe that Mr. Gunter may have connections to the Nazi Party."

"What? But that's impossible," she said.

"Consider how recently he moved to the United Kingdom," said Dennison.

"But I've read in the papers about how many academics are trying to leave Germany. The Nazi Party's condemned student groups," she said.

"That may be the case, but it's the responsibility of the Home Office to investigate these sorts of connections. Surely you understand." When he fixed her with a look, she hurried to nod. "Good. I'm glad you agree. It is imperative during a time of war that any acts of treason be stopped before they can damage our national security."

"Acts of treason?" she asked. She couldn't imagine her slightly eccentric boss doing anything treasonous.

"Did he ever say anything to you that made you suspect his loyalties?" Dennison asked.

"No. In fact, I'd say he was almost apolitical," she said, looking to Dr. Hughes for support. Instead of meeting her eye, the dean made a display of studying the contents of his cup.

"Very often those who are intent on committing treason do not show their true colors until sometime later," said Dennison.

"I thought he was a quiet man who wanted nothing more than to be left alone to read his books and write his articles," said Marie.

"That may have been the case, but loyalties are loyalties. One can only imagine the depths to which one might be willing to go for one's country," said Dennison.

"I can't believe it," Marie murmured.

"I suggest you begin to believe it, Miss Bohn," said Dennison sharply.

"Miss Bohn, it's important that you cooperate with Mr. Dennison's line of inquiry," said Dr. Hughes, his eyes darting to the Home Office man.

So this was how it would play out. Dr. Hughes would do everything he could to make this problem go away. Dennison would snoop around until he was satisfied that the German Department wasn't a secret den of Nazi sympathizers, and Marie would be left to pick up the pieces, tidy the office, and set things to rights again.

She tilted her chin up, forcing herself to meet the man's gaze. She had nothing to be afraid of. She'd done nothing wrong. "I will help however I can."

Dennison reached into his jacket pocket and pulled out a small black notebook held together by a rubber band and a silver pen. He flipped it open. "How long have you been Herr Gunter's secretary?"

"I'm the secretary for the German Department," she said. "He is— *was* the head of the department, but I also assist Herrs Lange, Fuchs, and Vogt."

Dennison scribbled something down and, without looking up, asked, "When did you begin working in the German Department?"

"In 1935," she said.

"And when did you meet Herr Gunter?"

"Last year. A little more than a year ago," she said.

"In that time, did you ever see Herr Gunter act in a suspicious manner?" he asked.

She scrunched up her nose. "I'm surrounded by academics every day, Mr. Dennison. You will have to be more specific."

Dr. Hughes cleared his throat, but Dennison didn't look up.

"Did he ever keep meetings from you or receive correspondence he didn't allow you to see?" Dennison asked.

"Not to my knowledge."

"Did he ever receive visitors but not introduce you to them?" he asked.

"Not that I'm aware of, although any number of students come through this office on any given day. He would not have necessarily introduced me to all of them."

"Did Herr Gunter have a safe in his office?" he asked.

"If he did, it was well hidden," she said.

"And would he allow you into his office when he was not there?" Dennison asked.

"Yes. I was always going in there when he forgot papers for department meetings or if he was running late for something. I have a second set of keys," she said.

"May I see them?" asked Dennison.

Marie reached into her desk drawer, unsnapped the top of her handbag, and drew out the keys.

"Could you please show me?" asked Dennison.

She rose and demonstrated that the key for Herr Gunter's door went smoothly into the lock.

"And did the professor always keep his office locked?" asked Dennison.

"When he was not in it, yes. He was particular about that," she said.

"Why do you think that was?"

She shrugged. "He kept manuscripts there, and he has a painting that he seemed to think had some value."

"A painting?" Dennison asked. "Did you see it this morning?"

She shook her head, and he wrote something down.

"Miss Bohn, were you aware that Herr Gunter kept a personal diary for his appointments in addition to the one that is on his desk?" he asked.

"No, he didn't."

"He did," said Dennison, drawing a green leather book embossed with a G out of his jacket pocket. The book was no larger than a cigarette case.

"I've never seen that before," she said.

He handed it to her. "Could you please look at last week's appointments and verify that they are the same that appear in the diary you have?"

Picking through the mess of papers, Marie went to Herr Gunter's desk and retrieved the large leather desk diary that she left there each night. After reviewing it with him every morning, she would take it back to her desk and add to it throughout the day before starting the entire process over again.

Back at her desk, she flipped to the last week and began checking the dates against the one in the green book Dennison had shown her. Everything seemed in order until she reached last Thursday.

"This," she said, turning both diaries around and tapping on the entry in the green book with her short fingernail. "'Emily, half past seven, American Bar.'"

Dennison nodded. "Very good. And do you know who Emily is?"

She hesitated. "I don't, no, but he did mention an Emily once."

"When was this?" asked Dennison.

Herr Gunter was her employer, but she wasn't going to lie, either for him or against him, and so she said, "The day that Germany invaded Poland."

Dennison's eyes narrowed. "Is that right?"

"Herr Gunter was upset—we all were. He was in a rush and asked me to call Emily and cancel his dinner with her. When I told him I didn't know who that was, he said that he would do it himself."

Dennison sat back, his chair creaking with the shift in his weight.

"Who is Emily?" Dr. Hughes asked.

Dennison ignored him. "Miss Bohn, were you aware that in the last few months, Herr Gunter had begun to see a woman? Romantically?"

"No," she said. Herr Gunter had never so much as made a murmur about his social life outside of Royal Imperial.

"Then you did not know that your employer had used an agency to arrange to meet a woman?" Dennison asked.

Marie spread her hands over the desk to brace herself. "What kind of agency?"

Dennison looked down at his notes before fixing her with a stare she felt to her bones. "The Mayfair Matrimonial Agency. Now, Miss Bohn, I think you'd better come with me."

seven

Dennison bundled Marie into the back of a large black Morris that was parked in front of the university gates. She sat with her hands clasped tight, trying to hold on to her last shred of composure. Herr Gunter had never once mentioned to her that he had been to Hazel's agency, but it couldn't be a coincidence. And why had Hazel never mentioned that Marie's boss was a client?

Of course she wouldn't, Marie reasoned. Hazel might tell stories from the agency, but she rarely used names.

Dennison drove like a man who expected traffic to part like the Red Sea for him. Granted, there were fewer cars clogging up the roads now, making it easier to race down Piccadilly. The petrol ration that had been put into place meant people were far more considered about how they used their fuel. In just four weeks, the streets had been given over to official vehicles and buses as even cabs were abandoned by the young drivers who were signing up in droves to serve.

In Mayfair, Dennison swung the Morris into an open spot just a few doors down from Hazel's building and killed the ignition. The seats squeaked in protest as he shifted to look over his shoulder at Marie.

"This is the building of the agency Gunter visited," he said.

A growing unease churned in her stomach.

"We're going to go in and speak to the proprietor. Miss Bohn, I want to remind you that this is an investigation. When we go inside, you'll only answer questions that I put to you. Is that clear?"

Then why bring me at all?

He didn't know. The realization struck her like lightning. However he'd found out about Herr Gunter, the matchmaking agency, and his mysterious Emily, Dennison hadn't put together the fact that Marie might be the connection between her boss and Hazel's agency.

Dennison stepped around the car to open her door, and he led her into the building. They climbed the stairs just as Marie had done so many times before. On the occasions when Herr Gunter decided not to work in his office on the last Friday of the month, she would come here early to collect Hazel before walking over to the Harlan, just a few blocks away. Marie had always liked the agency. It was a place of warmth, feminine and welcoming. Lady Moreton, the proprietor and Hazel's mentor of sorts, insisted that she wanted clients to feel at home while they asked for help making one of the most important decisions of their lives.

The light was on behind the frosted glass panel of the agency's door. Dennison leaned on the small brass doorbell embedded in the frame, and a moment later Nancy, Hazel's secretary, opened the door with a smile.

Marie inched back from Dennison and shook her head emphatically, praying that Nancy wouldn't reveal that she knew Marie. She needed to speak to Hazel first and figure out why Herr Gunter had come here and warn her friend that Dennison seemed far too interested in finding out why.

"Hello," said Nancy brightly, looking from Dennison to Marie. A flicker of doubt flashed over the secretary's face, but just as fast she turned her smile back to Dennison. "Welcome to the Mayfair Matrimonial Agency. How can I help you?"

Dennison pushed forward, angling his body around Nancy as he said, "I need to speak to Mrs. Carey."

With Dennison behind her, the secretary dropped her smile and shot Marie an alarmed look.

"I'm afraid Mrs. Carey is with a client at the moment," said Nancy.

"Perhaps we should come back at another time," said Marie, stepping into the reception.

Dennison glared at her. "I'm here on Home Office business. It's a matter of great importance."

"I can see if she—"

Hazel's door opened, and she appeared, a laugh on her lips as she looked over her shoulder at the client following her. He was a good-looking, solid sort of man with light brown hair brushed back from his forehead in waves. He looked as though he might've spent his youth on the rugby pitch but had left the mud behind for well-cut suits and a leather briefcase. He was chuckling at something her friend had said, but he carried a sadness about him as well, as though life had somehow disappointed him along the way.

"Mrs. Carey, a gentleman from the Home Office is here to see you," said Nancy.

Hazel's laugh died as she took in the players in the room. Marie prayed that her friend would pick up on Nancy's discomfort.

"The Home Office, you said?" Hazel asked.

"Thomas Dennison. I have some questions for you about a client." He pulled that little black notebook out of his jacket pocket just as he'd done with Marie.

Hazel put her hand up. "Mr. Dennison, will you please allow me to see Mr. Calloway out first?"

Calloway . . . Calloway . . . Marie turned the name over in her head until it snapped into place. Richard Calloway, the widower with the wife who'd died tragically young. That, she thought, accounted for his slight air of melancholy. She felt a pang of sympathy for this man who had lost so much, yet was trying to find love when so many stood to lose again.

"I'll see myself out," said Richard, shaking Hazel's hand.

"We'll find you a more suitable match. Sometimes it simply takes a few attempts," said Hazel.

"I place myself entirely at your mercy," he said.

"You're very trusting," said Hazel.

"Only when I know that there's good reason to trust." Richard said goodbye to Nancy and nodded at Dennison. But when he came to Marie, he stopped and offered her a kind smile. "You're in good hands with Mrs. Carey."

"Thank you. I would certainly hope so," she said.

Over Richard's shoulder, she could see Hazel tilt her head in question. But by the time he gathered up his coat and hat to leave, Hazel's usual composure was back in place.

"If you'd like to come through, Mr. Dennison," said Hazel, gesturing to her office door.

Dennison gestured for Marie to lead, and they settled themselves into the chairs angled before Hazel's desk.

"Mrs. Carey, this is Marie Bohn. She is the secretary of Pieter Gunter, a professor of German at Royal Imperial University," said Dennison.

Marie's heart pounded as Hazel slowly said, "It's a pleasure to meet you, Miss Bohn."

"The pleasure is mine, Mrs. Carey," she managed.

"Yesterday, Miss Bohn's employer fled the country. We believe that he booked a place on a ship out of Southampton. It's likely that he is going to either America or Australia, but we've wired all passenger ships at sea and he doesn't appear on any manifest. In all likelihood, Gunter is using a false name and false papers," said Dennison.

"Why are you looking for him?" asked Hazel.

"When he was a university student, he was intimate friends with several men who now hold positions of some power in Berlin. We have reason to believe that he is still in contact with them and may be sympathetic to their cause," said Dennison.

"But that can't be." The words were out of Marie's mouth before she could stop herself.

"Several letters addressed to him that have been intercepted led me to believe otherwise, Miss Bohn."

"But what could he possibly do as a German professor at a university? It isn't as though he has access to any great state secrets," she said.

"We must investigate all potential sympathizers. A name came up in our investigation: Emily Boyne. I believe Mr. Gunter met her through this agency," said Dennison.

"I don't usually speak about clients, but given the circumstances, I can say that Mrs. Boyne is an older woman, quite respectable. Her husband died eight or nine years back, and she's only just now felt strong enough to think about starting a new life."

"What nationality is Mrs. Boyne?" asked Dennison.

"British."

"When was the last time that you made an arrangement for Mrs. Boyne?"

"When I introduced her to Herr Gunter," said Hazel. "But that was some time ago."

"You are remarkably confident about your answers without referring to any notes," said Dennison.

Marie fought to keep her eyes on Hazel's face and not the small key that hung from a ribbon tied to Hazel's skirts. It was the key to the safe—a key- and combination-operated contraption—that held the agency's hundreds of client cards. Marie had seen Hazel sort through them before, but she'd never been allowed to see what was written on any card. The information on there was extremely private.

"I've often been told that I have a remarkable memory, Mr. Dennison. It's useful in my trade," said Hazel.

Dennison grunted. "Did Gunter specifically ask for Mrs. Boyne?"

"No. He wouldn't have known her identity until I had secured permission from the lady to make the introduction. It helps preserve the privacy and safety of our clients."

"Are you aware that Mrs. Boyne's father is a government official?"

"Yes," said Hazel.

"And you don't think it suspicious that a woman with a father in government was being courted by a man who is a German sympathizer?" asked Dennison.

"Unless your investigation is a foregone conclusion, I believe you mean to say *if* he was a sympathizer." When Dennison didn't amend his statement, Hazel folded her arms and leaned back in her leather chair. "I find it strange that you should consider this match suspicious. There's little extraordinary about it. Mrs. Boyne and Herr Gunter met months before war was declared. I never mentioned the lady's parentage, and he did not make any specific request to be matched with Mrs. Boyne. If he had, I wouldn't have been needed because presumably he would've been able to effect an introduction himself. And so, Mr. Dennison, I believe you're chasing ghosts."

Dennison grunted again and turned to Marie. "Miss Bohn, you were Herr Gunter's secretary."

"I was the department's secretary," Marie said, correcting him again.

"Yet you claim to have no knowledge of Mrs. Boyne?" asked Dennison.

"Except for the one time he mentioned an Emily right after we'd found out about the invasion," Marie replied. She felt as though she were dancing on the edge of a knife blade, lying to him about Hazel and the agency. Lying to him about anything else would only spin a larger web.

"Did you ever make bookings for Gunter? Arrange any of his domestic duties?" Dennison asked her.

"Yes. I did on occasion," she said, thinking back to all of the theater tickets, dinner and lunch reservations, and train journeys she'd booked for him. Sometimes Herr Gunter had treated her more like a personal secretary than the woman who ran the university's office should've been, but wasn't that what all slightly puffed-up men like him did?

"And yet he did not see fit to use your services when he was going to see Mrs. Boyne," said Dennison.

"He was a private man," said Marie with a shrug.

"I think that we can assume that Gunter was taking pains to cover up his relationship with Mrs. Boyne," said Dennison.

"That's sounding like rather a stretch, Mr. Dennison," said Hazel with a laugh.

"I'd like to see your records, Mrs. Carey. The ones you claim you don't need in order to remember a client you matched so many months ago," said Dennison.

"No," said Hazel.

"I'm sorry?" asked Dennison.

"No," Hazel repeated.

"It is not wise to say no to the Home Office," said Dennison.

"And yet here I am, doing just that," said Hazel. "If you would like to complain, you may speak to my employer, Lady Moreton."

For the first time since he'd walked into the German Department, Dennison looked thrown. "The wife of Sir Gregory Moreton?"

Marie smiled at the way the prominent banker's name seemed to shake the man.

"That's right," said Hazel, clearly enjoying Dennison's discomfort, too.

"Then you are not the owner?" he asked.

"No. I am the primary matchmaker and run the day-to-day business, but Lady Moreton owns the establishment," said Hazel.

Dennison snapped his mouth shut, and for a moment Marie thought he might let all of this go, but then he straightened his shoulders. "Mrs. Carey, I'll be frank with you. Agencies such as this one have come under scrutiny by the Home Office due to the nature of your business."

"What is that nature?" Hazel asked.

"Engineering marriages."

Hazel threw her head back and laughed loud, some of the brassiness Marie knew she'd fought to refine over the years peeking through. "Some would say that we're in the business of love and happiness, but if you must insist on calling it engineering . . ."

"We are at war, Mrs. Carey. This is not a time for bright-eyed idealism. The Home Office has identified a number of ways that enemy agents may try to infiltrate Britain."

"Are you really that worried about German men marrying British women?" Hazel asked.

"Or Austrian men. And women, too. The Germans aren't above exploiting the weaker sex. We learned that in the last war," said Dennison. "I believe that Gunter was attempting to marry Emily Boyne in order to establish a stronger claim to this country and avoid any restrictive designation when he went before his tribunal. This would allow him to continue to operate as an informant for his friends back at home in Germany."

"I can assure you that we vet all of our clients," Hazel said.

"How?" he asked.

"References. Identification cards. Service records. University degrees. We want to ensure that everyone is being honest. We also require documentation of all letters of patent in the case of peers," Hazel said.

"You have members of the peerage using your service?" he asked.

"Mr. Dennison, it would shock you who I have matched with their spouse," Hazel said. Marie could feel the implied power hang in the air.

Still, Dennison said, "I would like to see your record books and your correspondence. As Miss Bohn is Gunter's secretary, she should be more than equipped to identify his handwriting."

Before Marie could protest, Hazel smiled at the man. "I'm afraid that will be rather difficult."

"Why?" Dennison asked.

Outside in the reception, a woman's bright, "Wonderful day to help people fall in love, darlings!" rang out.

"Who is that?" Dennison asked.

Hazel's lips twitched. "That would be Lady Moreton. Perhaps you would like to make your request to open up our books to her yourself."

All the years that Marie had been coming to the agency, she'd never met Lady Moreton. Part of it was her own doing. There was something intimidating about a regular girl meeting a baron's wife. But in that moment Marie couldn't have been happier for Lady Moreton's elevated status because it unsettled Dennison. He couldn't bully or demand from Lady Moreton in the way he might with Marie or Hazel. Lifting his chin, though, he said, "I shall do just that."

Dennison was the first through Hazel's door, giving Marie just enough time to grab Hazel's hand as she rounded her desk. "I haven't told him that we know each other."

"I gathered as much. I think it's best to keep him in the dark. I don't like the things he's hinting at one bit," whispered Hazel.

Out in the reception, Dennison appeared already to have introduced himself to Lady Moreton, because she was staring him down as though he were lower than pond scum.

"Does the Home Office not have enough to do without involving itself in the personal lives of British citizens?" asked Lady Moreton with a sniff.

"It is precisely because there is a war on that I'm here, my lady," said Dennison.

"What is it that you want then?" Lady Moreton asked.

"I would like you to open your records for our inspection."

"Lady Moreton, I've already informed Mr. Dennison that we will not do that," said Hazel.

"Well, what do you have to say to that, Mr. Dennison?" Lady Moreton asked as she removed a cigarette from a gold case she'd produced from her handbag.

"I will need to see *all* of your records. Matches, correspondence, receipts," he pressed.

Lady Moreton lit her cigarette, taking her time as she drew on it and blew the smoke out to the ceiling. Then she said, "No, I think not."

"I'm sorry?" he asked.

"I refuse to have you snooping around in my business dealings without a judge's order."

Dennison stiffened. "There is a war on."

Marie was beginning to understand that he used the refrain like a bludgeon to get his way.

"The papers don't seem to be convinced that there's much happening at all at the moment. So anticlimactic after all the fuss when Hitler invaded Poland. So far, all this war seems to have done is produce a lot of pesky false air raid sirens. And did you know, they told my nephew there will be a wait before he's called up because too many young men have tried to join the army? Of course, my sister's overjoyed, even though he'll look dashing in an officer's dress uniform," said Lady Moreton.

"Ma'am, the records," Dennison prompted.

The baroness arched a brow. "Mr. Dennison, the last time I checked, none of this changes the fact that you have no legal grounds to come in here and make such demands of a private business."

"I can compel you on legal grounds." Dennison practically ground out the words.

"Then I suggest you do that, or else I shall have to pay a visit to the Lord Chief Justice. He was up in the country with us in June, you see. He's mad about cricket."

"You have a duty to your country, madam," he said.

"I am acutely aware of my duty, and it does not include helping men like you persecute people when you cannot produce solid evidence of any wrongdoing. Good day, Mr. Dennison. You'll forgive us for not seeing you out."

Dennison clenched his hands into fists, but nonetheless made a small bow. The door slammed behind him.

Lady Moreton let out a long breath. "If ever there was a time for a stiff drink, this is it. Still, if we start drinking before luncheon, where will we be? Nancy, if you would brew a pot of tea?" Then the agency owner turned to Marie. "Now, who are you?"

Marie would've laughed if she hadn't been quite so shaken by the events of the morning. "I'm Marie Bohn."

"Oh, you're the friend from boarding school," said Lady Moreton.

Marie glanced over at Hazel. "Yes, Ethelbrook. We lived with our friend Nora."

"Nora Walcott, now it's all coming back to me," said Lady Moreton. "Do you know Mrs. Walcott? Horrible woman. Nose stuck so high up in the air it's a wonder she can see where to walk. Now, Hazel"—Lady Moreton turned to her head matchmaker—"what is all this nonsense about?"

In a few sentences, Hazel filled her employer in on Dennison's visit.

"Do you know Herr Gunter?" Lady Moreton asked.

"Yes, I matched him with Mrs. Boyne," said Hazel, her eyes sliding to Marie. "I'm sorry I didn't tell you. He contacted me ages ago and said that he had heard you mention me and the agency when you were talking to one of your friends in the office."

"What's happened to the man?" Lady Moreton asked.

"They think he set sail on one of the passenger ships under a false name. I doubt they'll ever find him," said Marie. *I doubt I'll ever hear from him again.*

"Well, what's done is done," said Lady Moreton, stubbing out her cigarette.

"What shall I do if Dennison comes back?" Hazel asked.

"Ring round to the house. I'll speak to our solicitor to see what legal ground we have," said Lady Moreton with a definitive nod. "War or not, I refuse to be ordered around by a man who's clearly never even heard of a good tailor."

eight

To the editor:
It is time for this government to consider the very real threat of the people living among us. There may be some Germans who look upon Britain fondly, but it is too much to ask the British people to risk their safety to keep those innocent few free. Intern them. Deport them. It is vital for the safety of this country that the German population be monitored and contained.

—*Albion Evening Courier*, October 9, 1939

A light mist of rain drifted down on Tottenham, dancing in the dim light of the streetlamps nearly entirely covered in accordance with the blackout. Marie tugged her coat closed at the throat and resisted the urge to pat the scarf that covered her hair again. Fussing with it would only cause the silk to slip off and bag around her neck.

She would've come to the party meeting with Neil, only he had headed off early from campus, telling her he was determined to arrive well ahead of the start. He was supposed to speak that evening, so it only made sense, except a selfish part of her wished that she'd traveled with him as they usually had.

She hadn't been able to shake the unsettled feeling that had crept under her skin since the day of Herr Gunter's disappearance. Everywhere she looked, she expected Dennison to pop out from hiding and arrest her on the spot even though she'd done nothing wrong.

But you don't need to do anything wrong, do you?

On Wednesday morning, the Müller family and Marie's tribunal hearing letters had come in the morning post. Tante Matilda had been waiting when Marie came home, her own letter already open on the sofa next to her. She'd handed Marie her own envelope and began to cry. Marie opened it carefully and slid the letter out. She was required to report to her hearing on October 26 at half past two. She would be permitted to bring character witnesses who were not related to her. She waited until Onkel Albrecht came home and then telephoned Hazel and Nora to ask them to stand with her. They'd both said yes.

A few days later, Tante Matilda and Onkel Albrecht had entertained two other couples—both German. She'd just been leaving to go to the cinema with Nora when she overheard them as she passed the sitting room door.

"But how could someone throw paint by accident?" one of the men had asked in German.

"I don't know, but surely—"

The same man cut Onkel Albrecht off with a derisive laugh. "And how many projects have you been put on since war has been declared?"

There was a slight pause. "It is a slow time. That's only normal. People are more worried about fighting than they are about building," her uncle said.

"Six of my British patients have canceled their appointments. I have enough German patients for now, but what happens if they decide to send them away to one of these internment camps they're opening in North London? That will be the end of my practice," said Herr Scharr, whom Marie recognized from the few times she'd accompanied her aunt to church.

"Things are changing, and not for the better," said Frau Scharr.

"These people are not your friends, Albrecht. The longer it takes for you to accept that, the more painful it will all be in the end," said the first man.

"But England is our home." Her aunt's voice was muffled, as though she was losing the belief in her own words.

"It won't be for very much longer, Matilda," said Frau Scharr.

Marie had squeezed her eyes closed so hard that she saw starbursts behind her lids, but forced herself to walk out the door and into the already darkening street. By the time she arrived at the cinema it was already pitch-black out, and she had to use her torch in the blackout. Once she passed through the black-cloth-covered doors, she'd blinked in the light and fixed a smile firmly in place to greet her friend.

But the moment Marie was alone, her forced jolliness had slipped away. Back at home, she hurried past the door and locked her bedroom door behind her. She applied her thick cold cream, just as usual, and slipped into bed, praying she might dream it all away. But the next morning the newspaper next to her uncle's breakfast plate ran another headline, another reminder that there was no escaping any of this.

In the CPGB's meeting hall, young couples—too young for the men to be able to join up—walked arm in arm, while stern middle-aged ladies stood in buttoned-up cloth coats, surveying the room. There were far fewer men about than had been at any other meeting Marie'd attended, but she'd missed the last couple so she supposed she shouldn't be surprised. Half of the university's campus seemed to be donning tan or blue uniforms, and there was talk around campus that a few of the department secretaries might even join the WRNS or the WAAFs or another of the women's auxiliary branches.

Marie finally spotted Neil near the stage. His tweed jacket hung unbuttoned, revealing a crisp white shirt and a red tie. He was speaking to another man, and as she drifted up his companion glanced at her.

"Who is this?" the man asked with a nod.

Neil started when he saw her, as though he'd forgotten that they'd agreed she would meet him. But then he gave her a little smile.

"Marie, meet Harvey Lambeth," Neil said.

"Like the neighborhood." Harvey laughed. "South of the river, just like me."

"Or like 'The Lambeth Walk,'" she said, shaking the hand that engulfed her own.

"What's that?" Harvey asked.

"'The Lambeth Walk'? From the musical? The film came out earlier this year," she said.

Harvey stuck his thumbs in his suspenders and rocked back on his heels as though mulling this over. "Don't go in much for trips to the cinema. There's too much needs changing in this country. Where are you from?"

Marie swallowed. "Munich, but I've lived here for my whole life." It was almost true.

Harvey ran an assessing eye over her again, but this time there was a hint of suspicion there. "And what do you think of this war?"

"I hate it."

Harvey grunted and turned his attention back to Neil so fully that he gave Marie his back. "Think about what I said. It'll be a sacrifice, but it would be well worth it in the end." Then Harvey walked away.

"I didn't think you'd actually come," Neil said, turning his attention on her.

"I told my aunt and uncle I was having dinner with a friend and her mother. They worry whenever I leave the house now, but they also know that they can't keep me locked up," she said.

"Like Cinderella in her tower?" he asked, his eyes darting to something over her shoulder.

"You mean Rapunzel?" He frowned, so she clarified, "The damsel locked in her tower was Rapunzel."

"Yes," he said.

Something hung between them, heavy yet unacknowledged. She didn't know what it was, but she didn't like it.

"Are you ready for your speech?" she asked, attempting to find something—anything—that would once again forge the connection that she'd felt the night he'd kissed her.

This time she was rewarded. He gave her a little smile and let out a long, shaky breath.

"As ready as I'll ever be, *kleine Maus*," he said.

If Marie was being completely honest, Neil's speech was adequate. He'd asked her to look over the draft a few weeks ago, before the entire world had gone mad. She'd rewritten large parts of it, smoothing out the language and coaxing poetry out of the prose of a man who seemed intent on transporting his audience but wrote more eloquently of facts and figures. However, as she watched him deliver the words at the podium on the stage, it was clear that the written word could only do so much. A speaker needed passion and conviction, and while Neil had those in spades, he didn't have the charisma that made it impossible to look away from him when he spoke.

He was nearing the final page, Marie half following in her head, when suddenly he veered wildly off course from what she'd edited.

". . . This organization has long stood up to the tyranny of the British government, ruled by corrupt politicians who have no greater aspiration than to sit in Parliament and tell us how it is that we should live our lives," Neil said. "Well, it is time for that to end. Just as our brothers and sisters in Germany and Russia and all over Europe are struggling in the wake of war, we must demand an end to the government's warmongering!"

Marie sat up straight. She'd expected him to change bits and pieces of it to address the war, but this was vastly different. Just a few weeks ago, at her last meeting, they were raging against the scourge of fascism spreading across Europe. Now Germany was their brother and the British were the ones agitating for war?

"Responsibility for this war lies at the feet of Prime Minister Chamberlain, who allowed us to fall prey to our own hubris. Do not allow the politicians to convince you that the cause of this is anything more than the pride of a few stubborn men sitting in their ivory towers. We must stand up against the government. Stand up against those who would bring war to our doorsteps!"

Around her, people began clapping as they sensed Neil was building to the end.

"We welcome our brothers and sisters in arms and say we stand with you! We know what it is to hurt. We know what it is that must be done!"

Neil pushed back from the podium, triumphant, waved to the crowd, and stepped off the stage. People were on their feet applauding as he pulled his handkerchief out of his pocket and dabbed at his brow. He shot her a grin, broader than any he'd offered her all night. "I made some changes."

"Neil, you were asking the people here to rise up against the government. In a time of war!" she shouted over the din.

He stuffed his handkerchief back into his pocket and shrugged one shoulder. "We *want* to see the government overthrown. 'Workers of the world unite; you have nothing to lose but your chains.'"

People around them had begun to sit down, drawing attention to the fact that the last speaker seemed to be having an impassioned conversation with a young woman. The attention would've made her uncomfortable on any given day, but now, with things as they were, she wanted to hide.

"Can we step outside, please?" she asked, keeping her voice low as the applause was replaced by the buzz of anticipation for the next speaker.

Neil looked around, as though only just realizing how many eyes were on them. "Come on," he said, pulling her by her elbow toward a side door.

They pushed outside into the night. It was pouring, and they huddled under an awning that provided two feet of protection from the elements.

"Why did you change the speech?" she asked. "In August, all anyone could talk about was how we needed to defeat Germany and the fascists. Now the war is Britain's fault and Germany is our brother in arms?"

He scrubbed a hand over his face. "You're deliberately misunderstanding the politics of the situation. You don't know—"

"I'm not misunderstanding things, Neil. I'm fully capable of understanding." *I practically write your speeches for you.*

"Moscow decreed that we were no longer meant to focus on Germany as the enemy. We should be striving for peace, and the blame for all of this lies directly at the feet of the prime minister."

"You changed your politics because Moscow told you to? You're in London, Neil," she said.

"It's what I have to do, *kleine Maus.* You understand that, don't you?" he asked, his voice a little tender. "Sometimes doing things you don't want to?"

He tucked her into his chest so he could rest his chin on the top of her head. She breathed deep, the scent of wool and Brylcreem mixing with wet leaves underfoot. But even as they stood there, a question with hazy edges formed in her head.

"Or else what?" she asked.

"What?"

"You said, 'It's what I have to do,' as though someone is going to take something from you if you don't follow instructions," she said.

He peeled away from her, setting her from him at arm's length, and smoothed his hand over his hair even though not a strand was out of place.

"That man you met earlier? Harvey? He thinks I could have a career in politics after the war," said Neil.

"Neil, that's wonderful!"

"Yes," he said, his head hanging down. "Yes, it is."

She frowned. "Why aren't you happier about this?"

"I'll have to join up. Probably the army. That way I'll have a service record and all of the respect that comes with it. No one will vote for a man who didn't fight if he was capable, not even if his politics mean he disagrees with it," he said.

"You don't want to fight," she said slowly.

"I'll do my bit, but there are other things I'd rather be doing. And there are things I would have to give up. People."

"I don't understand," she said.

"You're German, *kleine Maus*."

Immediately she understood his halting words. She took a step back, bile rising in her throat. "Harvey wants you to give me up."

"You must understand that me being with a German woman . . . after two wars . . ."

"You're saying that you need to put me to the side just so you can maybe stand for office if you make it through this war. You *kissed* me, Neil."

He toed the ground with his brogue like a chastised child. "Just once. And this is my career. I could become one of the youngest members of Parliament ever to serve the North London boroughs. But not if there's anything that will make voters think twice about me."

"And I'm something to make people doubt your judgment."

He refused to look at her. "The CPGB is still fighting for constituents across the country."

To hear him lay out in such uncertain terms that his political ambitions were more important than her stung. It was as though the man who'd stopped by her desk to flirt and make her blush had dissolved and the true Neil stood before her. One who was as ambitious as he was craven.

"I thought better of you," she said.

She turned to leave, but he grabbed her arm. "*Kleine Maus*."

Through gritted teeth, she ground out, "Why do you call me that? It's a nickname people use when they feel affection for one another." *Not when they see someone as a burden.*

He spread his hands before him. "The first day I saw you, you were sitting behind that big desk looking so small. Just like a little mouse. It just popped into my head."

The cracks around her heart he'd been tapping at all evening shattered. That nickname—the one that had made her hope for so long—had been nothing more than a joking acknowledgment that he thought her small and meek. She'd spent so much time wishing that he'd notice her as a woman. Instead, he thought of her as nothing more than an amusement he could set aside when he no longer needed her.

"Marie, I *do* like you."

"But not enough to fight for me when people like Mr. Lambeth say you should set me aside," she said.

He threw up his hands. "I don't know what you want me to say. That I've secretly been in love with you for years and that I'd marry you no matter whether there's a war on or not?"

All she could do was stare.

"Oh, Marie." He chucked her under the chin. "You're a great girl. You have no idea how much I'll miss your cups of coffee when I'm at the front."

All of her memories of him reshuffled and reversed themselves, and she saw with clarity what should have been right in front of her since she'd met him. He didn't care for her. All she was to him was the girl who fetched the coffee, edited his speeches, and told him he was brilliant.

"I can't believe I thought you would ever be good enough for me," she whispered.

He had the audacity to look put out. "Well, there's no need to be mean-spirited about it."

"Goodbye, Neil." Dropping her shoulder, she walked around him and out into the rain, not bothering to cover her hair as she went.

nine

ROYAL OAK SUNK!
German U-Boat Breaks British Fleet
at Scapa Flow to Sink Battleship
—*Liverpool Intelligencer*, October 14, 1939

M arie spent three days furious at Neil, but it turned out that the best way to overcome a man's rejection was to have a tribunal hearing to worry about. Marie spent most of her free time shuttling between the Müllers' Bloomsbury flat and Hazel's office, where her friends were helping her study her own biography. For hours the three would go over again and again the details of her life, making sure that nothing the tribunal panel might ask would trip her up.

"Are you sure Nathaniel doesn't mind us taking you away from him for so many evenings?" she asked Hazel one night over packets of egg and cress sandwiches from the shop around the corner.

Hazel waved her hand. "The agency has been so busy he hardly notices when I'm not home these days. It's been like this for months."

Marie frowned. It was difficult to imagine the man who had been madly in love with her friend during the first flush of their marriage not minding his wife spending so much time away at night.

"Back to it, then," said Nora, brushing the crumbs off her white silk blouse, having discarded the jacket to her suit as soon as she'd arrived. She cleared her throat and put on a deeper male voice. "Tell us about your employment history, Miss Bohn."

"I was a switchboard operator at the Lindwood hotel," said Marie.

"When did you begin working there?" Hazel asked.

"June 1932."

"What were you doing before that?" Nora asked.

"I was at school in Herefordshire."

"And how long did you work as a switchboard operator?" Hazel asked.

"Until August 1933, when I began to work in the administrative offices for Royal Imperial University. I was promoted to my role as the German Department secretary in 1935," said Marie.

"When was the last time you went back to Germany?" Hazel asked.

Marie hesitated as she thought about the answer. "I attended a funeral for my maternal grandmother when I was sixteen. It was over the school holidays, so I was able to make the trip with my aunt. Before that, I would go to visit my parents for a few weeks in the summers." Cold, uncomfortable visits that she was relieved had come to an end as she grew older.

"Why didn't you return to Germany after leaving school?" Nora asked.

"England had become my home," Marie said.

Hazel leaned forward, her chair squeaking in protest, and asked in a gravelly voice, "But what about your parents?"

"Need we be so dramatic?" Nora asked.

"If you can put on funny voices, so can I," said Hazel. "So, Miss Bohn, what about your parents?"

"You know about my parents," said Marie, shifting in her seat.

"I don't know anything," said Hazel. "I'm Lawrence Humperdinck, underpaid, overworked civil servant who thinks that this whole thing is a waste of my time. But my supervisor is watching my every move, so I'm vigilant in my job."

"Lawrence Humperdinck?" Nora laughed.

Hazel shrugged.

Marie drew in a breath. "Well, Mr. Humperdinck, the truth is that my parents and I were never close. They sent me away to school in England and never visited. I stayed with my aunt and uncle during breaks."

Marie could still remember the day she met Tante Matilda. She was conjugating French verbs under her governess's watchful eye when a maid slipped into the nursery and whispered in her governess's ear. All at once, the French exercise books were put away, and Marie found herself being hurried to Mutter's morning room.

Mutter was not alone. Marie recognized Tante Matilda from her photograph, a little older but still the same pretty woman with thick blond hair caught up in a chignon.

"Marie, say hello to your aunt, Frau Müller," Mutter said with a wave of her hand.

Tante Matilda laughed at the formality and said in the low, warm voice that would become so familiar, "Please, call me Tante Matilda."

"Hello, Tante Matilda," Marie said, biting her lip to hold back a grin.

Tante Matilda stretched out her hands to Marie. "Oh, let me look at you." Her aunt's gray leather gloves had felt divine, and the light floral scent of Tante Matilda's perfume hugged her.

"You've grown into quite the young lady, haven't you?" Tante Matilda looked back over her shoulder at Marie's mother. "The last time you sent me a photograph, she was barely at her father's knee."

Mutter selected a cigarette from a box on the table. "We keep such a social calendar, it's nearly impossible to find the time to write."

Even at twelve, Marie saw the tightening around Tante Matilda's lips.

Everything moved in a flash after that. Brusque and businesslike, Marie's mother explained to her that she'd been enrolled in a girls' school in England called Ethelbrook. On holidays, she would stay with Tante Matilda and Onkel Albrecht in London. When she was finished with school, she would return to Munich to take up a social calendar of her own. The words washed over Marie, as though she was hearing them from a distance. She didn't understand. What had she done to be sent away?

The morning of her departure for Britain, Marie's mother and father emerged from their morning room and study, respectively, which was more than she'd expected.

"Be a credit to the Bohn family," her father said. "Make sure that you meet the right sort of people."

"Do as your aunt tells you, and be a good girl," said her mother, bussing her cheek so lightly no smudge of carmine lipstick was left behind. Marie gripped the handle of her little attaché case. Later in the car, she would see that it had left crescent imprints in the leather of her gloves.

Tante Matilda gently steered her to the car, where the family's chauffeur stood waiting at the open door. They climbed in and were off.

They crossed Europe by trains before taking a boat across the Channel. In London there had been shopping for seemingly endless things Marie would need for her uniform and for her schoolwork. Most of it felt like a fog until the morning they drove up to Ethelbrook.

Tante Matilda grasped her hand so tightly one might've thought that it was her rather than Marie who was meant to start classes. A soft-spoken lady told them that the headmistress expected them, showed them into an office, and gave them tea in delicate china cups. Marie hardly sipped at all because she feared breaking hers.

The head mistress, Mrs. Osborn, strode in a few moments later, and immediately began firing questions at Tante Matilda, who answered them all in her gentle voice. Yes, it was highly unusual to enroll a foreign girl in school midterm, but Marie was bright and would catch up with her classes quickly. Yes, Marie did have a full command of English, as she had been tutored by an English governess. Yes, the Bohns had authorized Tante Matilda to pay the rest of the year's tuition in full, as well as the next.

And, just like that, twelve-year-old Marie was officially an Ethelbrook girl. Tante Matilda kissed her on the cheek and promised to send for her at Christmas.

"Make friends, and make your mother and father proud, *mein Lieb-chen*," said her aunt before leaning in. "But don't forget that who you are is always good enough for Albrecht and me."

For the first time since she'd left Munich, Marie felt her shoulders inch down from around her ears.

After her aunt left, Mrs. Osborn introduced her to the matron, a tall, solid woman with hair pulled back into a severe bun. The matron rattled off everything Marie needed to know as they walked. Class schedules, bathing schedules, dining schedules. Everything seemed to have a time or procedure to follow.

Finally, they reached a room tucked away in one of Ethelbrook's four turrets. "We already had an odd situation with a girl coming in a week into term, so we might as well put you in with her and the scholarship girl she's housed with. They're one year apart, but we'll sort things out next year if you all last."

Without knocking, the matron opened the door. Two other girls jumped off their beds. A book clattered to the floor on the raven-haired girl's side of the room.

"Miss Walcott, pick that up," the matron barked.

The gangly girl Marie would soon learn was Nora bent to scoop the book up and resettled her glasses, but not before shooting Marie a cheeky grin.

"This is Marie Bohn. German. She'll take the third bed. Your trunk will be up when the porter gets around to it."

Then the matron was gone, and Marie was left staring at her two new roommates.

"Well, come in," said the pretty strawberry blonde with a laugh. "I'm Hazel Ricci. Thirteen years old, which I suspect means I'm a year older than you. And before anyone else can tell you, yes, I'm a scholarship girl and, yes, my mother has a *reputation*."

Marie, who'd met few children she wasn't related to, started when she realized Hazel's hand was outstretched expectantly.

"And I'm Nora Walcott." Another hand, another shake. "Are you twelve? I am. I like your hair. It's so blond. Are you really German?"

Marie blinked a few times at the onslaught of words, but then, realizing she was meant to respond to all of this, nodded. "Yes. I'm twelve and German."

Who are these girls and why do they speak so quickly?

"Your English is very good," said Nora. "My father said that I should learn German, but my mother prefers French and Italian. Would you like a biscuit?"

"A what?"

"Biscuit," said Nora with a grin. "I smuggled them in. Here."

Nora stuck out a packet of half-smashed biscuits. Marie took one, bit into it, and realized she could be friends with these girls.

Now, eleven years later, they were still her confidants, her champions, her best friends. Yet she knew she wasn't being completely honest with them. She'd been holding parts of herself back—the party meetings, the speeches, Neil.

She looked from friend to friend as Nora and Hazel bickered yet again about whether Hazel should testify at the tribunal.

"I've known Marie as long as you have," Hazel said.

"Yes, but this Dennison isn't coming to *my* office door and asking a lot of questions that could land Marie in the thick of it," said Nora.

"He works in the Home Office, just like you!" argued Hazel.

"The Foreign and Commonwealth Office building houses the Home, Foreign, Colonial, and India offices," Nora said, ticking off the departments on her fingers. "So many people wander through it there's no reason to think we'll ever run into each other. Besides, he doesn't even know who I am."

"How can you be sure?" Marie asked, voicing a worry that had nagged at her since Dennison had shown up in the German Department offices. No doubt the man had looked into her background. The question was: How far back had he dug?

"I can't," admitted Nora.

"I think I need to tell you something," Marie said, her voice halting. "It's . . . It's nothing *bad*. It's just . . ."

"Embarrassing?" Hazel asked.

She nodded.

"You know that we'd never laugh at you," said Nora. "Even I know when not to tease."

Marie nodded. "Do you know how I could rarely go to the cinema on Monday nights when you would ring around? Well, I wasn't working late."

Nora's eyes widened. "Marie Bohn, you dark horse. You have a man."

"No, it isn't anything like that," said Marie quickly. "There wasn't a man involved. At least, not really." She took a breath. "I was attending CPGB meetings."

Her friends stared at her openmouthed.

"Commie meetings?" Nora asked.

"There was a graduate student in the department who invited me," said Marie.

"His name?" Hazel prompted.

"Neil Havitt. He was speaking one night, so I went along. Then I just sort of kept going back."

"How often?" Nora asked.

Marie winced. "Every other Monday for months. Neil asked me to read over his speeches. I would rewrite them, and I liked watching him say them out loud to all of those people. Sometimes, when they were clapping or yelling, I felt like they were applauding for me even though they had no idea who I was or what I'd done."

"Are you a Communist?" Nora asked.

"No, I don't think so. I listened to all of the speeches, and I agreed with the things the speakers said. People should be paid more fairly. There should be better conditions. But I don't think the government is all wrong. I don't think there should be a revolution." She paused. "To be honest, I don't know that I'm really a political person." She'd never believed in it the way others did. Instead, she'd come along because she'd been infatuated with a man who was too self-involved to ever see her as anything more than a tool to bolster his confidence.

"It might come up in the tribunal hearing," said Nora. "You won't know what they know about you until you're in there."

"I know."

"It might compromise you. No one's looking very favorably on Communists these days," Nora continued.

"I know that, but hindsight doesn't help me." She sighed. "It's too late to tell me what a stupid thing it was to go to those meetings."

"It wasn't stupid," said Nora carefully. "Just potentially dangerous now."

"You went because you liked him, didn't you?" Hazel asked softly.

"Yes," she admitted.

"And that's why you've been keeping him a secret?" Hazel asked.

A fierce blush colored Marie's cheeks. "I thought he might actually like me. He seemed to enjoy my company. He was always asking me to join him when he spoke, and then giving me his writing to look at before anyone else. I was flattered. I thought . . . I thought if I told you that it might not be true. It turns out, I didn't need to have bothered. He was never truly interested in me at all."

"Oh, Marie." Hazel sat down next to her to pull her into a side hug. "How did you find out?"

"We kissed just before the invasion, but then I went to a meeting the other day and he told me he would have to drop me. He has political aspirations after the war, you see."

"He dropped you?" Nora asked at the same time Hazel said, "You kissed him?"

"How is that more important?" Nora asked.

"Because if he dropped her as a friend that's one thing. Adding a kiss to it would only make it more painful," said Hazel.

Hazel was right, except it was more embarrassing than painful.

"It doesn't matter anyway," said Marie. "It's all over now."

"Oh, Marie. It might not be," said Nora. "Did you register for membership? Did you march?"

"I never marched, but the membership . . . Maybe? They were asking people to put their names down at my first meeting. Neil said I should write my name so he could show that he'd brought people with him. He was supposed to help 'grow the cause' or something along those lines."

"Then you'll be on the rolls, and you can be sure that the Aliens Department will have record of that," she said.

"But surely that can't be so unusual. Communism was positively fashionable ten years ago. I'm sure even Mama went to Communist Party meetings in the twenties. All of the bohemians and writers and poets did," said Hazel.

"I suspect that if your mother was alive, it wouldn't matter at all for her. However, it's going to be different for Marie." Nora turned a sympathetic eye on Marie. "I'm sorry to be so blunt, but we have to be prepared that this could come up."

"What if she doesn't say anything about it at all?" asked Hazel.

"Like I said, I'd be very surprised if they don't already know about the party affiliation. Between this and Herr Gunter's behavior . . ."

"I might not get a category C classification," Marie finished Nora's thought.

"I'm sorry, darling," said Nora.

"Well." Marie took a deep breath and hoped her friends hadn't noticed how it shuddered a little. "I think we've been at it long enough."

"I would encourage you to stay, but in all honesty, I'm beginning to feel as though I live here," said Hazel with a yawn.

Nora glanced at her watch. "I should be going anyway. It's impossible to navigate the mews in the blackout, and last time an air raid warden yelled at me for shining my torch too high."

They all put their coats on and made their way to the street after Hazel locked up. Once they'd said goodbye on the street corner, Nora peeled off toward Hyde Park Corner.

Marie was about to turn north to her bus when Hazel gripped her arm. "Wait."

"What's wrong?"

"This Neil fellow is not worth being upset over," said Hazel.

"Thank you for saying that. I just . . ." *I want someone to love me. Unconditionally and without reservation.* She had the love of her aunt and uncle, but she could never quite shake the feeling that she'd been foisted on them. She wanted someone to choose to love her.

"I don't know if you remember, but there was a gentleman in my office that day Dennison brought you to the agency. Do you remember?" Hazel asked.

"Mr. Calloway?" Marie asked.

"Yes. He mentioned you the next time we spoke over the phone. He sounded quite taken with you. You don't have to if you don't want to, but if you'd like to go to dinner with him, I could arrange it," said Hazel.

"I don't know," she said slowly. Was she ready for another man's rejection so soon after Neil? Should she even be thinking about dinner with any man so close to her tribunal date?

"Here." Hazel pulled out the little pencil and pad she always carried around with her. "This is his exchange. You can ring him if you feel like it. I don't have to be involved at all except to say that it might do you some good to go out with a nice man."

Hazel ripped out the paper and handed it to her. Marie stared at it for a moment before taking it and stuffing it into her bag.

"I'll think about it."

ten

On the day of her tribunal hearing, Marie found herself in a crowded but eerily quiet waiting room on the second floor of a nondescript office building on a side street not far from the university. Nora sat on her right and Hazel on her left, because in the end, Marie had decided it wouldn't hurt to have a respectably married woman in her corner. Everyone who had received a letter had to attend their hearing, so they were surrounded by men in tired suits and women who looked as though they'd just walked out of a Parisian couturier. A handful of children squirmed in their seats, threatening to melt onto the floor until their parents pulled them back to sitting. Hardly anyone spoke, and when they did it was in hushed tones, German and English mixing together.

The whole atmosphere was oppressive, and Marie dragged a deep breath through her nose, trying to calm herself.

"You're squirming as badly as those children," said Hazel in a low voice.

"I can't help it. Besides, I'm not as bad as Nora." She elbowed her friend. "I'm supposed to be the nervous one. It's my tribunal."

"Are you nervous?" Nora asked.

"No," she said, but she was certain her friends could feel her whole body shake.

"It will be over soon enough," said Hazel.

A woman wearing a boxy blue suit stepped into the waiting area, and there was a collective intake of breath.

The woman glanced down at the stack of papers she held, the crisp crackle of them between her fingers punctuating the tension. "Marie Bohn."

Nora squeezed her hand. "Are you ready?"

Marie gave her a thin smile. "I'll have to be."

The three of them walked through the door arm in arm, the woman with the papers leading the way.

Inside was a long table with three men sitting at the head. For all of the fear outside in the waiting room, they were innocuous looking enough. Two were balding, and one kept touching a plain white handkerchief to his nose as he sniffled. They looked up in unison as Marie approached.

"Which one of you is Miss Bohn?" asked one of the balding men.

Marie stopped a few feet from the table and unlinked her arms from her friends' in order to step forward. "I am, sir."

"And these are your witnesses?" he asked.

"Yes. Miss Nora Walcott and—"

"Do you have your papers with you?" the other hairless man cut her off.

Marie nodded, a little shaken.

"Bring them here."

She approached the table and handed over her identifying documents. *You're fine. You're fine. You're fine.*

The sniffling man looked over her papers and, without looking at Marie, gestured to the hairless man on his left. "This is Mr. Renaut. And to my right is Mr. Elliot. I am Mr. Perry. So, Miss . . . Bohn, what brought you to Britain?"

"I was educated at Ethelbrook School for Girls in Herefordshire. I arrived in the autumn of 1928," said Marie.

"And did you remain at Ethelbrook for the duration of your education?" Mr. Renault asked.

"I did. I left in June of 1932," said Marie.

"And what have you been doing since then?" asked Mr. Perry.

"First I was a switchboard operator."

"Where did you live at this time?" asked Mr. Elliot.

"With my aunt and uncle."

"Never by yourself?" he asked.

"No."

"Are you still a switchboard operator?" asked Mr. Renault.

"No. I took a job as a secretary at Royal Imperial University," Marie said.

"Are you still employed there?" asked Mr. Renault.

"I am," said Marie.

"I have a note here that you were secretary to a Pieter Gunter, a man who is wanted by the Home Office," said Mr. Perry.

Breathe. It would do her no good to faint in the tribunal hearing.

"He fled the country shortly after Germany's invasion of Poland," she said in as steady a voice as she could muster.

"Your employer fled?" Mr. Elliot said, peering over his glasses. "That is most concerning."

Her chest felt like someone was squeezing it from all sides, and her heart rammed against her rib cage.

"To clarify, sir, the university is my employer. I was attached, by the university, to Herr Gunter's department," she said.

"But you were this man's secretary," said Mr. Perry.

"I was the secretary for the German Department," she said. "There were several other professors in the department as well. I also performed administrative tasks for them."

There was a great shuffling of papers at that, and the men looked at one another before moving on.

"Where are you currently living, Miss Bohn?" asked Mr. Renault.

"Number 5 Taviton Street with my aunt, uncle, and cousin. It's in Bloomsbury."

"Who is your first witness?" asked Mr. Renault.

Marie gestured behind her. "My friend Nora Walcott."

"Miss Walcott, where do you reside?" asked Mr. Elliot.

"My house is at 22 Crawley Mews," said Nora, stepping forward.

"*Your* house?" Mr. Perry asked.

"Yes. I own it," said Nora.

"You mean your father owns it?" Mr. Perry asked with an indulgent smile.

Marie could feel Nora tense next to her. "I own it. The deed is in my name. It was my solicitor who brokered the sale under my direction. After my father died."

"That is most unusual," muttered Mr. Elliot.

"If you're such a modern woman, I can only assume that you work, Miss Walcott?" asked Mr. Perry.

"I do."

"Where is it that you are employed?" he asked.

Marie cast a glance at Nora as her friend adjusted her glasses. She knew Nora was buying herself time because they hadn't discussed this. The questions were meant to be for Marie. Nora's job at the Home Office was never meant to come into this, otherwise she never would have allowed her to come here and risk it.

"I am also a secretary," Nora finally said.

Marie knew what it must've cost Nora to distill a job she'd fought so hard for into five simple words, and she shifted a little closer so her arm just brushed Nora's.

"All right, Miss Walcott. What have you to say about Miss Bohn's character?" asked the rather bored-sounding Mr. Elliot.

"I have known Marie since I was twelve years old. She has always been a dear friend, and one of the few people in this world I trust without reservation. I have no doubt as to the quality of her character. She is no threat to me or this country. She never has been," said Nora.

"And am I to presume you will say more of the same, Miss . . ." Mr. Perry looked at Hazel.

"Mrs. Nathaniel Carey."

"You're married?" asked Mr. Renault.

"For five years, yes," said Hazel.

"Then I presume you're a homemaker," said Mr. Renault.

"I am not," said Hazel.

All three men frowned, and Mr. Elliot asked, "Where are you employed?"

"I am a matchmaker at Mayfair Matrimonial Agency."

"That is Lady Moreton's matchmaking business, isn't it? I've read of it in the papers," said Mr. Elliot, obviously a little impressed by Hazel's connection to the peerage.

"That's correct," said Hazel.

"Extraordinary," Mr. Elliot murmured. "A married matchmaker."

"Who better to advise people in love?" quipped Hazel.

"And do you also feel as strongly about Miss Bohn's character as your friend does?" asked Mr. Renault.

"I do. Marie was a bridesmaid at my wedding. She attended my mother's funeral. She has been with me through every moment of celebration and struggle since we were schoolgirls."

"This is all very touching, but it really tells us nothing about whether Miss Bohn is a threat to this country," said Mr. Perry.

"That's because she isn't a threat," Nora burst out.

Out of the corner of her eye, Marie saw Hazel tug on Nora's arm.

"Mr. Perry, Mr. Elliot, Mr. Renault," said Hazel, turning on her most brilliant smile, the one that Nora had seen her use on their dormitory's matron just before Hazel had talked their way out of receiving punishment for breaking curfew. "Marie works at the German Department of Royal Imperial University because it was a natural place for a woman with such fluency, which—I must say—she would gladly use for the good of this country if she were called upon to do so. However, I know that her greatest ambition is to become a wife and mother. All she wants is a chance to settle into the domestic life that all women wish for. In fact, just the other week she asked me to arrange a connection between her and a well-respected gentlemen who is also a client of mine."

Marie watched her friend, a little smile playing over her face. The truth was, despite manufacturing matches with an eye for marriage, Marie knew Hazel had a fierce streak of independence, just like her infamous mother. Hazel *enjoyed* working, and she was always the first to encourage her friends. It had been Hazel who had suggested meeting Nora outside of the Home Office after her first day of work with a bouquet of flowers. It was Hazel who would always say, "I want to understand what your day at the university is like," and Marie would laugh and tell her the intricacies of typing and filing and answering the phone before admitting that running an office with so many different professorial personalities as well as graduate and undergraduate students took skill.

Still, Hazel's picture of Marie as a woman whose sole desire was for a life of domesticity seemed to be working. The three men had sat back in their seats, and although Mr. Elliot remained bored, Mr. Perry and Mr. Renault were slowly nodding.

"Thank you, Mrs. Carey," said Mr. Renault. "Your testimony is noted."

"I'd like to return to the matter at hand if that suits my esteemed colleagues," said Mr. Elliot. "You say you live with your aunt and uncle, Miss Bohn. What sort of people are they?"

"My uncle is an engineer at an architecture firm. My aunt is a homemaker. Their son, Henrik, clerks at my uncle's firm. He is meant to be learning the trade."

The questioning continued, back and forth, back and forth, for what seemed like an age. They wanted to know about Marie's habits, where she spent her time, the kinds of films she went to and books she read. The entire time, she held her breath, waiting for one of the men to mention the CPGB, but the meetings never came up. Instead, there were more questions specifically for Nora and Hazel. They recounted meeting

Marie and answered questions about whether she regularly disclosed the contents of her letters from her parents.

Finally, the three men looked at one another and declared that they were finished. Marie was directed to wait for her classification designation in the post.

As soon as they were released and the door shut behind them, Marie could feel all the energy drain from her.

"It's done," said Hazel, seeming to sense that Marie felt as though she had bags of sand tied to her limbs.

"What on earth was that about wanting to find a man?" Nora hissed as they hurried out of the waiting room.

"They ate it up with a spoon," said Hazel.

Nora shook her head. "Sometimes I can't tell when you're being serious about that sort of thing."

"Oh, please. You've known me for long enough to know I don't believe in all that tosh, but I know what men want to think about women," said Hazel.

Her friends continued to bicker around her, but Marie had stopped listening. She had made it through the tribunal, but those men held her fate in their hands. One decision from them, and she'd be confined to an internment camp. What if they found out about the CPGB? What if someone had told them, like Neil, or one of his friends who'd decided that she wasn't really behind the cause? What if Herr Gunter really was as nefarious as Dennison seemed to think he was? She could be locked away, her freedom gone for the duration the entire war. And if she was sent away, surely that would mean more scrutiny for her aunt, uncle, and Henrik. Would she be condemning them to a war spent in internment, too?

What happened if Britain won?

What if Germany won?

Her thoughts spiraled faster and faster. The vise around her chest squeezed tight. No matter how hard she tried, she couldn't seem to get enough air into her lungs. She breathed deep, deeper, but—

"Marie, what's wrong?" Nora asked, rounding on her.

That was when Marie realized she was gasping for breath. "I can't—I can't—"

"Here," said Nora, guiding her to a nicked wooden bench in the hallway of the municipal building. "Just sit here for a moment."

Her entire body felt hot, and it took everything not to rip at the buttons of her suit jacket. She half slumped, half fell onto the bench.

"Marie!" Hazel exclaimed.

"It's fine. You're fine," said Nora, shooting a look over her shoulder at Hazel before putting one hand on either of Marie's shoulders. "I want you to listen to me. You're going to breathe in through your nose when I say so, and you're going to breathe out through your mouth when I say so. Do you understand?"

She nodded weakly, fighting for breath.

"Breathe in," ordered Nora.

She breathed in.

"Now, slow and steady, breathe out," said Nora.

She did, and Nora hummed encouragement.

They sat like that, Marie letting Nora dictate her breath, until her heart stopped pounding and her lungs seemed to fill with air again. The sheen of sweat over her brow had cooled, and she felt clammy all over. But better. She certainly felt better.

"What happened?" Hazel asked softly.

"She had an attack," said Nora. "I've had them before, mostly during my debut. Mother would stand there and watch my every move, and I knew that if I wasn't perfect, she would be disappointed. I hated it."

"What did you do to stop them?" Marie asked shakily.

Nora gave her a sad smile. "After Papa died, I found I didn't care about any of that any longer. I had you two, and that was family enough for me."

The bridge of Marie's nose tingled, and she could feel the tears welling up in her eyes. "I don't know what I would do without you."

Without a word, they all leaned in, arms wrapping around one another. They stayed like that until a lady walked by and tutted.

"You've made me all watery," said Nora, pulling out a handkerchief to wipe her glasses.

"Hazel started it," said Marie with a laugh.

"I did not," said Hazel.

"Enough of this," said Nora, holding up her hands. "Five o'clock isn't too far off. What say you to martinis in the privacy of this 'modern woman's' own home?"

"I think," said Marie, "that's the best idea anyone's had all day."

eleven

Since Herr Gunter's disappearance, Marie had begun to feel super-fluous in the department she'd quietly run for years. She'd never realized just how much of her day was occupied by the head of the department's demands. Now she found herself missing them.

Already she'd tidied Herr Gunter's office, with the Home Office's permission delivered via a message from Dr. Hugh's secretary. Last week she'd reorganized all of the department's files stored in the towering bank of cabinets lining the wall opposite the door. And the day after Neil had told her that he didn't like her *in that way*, she'd set about cleaning the office from top to bottom.

She had the radio on now, since most of the professors had decided it was safer to hole up in their homes in case the Home Office—or the police—came around again. The BBC was airing a program to promote the Dig for Victory campaign, which was all very well and good if you had a plot of land to cultivate vegetables on, but was rather difficult in a block of mansion flats in Bloomsbury.

"Leeks and onions are suitable for planting this time of year, but don't forget the humble potato," the presenter was saying.

Neil had never really *been interested*, she reminded herself as her mind wandered. The flirtation and the kiss had merely been a game to him.

"Maybe I'm just as bad as him," she muttered to herself as she dampened the rag in her hand with wood cleaner and gave the top of a cabinet a good, hard swipe. A cloud of dust exploded into the air and sent her hand diving into her pocket for a handkerchief.

No, she told herself as she picked up the rag again, she hadn't played games. Her kiss had been genuine. Her enthusiasm for him had been real. Yet to him she'd been nothing more than a doting girl who'd tell him how wonderful he'd been when he spoke. She'd propped up a mediocre man, and that wasn't enough for her.

She thought about the telephone number Hazel had given her. Mr. Richard Calloway. They'd met so briefly with all of those other people around that it was impossible to say what she really thought about him, but he seemed kind and Hazel approved of him. Those were two marks for him in the "good" column. Perhaps she might consider ringing him if she could get up the courage. One day.

The hinges on the office door squeaked, and she peered over her shoulder just in time to see Dr. Hughes stick his head in and look at her in bewilderment.

"Dr. Hughes, how can I help you?" she asked, scrambling down from the chair she stood on.

"What are you doing up there?" he asked.

She held out the rag and the bottle of cleaning solution. "Cleaning."

"I see. I believe we employ a staff to do that very thing, Miss Bohn," he said.

Yes, but she was going to go crazy if she stayed in this office for any longer with so little to do. Never mind that the cleaning staff clearly neglected the tops of filing cabinets.

"It has been quiet in the department the last few weeks," she said.

Dr. Hughes readjusted his glasses on the bridge of his nose and peered down at her. "Are you not assisting the department's other professors?"

She'd tried—oh, how she'd tried. As soon as she'd made her way back to the office from Hazel's matchmaking agency and the meeting with Dennison, she'd gone to each professor and explained the situation at hand. She kept things clear and to the point, and when it came to the end of the story she said to each one of them, "It would be my pleasure to support you however I can."

Not a one had taken her up on her offer.

It was as though the stench of Herr Gunter—unconvicted though he might be—clung to her. She was tainted by association. The few times the German-born professors in the department came to the office, they gave her a wide berth, as though merely speaking to her might be considered some sort of collusion that would see them rounded up and thrown into a camp. The British ones looked at her with sympathy, but still murmured that they were "fine, fine." Marie wasn't sure which rejection unsettled her more.

"How can I help you, Dr. Hughes?" she asked, setting her supplies down.

"Please sit," the dean said.

She hesitated but moved to her desk and took her place behind the typewriter. Dr. Hughes sat opposite, pulled off his glasses, and polished them on a bright red handkerchief. He put the glasses back on, looked around, and began drumming this fingers on the arm of his chair.

"Dr. Hughes, is something wrong?" she asked.

He glanced over at her. "I don't suppose there's any easy way to say this, Miss Bohn, so I'll just have out with it. There has been a great deal of scrutiny on this department after Herr Gunter ran out with no word."

The way he said it made it sound as though Herr Gunter was a foolish schoolboy who had played an unfortunate prank.

"I can imagine that it has set everyone on edge," she said.

"Precisely. And that is why we must be so very careful with what we do. We are at war, after all."

As though either of them needed a reminder. The war was everywhere. Newspapers, radio programs, newsreels. Already two of the other families in her aunt and uncle's building had seen their boys off to the railway station, packs on their backs, to be trained. Only there didn't seem to be much fighting going on at all at the moment. It wasn't quite a stalemate, but with all of the bluster and brashness that had sparked the entire affair, the last few weeks had been more whimper than roar.

"I'm afraid that all of this leaves us in the difficult position of what to do with you, Miss Bohn."

"Me?" she asked.

"Well, clearly you don't have enough to occupy your time."

She swallowed. "I don't understand, sir."

"I think, given the circumstances, it's best if we terminate your employment with the German Department, don't you?"

"No!" The word burst forth from her before she could stop herself, and the dean looked stunned. Quickly, she said, "I only mean, is there nowhere else in the university I could work?"

Since the declaration of war, her position had become more than a job. It was a lifeline, a comfort. In a world where merely opening her mouth could expose her to derision and distrust, her little corner of Royal Imperial was a haven. Now Dr. Hughes seemed intent on taking that away from her.

"I think, given the circumstances, it would be inappropriate for you to continue your employment at Royal Imperial," he said.

"The circumstances?" she asked, her mouth gone dry. "But I haven't done anything wrong."

"Come now, Miss Bohn. You must understand how it looks. The Home Office shows up in my office the morning that Herr Gunter flees. The investigation is still active. Mr. Dennison dropped by just yesterday to make further inquiries. He asked about you."

"Me?" she asked. But she and Hazel had been so careful. There had been nothing to indicate that Dennison knew anything of her connection to the Mayfair Matrimonial Agency.

"And now you want me to move you to another department," Dr. Hughes went on. "Where? The sciences and engineering will be engaged in projects for the government. *That* certainly would not be an appropriate place given the suspicion that's fallen on you."

"I could stay in the Humanities."

"Where we have a full secretarial staff." He folded his hands and looked at her, his gaze not unkind but carrying no sign of softening. "Think of what people will say—what they're already saying. Herr Gunter's German-born secretary, a woman who was privy to all of his meetings, his diary, his correspondence, is bound to raise suspicions. It's high time that the gossip be handled or we risk even another investigation from our friend Mr. Dennison. No one wants that."

"But I haven't done anything wrong," she protested.

"You're German, Miss Bohn."

And with those words, he cut each of her arguments off at the knees. She was German, and nothing would change that.

⌒⌢

Don't cry. Don't *cry.*

Marie sat on the now-empty bus, staring out the window at the unfamiliar bustle of a working day as she blinked back tears. This was the first time she'd been out of work for any reason other than holiday or sickness since she had left school. She'd been *sacked.*

The sourness in her stomach rose up again. Dr. Hughes hadn't even stayed to see her off. She was so little threat that even a security guard was unwarranted. Yet after four years of service to Royal Imperial, she had been banished, exiled from the place where she'd found at least some satisfaction in being useful. Belonging.

She squeezed her eyes closed and forced herself to breathe slowly through her nose like Nora'd taught her. What was she going to tell her aunt and uncle? What was she going to tell her friends?

The bus screeched to a halt at the stop half a block down from the flat, and Marie scrambled off. Desperate for the sanctuary of home, she fumbled for her keys to unlatch the door and ran up the stairs of her aunt and uncle's building.

"Tante Matilda," she called out as she shut the flat door behind her. Her uncle would be at work until at least six o'clock, but her aunt should be at home unless she was playing bridge with her friends.

There was a shuffling from behind her bedroom door as she pulled off her coat and the thin scarf she'd worn tucked into her lapels. But when the door opened, it wasn't her aunt or Frau Hafner tidying up. It was Henrik.

"What are you doing?" she asked, taking in her bedroom. He'd clearly gone through her things, because a pair of stockings was hanging out of the side of a drawer that had been hastily pushed in, and he'd knocked over a pile of books on her desk.

Henrik straightened, a stack of papers in his hand. "I should ask you the same thing."

"This is my bedroom. What are you doing with those?" she asked, snatching the papers out of his hands. It was one of Neil's speeches.

"You're a commie," he sneered.

"It's just a speech a friend asked me to look over," she said, but even she could hear how unconvincing that sounded.

"You listen to that rubbish they spout?" Henrik asked.

"Not since Germany and Russia decided they were on the same side," she muttered.

His eyes narrowed. "What are you doing home?"

There was no point in hiding it from him. He'd find out when she told her aunt and uncle.

"I was fired today," she said.

His eyes bulged out. "Why?"

She told him about the investigation, unsure whether his parents had told him about the day when she'd come home pale-faced after Dennison and his questions.

"And you knew about it?" he asked.

She shook her head. "Not that it matters. The dean of the Humanities sat me down and told me I had to go." She waited for him to express some sympathy, but instead he simply stared. "Where is Tante Matilda? Is she playing cards at Mrs. Lang's?"

"Leave."

"What?"

"If you were fired from your job because the Home Office is investigating you and you're a commie, the best thing you can do for this family is leave," said her cousin.

"The Home Office isn't investigating me."

"But they are—or they will be if they haven't begun yet. Everyone knows that secretaries hold their bosses' lives in order. You had to know that he was doing something wrong."

"I didn't know anything of the sort," she said.

"Don't be naive, Marie. The Home Office probably has a file an inch thick on you by now. Everything you've ever done wrong, all written up and ready for them to pull out when they need to rank your classification."

The classification. It hung over her head like an executioner's ax, poised and waiting for the order.

"They'll dig even deeper into the lives of everyone you know. Me. Mutter and Vatter. Your parents," he said.

"They won't find anything. There isn't anything to find." She could say that about her aunt and uncle, but could she really answer for her parents? Their letters read like society columns of who had done what with whom. She hardly knew them any longer—not that she ever truly had. They weren't a family.

Henrik advanced on her now, crowding her until she was forced to trip backward over her feet. She slammed into the door, the knob hitting her back. Even with her body pressed against the wood, he stepped forward until they were so close she could smell raw onion on his breath.

"I will not let any of this to chance. You will leave, or I will report you to the Home Office myself," he said.

"Report what?"

He tilted his head, a sick smile stretching his lips. "Does it matter? They'll believe anything about any of us. That's why I can't risk you being here."

"Henrik—"

"If you condemn your beloved Tante Matilda to an internment camp, will you be able to live with that guilt?"

How could this dolt of a man cut straight to the heart of her worst fears? She was more exposed than any of them. She was the one putting the family at risk. And if she became the reason they all were interned, she'd never forgive herself.

Still, a selfish part of her wanted to cling to the only home she had ever known.

"I can't leave. Where will I go?" she asked.

"I don't care."

"Henrik, I'm your cousin," she pleaded.

"Go see how your British friends like you now. A pretentious snob and the daughter of a slut," he spat.

She pushed off the door, blood roaring in her ears, and her cousin stumbled back a few steps. "Don't you ever speak about Nora and Hazel that way again."

"I can't believe my mother and father allowed you to spend time with them. You're all so trusting of the British, as though you forget what they did to us during the last war."

"You weren't even born during the last war," she said.

His nostrils flared. "Leave, or I'll call the police myself."

Helpless. She felt helpless standing in her aunt and uncle's corridor, facing off against their son, whom they loved more than anything in this world, just as they should. She wanted to scream the house down, to slap and claw at him, but he was right. Her aunt and uncle had done everything they could to love and protect her, but she was not their daughter. She would not jeopardize their safety because she was too selfish and scared to leave when it was the right thing to do. To protect them.

"Why are you doing this?" she gritted out through clenched teeth.

"I know what you all think. I'm lazy. I drink too much. But I see what's happening. I know what this war is going to bring. You aren't a Müller, and I'm doing what I need to protect my family. *You* are not my family."

He walked to the door, but paused long enough to throw over his shoulder, "If you aren't gone in a half hour, I'll call the police myself."

The tears she'd held back on the bus began to streak down her face, but she wasn't going to stay and give him the satisfaction of seeing her pain. Instead, she hauled the suitcase she'd once used to travel to and from Ethelbrook from underneath her bed and began to deliberately transfer clothing from her chest of drawers. She would take only what she needed. Nora or Hazel could come for the rest and send them to— wherever she was going.

All while she packed, Marie prayed that the clatter of Tante Matilda's mules on the hardwood floors would signal her return and this would all be over. But her aunt didn't return, and what would it have mattered even if she had? There was still Henrik lurking in the background. She and her aunt and uncle might be able to stop him now, but he was a loose cannon, ready to strike out in retribution for years of pent-up resentment. He'd always hated her intrusion on the family. Her intelligence when she brought home strong marks from school and he floundered in mediocrity. Her tenderness toward his mother and father.

Marie latched her suitcase and hauled it off her bed. The solid leather bag hit her leg, but she hardly noticed. Miserable, she gathered up her coat and purse and sidestepped her way out into the hall. Henrik was nowhere to be seen, but she knew he was hiding somewhere. He would make sure that she left the house.

She made her way down to the street. It had started to rain, so she sheltered in the doorway of her aunt and uncle's building for a moment, peering up at the sky. She couldn't go wandering around for hours on end. She would wind up soaked to the core, even more downtrodden than she was now. She needed a place that was dry and safe where she could collect her thoughts and figure out how to pick herself up out of the ashes of this burning day.

A cab rolled by—a rarer and rarer sight these days—and inspiration struck her. She stuck out her arm and rushed to the curb as quickly as her bag would allow her. The cabbie glided to a stop. She told him she was going to Whitehall, and he leaped out to help with her bag. A tiny gesture of empathy from one human to another, but it made her heart ache just that little bit less.

It didn't take long to cross to Central London, and they only had to yield once for a motorcade carrying some cabinet official or another. When the cab glided to a stop, she paid the driver and waved him off when he offered to carry her bag into the imposing building. Instead, she maneuvered the bag through the doors herself and gave her name to a guard at the front desk who telephoned up. Then Marie settled down into one of the chairs lining the lobby wall to wait.

Five minutes later, the rush of click-clacking heels across the marble floor jerked her to attention as Nora stopped in front of her. "Marie, what are you doing here?"

Marie hauled herself to her feet. "After all this time, can you believe this is the first time I've been inside your office building?"

Nora looked at the floor. "Why do you have a suitcase?"

She pulled her shoulders back and mustered as much pride as she could. "I find myself between homes. I know it's an imposition, but could I please stay with you until I can find myself a place to live?"

Nora's mouth gaped open. "Between homes? What do you mean? What happened to your aunt and uncle? Are they all right?"

"Henrik threatened me, and I left." The truth stung like acid on her tongue.

"Threatened?" Nora shook her head. "Never mind that. There's plenty of time for you to tell me about it later. Of course you can come live with me as long as you like. As though that were even a question."

"You were so happy to have your independence, I wasn't entirely sure how you'd feel about sharing a house."

"No, we'll have none of that. There will be plenty of time for self-pity, but first let's get you home. You can have a bath to warm up while I make up the spare bedroom."

"Thank you," said Marie. And with that, all her resolve broke. She began to sob, and Nora gathered her up to hold her close.

SAMANTHA

Now

twelve

"I think," said Nora, "that is enough for today."

"There's more?" asked Samantha.

Nora offered her a weary grin. "We're only at the beginning, but I'm an old woman and it's my prerogative to be tired."

"Of course."

Samantha sank back into the cushions of the sofa. At some point during Nora's story, she'd edged her shoes off and tucked her feet under her. Six mugs of tea, some empty and others only half drunk, lay forgotten on the coffee table, courtesy of David, who'd kept them well supplied with drinks, even slipping off to make lunch somewhere in the back of the house. Samantha hardly noticed any of it, grateful though she was.

She'd had no idea about any of the story Nora was slowly unwinding for her. Sure, she'd heard inklings of the past. She knew her grandmother had gone to school in England. Simple math told her that Grandma would've lived through the war. But all of the rest . . .

One day, when you're ready, come ask me about what happened during the war, mein Liebling. *Then maybe I'll tell you.*

But for all of her curiosity, Samantha had never gone back for those stories. Instead, she'd left for college in Chicago, and suddenly her world seemed so much larger. She had friends, boyfriends, school. Then it was a master's program, a career. The visits to her grandmother had become fewer and further between, and when they did happen they were dominated by holiday traditions, a controlled chaos that hardly left time for sitting leisurely in the living room, listening to old records with a cup of hot chocolate warming her hands.

She should've made the time. She should've asked about the war, the friends Grandma had left behind, all of it. And now it was too late.

"David," said Nora. "Why don't you take Samantha to that pub down the road? The one with the garden. It'll be light for hours, and she should enjoy the sunshine while we have it."

"Of course," said David, straightening in his chair and looking to Samantha. "If you'd like to, that is."

"If you don't mind," said Samantha.

"Not at all. I'll just take these things back to the kitchen."

When he bent to gather up some of the mugs, Samantha stole another look at him. He was tall with dark—almost black—hair and blue eyes much like his grandmother's. A touch of stubble covered his jaw, but his hair looked as though it had just been freshly cut and cleaned up along the back of his neck. He wore his moss-green sweater—or jumper, she supposed he would call it—with the sleeves pushed up to his elbows and a crisp white shirt poking out from the V at his neck.

He moved off, revealing his grandmother watching her with a knowing expression. Samantha blushed and asked, "Won't you join us?"

Nora laughed. "It's good of you to ask, but Muriel, the woman who comes to help me in the evenings, will be here any moment. Also, it's a production to take me anywhere these days."

"You seem so fit," she said.

Nora tapped her temple. "In my mind, yes. In my body, most days, although I move slowly and need a wheelchair if I'm out of this house. But that doesn't change the fact that I was born during the First World War. These days, if I go out, it's usually with twenty-four hours' notice and one of my boys will bring his car around."

"Your boys?" she asked.

"David or his father, or Colin and his partner, Greg. Greg especially loves my club, so sometimes he'll whisk me off for tea."

"The Harlan?"

"The very one. I have the honor of holding the longest membership in the club's history. Ah, here's David."

He was holding Samantha's green military-style jacket. She stood, thinking he would hand it to her, but instead he held it out and helped her slip it on, as though it were made of the finest cashmere rather than plain heavy-gauge cotton.

They said their goodbyes to Nora—David promising to be respectful of Samantha's jet lag and have her back at a reasonable hour—and made their way down the road to the pub.

"If you'll let me know what you'd like and find a table, I'll get us drinks," said David.

"Since I'm in Britain, I feel as though I should have a pint of ale," she said.

"Good choice. I'll just be a minute."

He disappeared through the pub doors, and she wove her way to the back of the garden, where a table stood empty next to a wall of climbing ivy. All around, women in sunglasses and light jackets sat behind glasses of wine, and to her right a group of men in suits sat with their ties pulled off, barking laughter at a story involving someone called Cy.

She made a quick check of her phone, firing off a message to tell Marisol she'd managed to stay awake and she'd call tomorrow. Then she hesitated before sending a message to Dad to convey to her texting-averse mother:

Can you ask Mom if Grandma ever talked to her about the war when she was growing up?

Almost immediately, the phone dinged:

She says not much.

Your grandfather told her a little bit about his time in the RAF.

She frowned and messaged back:

Did you know Grandma Marie thought she might be interned?

A message back:

Your mom says she had no idea.
I didn't know either.
I guess it makes sense because she was born in Germany.

Samantha asked:

Why did Grandma never talk about it?

Dad, reliable as always, sent her a message back within the minute:

Mom says: I got the impression she missed people too much.
After the war, she and your grandfather didn't have much money,
but they were a lot more comfortable by the time I was born.
They would go over to England every five years or so.
Never took us kids.

She spotted David coming through the door to the pub, so she put her phone away and stuck up her hand to wave. When he arrived, he set their beers down along with two menus.

"It's just pub food, but it's good," he said.

"That sounds perfect," she said, studying her menu even though she knew immediately that she would have the chicken and leek pie.

"So your grandmother never told you any of that story . . ." he started as soon as she picked up her beer.

She took a sip and licked away the caramel-flavored foam that lingered on her lips. More than one pint and she'd be asleep in her food in ten minutes flat, but this was good. The sunshine, the chatter, the drinks, David.

"I can't believe that I didn't know any of it," she said. "It sounds like Mom knew bits and pieces about the war, but I don't think she has any idea that her mother thought she might be interned." She paused, pressing her fingernail into the soft cardboard of a coaster. "I was telling the truth when I said that my grandmother and I used to be close. I grew up just a few miles from her house, and I used to go around after school at least once a week, especially after Grandpa died when I was about thirteen. I used to ask her to tell me old stories. I know all about her childhood in Germany, but she always told me she'd tell me the rest later. My biggest regret is not following up on that promise. I don't even know much about how she and Grandpa met. And now I have a eulogy I don't know how to write about a woman I feel like I hardly knew."

She saw him move before she fully processed what he was doing, but that didn't mean she was prepared for the moment when his hand covered hers. "We're all guilty of looking at the people in our lives with blinders on, especially parents and grandparents. It's hard to imagine that they could have lived lives outside of the ones we see them in every day."

"It doesn't seem like you have that problem with Nora," she said.

He grinned. "That's because if she ever thought I believed that her life started and stopped at being a grandmother, she'd probably banish me from her house. We've been close my entire life, but when I grew up, I began to realize just how special she is.

"You're also catching me between projects," he added. "I have more time than usual to spend with her right now."

"She obviously adores you."

"The feeling is mutual. Now, I've been thinking about your eulogy. Do you think it would help to see some of the places where Marie spent her time during the war? I'm sure I could find the Müllers' house in Bloomsbury if it survived the bombing and the developers. And Royal Imperial University is simple enough."

"I'd love to see them." Anything to understand even that little bit more about the life her grandmother had led.

"Then we'll go on Wednesday. Muriel is taking Gran to an appointment at her GP in the afternoon, so I'll work in the morning and come around to pick you up around two if that's all right with you," he said.

Samantha beamed, even though it was the sort offer anyone might make for a visiting guest. It felt, for all intents and purposes, like a date. And it had been a very long time since Samantha Morris had been on a date.

"That would be great," she said, hiding her smile behind another sip of beer.

"Good, good. If you're feeling up for it, we could go to dinner as well," he said. He smiled that crooked little smile she'd come to like. "I wouldn't want you to come to London and never venture out of West Kensington for food."

"Yes, that would be a shame," she agreed with a grin.

One chicken and leek pie and a daring second pint of beer later, David walked Samantha home. He unlocked his grandmother's front door and, after several reassurances that she would be able to find her way up to the bedroom where she'd dropped her things earlier, they said goodbye.

Samantha closed the front door carefully, smiling as she heard David's key lock the additional dead bolt that he'd told her his grandmother only locked at night. Despite the beer and the jet lag, she found herself feeling light as ever as she climbed the stairs.

In her room, she took off her makeup, brushed her teeth, and removed her contacts. On went glasses, yoga pants, and a loose cotton top. Up went her hair. Then, situated under the covers, she reached into her purse and pulled out the notebook that had weighed her down with dread in the eight months since she'd learned that Grandma Marie expected her to deliver a eulogy.

At first it had been the enormity of the task that had stopped her. Summing up a person's life in ten minutes felt impossible. Then she'd spent a good two months worrying about how to write a eulogy that followed her grandmother's edict that there be nothing funerary about the memorial. But mostly she worried that putting pen to paper would make it impossible to ignore the fact that she didn't really *know* who Grandma Marie was. And that would mean confronting her very deep guilt.

But that evening, armed with Nora's stories and David's confidence, she turned to a fresh page of her notebook and began to write.

HAZEL

November 1939 to March 1940

thirteen

"Twelve bombs fell on the Shetlands yesterday in a raid by Luftwaffe planes. Those that hit land left craters nine feet deep. There were no injuries reported except to a rabbit."

—1 p.m. radio bulletin, November 14, 1939

Dinner was, without a doubt, Hazel's least favorite meal. If she wasn't working late, she usually rushed home from Mayfair, hopping on a bus and then catching the train out of Victoria back to Peckham in a desperate dash to get something—anything—on the table. The rush was exhausting, but at least it came with the satisfaction of watching Nathaniel push back from the table and give her a perfunctory thanks at the end of the meal. Late nights, however, meant rising early to make something he could reheat for his supper. All she got out of that was guilt, heightened by the tiniest drop of relief to have an evening to herself.

That Tuesday, Hazel rose, unpinned her hair from its curlers, powdered her face, hooked herself into her girdle and stockings, put on her dress, lipsticked her mouth, retrieved the paper from the front walk, and pulled on an apron to begin cooking.

Whispers of rationing abounded, but so far the Ministry of Food had issued no formal order. Hazel, already a middling cook at best, couldn't help but cringe at the thought of having to find substitutes for her already limited repertoire of dishes. That morning, she found a little bit of sausage in the larder and a now-stale end of the brown bread Nathaniel made a face at every morning when he scraped margarine over it. She sighed. Sausage ring it would have to be. Again.

Hazel turned on the tap and wet the bread before tearing and crumbling it into the meat with a good dash of salt. Then she set about pressing it into a metal mold she'd greased.

She'd heard some women enjoyed cooking, but it had never been anything but a chore to her. Between her mother's modeling work and the settlement from Hazel's father, they'd had more than enough money to spare when she was growing up. Mundane tasks like cooking and cleaning were left to Mrs. Macmillan, their housekeeper who came in every day. So while some girls might've been encouraged by their mothers to learn a few basic homemaking skills, Penelope Ricci had other ideas about what constituted an appropriate education for her daughter.

Until Hazel turned twelve, Penelope would sweep her off to the theater, opera, concerts, salons, readings, and even a portrait sitting or two, seeing no reason why a child shouldn't come along. It had been heaven, but then there had been the other nights—ones where Hazel woke up and wandered blurry-eyed into late-night parties of people sloppy on champagne and whatever drug was fashionable that month. At eight, she'd taken to locking her bedroom door so revelers couldn't get in, and pulling the pillow over her head when the groans of Penelope's latest gentleman had become too much to bear.

Then Hazel's father died, and the decadent whirlwind abruptly stopped. Penelope had come back from a meeting with her solicitor pale faced. Hazel's father's family had declared that his obligation to keep Penelope and her had ended with his death; there would be no more money.

The parties dried up, and all the people who'd crashed through their lives amid the seductive chaos moved on to other, luckier women. Penelope's modeling work soon went the same way, for there were younger beauties to paint and photograph. Thus mother and daughter moved south of the Thames into a flat that Penelope learned to cleaned herself.

A little part of Hazel had hoped that their life would settle down into a quieter existence and they might become a bit more like the other families she saw in the park or shopping at Harrods, but her mother, always full of surprises, had done something extraordinary. Using every connection she could, she'd secured a place for Hazel at the prestigious Ethelbrook School for Girls—with a scholarship to boot. The happiest day of Hazel's twelve-year-old life had been when she'd boarded the train and sped off to the countryside and a new life of normalcy.

Of course, no one at Ethelbrook had thought to teach the schoolgirls about cooking or cleaning or any domestic matters either. It had generally been assumed that the girls would have some sort of help, because most of their families paid the breathtaking fees to board and educate their daughters. In turn, they were expected to marry a man of at least enough ambition to advance his career modestly every few years while they kept a small household and had several children. A few lucky girls might even do well enough for themselves as to move in the same circles as the Cunards, Ashley-Coopers, Plunket-Greens, and Mitfords.

Hazel's ambitions weren't so lofty. She'd needed a job after school and found one working as a secretary at the Mayfair Matrimonial Agency while she lived with her mother. It had taken several months before Hazel, distracted by the excitement of her first job, realized her mother's beauty seemed to be rushing from her like an ebbing tide. Penelope became gaunt and sickly in a matter of months, hardly able to eat and too weak to do more than read on the old gray sofa in their sitting room. When Hazel finally convinced her mother to see her doctor, he told them that it was cancer of the stomach. Her mother's death had been slow and painful, and it had torn Hazel—who now understood more of the world and the sacrifices Penelope had made by having her—to pieces.

A creaking above Hazel's head announced that Nathaniel was awake as she put the sausage ring into the oven. She knew that the women who lived on their street gossiped about her, the neighborhood oddity who made her husband suffer through late meals and laundry *sent out*. Her own mother-in-law seemed to find Hazel's career a moral failing. She did her best to compensate for it by cooking him breakfast every morning. That was a little daily ritual she could give him.

Hazel set about laying things out for breakfast. First came the place mats, and then the plates, glasses, and teacups. Then, just as she did every morning, she took a deep breath and opened the silverware drawer. Nestled next to the knives, forks, and spoons was a smaller silver set. The child's flatware had been a gift from her mother-in-law—silver, Gertrude had proudly announced. Hazel's breath hitched every morning when she saw it.

Deliberately, she pulled out full-sized silverware and closed the drawer with a quiet click. It was still too soon to expect her period, but she'd checked this morning just in case. As always, she'd felt her heart lift a little when she'd seen no blood. Maybe this would be the month.

By the time Nathaniel shuffled into the kitchen in his gray house slippers, yawning and stretching, she had restored her usual, pleasant expression and had the kettle on the boil and eggs frying in the pan.

"It'll all be ready in a minute, dearest," she said brightly, turning toward him and trying not to flinch when hot oil spat on her exposed arm.

He nodded and brushed by her. When they'd first married, he would sweep her up in his arms and away from the stove, bending her backward with a deep kiss.

Her hand gripped the metal spatula she held, and she turned back to the stove.

"The paper was wet again this morning. Could you speak to the boy about tossing it onto the step so it's out of the rain?" she asked.

"I thought you were going to say something the next time you paid him," he said around a deep, hacking cough.

"Are you ill?" she asked.

He grunted. "Just my usual cough," he said as he reached into the pocket of his sweater for his cigarettes and shook one out of the packet.

She frowned. "I wish you wouldn't smoke at the table."

He looked up, a match poised in his hands to strike it against the back of the book. "What?"

"Please don't smoke at the table," she said.

His face contorted, but his expression was gone so quickly she must've imagined it. Deliberately, he took the cigarette out of his mouth and un- folded the paper to hold it to block his face from view. "First British De- stroyer Lost in War: HMS *Blanche* Sunk by Mine in Thames Estuary" read the headline, but all Hazel could see was the bloom of a wet stain running down the middle of the paper.

"The ship was accompanying her sister, Basilisk, when they entered a mine- field laid the night before by German destroyers," droned the radio bulletin as Hazel tried to focus on the agency's accounts at her desk that after- noon. The war had brought with it a surge in lonely hearts looking for companionship, and with the clients came long hours of interviews and late nights making matches. She'd taken to grabbing time wherever she could to do the more mundane tasks of running the agency such as pay- ing the bills, but today she was struggling to focus.

The look on Nathaniel's face as he put away his cigarettes was to blame. It had followed Hazel like a specter the entire day. She thought about it as she called her matches that morning and received reports about how their previous evenings' dinners had gone. It had been with her while she went over the accounts with Nancy to review who should receive a firm letter reminding them of their obligation to pay the agency for successfully matching them. And when she'd interviewed two women and a man all looking for love or, at the very least, companionship, she couldn't keep her thoughts from turning back to the man she shared a life with.

It all seemed clear: Nathaniel resented her.

"Men are never true," her mother had told her so many times, but Hazel hadn't listened. Nathaniel had appeared in her life like a beacon to guide her down the path of respectability and she'd never looked back.

He'd asked her out, and one dinner became a string of dates. She'd felt proud walking into the cinema on his arm or sitting across from him at a little Italian restaurant in Kennington in a dress borrowed from Nora. Nathaniel was a clerk in the Ministry of Fisheries and Agriculture—a junior clerk, yes, but one with prospects. A few years older than her, he had opinions and seemed to know about the world in a way the handful of boys she knew never did. He told her she was beautiful and, even if she didn't fully believe him, he made her feel as though to *him* it was true. He'd charmed her so utterly that it had taken hardly any persuasion for him to convince her to break one rule the daughter of an unwed mother knew by heart. Six weeks later, she'd found out she was pregnant.

Like mother, like daughter. Except Hazel had been determined she wouldn't bring another bastard into this world.

A man cleared his throat, and Hazel froze. Dennison, the man from the Home Office, pushed her door until it was fully open, the hinges' squeak prickling the hairs on the back of her neck.

"Mrs. Carey," he said.

Carefully, Hazel closed the ledger she was working in and folded her hands across the top of it.

All of the matches were legitimate, she reminded herself. The agency had done nothing wrong. *She'd* done nothing wrong. But Hazel's heart pounded a little faster as Dennison walked through the door and took one of the seats in front of her desk, uninvited.

"I'm sorry," said Nancy, glaring at the man from the doorway. "I told Mr. Dennison you were occupied but he came in anyway"

"It's fine, Nancy. Please give my apologies to my next appointment and ask them to wait. I'm sure this will only take a moment." Hazel lifted her brow, and Dennison inclined his head.

"Yes, Mrs. Carey," said Nancy before shutting the door.

Hazel sucked in a breath. "Mr. Dennison, to what do I owe the pleasure of a visit?"

His eyes darted around the room as though a German spy might materialize from behind the floor lamp. "I thought it might be prudent to stop by and remind you of your obligations."

"My obligations?"

"As a British woman. To report any suspicious foreigners trying to use your agency. I haven't heard from you since my last visit," he said.

"Your last visit was just a few weeks ago," she said.

"It was September. Now it is November."

"Mr. Dennison, if I had seen anything nefarious, I should've telephoned," she said.

"Have any Germans attempted to use your agency?" he asked.

"I have had people of many nationalities and backgrounds come to me. I'm a matchmaker," she said.

"Have any of them seemed suspicious?" he asked.

"One man swore up and down that he'd never been married, but his wedding ring fell out of his pocket when he stood up at the end of our interview. He had a hole in his trouser pocket, you see," she said.

"Mrs. Carey, you know very well what I mean, and it is not that," said Dennison.

"No? Then I'm afraid that you're going to have to be more specific, Mr. Dennison, because I will not simply guess as to what it is that you want."

"Your insistence upon making a joke of this is very concerning, Mrs. Carey," he said.

"It is not a joke," she said sharply. "All of us know men who fought in the last war."

She remembered them, the artists and poets who'd buzzed around her mother. One, who had lost a hand at the Somme, would grow quiet, eyes hollow, whenever someone mentioned the Great War. And then there was the time someone had popped a bottle of champagne too close to an actor at an opening night celebration. He'd dropped to the floor in a ball, shaking and whimpering as piss soaked his evening trousers. It had taken two men to carry him off to another room.

"Let me tell you something about being an investigator, Mrs. Carey," said Dennison, switching tacks. "You quickly learn that the devil's in the details. You need to investigate every possibility in order to gain a full understanding of someone's motivation. If Pieter Gunter chose to use your agency, there is a reason."

"Clearly this agency's reputation precedes it."

Dennison leaned forward. "I need to see your records. I need to see how many Germans have used your agency."

Hazel mirrored him and tilted over her desk. "No."

"I'm not implying that you did anything wrong, Mrs. Carey. Enemies of the state are very clever about getting what they want without raising suspicion."

"Do you have any actual evidence that anyone has used this agency for nefarious reasons?" she asked.

He sat back and crossed and uncrossed his legs twice. "We are following up on many leads."

A little smile played over her lips, but inside she was cheering. He had nothing.

"Open your records," he said.

"Not without being compelled by a judge or the government."

"It will take me longer if you don't cooperate, but the result will be the same. I will find out who you're protecting."

"The only thing I'm protecting is the privacy of my clients."

"Then you leave me no choice. I will have to dig into the backgrounds of every person associated with this agency," said Dennison.

"I can simplify things for you in my case. I'm the illegitimate daughter of an artist and his muse."

"Mrs. Carey—"

"I'm not ashamed of who I am, Mr. Dennison. I never met my father, and my mother is dead. I have no family. I've worked at this agency since

I left school in 1931. My loyalty is to Lady Moreton, this agency, and my friends."

"And your husband, surely," Dennison said.

Hazel blinked once. "Yes, of course. That goes without saying."

"I wonder what he would think if he were to find out that his wife was under suspicion because she refused to assist the Home Office in an investigation," said Dennison.

Nerves tingled along her skin. Hazel wanted to laugh off the implied threat, but she couldn't.

"My next appointment is waiting for me," she said, glancing at her watch.

He stood and buttoned his double-breasted suit jacket. "Don't be on the wrong side of this war, Mrs. Carey."

"I assure you, I'm firmly on the side of Britain," she said. But, she suspected, her Britain looked very different from Dennison's.

fourteen

"And what exactly are you hoping for in a husband?" Hazel asked Jacinda Reeves, a young woman wearing a bored expression who was dressed rather rakishly in loose green trousers and a slim-fitting cream jumper, two days after Dennison's visit.

Miss Reeves took a long draw on her cigarette before answering. "I'll be honest with you, Mrs. Carey, I don't really care who the man is. I just want out of my father's house."

Hazel set her pen down. So Miss Reeves was *that* kind of girl—all bravado and ennui masking a terrifying mixture of fear and purposelessness.

"Miss Reeves," she said, "I take my role as a matchmaker very seriously. If you're interested in meeting a man who will love you and make you happy, then we can work together. If you just want to marry because you're trying to escape your father's influence, I suggest that you join one of the women's auxiliary branches and become a military woman."

Miss Reeves looked at Hazel with interest for the first time since she'd sat down across from her. "I'm already a volunteer ambulance driver."

"And I commend you for it," said Hazel. "Now why don't you tell me what you really want."

Miss Reeves tapped her cigarette thoughtfully on the ashtray. "I would like to find someone I actually like. Mummy and Daddy have ideas about who that should be, but they haven't introduced me to a single man I can tolerate for the duration of a dinner party."

Hazel had seen these society girls before. They would all have been compatriots of Nora—had Nora ever taken any real interest in being a debutante rather than being forced into the Season by her mother. Most of them wore their affected boredom like a badge of honor, but Hazel had found that by cutting through and asking the right questions, she could often get at what was underneath: girls who had been educated, groomed, and shown a little bit of the world only to be told that they needed to turn their backs on that to become appealing to the right sort of man.

"Excellent news, Miss Reeves. I may be able to help you yet." Hazel picked up her pen again. "Now, in an ideal world, what qualities would this future husband of yours have?"

Forty-five minutes later, Hazel was shaking Miss Reeves' hand, convinced she would have no issues finding the young woman a match. The specifics of what Jacinda Reeves wanted weren't so extraordinary: a man with modern views on marriage who thought a wife was more than an accessory to keep his house and look pleasing next to him at cocktail parties. She didn't want to be dictated to, confessing that ambulance driving was the first time she'd felt as though she had made a choice of what to do in her life all on her own. She didn't want to lose that freedom when she married.

"I'll be in touch in a few days with a few potential matches. You can let me know how you like the sound of them," said Hazel.

Miss Reeves smiled, and there was a light in her eyes that hadn't been there when they'd started the interview. "I can't thank you enough for listening."

"You can choose the ending to your own story. Don't forget that," Hazel said.

"I won't. I shall look forward to hearing from you soon."

After Hazel showed the young woman to the door, she slipped into the powder room. She hiked up her skirt and slip and held her breath as she eased her knickers down from under her garter belt. Right in the middle was a crimson slash.

Her whole body sagged, and she had to bite her lip to hold back the tears that stung her eyes. Four Saturday nights with Nathaniel and nothing to show for it. She was exhausted from the hope and disappointment, again and again.

Hazel rearranged her clothes, closed the toilet seat, and sat down, head in hands. She'd been here before. She knew she and Nathaniel would just have to try again, like the doctors said.

"You're young. It could happen," the last one told her.

But five years and three miscarriages later, it·was becoming harder and harder to hold on to that shred of hope.

Swiping at the tears wetting her cheeks, she pushed back her hair and stood. Her mascara had run, but a quick dab with a tissue set her to rights. She'd slick on the lipstick in her purse and powder her nose, and no one would be any the wiser. By the time she made her way home to Nathaniel, she would be able to muster enough of a smile that he wouldn't notice any difference.

Striding back into the reception, she called out, "Time for both of us to go home, I think, Nancy."

The telephone rang. With a rueful smile, the secretary picked it up. "Mayfair Matrimonial Agency." Nancy's brow furrowed. "Yes, she's right here, Miss Walcott."

Hazel took the phone from her secretary. "Nora?"

"You need to come to the house. Now," said Nora.

"What's wrong? What's happened?" Hazel asked in a rush, her own disappointment forgotten.

There was a pause on the line, and Nora said simply, "It's Marie."

⌒

Hazel clutched the edge of the seat as the cab rumbled over Nora's cobblestone street. It was an extravagant expense taking a cab from Mayfair to Chelsea, but there was no time to wait for the bus. As soon as the cab rolled to a stop, Hazel shook out the fare from her coin purse, gathered up her things, and tumbled out onto the street.

Nora's black front door swung open before Hazel could raise her hand to the pineapple door knocker.

"What's happened?" Hazel asked as Nora stepped back to let her pass.

Nora caught her by the wrist to keep her from racing down the corridor. "Marie's in the front room. She's upset. She got a letter today with her classification from the tribunal."

Hazel sucked in a breath. "It's an A." But Marie couldn't have a category A classification, the harshest the government handed out. It didn't make sense.

Her thoughts flashed back to Dennison, who'd sat in her office just that week. If he'd found out somehow about Hazel and the matches and her connection to Pieter Gunter . . . Hazel shook herself. That was impossible. There was nothing connected to Marie because Marie hadn't known a thing about any of it.

"She isn't category A, thank goodness. She's category B," said Nora.

Her parentage being what it was, Hazel had never had much time for God outside of compulsory Sunday services at Ethelbrook, but standing in Nora's entryway she closed her eyes and sent up a prayer of thanks. "A category B is good, isn't it? It means she won't be sent away."

But from the way Nora's lips pressed into a line, Hazel could see she had it all wrong. "I wouldn't say that to her."

Hazel nodded. "Where is she?"

"The front room. Follow me."

Nora led her through to the small sitting room overlooking the mews, where Marie sat on the sofa. Her friend's shoulders were hunched, her straight blond hair hiding her face. She looked small as a schoolgirl.

"Marie," Hazel said.

Marie lifted her head, and Hazel was stunned. Her friend was pale enough that she could swear she saw the blue veins on Marie's neck even at a distance. In Marie's hand was a letter.

"May I?" Hazel asked, indicating the letter as Nora moved to the bar tray set on one of the built-in bookshelves to pour a finger of brandy into three snifters.

"I can tell you what it says," said Marie quietly. "They've decided to give me a category B classification. They say they have reason to believe that I should be restricted in my movements."

"What does that mean?" Hazel asked, glancing from Marie to Nora and back.

"I won't be arrested, but I can't travel without informing my local police station. I can't ride a bicycle." Marie looked over her shoulder at Nora. "We'll have to get rid of the radio. I'm sorry about that."

"I can find someone to take the radio," said Nora, handing around the brandy.

"When did the letter come?" Hazel asked.

"The afternoon post," said Marie.

"It came here, not to your aunt and uncle's?" Hazel asked.

"As soon as I moved in to Nora's house, I went to the local police station to register my address. I didn't want to give the Aliens Department any reason to think that I was trying to hide from them. I didn't want them digging any deeper, just in case they hadn't found out about the CPGB meetings." Marie lifted her glass, took a gulp, and immediately started sputtering and coughing. "I hate brandy. It's awful stuff."

"But strong, which is often what's needed," said Nora, sitting down on the sofa next to Marie.

"I suppose," said Marie. "As soon as I got the letter, I went to my aunt and uncle's."

Hazel stole a glance at Nora. Both of them had been urging Marie to go to the Müllers' and tell them what Henrik had done.

"Explain what happened," Hazel said gently.

"They received their letters today, too. Only Tante Matilda was home.

I found her sitting on the sofa, surrounded by all of the letters. It was just like when we got our hearing dates, except this time she'd opened all of them up. I'm the only one who is category B. The rest are category C." Marie pressed a hand to her heart. "Henrik was right. I'm a risk to my aunt and uncle. I need to stay away."

"No," Nora said. "No, that is not what this means. Don't isolate yourself so much that you might as well be imprisoned. Avoiding the people you love is not what living is supposed to be about."

Marie's head fell back against the sofa back. "I keep going over and over again in my head every wrong thing I've ever done in my life. I wish I could go back and unpick everything. Start again."

Marie's lip quivered just enough that Hazel knew her friend was fighting back tears. Marie had never liked to cry in front of anyone. When they were at school, it hadn't mattered if one of the older girls had smashed a hockey stick into Marie's shin, or if she'd received a letter from home telling her she was to stay in London for Christmas rather than go back home. Her shyness didn't mean Marie felt anything less than Hazel or Nora did, though. In fact, sometimes Hazel wondered if her friend didn't take cuts and slights deeper.

That was why, as Hazel sat there trying to comfort one of her best friends, the guilt of holding back from these women who knew her so well tugged at her. How could she ask Marie to share her hurt and grief when Hazel wasn't being completely honest with Marie and Nora?

Hazel set her glass aside and cleared her throat. "I think there's something I need to tell you both."

fifteen

Hazel shifted in her seat while Marie and Nora watched her expectantly. Finally, she said, "I haven't been entirely honest about that man Dennison."

"Dennison?" Nora asked.

"The one from the Home Office?" Marie asked.

"Yes," she said.

"What does he have to do with any of this?" Nora asked.

Hazel swallowed. "You know how I've been working such late nights? Business really has gone up since the war started, but there's more to it than that. Before war was declared, I was working with a different set of clients. Refugees who were escaping Germany."

"You're matching them up with British citizens," said Marie, comprehension and then shock spreading over her face.

Hazel nodded. "Single men in particular were having difficulties with their applications because the government was most sympathetic toward families with children. We found that applications for asylum were processed faster if a refugee could say that they were engaged to someone already living in Britain. The matching was all done by letter, of course, although the British women I matched the gentlemen with came in just like other clients."

"Was Herr Gunter a part of this group, or was he just a coincidence?" Marie asked.

"He was the one who convinced me to start helping after I'd matched him. He was trying to help some of his Jewish colleagues escape because it had become clear that they weren't safe any longer. What I told you in front of Dennison was true, though. Mr. Gunter had heard you mention my name and the agency when you were talking to one of the other departmental secretaries. That was all."

"So you were doing exactly what Dennison accused you of?" Nora asked.

Hazel jerked back. "No! There's nothing nefarious about it."

"Then why not tell this to Dennison?" Nora asked.

"Because I don't know what will happen if I do. What we were doing wasn't illegal, but it wasn't exactly something the government would look kindly on. We *were* manufacturing matches, and the refugees who were taken into this country would have lied in interviews about their relationships' origins.

"The people this group helped were all well-known intellectuals, not spies. Professors, artists, critics. It seems that in the last few years, the Nazis had begun to take exception to them. The stories Mr. Gunter told me when he first approached me—I didn't see how I couldn't help."

"Was he the only one you spoke to?" Marie asked.

"There was one other man—a backup in case something happened to Mr. Gunter. He was a printer who sometimes made up false papers if a refugee's had been confiscated before they escaped. I contacted him after Mr. Gunter disappeared, but he said he didn't know anything. The whole group has gone to ground." Hazel turned to Marie. "I hate that I lied to you about all of this, Marie. I'm so sorry."

"You didn't lie to me." But before Hazel could feel absolved of her guilt, Marie added, "But you didn't tell me the truth either. You held this back from me. From us."

"We tell each other everything," said Nora.

Marie put up her hand. "That's not fair to Hazel. Neither of you knew about Neil or the CPGB meetings for a long time."

The back of Hazel's neck went hot. This wasn't the only thing she was keeping from her friends, but that would require admitting that her marriage wasn't what she'd hoped it would be. Yes, she had the normalcy and stability that her mother hadn't, but all of the rest? It wasn't exactly what little girls dream of. However, to say any of that out loud would be to admit that she'd made a mistake, and her marriage was what it was. There was no changing it.

"I didn't tell you what I was doing for the refugees, not because I was ashamed or wanted to lie to you. To involve either of you would have been dangerous," said Hazel.

"You were shielding us," said Nora.

"Yes. At first it was just supposed to be a match or two, but then Mr. Gunter kept coming back to me with more people who needed help. There were so many after the Munich Agreement—as though none of the refugees believed for a second that Chamberlain would be able to control Hitler," she said.

"Smart of them," murmured Nora.

"When war broke out and you told us how worried you were about internment, I thought it would be best if you knew as little as possible—Marie, because of your connection to Mr. Gunter, and Nora, because of your place in the Home Office. If you didn't know, you couldn't be held accountable," said Hazel.

"But then Dennison showed up, and I still had to face him not knowing a thing about what was going on," said Marie, her voice rising steadily. "When he took me out of work and put me in the back of his car, I didn't know what was going to happen to me. And now look at me. I'm hardly making money working a few mornings a week in the stockroom of a shop. I'm afraid all of the time, and I don't even know if I'm part of Dennison's investigation or not."

Hazel hated this—not because of Marie's anger but because she worried she'd damaged her friend's trust. The three of them each had a role to play. Nora was the bold one, Hazel was the nurturer, and Marie—Marie was their strength. She'd sat by Hazel's side in the hospital when she lost her first baby, holding her hand and saying nothing because she seemed to know there were no words that would ease her pain. Marie had been her shoulder to lean on time and again.

"I'm truly sorry, Marie," said Hazel quietly.

Slowly, she replied, "I know that you both must think I'm weak. I've cried about my classification. I've been afraid."

"You're not weak at all," said Nora fiercely. "We know that."

"And you cried because that's a normal thing to do given the circumstances," said Hazel.

Marie stared at the brandy glass in her hand, rolling it from side to side so Hazel could see the last drops of brown liquid creep lazily along the glass.

"Then promise me you won't ever hide things from me because you think I can't handle hearing them. Let me decide for myself what is too much to bear," said Marie.

"I won't," said Hazel. "You have my word."

"One more question," Marie said. "Did you suggest I meet Richard Calloway because you thought I could do what your refugees have done?"

"Who is Richard Calloway?" Nora asked.

"He's one of my clients, remember? I thought you might know him because of his late wife." Hazel turned to Marie. "I genuinely thought you two would be a good match."

"We live in the same house. How did I not know that you have a fellow?" asked Nora.

"I don't have a fellow, and I probably never will have one because I keep picking up the telephone and then putting it back down again. I never even get as far as talking to the operator," said Marie.

"Why not?" Hazel said, her professional instincts itching to ask one hundred questions. She might've, but now was not the time.

Marie let out a sigh. "Which reason do you want? I've lost my job. I've been kicked out of my home. I've a category B classification hanging over my head. I've hardly anything to offer."

"That's not true," said Nora. "You're wonderful."

Marie laughed. "I'm glad you think so, because you're saddled with me. I have no other place to go. At least not in this country."

"You're not leaving," said Nora quickly. "You said it yourself. You're category B, so you have some restrictions, and—while that isn't nothing—you aren't about to be arrested and interned."

"Nora's right," said Hazel, "but if you're going to stay here, you need to live your life."

"I am living my life," said Marie.

"Not the way you want to. Do you like your job?" she asked.

"Do I enjoy being a stock girl stuck in the back room of a pokey shop because the owner doesn't want me scaring off customers with my accent? No, of course I don't," said Marie.

"Then change it," said Hazel.

"And who would want to hire me?" Marie asked.

"You're smart, you speak three languages, you work hard," said Nora, ticking off each point on her fingers. "Who would not want to hire you if they had any sense?"

"It's not that easy," said Marie.

"Have you really exhausted all of your options?" Hazel asked gently.

Marie made a noncommittal noise.

"It's the same with Mr. Calloway. If I thought you weren't hoping to meet someone one day, I would leave you be, but can you honestly tell me that you aren't at least curious to see if he might be the man for you?" Hazel asked.

Marie stared at the glass she held delicately between her fingers. "What if he doesn't want to meet me?"

"I think the better question is what if Mr. Calloway *does* want to meet you?" asked Hazel with a smile.

"Exactly. You're wonderful," said Nora.

"You have to say that, you're my friends," said Marie.

"That doesn't make it any less valid," said Nora.

"What if Mr. Calloway turns out to be Neil all over again?" Marie asked.

"Neil is an ass," said Nora.

Hazel rolled her eyes. "Yes, as Nora puts it so eloquently, the man clearly is an ass. But more importantly, you can't live your life being ruled by hypothetical questions."

"But my classification . . ."

"If he is scared off by something as arbitrary as a tribunal classification, he isn't the man I thought he was and I should retire from the matchmaking business," said Hazel.

Marie lifted her empty glass. "I wonder if I should have another."

Nora reached over and gently took the glass away. "As much as I would heartily endorse you getting properly sauced, I think it's probably best if all of us have a bite to eat first, don't you?"

"I suppose so, but dinner is probably ruined. I've left the chicken out for too long," said Marie.

"That's no matter. We'll go to Feliciano's," Nora said. "My treat. I owe them more than a little patronage. The last gentleman I went to dinner with there spilled an entire bottle of wine and nearly set the tablecloth on fire when he knocked over a candle trying to clean it up."

"And here you are protesting every time I suggest you go to dinner with one of my clients," said Hazel with a laugh.

"That dinner was eight months ago," said Nora.

She rolled her eyes again. "You are hopeless." Then she smiled at Marie. "Now, how about it? Come to dinner. We don't have to talk about anything you don't want to. In fact, I might spend the whole time making you both help me figure out what on earth I'm meant to get my mother-in-law for Christmas."

"A teapot?" Nora suggested as they all rose.

Hazel groaned. "Don't talk to me about teapots. I'll have to get out that horrid cabbage rose set Gertrude gave us as a wedding present even though I specifically asked for a simple pattern. But she saw this one in a magazine saying that the duchess of something or another used it as her day set."

"I remember that. It is remarkably . . . flowery," said Marie.

153

"If my mother could have seen me with something as bourgeois as cabbage rose teacups . . ." Hazel trailed off.

Nora nudged her with her hip. "Maybe if you're very nice, I'll give you the perfect Christmas present."

"What's that?"

"I'll knock the whole set off the table at our Christmas lunch," said Nora.

"Would you? Then perhaps Gertrude will find something to complain about other than my cooking," said Hazel.

Nora grinned. "That's a promise."

❧

Apparently Mr. Feliciano had forgiven Nora for her last date's clumsiness, because by the time the three women had finished their dinner, each of them was comfortably squiffy. It had been the bottle of Chianti wrapped in a woven straw basket that had done it. Or perhaps the grappa at the end of the meal. Either way, for a short time, Marie had appeared to forget about her classification and Henrik and the war. She'd smiled—really smiled, for the first time in a long time—and Hazel wouldn't have traded that for the world.

She walked Nora and Marie back to Crawley Mews, where Nora gracelessly tripped over a cobblestone.

Marie cackled out a laugh. "Look at you!"

"Shhh, you'll wake the neighbors. And I wouldn't say anything if I were you. You're a glass of wine away from singing Irving Berlin in the streets," Nora retorted.

"'Heaven, I'm in heaven,'" Marie sang, swaying back and forth.

"Ginger Rogers, my dear, you are not," said Hazel.

Marie drew herself up to her full height. "Are you insinuating that I'm drunk?"

"Or that you can't dance," Nora offered.

"I beg your pardon," Marie said. Whether the offense in her voice was real or fake was difficult to tell.

"Hazel's not insinuating a thing. She's saying it plainly. Now go to bed," said Nora.

If ever there were a confirmation that Marie was tipsy, it was when their normally undemonstrative friend flung her arms around both of their necks at once and squeezed them tight. "Thank you, again."

"You're welcome, dearest," said Hazel.

"Oh, stop thanking me or I shall have to stop doing nice things for you," Nora said with a laugh before turning to Hazel. "Are you sure you don't want to stay over?"

Hazel had glanced at her watch. Nearly eleven o'clock. "Nathaniel will be worried sick about me."

Hopefully.

"Go, then. I'll ring you in the morning," said Nora.

"We'll talk more about Christmas lunch," Hazel promised.

Inside the house, Marie began to warble again. "'And my heart beats so that I can hardly speak.'"

"Lord," Nora muttered, rolling her eyes before waving Hazel off and shutting the door.

During the trip back to Peckham, Hazel learned that running for the bus while half tight was not the ideal way to end an evening. Neither was sprinting through the gates at Victoria Station, shoving her train ticket into the hands of the waiting attendant. She only just made the train.

Sitting with her forehead against the cool glass of the window, she felt all of the joyfulness of an impromptu dinner with her friends slip away. Now that Hazel was alone, it was hard not to let worry set in.

Marie couldn't visit the agency anymore, that was clear. There was too much risk that Dennison might show up the way he had earlier that week and run into her. There would be no way to explain away the connection between Marie and Hazel then.

At least it would be difficult to trace Hazel's name through to the refugee program. She'd worked with just Mr. Gunter and the printer, the group seeming to operate on the principle that too many connections meant too many chances for the entire network to fall apart. And she hadn't done any matches for them since the summer—months before the war had broken out. The gray area they were operating in was too dangerous, Mr. Gunter had told her the last time they'd spoken in August.

Hazel shook her head as she fumbled the key in the lock of her front door. She managed to get it open, plunging into the darkened corridor.

She dropped her things onto the floor, suddenly exhausted. She would pick them up tomorrow. She was always the first one awake anyway.

Hazel climbed the stairs to the bedroom, her feet dragging with each step. Every light in the house was off, so she turned on just her little bedside lamp. The artificial light cast a harsh yellow glow over Nathaniel where he lay in bed. He didn't stir.

As quick as she could, she undressed, put on a nightgown, cleaned her teeth, and applied cold cream to her face. She really should put her hair up in curlers to better preserve her hairdresser's work, but instead she just tied it up in a silk scarf to try to keep it from looking too much of a mess the next morning. She'd be up and making breakfast soon enough.

As Hazel slid into bed and turned off the light, Nathaniel stretched and rolled toward her. He reached for her, just as he used to do when they were first married, and pulled her against him. She could feel the heat of his breath against the back of her neck as he settled his leg over hers.

"I'm sorry I'm home late," she whispered into the dark.

"You're always late," he murmured.

She stiffened. Was there a hint of censure there or had she just imagined it?

"Marie got her enemy alien classification from the tribunal today. She's category B," she said.

"She'll be fine."

"She's upset. I don't know what there is to do and—"

"It's late," said Nathaniel, sharper now. "We'll talk about this in the morning."

He rolled over then, leaving a cold stretch of sheet between them. Hazel lay there listening to his breath lengthen and become shallow as he fell asleep again.

It was a very long time before she did the same.

sixteen

A wartime Christmas needn't be somber. The blackout may mean Christmas trees do not have their lights, but that hasn't stopped families from hanging tinsel and decking the halls. The Ministry of Food will start rationing bacon and butter after the New Year, but that's meant good business for restaurants and hotels. They're fully booked and ready to welcome all those looking for festive cheer outside of their homes.

—*The Lady's Day*, December 22, 1939

The last of the Christmas crackers lay abandoned on the dining room table in piles of brightly colored paper and cardboard amid the remnants of the goose and all of the trimmings. After what was likely to have been their last lavish meal for who knew how long, Hazel, Nathaniel, his brother Ross, Hazel's mother-in-law Gertrude, Nora, and Marie had all decamped to the front room of Hazel's house to exchange gifts.

The last few weeks had been laced with a forced jolliness that hid a particular desperation. It was as though everyone in the country had decided this *must* be a glorious Christmas because little progress had been made at the front and it was growing increasingly clear that this war would not be ending anytime soon.

No matter. Hazel was determined to make the best of it all. She had strung popcorn in garlands on the tree and wrapped presents in brightly colored paper she'd saved over the years. Nora had brought a bottle of sherry, and even Gertrude hadn't turned down a tiny glass of the sweet liquor.

However, if Hazel had hoped the liquor would make her mother-in-law a little more jolly, she was sorely disappointed. The woman sat in the middle of the sofa, handbag firmly in her lap. Nathaniel had barely been able to persuade Gertrude to take off her coat when she'd arrived, and she'd only relinquished her handbag long enough to pick at Christmas lunch and criticize Hazel for letting the goose dry out while overdoing the roasted vegetables.

Now Hazel held her breath as her mother-in-law opened the last package under the tree with her name on it. Gertrude untied the cheerful gold and red bow slowly, as though suspicious. Finally, the wrapping paper fell apart and Gertrude opened the box to lift out a pair of chocolate-brown gloves. Hazel had agonized over them, wanting so badly to get the present right. Too impersonal or inexpensive and her mother-in-law might take exception to being an afterthought. Too obviously extravagant and she would snipe that Hazel was attempting to show off.

Gertrude looked at the gloves and then up at her son. "They're beautiful, Nathaniel. Thank you."

Her gaze flew to her husband, who lifted his head from the book on golf Nora had bought him on Hazel's recommendation.

"What's that?" Nathaniel asked with a frown. "Oh, the present. You're welcome."

Across the room, Ross, dressed in his army uniform, smirked.

Hazel's jaw went slack, and she stared down at her hands, which clutched the perfectly serviceable chintz apron Nathaniel had given her. An apron. And now this. She'd told him how long she'd searched for the right pair of gloves for his mother, how many shops she'd been to. When she'd showed her final selection to him, he'd given the gloves a perfunctory glance, said, "Very nice, dear," and gone back to his newspaper. Yet he wasn't going to say a thing to correct his mother's assumption?

Before she could say anything, Gertrude asked, "The leather is so soft. Where did you find them?"

Nathaniel scrunched up his brow as though trying to recall a shopping trip that never happened. Finally, he admitted, "I think Hazel bought them. Didn't you?"

"Yes," said Hazel through gritted teeth.

"I see," said Gertrude, carefully setting the gloves back in their box and putting it aside. "Well, you really shouldn't have. I have a perfectly good pair of gloves that will last me an age."

"Just two more presents under the tree," said Nora quickly, saving Hazel from the irrevocable damage that would be telling Gertrude exactly what she thought.

"I'll get them," said Marie, setting aside the blanket she was under and rising to her knees.

"Good, because I happen to know that one is for you," said Nora. "The other is for Hazel."

Hazel let out a long, slow breath and tried to focus on her friends as Marie shuffled forward. She'd been determined to give Marie a good Christmas Day. The three Ethelbrook girls had never spent the day together before. Nora had joined the Careys after her father died, but Marie had always been with her aunt and uncle on Christmas Day. Hazel couldn't help being selfishly glad about this year.

Marie hunched over to pull two small boxes wrapped in silver paper with bright green bows out from under the branches of the fir tree. "There aren't any labels."

Nora waved a hand. "They're both the same."

"Shall we open them at the same time?" Hazel asked as Marie handed her one of the boxes.

Marie nodded and began to count off, "One. Two. Three!"

Hazel laughed as she ripped open her wrapping. Inside was a small black box. When she opened it, she fell silent. On a black velvet cushion lay a delicate gold chain. From it hung a stunning round lapis lazuli in a gold claw setting.

"What is it?" asked Nathaniel, peering over her shoulder. She held it up for him to see, wondering if he was regretting his decision to give her an apron.

"Nora," said Marie, eyes wide, "where is your grandmother's bracelet?"

Hazel glanced up to see Nora pulling out the necklaces' triplet from her neckline. "I took it to a jeweler and asked him to break up the stones into three necklaces. He melted down the gold from the bangle to make the settings. I'm surprised you haven't noticed that I haven't been wearing the bracelet these last few weeks. I thought it would give the whole thing away."

Hazel shook her head.

"But you love that bracelet," Marie said.

"And I want you two to each have a piece of it. We can't know what's going to happen in this war, but this way we'll always have a reminder of each other."

Hazel touched her heart. "I don't know what to say."

Nora laughed. "Don't say anything. Try it on."

Marie smiled shyly as she unclasped the chain and smoothed the pendant against her skin. But Hazel didn't move.

"You don't have to if you don't like it," said Nora quickly.

"It's not that," she said.

"Are you sure? I can have it reset. I know jewelry can be such a personal thing."

Hazel shook her head slowly. The necklace hadn't made her pause, not really. Nathaniel had. It wasn't that Hazel wanted extravagant gifts—her mother's life had been cautionary tale enough—but she did want to believe that he'd done more than spend two minutes thinking about her Christmas present, and she couldn't muster enough denial to convince herself that was true.

"I love the necklace. Thank you." She turned to her husband. "Would you mind helping me with the clasp, Nathaniel?"

The delicate chain looked comical in his large, blunt fingers. He squinted, his attention focused on the small metal tab that would open the clasp. Hazel watched him wrestle with it and lifted her hair when he finally got it undone. His fingers brushed the back of her neck, and she couldn't help but shiver. How long had it been since he'd touched her intimately outside of Saturday nights, when he would give her a perfunctory kiss or two and then climb on top of her? Days? Weeks? All she knew was that even on the nights when she wasn't home late, he was already in bed with the light off, his back turned.

The cool metal settled on her sternum. She'd carry her friends with her always.

"Now, I think it's time for cake and tea. Who would like some?" Hazel asked brightly, slipping on her hostessing mask once again.

"I'll have some if you're serving it," said Ross, kicking his feet out in front of him as he reached for a packet of cigarettes and lit one.

"Thank you, dear," said Nathaniel, his attention falling on his book again.

"Cake at a time like this?" Gertrude said with a sniff.

Hazel's smile faltered, but Nora jumped in. "A time like what, Mrs. Carey?"

Gertrude's fingertips touched her throat. "Why, a war, of course."

"What better time to celebrate what we have than when things are the most difficult?" Nora asked sweetly, but Hazel could hear the sharp edge of honed steel underneath.

"It's a time to enjoy each other," said Hazel, jumping in.

That earned her another sniff. "If you had children of your own, you would understand . . ."

The well-aimed insult plunged white-hot into Hazel's belly, and it took everything not to double over from the physical pain of it. This wasn't the first time Gertrude had gone after her inability to carry a child to term. It would not be the last. Yet it hurt fresh every single time.

Moving deliberately, Hazel stood, smoothed the skirt of her green dress, and excused herself. She counted silent steps to the door. One, two, three—just a few more and she could let the hard mask of calm she wore shatter. She just couldn't give Gertrude that power.

She was closing the front room door behind her when she heard Gertrude mutter, "She needn't be so sensitive about it, but then given her mother . . ."

Rage replaced hurt, and Hazel clutched at that forceful emotion. Rage was active, powerful. Hurt and grief had once left her in a fog so thick she couldn't pull herself out. It had taken Lady Moreton showing up at the house and insisting that Hazel come back to work after she'd physically healed from her first miscarriage. She'd needed purpose, and the agency had given that to her.

She pushed through the kitchen door and stopped in front of the sink. Her nails cut into the thick edge of the wood countertop.

She wasn't surprised when a few minutes later the door swung open and Nora announced, "Your mother-in-law is terrible."

Hazel gave a short laugh and let her head fall back. "She is the nightmare that everyone warns you about when you marry."

Marie circled an arm around her waist, and said, "She has no right to say those things to you."

"She doesn't always when she comes here, but every once in a while she'll bring up grandchildren." Hazel began to stack freshly washed plates and put them away in the cabinets above the countertops. "I can never predict it, and that means I'm on edge all of the time. Sometimes she wraps it up in criticism for me going back to work after the miscarriage. She thinks it's unnatural for women to want to work, and she's convinced that's why—" Hazel cleared her throat. "Why I can't seem to keep a pregnancy."

"That's ridiculous," said Nora.

That might be, but even Hazel herself wondered about it in her darkest moments.

"Anyway, it isn't anything I haven't heard before," she said.

"Why doesn't Nathaniel say anything?" Nora asked, not taking the hint that Hazel was trying to move the conversation on.

Hazel hesitated. It was only for a second—but it was enough that she knew her friends noticed it.

"It's no bother," she finally said, shutting the cabinet door. "They're just words."

Maybe if she told herself that often enough, she would begin to believe it.

"Perhaps this isn't the best time, but I wonder if I could ask a favor," said Marie quietly.

"Of course," she said.

Marie opened her mouth and then closed it, as though she couldn't form the right words.

"Are you all right? Is something the matter?" she asked.

A little smile played over Marie's lips. "There's nothing wrong. I'm sorry, I'm being ridiculous. I just don't know what exactly to say."

"About what?" Nora asked.

"Richard Calloway wants me to come to dinner."

Hazel's eyes widened. "You telephoned him." She'd nearly given up hope.

"When?" Nora asked.

"While you were at work," said Marie.

"You sneaky thing," said Nora with a laugh.

"I hope you don't mind. I can pay you back for the cost of the call," said Marie quickly.

"Don't you dare. I can't think of a better use for that telephone. Use it all you like, especially if it keeps the line tied up so my mother can't get through," said Nora.

"What did you talk about?" Hazel asked.

"He told me he'd hoped that I would call," said Marie. "That you'd said lovely things about me—"

"All of them true," said Hazel.

"—and we talked about . . . Oh, I don't know. Everything? He's easy to talk to. He reads quite a lot, and he enjoys going to the cinema, so we spoke about what we'd just seen. But mostly, he asked me about myself, and it was funny."

"What was?" Hazel asked.

"I think he actually really wanted to know the answers," said Marie.

Hazel grinned. It had been months since she'd given Marie Mr. Calloway's telephone number. She'd called him up right away and warned him that her friend might ring, but she'd just been through some heartbreak and could be cautious by nature. She was delighted to hear that he'd not only waited for Marie, but had shown genuine interest. Hazel would only chastise him a little the next time they spoke for not letting her know that Marie had telephoned.

"What sort of questions did he ask? What did you tell him?" Nora asked.

Marie blushed. "More than I meant to. I told him about going to school with both of you. I told him about what it's been like since the war broke out—how worried I am all the time that something is going to happen to me or to Tante Matilda or Onkel Albrecht."

"What did he say?" Nora asked.

"He just listened," said Marie.

"That, I think, is a good sign," said Hazel.

Marie bit her lip and then nodded. "I suppose it is. And then at the end of all of it, he asked me if I would like to have dinner with him in the New Year."

"That's wonderful, Marie," she said.

"Did you say yes?" Nora asked.

"Yes and no," said Marie.

"It's perfectly normal to be nervous, especially after Neil was so cruel," said Hazel.

"It's not that. Well, it isn't only that. Of course I'm nervous."

"Then what?" she asked.

Marie winced. "I sort of panicked and said I would only go if you went."

Hazel's brows popped. "Me?"

"You and Nathaniel. You—you'd offered to," said Marie.

Of course she had. She'd made the offer, thinking it would make Marie more comfortable. But that was before the cracks in the foundation of her marriage had become too deep to ignore.

Still, this was Marie asking, and she would do anything to see her friend happy.

"We'd love nothing more than to have dinner with you and Mr. Calloway," she said. She would figure out a way to explain it all to Nathaniel and make him promise he would be on his best behavior.

Marie blew out a breath. "Thank you."

"We'll have a wonderful time, don't worry. I'll ring around with a date next week. Do you care about the restaurant?" she asked.

"You know more about this than I do. I trust you," said Marie.

"Well, I should hope so. I am a matchmaker," she said with a laugh.

"Marie?" Nora asked.

"Yes?"

"Why did you decide you wanted to call this Calloway man now? What made you change your mind?"

"It was something Hazel said." Marie glanced at her. "You told me I can't live my life being ruled by worry. I've been so afraid for so long about the war, what will happen to my aunt and uncle, to me. But what's the point of staying free if I can't enjoy it?"

"And," Marie added, "I don't want to give Neil any more thought. You were right, Nora. The man is an ass."

Nora laughed. "I may not know much, but I do know that."

"You could come, too, Nora," Hazel said.

Her friend snorted. "And who would I bring with me? Joseph from work?"

Hazel arched a brow. This wasn't the first time she'd heard Nora casually throw out that name. She gathered that he was in the Air Raid Precautions Department, too, but neither she nor Marie had ever actually laid eyes on the man.

"In that case, we'll keep it dinner for four." Hazel planted her hands on her hips and stared down at the fondant-covered cake that sat under the glass bell of her cake stand. "Now I suppose it's time to serve my sinful cake."

"Is it sinful or decadent?" Nora asked.

She shrugged. "Either way, I can promise you that Gertrude will have a second slice. She might even have a second glass of sherry."

"The devil you say," said Nora.

"I don't know how you can stand her," said Marie.

"I hide in the kitchen as often as possible," said Hazel with a laugh, but there was more truth in that statement than she wanted to admit.

"The offer still stands to smash that ugly teapot right in front of her," said Nora.

"Don't tempt me," said Hazel.

"Just give the signal . . ."

She laughed but shook her head. "Go on, be useful and count how many for coffee and how many for tea. Marie, you can help me with the tray."

Nora strode off with such purpose Hazel had to chuckle. But as soon as she and Marie were alone, she turned to her friend. "I just wanted to say one more thing about Mr. Calloway."

"Yes?"

Hazel squeezed Marie's arm. "Don't worry about your classification. He won't care one bit."

"I hope you're right," said Marie.

"Either way, I'm proud of you," said Hazel. "Now, let's get this cake sliced. The sooner it's served, the sooner I can free my house of in-laws."

seventeen

To the editor,

I have been a loyal subscriber to the *London Herald* for twenty-three years, but I will be canceling my subscription because I cannot support a paper that will not condemn the continued freedom of those enemy aliens who live among us. This government made a serious error in judgment in not shipping all of the Germans back home at the start of the war. They are allowed to walk among us as though nothing changed when Chamberlain made his broadcast. A disgrace.

—*London Herald*, February 13, 1940

"I still don't understand why we're here," said Nathaniel, patting down his tie before passing a hand over his hair. He needn't have. Hazel could still see the sharp lines of the comb he'd scraped through it before leaving the Ministry of Food's offices.

They stopped on the street corner for a turning bus, and Hazel prepared herself to explain yet again because, she suspected, he saw dinner with Marie and Mr. Calloway as an inconvenience. That was part of the reason that it had taken so long to arrange. Hazel had given everyone enough time to put the holidays behind them before ringing Mr. Calloway in the first week of January. He'd been delighted that Marie had asked her to arrange dinner, but then Marie had fallen ill with a head cold. Then Nathaniel had rejected three weeks' worth of Hazel's suggestions for an alternative night. By the time January was closing, Hazel was itching to put a date—any date—into their diaries.

But the night was finally here, and Hazel was determined to be excited for her friend even if Nathaniel wasn't.

"It's just a double date, dear," she said.

"But you make these introductions all the time. Marie knows that," her husband pushed back.

"Marie has been so cautious about the idea of being matched that I made an exception this one time. I can do that to help her, and I know she will appreciate you being there, too."

Nathaniel began to cough, and she handed him a handkerchief. He waved it off, and as soon as he stopped, rolled his shoulders back as though uncomfortable in the navy suit that came out only for church services and those days when he had a meeting with the health minister. He'd frowned this morning when he'd seen that she had laid it out for him on their bed.

"And who is the chap you've set her up with? Has he been a client for long?" he asked.

"His name is Richard Calloway. He's a widower, and I've been trying to find him the right woman for months now, so be polite."

"I'm always polite." But the prickliness of his tone undercut the sincerity of his words.

They'd reached La Vieille Maison, a little French restaurant tucked into a side street in Marylebone not too far from the house where Hazel had grown up. Nathaniel opened the door for her and she nearly walked into Marie.

"Oh!"

"Hello, dear. We must have perfect timing," Hazel said, kissing her friend on either cheek.

"Hello, Nathaniel," said Marie as he bent awkwardly to kiss her on the cheek.

"How long have you been waiting?" asked Hazel.

Marie turned a tortured look to her. "Five minutes. I was hoping you would all arrive before me."

"Madam preferred to wait here rather than sit with the gentleman," said the maître d' with a sniff of disdain, as though having a nervous woman anywhere near his entrance would somehow lower the level of his restaurant.

"How strange then that you didn't offer to make Miss Bohn more comfortable by taking her things," said Hazel with a raised brow.

The white-jacketed man gave a little cough and swiftly moved to help Marie out of her black wool coat. Nathaniel helped Hazel slide off her rabbit jacket. It was nothing compared to one of the minks that had once hung in her mother's wardrobe, but it was what he'd been able to afford as a wedding gift, and she'd always loved it for that.

As soon as Nathaniel was occupied with checking their coats, Hazel leaned in to Marie. "What's the matter?"

Marie bit her lip. "I don't know if I can do this. My dress is all wrong, and I'm nervous."

"You look perfect," said Hazel, giving the plum silk dress with a deep V at the neck a once-over. She remembered coming with Marie to choose the fabric for the cocktail dress years ago when Marie had a rare university event to attend.

"What if we don't like each other?" Marie asked.

"You liked him enough after speaking over the telephone to say yes to dinner," Hazel pointed out.

"But we've never *met*. That's different."

"If you don't like him, then you'll say goodbye at the end of the night and that will be that."

Marie hugged an arm across her stomach. "What if we have nothing to say to one another?"

"I thought we talked about how Mr. Calloway is not Neil."

"It isn't that. I wouldn't have said yes unless I thought he would be different from Neil."

"Then what's the worry?" asked Hazel

The crease in Marie's forehead furrowed deep. "What if you're right and he is the right man for me?"

She smiled softly. Her friend *deserved* to have as lovely a meal as her ration book would allow in the company of a man who might very well suit her. And Hazel was going to be there to support her the entire time.

"I'm being ridiculous," said Marie.

"I never said that," she said.

Marie closed her eyes and breathed in deep. "How do your regular clients do this? How are they not afraid all the time?"

"I'm sure some of them are, but they want what I can give them more than they want to avoid nervousness. They think it's worth it."

"What is that?"

Hazel shrugged. "Companionship. Connection. Love. It's what all of us are searching for—now more than ever."

Marie took a deep breath. "You're right. You're right. You're right."

"He won't be able to help but adore you when he meets you," said Hazel.

She gave her friend's hand a squeeze just as Nathaniel came back. "Ready?" he asked.

Marie nodded. "Yes."

The dining room was half full, just as Hazel had hoped it would be. Atmosphere mattered. She'd wanted a location with enough patrons that they could speak freely, but not so many that they needed to shout.

The night she'd met Nathaniel it had been a crush, everyone drunk on jazz and dancing—and perhaps a few nips from a hip flask. He'd caught her eye earlier, and slowly she'd wound her way around the room, dancing her way to where he stood. He'd danced with a few girls throughout the evening, but mostly he'd watched as his friends navigated the rhumba, fox-trot, Charleston, dance upon dance until their heads must've been spinning. Finally, Hazel's partner had dropped her right next to Nathaniel and she'd looked up at him with what she hoped were bright eyes.

"Hello, there. You've been dancing up a storm this evening," he'd said.

"I love dancing. There's nothing quite like it."

"I'm afraid I'm not very good at it," he said.

"You should practice more," said Hazel.

"There isn't much call for it in my line of work," he said.

"What work is that?"

"The Ministry of Agriculture and Fisheries," he said.

A civil servant. A perfectly ordinary, respectable position. Hazel edged a little closer. "What do you do there?"

He caught her eye and smiled. "I'm a junior clerk. It's rather dull."

He might've meant it as a warning, but to a girl who didn't want glamour, it was a balm. And so Hazel, emboldened by the knowledge that a junior clerk would stand for the quiet life she craved, had turned to this man, looked him square in the eye, and said, "I don't think your job sounds dull at all, and to prove it to you, I think you should ask me to dance."

She couldn't have timed her proposal any better, because the band struck up the first notes of a fox-trot just as she finished. He'd looked at her, a little shocked, and then chuckled. "You're asking *me* to dance?"

"If I'd waited any longer, you might have been swept up by some other lady," she'd said.

"But there's no other lady I'd like to dance with more." He'd put out his hand to her, and she'd taken it. She could remember how solid his hand felt in the middle of her back and thinking that all she would have to do is lean her head a little to the left to rest it on his shoulder.

Halfway through the song, he'd said, "I don't know your name."

She'd looked up and found him gazing down at her. "Hazel Ricci."

"Are you Italian?" he asked.

"If you'd asked my mother," she said, although she suspected the surname was an affectation that Penelope had adopted early in her modeling years to lend her an exotic quality.

"I'm Nathaniel Carey. I think I'd like to get to know you better, Miss Ricci."

Now, walking through the restaurant with Nathaniel at her side, she wondered if Hazel would feel that same instantaneous spark with Mr. Calloway. And if it would last longer.

She spotted her client at the back of the restaurant, away from the distraction of the windows. If he'd requested that table, it was a good choice. Discreet and quiet.

When they were a few feet away, he looked up and his eyes crinkled into a smile as he rose to greet their party. "Hello," he said in a voice of deep, polished vowels.

Hazel stole a glance at Marie, who looked up at him cautiously through her lashes.

"Mr. Calloway, this is Marie Bohn, one of my dearest friends, but of course you already know that," she said, jumping in to perform introductions before Marie's nerves could beset her. "And this is my husband, Nathaniel."

Everyone shook hands, and then they took their seats. Mr. Calloway waved the maître d' away so he could help Marie with her chair, checking that she was quite comfortable before sitting down himself.

"I'm so pleased you agreed to dinner, Miss Bohn," he said to Marie.

"I think you should call me Marie," said her friend haltingly.

He smiled. "I'd like that, and if you would all call me Richard, I would be grateful. I'll confess, Marie, I was pleased when Mrs. Carey offered to introduce us in the autumn. She spoke very highly of you."

"Hazel is always generous with her praise," said Marie with a blush.

"Marie and I have known each other for years. We went to school together," said Hazel.

"I came at midterm. I don't think the headmistress knew what to do with me, so they stuck me in the first room they could find," said Marie.

"Even though I was a year ahead of the other girls," said Hazel with a laugh.

"So there's more than just the two of you?" Richard asked.

"Oh yes, they come as a trio," said Nathaniel. "You can't have Hazel without Marie and Nora. They even have this silly thing they say to each other."

It was an offhanded comment, but Hazel couldn't help but wonder at the edge to his tone.

"What is that?" asked Richard.

Hazel glanced at Marie, who was burning bright pink. It did feel a little childish, their motto, but she wasn't going to apologize for it.

"We'll always be," she started.

"Just us three," Marie finished automatically.

Richard tilted his head. "It sounds as though you're musketeers."

"It felt that way sometimes," said Marie.

"Well, I should very much like to meet your friend Nora one day as well," said Richard.

"You would like her, I think," said Hazel.

"She's quite something," murmured Nathaniel.

Hazel fought the urge to kick him with her heel under the table, settling for a glare.

Nathaniel cleared his throat. "She's a good sort, but she is one of those forceful women one half expects to be running a unit in a women's auxiliary service."

"She's already doing her part. She used to be a deb, but now she works for the Home Office," Hazel clarified.

"Not exactly where one pictures a society girl," said Richard.

"Nora was an atrocious debutante and rather proud of it," said Hazel.

Richard leaned back. "How would you spend your days, then, if you had a choice, Marie? Painting still lifes of fruit while listening to Wagner arias?"

Marie laughed. "To begin with, it wouldn't be Wagner. That would be far too obvious for a German woman."

"I must beg your apology," he said, hand over his heart. "I should've known that you would only listen to Verdi."

"American jazz records when I can get them, but thank you," said Marie, accepting the gentle teasing.

"Very modern," said Richard.

Hazel could hardly contain her grin as the feeling around the table settled. There was something flitting back and forth between her matches. Marie's shoulders had come down from around her ears and she was smiling quite openly now. Hazel was grateful to Richard for that.

"I'm so pleased that you said yes to dinner, Marie," said Richard. "When we first met, I had come in to see Mrs. Carey a second time after a dinner that didn't get off the ground. You were wearing a green dress, and I hoped that Mrs. Carey would match us."

"It did take some convincing," Marie admitted.

"It's a matchmaker's curse that her own friends always seem the most cautious about using her services," said Hazel.

"Well, I'm very glad that you did, Marie." Richard paused to straighten his knife and fork. When he looked up, he grinned and folded his hands in his lap a little sheepishly. "Perhaps this is as good a time as any to lay my cards out on the table, as our American friends might say."

"Hardly our friends if they keep neutral," Nathaniel grumbled. This time Hazel pinched his leg under the table. He winced, but Richard didn't seem to notice. His attention was fixed firmly on Marie.

"I told you before that I'm a widower." Richard paused. "I deeply respected my wife. We were opposites—she was vivacious and friendly, while I'm more inclined to quiet nights—but she brought out a better side of me. I won't pretend ours was some great love affair, but we were happy enough. I mourned her when she died but decided some months ago that I'm ready for marriage once again.

"I have no children, but I would like them one day if I found a woman who wants to be a mother. I have a good living, and I'm fortunate enough to be doing work that is helping our men in Europe, even if it means I can't join them because mine is a reserved occupation. I have a sister I see every other month for Sunday lunch and a brother-in-law who I tolerate, although I won't pretend that I like the man. I have a little house in Belsize Park and a car—although, with the petrol ration, it's doing little besides sitting parked on the street. That is about the sum of my parts."

Out of the corner of her eye, Hazel watched Marie stare at Richard quite openly until, without warning, a laugh bubbled up.

"I'm sorry." Marie slapped a hand over her mouth. "I'm so sorry."

He gave her a wry smile. "I don't think I've ever made a lady laugh with so little effort before. My life must truly seem uninteresting."

"It's not that at *all*. It's just . . . Why should you feel you need to be blunt about any of this?" asked Marie.

"If the last few years have taught me anything, it's that nothing is gained by concealing my faults."

"*Your* faults? Ever since we spoke on the telephone, I worried that you would decide you weren't interested in someone like me," said Marie.

"Someone like you?" Richard asked.

"A German."

Hazel held her breath, hardly daring to move. This, she knew, was why Marie told herself she had been so fearful of this meeting. But in her opinion, that wasn't the full story. Just like Nora and Hazel, Marie had been looking for people to belong to since she'd shown up at Ethelbrook. Her parents had sent her away, and, even now as a grown woman, she craved that same connection, love, loyalty—all without condition—that each of Hazel's clients were looking for.

"Whether you're German or not doesn't matter to me." Richard sounded so genuine Hazel could've kissed him for it.

"Just yesterday, a pair of boys called me a dirty Jerry when they bumped into me in the street and I apologized. I've been told by women that their husbands were off to kill my kind, and all of the Bosch should be locked up and shot."

"I cannot believe someone would ever think—"

"But they do," said Marie, holding up her hand to stop Richard. "And it's only become worse after Christmas. So many people thought this war would be over quickly, but now it's been almost six months. People are starting to become afraid it will go on for years like the last one."

"Did you make the decision to invade Poland?" Richard asked.

"Of course not," said Marie.

"And do you support what Hitler and his troops are doing in Europe?" he asked.

"Absolutely not." There was a hint of ferocity behind Marie's answer.

"If women were able to fight, who would you fight for?" Richard asked.

"Britain."

"That's all the answer I need," he said. "And no one should be allowed to speak to you the way those people did."

Hazel watched her friend's expression soften.

"Thank you for saying that," said Marie.

"I'm not just saying it. I mean it. Now, I think we can begin with some of the conversational prompts that Hazel recommends to her clients," said Richard, tilting his head to her.

"Oh, don't do that," said Hazel. "I'll die of embarrassment. We hand that sheet out to everyone!"

"In that case, I think we should certainly go through Hazel's questions," said Marie with a laugh.

"Right then. Miss Bohn," said Richard, folding his hands in front of him and assuming an overly serious expression. "I would love very much to know what the last book you read was."

eighteen

Somehow, after dessert was served, Hazel managed to maneuver things so she and Nathaniel sat at the long bar of La Vieille Maison and Marie and Nathaniel were alone at their cleared table. From this vantage point, she could watch them like a chaperone in a Victorian novel, although she would allow more than a lingering glance or two. Twice during the meal, Richard had brushed his fingertips over Marie's as she'd passed him a dish. It looked accidental enough, but Hazel suspected that it was, in fact, intentional. She knew the excitement that came with the first sparks of a new relationship and the craving for touch that came with it, almost as though it was impossible to believe that the other person really existed.

Her husband's fingers drummed the polished wood just inches away from where her hand lay. But she knew that no matter how long she left it there, palm facing up or down, Nathaniel wouldn't reach for her.

"They seem to be getting along well," said Hazel with a smile at him.

His fingers stopped drumming. "Are they?"

"He's been so attentive, following everything she says."

Nathaniel threw a look back over his shoulder. "I suppose."

She frowned. She wanted him to be more enthusiastic than this. This was her work. She brought people together, gauging what might spark that little bit of interest that could grow if fed and nurtured. She wanted people to love the way she'd loved Nathaniel when they'd first met because it had felt incredible, like a gift.

"You fascinate me," he'd whispered to her after he'd kissed her for the first time. He'd wanted to know everything about her, quizzing her endlessly about Ethelbrook, her job, and her childhood, which he'd told her seemed wild and a little wonderful because, as much as she'd wanted a normal family with a father and a mother and Sunday lunch and picnics in the countryside, it had been exciting. He'd even listened respectfully as she talked about her mother's death, so recent that time had yet to dull the sharp edges of her pain.

"My father was a gentleman painter, one of those men who have the privilege of painting for pleasure and not to survive," she remembered telling him. "He fell in love with my mother, his model, but he was Catholic. He wouldn't leave his wife, not even when my mother told him she was pregnant.

"He came to the house just once after I was born. My mother says that he spent a long time looking down at me in my cradle, and then he left without a word. The next week, she received a letter from his solicitor. He had decided that it was time for them to end their affair. He'd arranged an income for her for the duration of his lifetime. And then he was gone. I've never met him."

She remembered Nathaniel had picked up her hands and tenderly kissed the backs of them. That was the moment when Hazel knew she was in love. That she would marry this man.

She reached for his hand now, her fingers tentative as they brushed his knuckles. He didn't pull away, but neither did he offer her his palm.

"How are things in the ministry?" she asked, knowing how hard he'd fought to be brought along to the Ministry of Food, which had been created out of his old department just after the declaration of war.

"A challenge. We're trying to fight the black market that's cropped up for ration coupons."

"What are people doing?" she asked.

"Mostly it's merchants setting a bit extra aside for regular customers. Meat seems to be where most of the issue is, although the police recently raided a flat in Barking that had a print machine set up to make sugar coupons." He paused. "Do you really find this interesting?"

"I do," she insisted. "I want to know what it is that you do all day." *I want to know what worries you and what makes you happy, because I used to know those things and I don't anymore.*

He gave her a weary smile. "You don't have to try to make small talk with me. This is the way it is with married couples sometimes. It's the way my father and mother were."

But she didn't want what his father and mother had. Well, once she had, but that was before she realized that it meant nights sitting together in the front room, barely speaking to each other while trying to squash the insidious pull of loneliness that rose up when she least expected. They were like two planets orbiting around one other, never crossing paths.

"I can't imagine you would understand that," he added, "given that your mother never married."

"Nathaniel," she said sharply. "I cannot believe you would say something so callous."

"It's simply the truth," he said with a shrug.

His words stung like lemon juice on a fresh wound.

How have we come to this?

She'd once felt proud walking on his arm, knowing that he was a sturdy sort of man. One who would never abandon his responsibilities. And sure enough, when she told him she was pregnant just four months after they'd met, he'd proposed immediately.

She'd quit her job as a secretary at the Mayfair Matrimonial Agency, and as she'd stood in her wedding dress, a white satin bias-cut confection with long belled sleeves and a veil that stretched to the floor, surrounded by her best friends, she was *happy*. She was going to be Nathaniel Carey's wife. She was going to be a mother. She had done everything right, and—even if she had become pregnant before they married—she would have the life she wanted.

Then, just weeks later, it all shattered.

She'd been home alone. There had been blood—so much of it—and she'd stumbled out onto the street to pound on a neighbor's door. They'd taken her to the hospital, but the doctors could do nothing except make her comfortable. Nathaniel had sat by her bed, squeezing her hand, but his face betrayed nothing as he stared hard at a spot on the far wall.

When Hazel had returned from the hospital, everything had seemed to slow, as though the world was coated in thick golden syrup. She couldn't make herself leave the house, couldn't make herself stop crying. She'd hear Nathaniel come home from work, pots clanging as he ham-handedly tried to prepare dinner. Nora and Marie would come to sit with her on the weekends. The only time she'd left the house was on the last Friday of the month to go to the Harlan, where she would sit silently, half listening to her friends fill the space around her with chatter.

It had been like that for months until one day Lady Moreton had shown up at her door and offered her a purpose. Not her old job as a secretary, but a different one. One that would make use of talents she never knew she had. Matchmaking gave Hazel her life back.

"I went to the recruitment office today," said Nathaniel, yanking her attention around.

"What?"

"It was the army, in case you're curious."

Her heart skipped. "You enlisted? But we haven't talked about this. You never said—"

"I tried to enlist."

"I don't understand."

"They won't have me," he said, toying with his half-empty glass.

"I don't understand," she repeated.

"They say that my lungs aren't strong enough."

"Your cough," she said, finally understanding.

"They think the pneumonia I had as a child tore up my lungs. They don't want a defective soldier."

"Nathaniel." She placed a hand on his leg, but he shifted to knock her touch away.

"We're in public."

Her hand clenched until her knuckles went white. He didn't want her to touch him. It shouldn't shock her. January had been the first month in years that she hadn't wished her period away. There had been no point in hoping, since they hadn't been together since before Christmas.

Across from her, Nathaniel scrubbed a hand over his face. "I want this bloody night to be over."

"I'm sorry. I didn't even know you wanted to join up," she said quietly. It was the sort of thing a wife should know about her husband.

"Why wouldn't I want to? Every man worth his salt is doing it. Even the ones who don't have the stomach for it. You know the stories about the last one. Women walking up to men with white feathers, branding them cowards for not going off to fight."

"What those women did was cruel."

He snorted. "Do you want to know the worst of it?"

Empathy made her fingers itch, but she couldn't stand the thought of being rejected by her own husband again.

"I came out of the recruitment office, told I was a broken man, and all I wanted to do was go home to my wife. But your friends always come first."

"Nathaniel," she said sharply.

"No, no, you're right. The real problem is that we're here because you're a matchmaker at that bloody agency."

She swallowed. "Don't make this about the agency."

He lifted his head, eyes locking with hers. "Maybe it's time for you to stop working."

Feeling punched, she gasped for breath. "Why would you say that?"

"There's a war on. People have worries other than finding husbands," he argued.

"This is *exactly* the time that the agency should be working harder than ever. And that's what we're doing," she insisted.

"Then leave it to Lady Moreton. She owns it. Let her do the work while you come home to be a proper wife."

"Nathaniel, I don't want to stay home. I never did." The words were out of her mouth before she could think to stop herself.

His eyes narrowed. "You did when there was a baby on the way."

It had been true then, but now . . . She wasn't going to have a child. For all of her hope and all of her denial, she knew that.

"I understand that you're frustrated and angry and feeling sorry for yourself, but you needn't be cruel, Nathaniel," she said as firmly as she could.

"Why shouldn't I be?" His voice was starting to rise, and she could see his nostrils flare.

"Nathaniel—"

"Is it too much to expect my shirts to be clean, my dinner to be ready when I get home, and to know that I'm no longer the laughingstock of my office because I can't keep my wife from working?"

"Lower your voice. People are staring," she hissed.

He clamped his jaw shut, but between his gritted teeth said, "My mother thinks that if you stopped working, the pregnancies wouldn't be at risk."

"Your mother is not a doctor. And I'm not surprised she disapproves, given that she hates everything I do," she said.

"What does that mean?"

Hazel began to laugh, high and a little manic. "Do you never wonder at the way she speaks to me?"

"She's always polite," he said, defensiveness touching his tone.

"Nothing I do is good enough for Mrs. Carey. It never was going to be," she said. Her mother-in-law had been cold since the day Hazel had nervously sat next to her fiancé at the dinner table for her first Carey family supper. But Mrs. Carey had held back her disdain until it became clear that no child would come out of the lightning-fast marriage.

Hazel sighed and rubbed her temple. "I don't want to argue about this. Marie is doing so well tonight."

Her husband looked over his shoulder at her friend, who was laughing at something Richard had just said.

"Was that ever us?" Nathaniel asked after a long moment.

"Yes," she said. "And I loved you for it."

Nathaniel dropped his gaze to his glass, the fight gone from his body. "Forgive me. I'm not myself."

She forced a smile onto her face. "Everyone is on edge these days."

"It's not your fault that I couldn't pass my medical," he said. "And I really do want you to consider staying home, but I know that there isn't a single person on this planet who can make you do something you don't want to do."

It wasn't an apology, but Hazel wasn't going to stretch out a fight that was already beginning to cool. Instead, she took a sip of her drink and let the moment slip by, just like so many others.

⌒

The next morning, Marie wasted no time calling Hazel before Nancy had even arrived for work.

Hazel rushed out of her office to pick up the telephone. "Mayfair Matrimonial Agency. How can I direct your call?"

"Hazel, I'm so glad you're in. I've been waiting to ring you since half past six, but I didn't think I could stand it any longer. Thank you," Marie said in a rush.

"You're welcome." She laughed. "I take it this means you approve of my match."

"He was so kind. He's charming, and I think a little bit handsome, too."

"I'm glad that the real Richard Calloway stood up to the one you met over the telephone," said Hazel with a smile.

"I like him," said Marie, slower now, as though she was considering the weight of her words. "I like that he's kind and interesting and listens to other people when they talk. I don't understand why he didn't match with the other ladies you put him with."

"I've been thinking about that myself," she said. "He's told me before that he can be quiet and a little guarded."

"I didn't get that impression at all. He seemed positively gregarious to me," said Marie.

"That's because he likes you, too. Sometimes, if you meet the right person, you don't need to worry about all of those other things."

"I'd like to see him again," said Marie.

"Then you should ring him, although I suspect that he will be telephoning you very shortly."

"Do you think so? How do you know?" Marie asked.

"Call it matchmaker's intuition."

"I hate waiting," said Marie.

"Everyone does," she said.

"Thank you and Nathaniel for coming yesterday evening. I hope it wasn't too dull for you both," said Marie.

"We didn't mind at all," she lied.

"Are you sure? I didn't mean to impose upon Nathaniel's time. I know he's busy at work," said Marie.

It was an opening—a way for her to finally tell her friend what was going on in her marriage. Hazel shifted in her seat, but as soon as she opened her mouth, Nancy came through the door.

"Nathaniel wants to see you happy. He's very fond of you and Nora," she said firmly. "I should go. Nancy's just arrived."

The friends said goodbye, and Hazel settled into her routine of preparing for her first appointments of the morning. She'd just seen out a young girl who, Hazel had learned after several pointed questions, was just fifteen—far too young to be employing an agency to meet a soldier—when Nancy's telephone rang again. Nancy answered it, then covered the receiver. "It's Mr. Calloway."

"I'll take it in my office," said Hazel.

She hurried back to her desk and picked up.

"How are you this morning, Mr. Calloway?"

"Richard, I really do insist." He laughed. "And it sounds as though you've been expecting me."

"I'd suspected you might call, yes," she said.

"Now I'm wondering if I've called too quickly, but I don't care. I feel as though I've been waiting all morning to speak to you."

"I hope that is a good indication of how you feel about Marie," she said.

A pause stretched on the other line, and the longer it edged on the more she doubted herself. What if she'd misjudged Richard completely, and Marie hadn't been as suitable a match for him as she'd hoped? Poor Marie would be heartbroken.

"I'd like you to remove me from your files," he finally said.

Hazel's stomach sank. "Oh."

"I don't want to see anyone else. Only Marie."

"Only Marie?" A huge smile broke out over her face.

"I can't explain it. I just know."

"She's truly one of the best people I know," she said.

"I can see why, and I'm honored that you thought that she might take a fancy to me." He paused. "I'd like to take her to dinner again. Whenever she likes. I just want the chance to be with her."

"Maybe this time you'd like to be alone," said Hazel as Lady Moreton slipped into her office. She held up one finger, and the proprietor made herself comfortable in one of the chairs facing Hazel's desk, settling her crocodile bag on the edge.

He laughed. "Yes. Yes, if she's willing."

"I don't want to speak for my friend, but I think that if you ring around to Marie's today, you'll find that she'd be happy to accept an invitation."

"I'll that do. And Mrs. Carey? Thank you, sincerely."

As soon as she hung up, Lady Moreton said, "Was that your friend?"

"The man I matched her with, Mr. Calloway. The dinner was a success."

"I'm glad to hear that. Your friend deserves a bit of happiness."

"I think so, too. They seemed to get along so well."

Lady Moreton paused. "You were at the dinner?"

"That's right," she said.

"With your husband?"

Hazel tilted her head a little in question.

"How did he enjoy it?" Lady Moreton's voice was too high, as though she was fighting to keep her tone light.

"Why do you ask?" Hazel asked.

"You've been working very late for months," said Lady Moreton, picking at the hem of her simple black suit skirt Hazel knew she'd had made in Paris just last year.

"Your business is thriving. More so than any of us imagined it would."

"Perhaps we should take on another matchmaker."

"No! That is, if we need to take on another matchmaker, we should, but I don't need less work."

Lady Moreton arched a brow. "Perhaps the problem isn't the work, then. You're avoiding going home."

Hazel opened her mouth to protest, but Lady Moreton wasn't done.

"I know that the agency is important to you. After you, well, returned to work, it seemed to give you some life back," said Lady Moreton. "But now I'm worried that it's becoming the problem."

"It's Nathaniel. Or maybe I'm the problem," said Hazel, rubbing her forehead without a thought to the fact that doing so would smear her Pan-Cake makeup. "Maybe it all happened too fast."

"You met him just after your mother died," said Lady Moreton gently. "Sometimes we can be so desperate to free ourselves from grief that we rush into things because we think that they will make things better."

"Maybe," said Hazel. Even if she'd sometimes resented her mother's vivaciousness, Penelope's death had stolen the color from Hazel's life. Dancing with Nathaniel had been the first time in a long while that she didn't feel lost.

"Do you know, even with all of this mess with Germany, I'm grateful for the time we live in. Do you know why?" asked Lady Moreton.

"Tell me," said Hazel with a sigh.

Lady Moreton leaned in. "Women can petition for divorce."

"I'm not going to divorce my husband."

Lady Moreton inclined her head slightly. "If any one of my grandmother's or even my mother's friends had the slightest hint of a rumor of divorce whispered about her, her social life would be over," said Lady Moreton. "But things are different now. Look at Ginger Rogers in that *Gay Divorcee* film, darling. She even ends up happy! And with Fred Astaire!"

"It's just a film," said Hazel.

"It's a sign." Lady Moreton gathered her purse and stood. "I just think you should consider some of the advice I've heard you give to your clients before."

"What's that?" she asked.

"Don't let yourself believe that there's only one ending for your life's story."

The proprietor stood to leave, when Hazel blurted out, "Lady Moreton, I need to tell you something."

"I beg your pardon?" Lady Moreton said.

"Do you recall that man Dennison? He was here a few days ago, snooping around. If he's taken up the investigation into the group that was bringing refugees into Britain and trying to expedite their applications, he's going to dig deeper into the agency's records."

"So let him dig," said Lady Moreton. "What is the worst that he could find?"

"That I was arranging marriages for German refugees to help ease their applications along," said Hazel.

A long pause stretched between them until finally Lady Moreton asked, "Did you do it because you wanted to help German spies?"

"No!"

"To your knowledge, were any of them sympathizers?"

"Of course not. I wouldn't have had anything to do with them if they were," she said.

"And did you match them with people you thought they might actually get on with?" Lady Moreton asked.

"The only thing different from the norm about these matches was that a network of people contacted me with a list of names, and the couples corresponded by letter. If they decided to marry, it was their decision," she said.

"Then what's the matter?" Lady Moreton asked.

"If Dennison finds out, he's going to twist what I did into knots. It could mean trouble for all of us."

The woman laughed. "If I was worried about every little man who thought he was more important than he is, I would have pulled the duvet over my head and given up long ago. You thought you were doing the right thing in making these matches, and that is enough for me."

"Thank you," said Hazel.

Lady Moreton paused at the door. "Next time, perhaps let me know before launching a one-woman rescue mission from this office. I'd like to be involved. There's nothing like a little seditious do-gooding to keep the spirits up in wartime."

nineteen

OSLO FALLS!
Germany Invades Norway by Sea,
Lands at Bergen, Trondheim, Narvik

—*Chelsea Evening News*, April 9, 1940

Despite her excitement, Marie was cautious by nature, and it was two weeks before she agreed to have dinner with Richard again—this time on their own. Afterward she'd done little more than blush at Hazel and Nora's interrogation.

"But what did you *do*?" Nora had asked as they entered the cinema one early spring evening.

"We talked," Marie replied.

"About what?" Nora demanded.

"Oh, leave her alone," Hazel stepped in with a laugh. "If she wants to tell us, she will."

Marie had looked gratefully to her, and Hazel had forced herself to follow her own advice. Marie would tell them what she wanted about her time with Richard. Slowly Hazel pieced together the story of their courtship as it progressed through dinners and a picnic in Regents Park on a particularly fine day in March. There had been a trip to the cinema to see a Hollywood romance, and just last week, Marie had haltingly told them that Richard had given her a gift.

"A typewriter," Marie had said.

"A typewriter?" Nora asked.

Marie nodded.

"That's unorthodox," said Hazel. She really hadn't known what else to say.

"It's secondhand," said Marie quickly. "We were walking by a shop, and I stopped to admire it. He insisted upon going in to look at it. Before I could protest, he'd bought it."

"But why?" Nora asked, clearly stumped.

Marie stared at her hands. "I told him that I used to help edit speeches for someone in the German Department—and, no, I didn't mention Neil's name. Somehow that story led to another, and I found myself admitting that I've always wanted to try my hand at writing something of my own."

It had been Hazel's turn to sit back then, a little stumped. "I didn't know you had literary aspirations."

"I don't know that I do, but I think it's worth a try," Marie had said. "And it is a beautiful typewriter."

Now, as the days stretched into mid-April, Hazel wondered whether she should ask Marie for a more frank conversation about Richard. She snuck a glance at Nathaniel, who sat in his wing chair across from her in their front room. He'd put a record on earlier—Mahler's *Fifth*, he'd announced—but he hadn't bothered to switch it for another when it had come to the end of the second side. Instead, they sat in silence, Hazel with Stella Gibbons' *Cold Comfort Farm* forgotten on her lap while Nathaniel had his nose buried in a Graham Greene novel.

With a sigh she closed her book and folded back the cable-knit blanket that covered her knees. "I think I'll head to bed."

Nathaniel's gaze flicked up, he gave her a weak smile, and then he lowered his eyes to his book again. "Good night."

This was absurd. All of this tiptoeing around each other, never actually saying what was wrong.

Perhaps the problem isn't the work, then. Lady Moreton's words had been following her around for weeks, twisting and turning in her mind and always coming back to the same conclusion: He didn't love her anymore. As for her own mind, she questioned whether she ever had loved him, or if she'd merely loved everything he'd represented. All she had to do was say that aloud, name the monster that gnawed at her every day. Accept that their marriage was a failure.

"Nathaniel, do you ever wonder—"

A knock cut through the quiet house.

"What the devil? It's nearly eleven," said Nathaniel, glancing at the clock.

She surged up out of her chair, grasping to put off the conversation. "I'll get it."

"No, no, I'll go. You stay here," he said.

Another round of knocking sounded through the house, and she heard Nathaniel call out, "I'm coming!"

Her slippers shuffled on the carpet as she followed a few steps behind him, her heart lodged high in her throat. People did not just knock on doors in the middle of the night unless there was something wrong. She half hid her body around the doorframe that led from the front room to the short entryway.

Nathaniel opened the door, but his wide shoulders blocked the view so she couldn't see who it was.

"Can I help you?" he asked.

"Mr. Nathaniel Carey? I need to speak to you on a matter of great importance. It's about your wife."

Dennison.

Anger pushed her fear away, and she stepped into full view of the door. "It isn't enough that you badger me at my place of business? Now you insist on coming to my home?"

Nathaniel turned to cast a look over his shoulder, and she saw Dennison illuminated by their front light.

"Mrs. Carey, it's a pleasure as always," said Dennison, lifting his hat.

"You have no right to come here in the dead of night," she said.

"I assure you that I do so with the full power of the Home Office," the man said.

That, she knew, was difficult to argue against. Still, she wasn't going to back down. "You can state your business and then leave. I've had enough of you harassing me." She would call Lady Moreton first thing in the morning and send the baroness's solicitor after Dennison. Surely this had to be a violation of some law or code or ordinance.

"Hazel, who is this man?" Nathaniel asked.

"Thomas Dennison of the Aliens Department. I am investigating the disappearance of a German national we suspect of wrongdoing, and your wife has blocked me every way I've turned."

"Don't be absurd. I've done nothing of the kind," said Hazel.

Nathaniel put a hand up, confusion etched on his brow. "I don't understand. My wife is a matchmaker. What business does the Home Office have with a marriage agency?"

"Were you aware, Mr. Carey, that for months before the war, your wife was helping Germans marry British citizens so they could live in this country?" asked Dennison. "And we have reason to believe that she has not stopped. In fact, she's graduated from matching refugees to matching sympathizers."

"What?" Nathaniel asked.

"I've never had a Nazi sympathizer in my office," she said, indignant.

Dennison pointed at her. "You've been playing a dangerous game, madam, and it has only become more dangerous."

Across the way, a light went on and Hazel could've sworn she saw the curtains twitch. Nathaniel must've seen it, too, because he said, "Maybe it would be best if we all sat down inside."

Clenching her fists, she led the men into the front room, sitting back down in her armchair. Dennison perched awkwardly on one end of the sofa while Nathaniel sat bolt upright in his chair, his hands on his knees.

"You said that Hazel has been blocking your efforts in this investigation. That does not sound like my wife," said Nathaniel.

"She refuses to divulge her client list," said Dennison.

"That is because it is a violation of my clients' privacy and completely unreasonable. You have no reason to believe that any of them are German spies or bad actors or whatever it is you're looking for," she said.

"Other investigators have made progress in the investigation into a group of Nazi sympathizers believed to be living and operating in London. This new information means that it is possible my investigation dovetails with—"

"Possible? Is that how you're justifying harassing me in my home? Where is your evidence, Mr. Dennison?" Hazel asked sharply. "Where is your order from the government compelling me to comply?"

The man went bright red.

"You don't have one, because you're grasping at straws," she said.

Dennison turned his body fully to Nathaniel. "I'd like to search your house. If your wife has nothing to hide, surely she won't try to stop me."

"No."

Hazel jerked her gaze to her husband. His jaw was set, and he was glaring at their interloper. She could feel his anger simmering just below the surface. She hadn't seen him this defensive in years.

"Excuse me?" Dennison asked.

"My wife has said no to your requests before. I would be a sorry excuse for a husband if I were to override her wishes simply because you told me to," Nathaniel said.

Dennison obviously thought that changing tactics might help, because he affected a chummy smile and said, "I know the feeling. Wouldn't want to make the wife angry."

"My wife's never displayed a particularly volatile temper, Mr. Dennison," said Nathaniel.

She was, however, beginning to see the appeal of one, and now seemed as good a time as any to begin cultivating it.

"Mr. Dennison," said Hazel, rising from her chair to loom over the man. "If you are quite finished trying to bully me using my husband, I will ask you to leave."

Dennison shot to his feet. "You think you're being loyal to your clients, but you're putting yourself in a dangerous position, Mrs. Carey." He stuck his finger in her face. "Things are changing, and soon people like you will have to cooperate or face the consequences."

A shiver ran down her spine, but still Hazel leaned in, hands on her hips. "Who, exactly, are people like me? Because I have never done anything but act in the best interest of my country, but neither will I stand back and allow my clients to be harassed by a man who is no more than a bully with a government office backing him. Yes, I have had German clients. People like them are *good* for Britain, and *you* are the one who is hurting innocent people by wasting your time pursuing those who have done nothing but try to build a life for themselves and find love in our country.

"You can bully me and threaten me and say all of the things you like, but if you think for one moment that I am scared of you, you are sorely mistaken, Mr. Dennison. Now leave my house."

Dennison, beet red, rounded on Nathaniel. "I would suggest that you control your wife, sir."

"Why would I want to control her? I think she's rather spectacular," said Nathaniel.

Hazel caught a little smile playing at the corner of his lips. It was the first genuine smile he'd given her in months.

"This is not over," said Dennison.

"The next time you come back, I would advise you to have a warrant or I will go straight to the Home Office and to Parliament," she said.

Dennison laughed. "And I suppose you know a whole flock of MPs."

"One of my closest friends is daughter of the late Honorable Neville Walcott. It would be no trouble for her to rally support from her father's old colleagues." Her eyes narrowed. "You do not want to test me, Mr. Dennison."

The depths of her satisfaction at seeing the Home Office man blanch just a little at that were too great to describe. Seeing the man march out the door and slam it, even more so.

Nathaniel and Hazel stood there for a moment, eyeing each other. He lifted a hand and waved vaguely to the entryway. "I'll just go lock the front door."

As soon as he was out of the room, Hazel deflated. The adrenaline that had pumped through her was gone, replaced by deep, aching fatigue.

Nathaniel dropped into the chair across from her and leaned back. "Are you going to tell me what's going on?"

She looked at him and it all came spilling out, every last detail, from helping the refugees to Dennison's first visit to Marie's connection to it through Pieter Gunter. When she was done, he sat silent.

"Aren't you going to say something?" she asked cautiously.

"What should a man say when his wife is defying the British government, going against direct orders from a Home Office official, and really has been doing some of the things that she's being accused of?"

"Dennison thinks I've been helping spies, which couldn't be further from the truth."

"He doesn't care whether the Germans you were matching were spies or practically saints. If he finds a connection from you to this group, he will put you in jail," said Nathaniel.

Hazel breathed deep, trying to calm herself. "He won't find out. The rumor is that the network has all gone to ground since war was declared."

"And Marie's boss?"

She shook her head. "I don't even know if he made it out of the country."

"Hazel, I don't know what to say—"

"Then don't say anything," she cut in.

"If you'll let me finish, I think you'll find that I was going to say that I don't know what to say when my wife has been working to help people so many others would ignore and I couldn't be prouder."

She stilled. "What?"

"I couldn't be prouder." He offered her a little smile. "Is that so hard to believe?"

"Yes."

His hand rasped over his chin. "I suppose that's my fault."

"No. No, it's not."

He shook his head. "This hasn't been a marriage for a long time, has it, dear?"

His question sliced through her, even if she'd been thinking the same thing just a half hour before. But to hear him say that out loud? It hurt.

"It's my fault," he said again.

Tears started to brim in her eyes. "I've been neglectful. If I were the sort of wife you deserved—"

"Stop that," he said. "You've been nothing but the best wife a man could wish for. I've been the one who's come up short. It's just . . . after the baby, I couldn't think."

There it was, this hurt they'd skirted around for years. They hadn't spoken about the first child they were supposed to have since Hazel had packed away her knitting needles with a half-finished baby jumper still looped on them. Every month for years, she'd cried by herself in the bathroom when her monthlies came until she learned to expect the dull ache of disappointment. Never once had they talked about any of it.

"I wasn't the husband you needed me to be," he said quietly. "When you were grieving, I tried to help, but then you seemed to heal without me, and I couldn't stand the thought that you didn't need me. I pulled away, and by the time I realized what was happening you'd become this woman I hardly knew."

"I didn't know what else to do," she said, tears falling into her lap. "I needed you once. I wanted to love you so much when we met."

He was across the room, arms around her, before she realized he'd moved. She leaned into him, unable to stop wanting comfort and contact. It had been so long since he'd just held her.

"I know. I know that now," he said, stroking her hair.

They sat like that until her crying slowed to shuddering breaths. Finally, she looked up. "I can't do this any longer. I'm not happy. I haven't been for years."

He closed his eyes but nodded once. "If that's what you really want."

"It is," she whispered. At first she'd been lost in the dream she'd wanted so badly her whole life. But at twenty-four, she knew there must be more to life than predictability. She wanted to find out what it was.

"Neither have I," he admitted.

She gave a little laugh through her tears. "And it's as simple as that?"

He sighed. "Nothing is ever simple, but for the first time since we met, I think we're finally being honest. We should've done this before things became so broken they couldn't be fixed."

"I just think we got carried away," she said quietly.

"I wanted to do the right thing."

"I need more than that now," she said, the truth sending prickles throughout her entire body. She wanted more. She deserved more.

"Do you know, the first night that we met, I saw you making your way around the room toward me," he said. "You were so beautiful."

"My mother was beautiful, not me," she said.

"You're beautiful. You still are."

He kissed her on the temple. She thought he might hug her again, but instead he stood and crossed the room to the record player. With his back turned, she couldn't see which record he selected, but he pulled one out of its paper sleeve and replaced Mahler with it. After a moment, a dance band filled the drawing room with the sweet notes of "Deed I Do." Extending his hand to her, he said, "One last one? For old times' sake?"

Slowly, Hazel unfurled her hands and placed her right into his left. "I would love to."

He pulled her close. She tucked her head onto his shoulder and felt at honest peace for the first time in years.

It was nearly half past two in the morning when Hazel rang Nora's doorbell. She leaned on it, armed with the knowledge that her friend could sleep through a stampede of elephants. The lights went on in Marie's second-floor room first and then Nora's.

She glanced back at the car idling behind her, but the thump of feet on carpeted stairs drew her attention back to the house. The key scraped in the lock, and the door opened to Nora wrapped in a dressing gown, her pin curls tied up in a silk scarf.

"Hazel! What's wrong?" Nora asked in a rush.

She lifted her two suitcases. "Do you think you could stand a second houseguest?"

"What's going on?" Marie asked, appearing at the bottom of the stairs. "Hazel?"

"I'm leaving Nathaniel. Or rather, we're leaving each other," she said with a frown. The words still felt strange in her mouth, but she supposed they would come easier with time.

"Isn't that his car?" Nora asked, nodding over her shoulder.

"Yes. He insisted on driving me. He wanted to be sure that I made it to your house safely, since it's so late."

Nora opened her mouth, but instead of the barrage of questions Hazel was expecting, Nora snapped it shut and nodded firmly. "Well, you'd better come in, then. We'll get you settled and then you can tell us whatever you want to tell us in the morning."

"Yes, a good night's sleep is what you need," said Marie.

In that moment, Hazel's gratitude for her friends' acceptance—completely and without any questions—was almost overwhelming.

"Thank you," she said.

Nora stepped back to let her through the door. As soon as she was inside, Nora waved to Nathaniel and called out, "Don't worry! We have her now!"

One last time, Hazel looked back at her husband. He'd rolled down the window and now lifted his hand. She returned the gesture, then he put the car into gear and the man she'd once loved drove away.

SAMANTHA

Now

twenty

Samantha stood in the light drizzle in front of 5 Taviton Street, looking up at the brick facade. Poured concrete detail topped the highest windows and formed a cornice over the front door with a set of brass buzzers to the right of the door handle. This was the third stop on their tour of her grandmother's life.

After her morning session with Nora, David had come to pick up Samantha as planned. They'd started in Chelsea, where Colin and Greg had given them a late lunch after a tour of Nora's old mews house. It was, they admitted with some regret, very different from how it had been when Nora had bought it before the war. Nora and her husband had rented it out for years until a particularly negligent tenant in 1982 had left the upstairs bath running and flooded the entire front sitting room and kitchen. When Colin had bought it from his parents, he'd opened up the ground floor, making the living room, dining room, and kitchen flow together. Still, it felt special to be standing in the home where Grandma Marie had spent some of the war, sheltered by one of her best friends.

The second stop had been Royal Imperial University, interesting enough but impersonal in comparison. But this. Standing on the Bloomsbury street next to David in front of the building her grandmother had called home for so long felt different.

"Do you think we can go inside?" she asked, glancing at David, who she discovered was watching her closely.

"I'm not sure anyone will be at home this time of day, but we can try," he said, stepping forward to the buzzers. "What was her flat number?"

"She was in flat C," she said.

David leaned heavily on the bell and stepped back to wait. Nothing.

"I'm sorry," he said. "Why don't I take you to the Harlan? Gran asked me to phone ahead so they know you're coming. Usually you have to be accompanied by a member, but they were happy to make an exception in this case."

"Anything for a Founding Few's granddaughter?" she asked with a smile, trying not to be disappointed that they couldn't step inside Grandma's old building. She wasn't sure what she'd expected. Surely the flat had changed hands several times since the war. It would have been painted and papered, redecorated and worked over many times, just like the house on Cranley Mews. There wouldn't be anything left of what Marie had known.

David placed a gentle hand on her elbow to guide her back down the street. But just as they turned, the door to the building swung open, and an older woman with a wild helmet of dyed black hair shuffled out.

"Excuse me," said Samantha before she could think better of it, "but you don't live in flat C, do you?"

The woman stopped, brow furrowed. "No. I don't," she said, her words touched with an Irish accent.

"Oh, thank you. Sorry to bother you," she said.

"They're a young couple who split their time between California and London. Computer people," said the woman before pausing. "Why do you ask?"

"My friend's grandmother used to live in the building before the war," said David, his hand still resting reassuringly on Samantha's elbow. "We had hoped we might be able to meet the owners and see the flat."

"They won't be back until next week," said the woman with great authority. "I sometimes take in their post for them if their box becomes too full, and they told me they'd be around to collect it on Wednesday. You might come back then."

"I'm afraid my flight is tomorrow afternoon," said Samantha, unable to hide her disappointment. "But thank you for your help anyway."

This time she and David got three steps down the street before the woman called after them, "Will you not be wanting to see the air raid shelter then?"

Samantha and David exchanged a look.

"Air raid shelter?" he asked.

"Well, it's really a basement, but they fitted it out to be an air raid shelter. Many places did. In you go, then, and I'll open it up for you." The woman pulled out a key and unlatched the front door, letting David hold it open for her. "I'm Joan, by the way."

"I'm Samantha, and this is David. Have you lived in the building long?" she asked.

"Since 1963. I've been here longest by about four years. That's when Mrs. Sully moved into F on the third floor," said Joan as she led them to a painted metal door with a large bolt keeping it shut. "Here it is. It's luggage storage now, but all they did was shore up the old bunks and stack cases on them."

David undid the bolt with a clang and opened the door. After searching for a moment, he found the light switch, illuminating a set of stairs.

"I'll wait for you up here if you'd like to have a look," said Joan.

Samantha nodded and took a deep breath before following David down the stairs. They were halfway when he stopped and looked up at her with a grin. "What are the chances she locks us in?" he asked.

She laughed. "Probably slim, but I'd be worried if I were you."

"Why is that?"

"If this were a horror movie, I'd be the last girl standing," she said. "*Halloween, Friday the 13th,* even *A Quiet Place*—it's a classic trope."

He barked a laugh. "So you're a horror film fan, Miss Morris. I'll have to remember that."

She was pretty sure he'd started down the stairs again before her blush became too obvious.

It was cool and a little musty down in the basement, but free from the humidity of the outside. Just as Joan said, a wall of bunks stacked with boxes and suitcases stood on one side. On the other was a row of benches.

"This must be the place your grandmother was telling us they went after the air raid siren went off the day of the declaration," she said.

David sat down on one of the benches, his wide-spread arms braced against the wood as he watched her. "What she's told you over the last few days—it seems incredible. I can't imagine London during that time."

Samantha wandered over to the bunks and ran her fingers over them. "They must've been terrified."

"Your grandmother more than most, I think."

"The way Nora tells the story, it sounds like Grandma Marie had no doubt that this was her home, even if other people didn't understand."

"People can become ugly when they're afraid. It isn't an excuse. More a statement of fact."

"I just hate to think that she was so afraid of what might happen next to her and her family," she said.

David didn't say anything, instead letting her stand in silence, absorbing everything she'd learned over the last few days.

Finally, she sighed. "I wish I could stay for longer. There's so much more that I'd like to ask Nora."

"She's not done, then?" he asked.

"She told me I'll get the rest of the story tomorrow morning and not a moment sooner," she said.

"She never was one to shy away from a dramatic moment." He paused. "I'm glad you came to London."

"I am, too."

"Do you think you might come back one day?" he asked, something in his voice telling her it was more than just a polite question to pass the time.

"If I had a reason to come back," she said.

The fingers on his right hand twitched, and she thought for a moment that he might reach for her. Instead, he set his hands on his knees and stood, his head nearly touching the low ceiling. "Shall we go on to the Harlan?"

Samantha shook her head, trying to scatter the hope that had built up there. Then she glanced around the basement one last time and nodded. "Let's."

⁓

Samantha's things were neatly stacked in the hallway and her boarding pass downloaded to her phone when she sat down with Nora for the last time. The older woman was looking even more the grand dame than ever, wearing a white shirt with a high starched collar and a set of pearls so old they glowed creamy rose in the morning light.

She was going to miss Nora, she realized—not only for the stories, but because Nora was a link to her grandmother's past. Marie Bohn had been so much more than an old woman who was always ready with a smile and a soft word when Samantha skinned her knee or came up for the holidays to seek comfort in her family, her heart broken by a college boyfriend. If only Samantha had cared enough to see past her silver hair and the deep grooves of her laugh lines and ask about the past.

"Your final morning," said Nora as Samantha folded the ends of her cardigan around her as rain pinged against the bay windows. "How has your trip been?"

"I wish I could stay longer," she said truthfully.

Nora tilted her chin down and peered over her spectacles. "Is that a testament to my riveting storytelling or to a certain grandson of mine?"

A blush crept up the back of her neck as she thought about the moment in the basement of Taviton Street. She knew it didn't make any sense—the chances that she would ever see him again were slim—but part of her wished she'd been brave enough to pull him to her. To answer a question she'd had since she'd first spoken to the man with the sign in Heathrow Airport.

Instead, she said, "David has been very kind to me these last few days."

"Yes. He has, hasn't he?"

"I appreciate the time he took to show me around London. Seeing all of those places where Grandma used to go made it all feel more real," she said.

"Do you know, I never thought I would marry? I was convinced of it, which, you can imagine, drove Hazel batty. I managed to make it through the entire war without a man, got myself a job at the BBC in the programming department, and then when everyone thought I was too old to possibly be a bride, I was reintroduced to my husband at a party."

"Reintroduced?" Samantha asked.

"Yes." Nora smiled slyly. "I married Joseph Fowler, who I'd worked with before the war. He'd become a radio reporter after VE Day. He'd just been transferred back from Hong Kong and was supposed to go back, but then a well-meaning friend cornered us and told us we'd both worked in the Home Office before the war so we should have plenty in common. I've never seen a man more shocked in my life than Joseph was when he saw me again.

"We left the party and went to a little Cypriot restaurant for dinner to catch up. We talked for so long that the waiters had to tell us to leave. The day after that party he put in a request to transfer to London. We were married six months later."

"What made you change your mind?" Samantha asked.

"Hmmm?"

"What made you change your mind about getting married?"

"Joseph was the first man I'd ever met who didn't tell me what I was supposed to think or do. We could fight like cats and dogs sometimes, but he always respected what I had to say and listened. He didn't balk when I told him I didn't want to stop working. He didn't think it was 'unnatural' for a woman to love both her work and her children, because that was the kind of father he wanted to be. How could I not have fallen in love with him?

"So, all this is to say, sometimes you don't plan for things. They just happen."

But even as Nora said it, Samantha knew it wouldn't be true for her. There were so many reasons—an entire ocean's worth—it wouldn't work, but she liked knowing that she'd always remember David as the kind, considerate man who had picked her up from the airport when he didn't have to. Who'd chatted with her for hours to keep her awake from jet lag. Who'd gone with her on the most seemingly unremarkable sightseeing trip around London because the places were important to her.

"Then, of course, there's what Joseph did for Marie," Nora added.

"What he did for Marie?"

Nora's lips hitched up just a little on the left side—so reminiscent of David's smile that it made Samantha's heart squeeze—and she nodded slowly. "I think it's time for you to hear the end of the story."

NORA

May 1940 to June 1940

twenty-one

BRITISH TROOPS RETREAT AFTER GERMAN CAPTURE
OF DOMBÅS AS BATTLE FOR NORWAY INTENSIFIES
—*The Evening Crier*, May 1, 1940

"Good morning, Miss Walcott." Sir Gerald's booming voice filled the reception of the Air Raid Precautions Department as the door smacked against the wall behind him so hard it rattled the low set of windows that looked out into the corridor. "An early start for you today."

Nora looked up from the brief she was writing and folded her hands. She was not, in fact, particularly early, having come in at half past eight, like she normally did, to turn on all the lights in the reception and the adjoining bullpen, where a dozen young male civil servants sat. Not only did she oversee the typists assigned to the department, she managed much of the flow of work between the department's twelve regional commissioners and the main office, training in local councils across the country, and communication with the other four departments that made up the Ministry of Home Security in the Home Office. She knew everything that was happening at any given moment in the Air Raids Precautions Department and prided herself on being able to jump in and assist on any task that had to do with logistics, recruitment, or training. And yet, Sir Gerald had still walked in every day of the last three years surprised that she had shown up for work.

Pushing away from her desk, Nora grabbed the small diary with Sir Gerald's appointments in it. "Good morning, sir. Messages are on your desk. None are urgent, but you may want to return Mr. Grant's call first. Another shipment of gas masks sent to Leeds are defective."

"Defective?" he asked.

"Cracks in the rubber seals."

"Handle it, Miss Walcott, if you would," he said.

She placed a tick mark next to the item on her list. "You have a meeting with Mr. Elroy at one o'clock, and I've confirmed your table for dinner at the club with your wife. You have tickets to the Prince of Wales Theatre waiting on your desk."

"Thank you, Miss Walcott. Is that all?"

She hesitated. "You mentioned that you might look at my proposal for the Ministry of Information."

Sir Gerald leveled a direct look at her for the first time that day. "What was it about again?"

"A new group of recruitment materials aimed at women. The proposal is on your desk. I've included an estimate of costs for both color and black-and-white printing, as well as suggestions for geographical locations where we may increase the saturation of handbills and posters. There's also a suggestion for a media campaign that could run in conjunction—"

"A media campaign?"

"Yes." She hated that he suddenly made her doubt what she'd been sure only moments ago had been a very good idea. It *was* a good idea. Newsreel features and advertisements in women's magazines would reach far more women than the simple bus posters Huw in the department had suggested last week.

"There will be questions of budget around that," Sir Gerald said, a hint that budget would be the reason he didn't back her proposal strongly enough to pass it along to the Ministry of Information. They'd been down this path too many times before. Nora's ideas were good. They deserved a chance just as much as any of the department's civil servants'. Sometimes they were taken up—when one of the young men in the bullpen twisted them just enough so it couldn't be called stealing and pitched them. It made her want to put her heel through Sir Gerald's frosted glass door. Or it would have if shoes hadn't become so expensive.

"I would appreciate your thoughts on the proposal, sir. If adjustments need to be made, I would be happy to make them," she said.

"If there is time, I will give it a look. But only if there is time."

Nora's shoulders sagged. There was never time. She understood the importance of her work. Keeping a department like Air Raid Precautions running was vital, but it didn't feel like enough. She wanted to do more, to be challenged.

Her father had warned her that as a general rule men didn't listen to their secretaries' brilliant ideas about implementing new policies and programs. Yet she refused to believe that something wouldn't break through. All she needed was to hook Sir Gerald with the right idea and get him to show some interest. Then she could do more.

"Is that all, Miss Walcott?" Sir Gerald asked, pulling her back to the diary in her hand and the high-pitched hum of the overhead office lights.

"You're due at a meeting of the department heads of the Ministry of Home Security in fifteen minutes," she said, trying to keep the disappointment out of her voice. "Will you be wanting tea before you go?"

"No time. I'll need you for notes. Go and secure us seats." He tugged off his coat as he shuffled over to Maddie's desk. "Miss Emerson, if you would be so kind."

The typist dedicated to Sir Gerald's correspondence popped up from her seat like a cork, her hands outstretched to receive his coat and hat.

When Sir Gerald solidly shut the door to his office, Nora turned to Maddie. "If you don't stop letting him treat you like a glorified maid, he'll never change."

"Oh, I don't mind. I wouldn't want anyone to think I'm ungrateful," said Maddie as she hung up Sir Gerald's effects on the curved wooden coatrack next to the door.

"No one would ever believe you're ungrateful for wishing to do your actual job," Nora said, gathering up her steno pad and pen from the top drawer of her desk. Of course, the same sort of advice could be applied to her.

"Thank you, Miss Walcott. Oh, you have a message," said Maddie, holding up a scrap of paper. "Your mother called while you were fetching tea earlier."

"Would you put it on my desk? I'll have to ring her back later," said Nora. Telephoning her mother was the last thing she wanted to do that day.

She hurried out of the office, sidestepping two men arguing in hushed tones on her way to the stairs. She had too much to do to spend hours in a departmental meeting. Letters filled with requests formed stacks on her desk. Some local councils wanted Anderson shelters—essentially a tin tube that could be buried in a back garden to make an air raid shelter for a family, provided they were small in stature and didn't mind sitting in very close quarters in the dark. Others were pushing for more substantial shelters, but the question was where to put them. Air raid wardens wanted more official uniforms, schools needed a place to store their schoolchildren's gas masks. There was always something.

Inside the meeting room, the smoke from a dozen cigars and cigarettes already wafted above the large walnut table around which some of the most powerful men in the Home Office sat. Lining the wall behind them, their secretaries sat ready with steno pads and pencils in hand. She sat down behind an empty spot Sir Gerald took a few minutes later.

Voices droned as her hand flew across the page to record the meeting's proceedings in shorthand. The task was such second nature now that her mind wandered, as it so often did these days, to her friends.

She had a full house, and the selfish part of her couldn't have been happier. It had been anguishing seeing Hazel on her doorstep the night she'd left Nathaniel. Still, it had made the house feel like an adult version of their Ethelbrook dormitory. All three friends, back together again.

The following morning, Hazel had been stoic about the whole thing. She'd sat with a cup of tea at the kitchen table with Marie and Nora and told the entire story—not just about what had happened yesterday, but of all the loneliness she'd felt within her marriage.

"What happens next?" Marie asked.

"We haven't worked out who will take fault in court, but we will. So I'll become a divorcée. It's something I've never considered for myself, but I'm beginning to realize that there are far worse things in life."

Nora pressed a hand to her forearm. "You haven't seemed happy for a long time."

"Why didn't you tell me?" asked Hazel.

Before Nora could make an excuse, Marie said, "You weren't ready to hear it yet. It was too hard until it wasn't."

Hazel gave a laugh. "That much is certainly true. And what of your 'too hard' task? Have you reconsidered talking to your aunt and uncle?"

"I can't go back," Marie said.

"Why won't you tell them about Henrik?" Nora asked, just as she had been doing for months.

"Nora." Hazel's tone was warning.

"It's not right. He shouldn't be able to get away with this, Marie!" She could hear her voice rise, but it was wholly unfair. It had been Marie who nursed her aunt through a bout of pneumonia three years ago. And Albrecht Müller doted on his niece, listening first to Marie's stories of school and then to her tales from Royal Imperial University. Marie had even tolerated Henrik—a feat Nora considered akin to saintliness.

"This is more complicated than you think," Marie said.

"He can't just kick you to the curb," she pressed.

"Henrik can do it because I'm not a Müller! He has every right to ask me to leave—he is their son—and I have no right to stay. Not a single one. My mother dumped me on her sister years ago. It's only because they're good people that Tante Matilda and Onkel Albrecht put up with me for so long."

"They *love* you," said Nora.

"But they love their son more. What parent wouldn't?" Marie picked up her tea with shaky hands.

"I'm sorry for pushing," said Nora. "I just can't stand how unfair it all is."

"Neither of us can," said Hazel.

"It's all right. I know you don't mean anything by it."

And they'd all sipped their tea, knowing that there was no moving Marie when her mind was made up.

From the edges of her consciousness, Nora heard a man say, "And then there is the matter of the camps."

She started, her notepad nearly falling to the floor. Over his shoulder, Sir Gerald shot her a frown.

"Mass internment came up again in the last Cabinet meeting," said Sir John Anderson, home secretary and minister of home security, from his seat at the head of the table.

"Yes, sir," said Mr. Gilman, the gaunt undersecretary who headed up the Aliens Department, around a pipe clamped between his yellow teeth. "We're ready for the internment of all German and Austrian men in the south if the Home Office should order it."

Nora's pencil froze. This was the first time she'd heard about any such internment measures. The tribunals had finished up their work earlier that year, and only a few hundred people had been given a category A classification. Some, like Marie, were under restrictions, but most were free. The idea of mass internment of all men in a geographical location had never before been floated at a meeting she'd attended. And once that happened, it was just one step until the women who were enemy aliens found themselves in the same position.

"And the women?" a man Nora didn't recognize asked, echoing her fears.

"Not yet, but the Cabinet isn't ruling it out," said Gilman. "Nothing is off the table."

"Gilman, Aliens is getting ahead of itself. We're not ready for all of those men. There will be problems," said Mr. Williams, undersecretary for the Fire and Police Services Division.

"What kind of problems?" asked the deputy chief of the Public Relations and Civil Defense, Personnel Division.

"We haven't processed this many people at once," said Mr. Williams.

"Hold them in the jails," said Mr. Gilman.

"And when we quickly realize that we don't have room in the jails?" Williams shot back.

"Then we'll conscript official buildings that can be secured until they can be assigned a camp and moved," said Mr. Gilman.

"Gentlemen," said Sir John. Both men settled back into their seats. "The Cabinet made up its mind. The internment will move forward as planned on the seventh." There were murmurs around the table. "Williams, you have six days to find places for the people who will be detained. I suggest you use them wisely and look to the future. Some members of the Cabinet still think that it will be best for the public's psyche if all Germans—men and women—are interned now before the press begins to stir up concerns about an invasion."

The threat of mass internment hung like a cloud in the air, even as the undersecretary of the Aliens Department let a little smile slip. "Churchill's at it again."

"Yes, well, whatever the Lord of the Admiralty's opinion may be on the matter, it is still the business of this ministry." Sir John paused. "The air attacks and fighting on the ground in Norway should worry all of us. If Hitler's troops continue to press, and our boys can't hold their ground, we may very well find the tide of public opinion turning against leniency for the Germans. If the public are afraid and demand mass internment, I don't know how long I will be able to defend the idea that it is too great a burden for the government to shoulder."

As the men continued to snipe back and forth across department lines, Nora forced herself to start taking notes again, but the way they'd spoken about the internees set her on edge. People weren't just pawns to move around on a chessboard. They would lose their livelihoods, their homes. Some would be separated from their families, for she'd already heard stories of husbands who'd been given tribunal designations that didn't match those of their wives. They would be locked away within camps with barbed-wire-topped walls for the duration of the war.

That couldn't be Marie. She wouldn't let it be.

⁓

By the end of the meeting, Nora had chewed the inside of her right cheek so raw it stung. The conversation had swiftly moved on to other matters, but she'd absorbed little else.

As heads of departments stood to stretch their legs and secretaries gathered their things before running off to type up notes, she glanced at Sir Gerald, but he was engaged in a heated discussion with Mr. Williams. If he wanted her, he could find her back at her desk.

But first, a little fortification. She made her way down the hallway and into the canteen. Just after war had been declared, a rotation of tea ladies had been installed to provide hot cups of tea from huge silver urns no matter the time of day. It had been a blessing for secretaries like Nora, who now no longer had to faff about with gas rings and precariously perched kettles when their bosses wanted refreshment. They were also an excellent place to exchange snippets of gossip throughout the day, though at the moment, hearing who had asked whom to dinner was the last thing on her mind.

Nora nodded to the tea lady, who wore a bright white, nurse-like uniform.

"White tea, no sugar, love?" the woman asked, turning the spigot on the urn.

"Yes, thank you," she said.

"There you are." She poured in the milk for Nora. "Just brewed this one, so it's nice and hot."

"Thank you," said Nora again, taking the cup.

"That isn't your lunch, is it?" She turned around to find Joseph Fowler, one of the civil servants from her department, standing behind her.

"Is it lunchtime?" she asked, checking her wristwatch and finding, to her surprise, that it was nearly one. She had hoped to look over her notes about standardizing the methods by which local authorities requested shelter supplies from the department, but there likely wouldn't be time now.

"Will you be joining the young lady for a cup of tea, sir?" the tea lady asked Joseph.

"Yes, thank you."

As the older woman fixed Joseph his cup, Nora couldn't help but notice that he didn't have to confirm how he took his tea.

"Did you speak to Sir Gerald about your recruitment campaign?" Joseph asked, nodding to a small table in the corner of the canteen.

She sighed, remembering her boss's distinct lack of enthusiasm that morning. "I did."

"And?"

"He said he would look at it. If he has time."

"Perhaps he'll have time."

Nora snorted. "He's an undersecretary in a wartime Home Office department. Of course he won't have time."

"He looked at Miller's proposal for mobile tea relief stations just last week. Clever idea really. They'll follow the ambulances to bomb sites and hand out cups of tea to the survivors and workers. Miller seems to think they'll help with the shock that was so prevalent in the last war," said Joseph.

"I'm sure they'll be very comforting," said Nora.

"You don't sound convinced."

"Oh, it isn't that." She pushed a hand against her forehead, mussing her fringe in a way that probably would've made her hairdresser faint away. "One day I'm just going to have to accept that he doesn't want to consider any of my ideas because, not only am I a woman, I'm his secretary, and secretaries don't propose policy."

"That's not true," Joseph protested.

"Isn't it? I do more for the operational side of the department than anyone else. I know it inside and out, but if I suggest something myself, Sir Gerald won't seriously consider it. Do you remember when I said we should standardize the forms the councils used to request gas masks because every order was coming in a different way and half of the information was missing from most? Sir Gerald said no."

"But you made the new forms anyway and issued them behind his back," Joseph pointed out.

"And now those forms are used by every branch office. And Sir Gerald has never once mentioned it."

"You're right," he conceded.

"I know I'm right," she said.

"I don't know what to say, Nora. It's not fair."

"Thank you," she said. Somehow his acknowledgment of the injustice helped. A little.

"Was there anything interesting in the meeting you just came from?" Joseph asked.

"Internment," she said as they sat down.

"What about it?" he asked.

"If you ever repeat any of this, I will deny it up and down." Nora leaned in. "Some of the Cabinet is pushing for mass internment of all enemy aliens. As it is, they're going to issue the order to detain German men in the south next week."

"And I take it from your tone that you don't agree."

"I don't believe in internment at all," she said.

He chuckled until he saw that she wasn't doing the same. "You're serious? Even those who are category A?"

"I understand the need to find and jail sympathizers and those who are actively working against Britain, but mass internment? Of course not. Even if you set aside the morality of it, consider the expense. There are far better things for the government to be doing in the middle of a war than funding what is essentially the imprisonment of tens of thousands of people."

"On the other hand, what is expense when you consider the safety of British citizens and the state?" he shot back.

"And what of the last war? We interned thousands of innocent people in camps that were ill run and exposed them to disease. We couldn't feed or house them properly."

"We couldn't risk the possibility that some of those people would've done us harm if given the opportunity," he said.

"Interning that many people would mean guarding all of them, valuable labor that could be used at the front," she pointed out.

"The enlistment offices have queues out the door of men looking to join up and do their duty."

"But, Joseph, what about the little matter of what it means to be British? If we begin to lock people up purely because they happen to have been born in a different country—"

"A country we're at war with," he interjected.

"That makes us no better than Germany. You've been in the meetings. You know about the reports coming out of the War Office. You know about all of the Jewish people trying to flee before war was declared."

"The refugees," he said.

"People don't leave their home in droves for no reason," she said.

"Your compassion is admirable, but that doesn't mean there isn't merit to the idea of at least some internment. Besides, the tribunals sorted people out into their categories. There's a system in place to stop the young people from being interned en masse."

She scoffed. "A system put into place by fallible humans. You know there will be mistakes."

"Better some innocent people mistakenly taken in than people who mean to do us harm left free," he said, sitting back with crossed arms.

Nora's jaw fell open. This wasn't just an argument between two people on different sides of an issue. This was life—*Marie's* life—yet Joseph seemed to be almost blasé about the idea of locking up thousands of people indiscriminately.

"I cannot believe that you think that. I thought you would have compassion," she said, her voice starting to rise.

"We're at war. Compassion is a luxury we cannot afford."

"You're wrong." Two women across the room were openly staring now, their teacups raised halfway to their lips. Nora lowered her voice, but she could barely restrain the roil of anger under her words. "Compassion is a necessity we must maintain, otherwise what on earth are those boys we're training and shipping off fighting for?"

"Look," he said through gritted teeth. "If anyone is worried that they might be interned, they had ample opportunity to make their choice at the beginning of the war. They could've gone back to Germany. We gave them time."

She snorted. "'Z plus 7' day? How kind of us to say, 'Here, take seven days to pack up your entire life, make arrangements to sail, and wish your friends and neighbors a heartfelt goodbye.'"

"It's more than most countries would do in such circumstances," he said.

"And what about all of the people who don't think of Germany or Austria as home? What about them?"

His eyes narrowed. "Why do you care so much about this?"

The sudden question threw her off balance a little. "What?"

"This isn't merely a philosophical argument. You're invested."

She caught herself shifting in her seat, and forced herself still. Her friendship with Marie wasn't wrong, and she wouldn't be made to feel that it was.

"You know I have a German friend," she said.

"One of the girls you went to school with. Yes, I remember you mentioning her," he said.

"She's living with me now."

This time it was Joseph who's mouth fell open. "Living with you?"

"She has been for months. She had a disagreement with her family and had nowhere to go," said Nora.

"She could stay in a boardinghouse," he said.

"She lost her job the same day."

"Nora, you know it's not wise to have a German woman living with you, even if she is one of your closest friends," he said.

"Why not?" she asked.

"Think of where you work. How it looks," said Joseph.

"It looks as though I've helped a friend in a time of need," she said, even though she'd purposely avoided naming her place of employment during Marie's hearing. "I have a divorcée living with me now, too, if you find that morally objectionable."

He stared at her. "Nora, this is not a joke. You're making a mistake."

"If helping a friend is a mistake, it's one I'm happy to make. Now, if you'll excuse me, I think it's time for me to return to work. There's a great deal left to do, and Sir Gerald will be eager to get to work after his meeting with Mr. Elroy."

"You still haven't eaten lunch. At least let me bring you a sandwich," he said.

She could see the offer for the olive branch it was, yet she couldn't take it.

"I'm not hungry," she announced, and walked deliberately out of the room, leaving him and their cold cups of tea behind.

twenty-two

Nora threw down her keys on the entryway table when she got home and removed her hat, shaking off the rain as best she could. It had been a rotten day, and now she was going to have to tell Marie the bad news about the internment plans.

Keys rattled in the door, and Hazel pushed through, closing her umbrella so the water shook out into the street.

"Evening," Hazel said. "Did you get stuck in the storm?"

"Just as I was coming off the Tube," said Nora.

"Shame." Hazel held up the umbrella. "I had this, not that it did me much good."

"Fancy a drink before dinner?" Nora asked.

"Oh yes," said her friend.

"Dinner's at seven," Marie called from the kitchen.

Nora's heart twisted. She didn't want to drive away the lightness and cheer from the evening, but she had to tell Marie what she knew.

"Marie, will you join us for a cocktail?" she called back, heading through to the front room and making a beeline straight for the drinks tray with Hazel in tow.

"I will, thank you," Marie replied.

Nora set about making their usual drinks: a sidecar for Marie, a martini for Hazel, and a gimlet for her. She was just dropping a cocktail olive into Hazel's glass when Marie came through, pushing her blond hair back from her face with a smile.

"I hope you don't mind a simple casserole tonight. I thought we'd save our meat coupons for a nice roast on Sunday," said Marie.

"Whatever you choose is perfect as long as you don't make me cook it," said Nora, handing drinks around.

"Or me," said Hazel.

Marie laughed. "I promise, all you have to do is eat what I put in front of you."

Nora slipped off her shoes and settled onto the sofa. She watched her friends take up their favorite spots—Hazel in a Morris chair that caught the late afternoon sun and Marie on the other end of the sofa, a blanket tossed over her legs. It was almost like being back at school, except the conversations had become much more serious than which teacher seemed to dislike them and which of the girls they thought they would remain friends with after leaving Ethelbrook.

When Nora had bought this house she'd hoped to sit with her friends just like this. It hadn't been easy. Her father had left her the money, yes, but everything had to be arranged through a solicitor because she was an unmarried woman and the seller had been suspicious of why she would want a house all her own. As soon as the keys were in her hands, however, she marched into her mother's morning room and announced that she was leaving her family's Hanover Terrace home. The tongue-lashing she'd received had stung more than she wanted to admit, but that was that. The ending of her relationship with her mother. The opening of a home of her own. To now share it with her friends made it all worth it, but she also knew that with the sweet comes the bitter.

"Marie, there's something I need to tell you, but you can't tell anyone else. It'll cost me my job," she said.

Marie froze midway through pulling a blanket onto her lap. "What's wrong?"

"The Home Office is going to order the internment of German men living along the south coast."

Marie's hand covered her mouth. "When?"

"Next Tuesday."

"How can they do that? Those people all received their classifications and were found not to be dangerous," said Hazel.

"This is exactly what I worried would happen," murmured Marie.

Nora nodded grimly. "People are starting to grow concerned because of what's happened in Norway. And don't forget about Denmark." That country had taken a mere six hours to fall to Germany.

"But surely the Maginot Line—"

Nora cut Hazel off with a sharp shake of her head. "A few cement bunkers and some wall on the border of France? What good is that going to do against Hitler's army if they decide to circumvent it?"

"But if the Netherlands falls, and then Belgium . . ." Hazel trailed off.

"Then France will be next, and all that separates us from France is less than twenty-one miles of water." She glanced at Marie. "They're worried about an invasion."

"Who will be taken away?" Marie asked.

"All men between seventeen and sixty who aren't infirm. The police will begin to arrest them on the morning of the seventh," she said.

Very carefully, Marie set down her glass. "This isn't going to be the only internment order that comes out, is it?"

Nora gave a tight shake of her head. "We just have to hope that fears calm and people regain their sense of reason."

"Maybe it's time we reconsider appealing Marie's classification," said Hazel. It was an idea they'd tossed about after Marie's classification came through, but it had never really gotten off the ground.

"I still don't want to take the risk that it will make them dig any more into my past. If they don't know about the Communist Party meetings, I don't want to give them any more reason to believe I might be a threat," said Marie.

"At least we don't have to worry about your aunt and uncle with their category Cs," said Nora. Not yet, anyway.

"Which means that either I'm the unluckiest girl in the world to have worked for a man under Home Office scrutiny, or I was foolish enough to go to those bloody meetings," said Marie.

"But they aren't interning women yet, or ordering mass internment outside of the south coast. Surely that's a good sign," said Hazel.

"There's still a risk," said Marie.

"We will figure this out. I promise," said Nora.

"How?" asked Marie, shoving her hands through her hair.

"I don't know," said Nora.

The silence between them swelled, pressing against the walls and smothering any of the good cheer they'd walked in with. Finally, Marie said, "I think it's time."

"For what?" Nora asked.

"To make a plan."

"What do you mean?" Hazel asked.

Marie looked between them. "I don't want to be interned, even if there's only the slightest chance that it might happen. I will do whatever I can to make sure I'm not arrested and locked up—even if that means leaving."

The word hit Nora like a swift kick to the stomach. "Leaving?"

"I've heard of some Germans and Austrians trying to leave the country. They go to Canada, Australia. There are still ships sailing out of British ports," said Marie.

"Ships that have to sail past U-boats. The fighting at sea is very real," said Nora. "Look at what happened to the *Royal Oak* in the autumn."

"The risk is better than the thought of being locked away. At least if I emigrated, I would have a chance at living my life. Yes, I would have to leave the two of you and my aunt and uncle, but in an internment camp, I would have none of you and none of my freedom."

Nora sat back heavily. Marie was right—of course she was—but Nora didn't want to lose one of the most important people in the world. Not without a fight.

"You're restricted in how far from home you can travel," Hazel pointed out.

"That's a problem, yes. If I were category C, it would be easier. But I will need to book my passage under a false name. And I'll need a new passport," said Marie.

"You've thought about this," said Nora, trying to keep the accusation from her voice. She wanted what was best for Marie, yes, but she was selfish enough to not want to lose her friend.

Marie shrugged. "How could I not? I'm not saying that I'm going to leave tomorrow, but you can't tell me that it's safe for me here." When Nora gave a tiny nod, Marie continued. "Even when it was only a few hundred people interned at the start of the war, I thought about my tribunal all of the time. I know I should be grateful I wasn't locked up, but I can't help thinking about how I can't travel, I can't ride a bicycle. Nora even had to remove the radio from the house," said Marie.

"It was no bother. The BBC is so dreary," said Nora.

"I keep going over in my head again and again that if I had answered those three men's questions in a different way, maybe it would be different," said Marie. "But now I can't even be sure that any of that matters, because all of the people who will be arrested went through the same thing. The fighting has really started now. Things are beginning to change. Surely you can both feel it."

How could they not when rationing was restricting everyone's meals? When there were antiaircraft gun batteries set up in the parks? When every day it seemed like one of the girls in the office was seeing off a boyfriend or a husband? They all lived in fear of the wrath of an air raid warden scolding them for not doing the blackout correctly. They all knew where the closest air raid shelter was, false alarms sending them scurrying down to what they hoped was safety if this time bombing started in earnest.

"I don't want you to go," said Nora.

"I don't want to either," said Marie with a small smile. "Maybe I won't need to, but I won't feel comfortable unless I'm prepared for if things change and the internment orders widen."

Nora straightened her shoulders, determined to put away her own selfish wish that they could revert to a simpler time, a time when they lay in their beds at school and talked with such confidence that everything would turn out all right. "Tell us what you need us to do to make you feel as though you're ready."

"The first thing I'll need is a passport, and that is where I immediately start to feel overwhelmed because I have no idea how to go about getting one," said Marie.

"I may know someone who may be able to help with the passport," said Hazel quietly.

"You do?" Nora and Marie asked in unison.

Hazel held up her hands. "Don't become too excited. I don't know if the man I'm thinking of is still in the business of false papers. He could've been arrested, for all I know, because what he was doing was highly illegal."

"Was he the printer working with your refugees?" Nora asked, remembering Hazel had mentioned the man when she'd come clean about the scheme to secure matches for German citizens.

"That's the one," Hazel said.

"Will asking put you in danger of being arrested?" Marie asked.

Hazel shrugged. "Perhaps, but I'm happy to take the risk for you."

"I'll find you what I can in the way of ships' schedules," said Nora. "I don't want you to be the one asking about them. Someone might become suspicious and decide to report it to the authorities."

"I wouldn't give them my name," said Marie.

"Even so." The meeting that morning had rattled her, and so had her argument with Joseph. She might trust him—certainly enough that she'd told him about her aspirations in the department and about Marie—but she didn't know how far she could push that trust. The war was forcing people to take stands, to have opinions. She ran the risk of finding out that Joseph's were different from hers.

"Is there anything else that we can do?" asked Hazel.

Marie shook her head, but Nora wasn't so sure. She worked in the Home Office. Surely that must be worth something.

Still, she kept her thoughts to herself for now.

"Marie, when will dinner be ready?" she asked instead.

Marie glanced at her watch. "Thirty minutes?"

"Then I propose we sit here and enjoy our cocktails and let Hazel regale us with the latest stories of her clients," she said, lifting her glass to her friends.

Marie mirrored her, but before she took a sip, said, "Your mother called earlier."

The bite of gin from her gimlet helped Nora brace for the inevitable. "She didn't say anything cruel, did she?"

Marie smiled gamely. "Nothing."

Her eyes narrowed. "Really?"

"She sounded a little taken aback when I told her that I was staying with you now," Marie admitted.

"Did you mention me?" asked Hazel with a laugh.

"I didn't," said Marie.

"That's probably for the best. We wouldn't want to give Mrs. Walcott an aneurism," said Hazel.

"I am so sorry, Hazel," Nora apologized automatically.

Hazel waved her away. "If I was hurt every time someone disapproved of my parentage, I'd never get out of bed in the morning. Now, I won't use his name, but there was a gentleman who came into the agency today with a very particular request . . ."

❧

Later that evening, Nora stayed up late reading a report she'd brought home about the probability of Anderson shelters withstanding direct hits from a variety of bombs. It was nearly eleven when she put aside her papers, stuffed her feet into slippers, and knotted a claret silk dressing gown around her waist to shuffle down the hall to the bathroom. Her usual hair appointment was only a few days earlier, so she went through the annoyance of pinning up her curls. Then she applied her cold cream, wiped it off with a tissue, and cleaned her teeth.

When she shut off the light to the bathroom, she saw that a faint light was illuminating the way down the stairs. Marie's soft voice drifted up to her. She crept to the landing and leaned down as far as she could.

"Sometimes I feel as though I can't talk to anyone about it. As though no one will understand what it's like not to know what is going to happen the next day," Marie said.

There was a pause, and it took Nora a moment to realize that her friend was talking on the telephone. Given that Nora couldn't see Marie seated in the straight-backed chair next to the hallway telephone table, she could only assume her friend had stretched the cord as far as it could go in search of a bit of privacy. She knew she should respect that, but there were only so many times in one day Nora could restrain her natural instincts.

Nora hinged at the waist a little more, careful to spread her weight out so she didn't make the top step creak.

"You could just ask her who she's talking to."

Hazel's whisper from behind nearly make Nora jump out of her skin.

"I didn't even hear you come out of your room," she whispered.

"That's because you're too busy being a snoop," Hazel whispered back.

"Who is she talking to?"

"Richard Calloway." Hazel shot her a smug smile. "They speak nearly every night."

"I really should pay closer attention to my telephone bill," Nora muttered.

"I think you'll find that Marie has been slipping extra shillings into your coin purse every morning."

Her brows shot up. "Really? How do you know all of this?"

"She told me about the shillings because she feels guilty, and she knows that you wouldn't accept them if she told you outright," said Hazel.

That was very true. At first, Nora had insisted on paying for everything from groceries to drinks to the occasional new record. When Marie found a job at the real estate agent's and began to make a steady wage, Marie had sat Nora down and told her in no uncertain terms that she would be paying her own way. They'd argued about it, but finally Nora had conceded that Marie could pay a nominal rent and her share of the groceries. The telephone had not come into the conversation.

"Also, I haven't been sleeping well since I moved out of the house," Hazel continued. "I thought it wouldn't make such a difference, given that Nathaniel hardly seemed to notice if I was in bed. But it turns out you become used to sleeping next to a man over the years."

She squeezed her friend's hand. "I'm sorry."

Hazel shook her head. "I'm not unhappy. But it is a change. I never thought I would divorce. I thought I would have the life I always wanted."

"Conventional."

Hazel nodded. "But you know, I'm beginning to wonder whether my mother didn't make the best of it in her own way. She was her own woman. Even when my father was still alive and we were living at his generosity, she always chose what she wanted to do and who she wanted in her life. I'm beginning to appreciate the freedom of that."

Nora leaned into Hazel, silently sharing each other's comfort for a moment on the darkened landing. After a moment, however, she nudged her friend. "You're right. We should leave Marie alone."

They said good night, and Nora retreated to her bedroom, hoping that Marie would find whatever comfort she could on the other end of the phone.

twenty-three

To the editor,

Chamberlain must go. The prime minister has proven ineffectual at keeping his "peace in our times," and with the German offensive strengthening we can no longer rely upon him to lead this country in a time of war.

—*London Free Press Journal*, May 6, 1940

N ora knocked gently on Sir Gerald's door, her hands clasping a brown file folder. She tapped her foot as she waited. *This* was the proposal—the one that would finally convince Sir Gerald to move her from the desk in front of his office door to the bullpen where his staff sat. It should've been obvious to her earlier, given all the requests that came across her desk. The London councils were struggling to find enough shelter for all the people they would need to house if the Germans started to drop bombs on the capital. Anderson shelters weren't sufficient, because a family needed a back garden in which to bury one—a hot commodity in such a built-up area. But Nora had found a solution.

"Come in," called Sir Gerald from behind the frosted glass.

When Nora opened the door, her boss didn't bother to look up from the briefing book spread out on his desk. "What is it, Miss Walcott?"

"I had wondered—"

"If this is about your recruitment ideas for women air raid wardens, I haven't had the time to look at the proposal," he said.

She bit her lip. Of course he hadn't. Still, she pressed on. "This is about something different, actually, sir."

Sir Gerald put down his pen and gave a world-weary sigh. "What is it?"

She edged forward to his desk, nerves pooling in her stomach. "I've been thinking about the problem of shelters in London."

"The councils are making a fuss again?" he asked.

"Always," she said.

"You know what to tell them, Miss Walcott," he said, picking up his pen.

Except he wasn't the one writing to council representatives, telling them to magic the land to dig air raid shelters out of thin air. Those who had basements, like the Müllers' building, stood a bit more of a chance, but a direct hit from a high-explosive or incendiary bomb would devastate them. There could be a better way to protect people, Nora was certain of it.

"If you would take just one moment to look at my proposal, I think you'll find I've some ideas for a way that we could protect more people in London. And it could be brought to other cities as well," she said.

Sir Gerald slid a look at the file in her hand and tilted his head. "Is that it?"

"It is." She placed it on his desk.

"Summarize it for me."

"The Underground," she said.

"The Underground?" he repeated, his skepticism on full display.

"If you think about it, it really makes sense," she said quickly. "The stations are dug out deep underground. There is quite a bit of space. In many of them, there are facilities where police officers can keep law and order. And—"

"And the majority of London uses them every single day," he interrupted. "How do you propose using a station as an air raid shelter when trains need to run?"

He doesn't know any better than you. You *know this department inside and out.*

"I think you'll find in my report that I lay out a system that will clearly define when the stations can be used as shelters. It would only be after dark, naturally, to allow the commuters a chance to be home before a curfew that I propose instituting. I also have laid out a plan for how to inform people that the Underground stations are ready to be used as a shelter. There would be different-colored flags, you see."

Sir Gerald put up his hand to stop her. "Miss Walcott, your enthusiasm, as always, knows no bounds."

"Thank you, sir," she said, even though she wasn't sure it was a compliment.

"However, I reviewed a proposal about using the Underground as air raid shelters before the war even started. Howard Simmons wrote it up. It was dismissed because of the disruption it would cause across London."

"Yes, but, sir, if you read my proposal, I think you'll find I've offered solutions to some of those problems."

Sir Gerald smiled. "I think that we can both agree that if Mr. Simmons wasn't able to find an acceptable solution, it's unlikely one exists."

She wanted more than anything else to snatch up her report and beat Sir Gerald over the head with it.

"I'm glad you're here, though." He pointed to the full out-box on the right corner of his desk. "If you would be so good as to take those files to the Records Department." Reluctantly, she picked up the papers. "Oh, and don't forget this."

She watched her boss pick up her report and drop it onto the top of the stack. She was, without question, dismissed.

༄

Nora stomped down the hallway from the Air Raid Precautions Department, trying to hammer her fury into the polished floor. She was done, fed up, furious. About Sir Gerald treating her as though she was a mere annoyance. About his dismissing her outright. She could scream the bloody walls down.

She was walking so fast that when she whipped around a corner, she collided straight into a rather tall, solid object. Her files cascaded to the floor in a waterfall of brown and white paper, and she lunged for them.

A hand flew to her elbow. "Nora, Nora, wait. Let me help you."

She shot Joseph, the solid object himself, a glare. "I'm fine."

His other hand went to her elbow, stilling her enough that she was forced to look at him fully. The expression he wore was appropriately contrite. "I'm sorry for walking into you."

She shook her head and breathed. This was Joseph. Even if they didn't always see eye to eye, they were friends. "No, I should've looked where I was going."

"Is everything all right?"

"Can I ask you something?"

"Anything," he said.

"Are my ideas all that far-fetched?"

"I'm sorry?"

"Every time I suggest something that the department can do, Sir Gerald shoots me down. I'm beginning to wonder whether the problem is me," she said.

He shook his head. "The problem isn't you."

"At least there's that."

Joseph bent to begin collecting her files. "Sir Gerald is set in his ways."

"You mean he doesn't like the idea of a woman who can think," she muttered.

"Do you want me to tell you the truth?" he asked.

"Yes." She did, even though she knew she wasn't going to like it one bit.

"I think Sir Gerald still thinks you're going to waltz out of the office one day and never come back. He doesn't take you seriously because he still thinks of you as a deb."

"I've been running this department since I arrived at the Home Office. Sir Gerald's secretary was the one who handpicked me and trained me." That was precisely why her reception had been so frosty among the typing pool in the beginning. Those girls had felt as though she'd taken their chance to move up to a more prestigious position with better pay.

"Some days I don't know why I'm still here," she muttered.

He handed her back her files, his hand lingering when it brushed hers. "Don't say that. It wouldn't be the same without you."

Her gaze jerked up to his, and she found he was smiling down at her in that particular way—the one she'd only caught a glimpse of when he thought she wasn't looking.

She took a step back just to put a little bit of space between them.

Joseph cleared his throat and tapped the files. "What are all of these?"

"Authorizations, I think. Sir Gerald's exiled me down to Records."

"I was just down there a couple of weeks ago. The amount of paperwork this war has generated is incredible, and they're storing as much of it as they can here."

"Why?" she asked.

"They're worried that one of the usual storage facilities might be bombed. They're all aboveground. It's not a permanent solution, but at least it keeps all of the important things safe for now," he said.

"Like what?"

He shrugged. "Everything you can think of. Personnel records, invoices, tribunal hearing documents—"

She straightened. "Tribunal hearings?"

"The London ones, yes. The hearings meant a lot of paperwork because each classification justification had to be recorded, in case of an appeal. Why are you interested in—" He froze. "Nora, no."

"No, what?" she asked sweetly.

He grabbed her elbow. "Nora, you can't go to the Records Department to look at your friend's file."

She shifted her elbow out of his reach. "I have to go to Records to file Sir Gerald's papers. If I happened to accidentally stumble across a hearing file or two, who could blame me? You said yourself that the place is brimming with paperwork."

He leveled her with a look.

"Joseph, I told you that we still don't know why Marie was given her classification, and with the fighting being the way it is right now . . ."

"I know you're worried for your friend—"

"Of course I am. She's one of my best friends," she said.

"But," he interjected, "you can't go rooting around in the Records Department."

"Why not?" she demanded.

"Dennison!" a man called out from over Joseph's shoulder before Joseph could respond. Nora whipped around, catching sight of a little man in a cheap gray suit with a pair of glasses perched on the end of his nose acknowledging the caller. *That* was Dennison? The specter who'd haunted Hazel these last months? He hardly looked as though he could squash a fly, but looks could be deceiving. And if he managed to connect Hazel to Marie, then there was even more at stake. Both of her friends could find themselves locked away, Hazel in prison and Marie in an internment camp.

Dennison looked up, and their eyes locked across the hallway. Without thinking, Nora spun around and made for the stairs.

"Nora, what's wrong?" Joseph's question pulled her back. She looked down at his arm and realized she had grabbed for him without thinking.

"There's a man I don't want to see," she said.

"Who?" he asked, peering over his shoulder.

"Don't look," she mumbled as they began to clatter down the stairs. The last thing she needed was Dennison asking around, wondering who that strange woman staring at him was. A few questions would be all it would take for her name to strengthen the link between Marie and Hazel even more, and she had no doubt that if he was an investigator for the Aliens Department he would get there before she knew it.

Joseph frowned. "You're not running from Dennison, are you?"

"Is he following?"

"Has he asked you out to dinner, too?"

Nora nearly tripped over her own feet. "Asked me out to dinner?"

Joseph sighed. "The girls in the typing pool were talking about it the other day. Apparently he's been after all of them. He has a reputation of working from department to department, trying it on with any woman who will give him a smile."

"But he was wearing a wedding ring." He stared at her, and quickly she added, "That's exactly what he did. Back before Christmas. I've been trying to avoid him ever since. You know him?"

"Cambridge man," Joseph said, as though those two words declaring their shared alma mater was all she needed to know. And, in a way, it was.

"I'll have a word with him," he continued. "Tell him to stay away from you."

She let out a long breath. She could tell Joseph everything, and at one time she might have, but something had shifted in her since war had broken out. Loyalties weren't quite so simple as they once had been, and she couldn't be certain that Joseph wouldn't do what he thought was right and report her.

"There's no need, but thank you," she said.

"None of this changes the fact that you haven't promised me not to go snooping around the Records Department," he said.

She smiled at him. "Why would you ask me to make a promise I'm not going to keep?"

He sighed and shook his head. "No, silly me. Come on, then."

"What do you mean?" she asked.

"It'll be faster with two of us looking."

She blinked. "You're going to help me?"

"Yes. And one day I'm going to remind you of this," he muttered. Then he grabbed her hand and began to lead her down, down, down, until they finally reached the very lowest floor of the building. They turned off the stairs into a long corridor bathed in harsh overhead lights, and came to a stop in front of a wide set of double doors with Records written on a plaque over the top of the frame.

Joseph held open the door for her and she nearly walked straight into Mrs. Stowe. Nora'd crossed paths with the stern, white-haired lady who had ruled over the Records Department for the past forty years on occasion. She seemed to know every little thing that happened in her domain. Seeing her now turned Nora's blood cold.

"Miss Walcott," said Mrs. Stowe. "Returning Sir Gerald's files, I see. The girl he sent down to retrieve those tried to take them without properly signing them out."

Nora looked down at the folders in her hands. "I apologize on behalf of my department, Mrs. Stowe. I will speak to the girls upstairs and make sure it doesn't happen again."

That earned her a curt nod. "You do that. Mr. Fowler, what brings you here? It isn't often that the gentlemen of Air Raid Precautions grace us with their presence twice in one month."

Nora could've kicked herself for not realizing that Joseph would likely send up red flags. Filing was an act usually reserved for secretaries.

"He's helping me," said Nora. "On a project. At Sir Gerald's request."

"And what project would that be?" asked Mrs. Stowe.

Nora looked at Joseph. He stared back at her in panic. Sweet, useless man. So Nora said the first thing that came to her head. "Shipment records. For air raid wardens' helmets."

"Yes, I made an error and three thousand were lost in transit," said Joseph. "Completely my fault. I made quite the hash of it."

"And Sir Gerald thought I might be able to sort it out for him," Nora finished.

Mrs. Stowe huffed. "Go along, then. The Air Raid Precautions Department's supply records are on the right, halfway down. You'll find everything clearly labeled."

As they walked away, Nora thought she heard the woman mutter, "Men," under her breath.

Nora was acutely aware of her footsteps' echo in the large space filled with metal boxes. Neat little printed signs were pasted onto the ends of all of the columns, surely the work of Mrs. Stowe. There were personnel records, purchase orders, meeting minutes. Then, on her left, something caught her eye.

"There are the tribunal records," she said, nudging Joseph.

"We can't," he said out of his mouth. "She could be watching."

"But Joseph—"

"On your right, Miss Walcott. Just over there," called Mrs. Stowe.

Nora's jaw clamped shut, and she automatically turned into the aisle as directed.

"I told you, she's watching too closely," said Joseph in a low whisper.

"This could be my one chance. How often do I ever come down to Records? It's always the other girls who come down to fetch files."

"You could say that I botched another shipment," he offered, although even he sounded unconvinced.

She shook her head. "She'll become suspicious."

Joseph opened his mouth, but then his brow furrowed. "This is important to you." It was more statement than question.

"I think it will help Marie, and that's the most important thing to me in the world."

He blew out a breath. "I will figure something out. I promise."

"Why are you helping me?" she asked.

He looked at her for a long moment. "I had hoped you wouldn't need to ask that question."

"Joseph . . ." But she didn't know what to say. She knew that if she could give him more, he would take it. If she let him say what always seemed on the tip of his tongue, he would willingly. But that wasn't what she wanted. Not yet. Not before she'd had a chance to prove that she could be the woman she'd always hoped she'd become, independent and loyal. Someone who *mattered*.

"I will figure something out," he repeated. "I promise."

twenty-four

INVASION FEARS PROMPT INTERNMENT IN
COMMUNITIES ALONG SOUTHERN COAST

—*London Weekly Tribune*, May 7, 1940

Nora could hardly be accused of being the sort of girl who, from the three o'clock hour onward, sat at her desk and stared at the wall clock ticking its monotonous way until the hands read five. But with the wind rattling the windows of her office and pregnant gray clouds threatening rain on the dull Tuesday afternoon, she couldn't help but will time to move a little faster.

The morning had been a rush of activity. The internment orders had gone out, and all morning the Home Office had been abuzz with updates from the roundup of Germans and Austrians living along the coast. But as the day went on, it became clear that Mr. Williams' fears that there wouldn't be enough space to jail and process the men were unfounded. The rumor was that the Aliens Department was already realizing that there were fewer male enemy aliens living in the south than it had estimated.

The afternoon had given way to an onslaught of meetings, and when

Nora finally made it back to her desk, Sir Gerald had kept buzzing her intercom, pulling her away from her memo suggesting a standardized uniform for air raid wardens. Around teatime, however, she'd heard his phone ring and he'd shut his office door, making it clear she would not be needed.

She tried not to mind, telling herself that she had plenty of her own work to do, but it was hard not to be disappointed. Her hope that the war would mean Sir Gerald would entrust her with more had fizzled weeks ago. If anything, he seemed more intent than ever to keep her tied to her desk, handling his correspondence and reports.

With a shake of her head, Nora slid the buff dust cover over her typewriter as, across the room, Maddie—having just come back from an errand for Sir Gerald—took her cue to do the same. Nora was just pulling out her handbag and gloves when the telephone rang.

She stared at it, torn for just a moment as to whether to answer it. But a ringing phone could mean news. If she left it unanswered, she'd be up half the night fretting that she'd failed to do something important.

Unclipping her right earring, she picked up the receiver with her other hand. "Air Raid Precautions Department."

The line crackled and a woman's voice came on amid the thunk of wires being unplugged and the chatter of dozens of switchboard operators' voices. "I have a call for Miss Walcott."

"This is Miss Walcott. Who is the caller?" she asked.

"Regent 4621," said the operator.

Nora stifled a groan. No amount of worry about news from the front was worth a call from her mother. She wanted desperately to beg the operator to tell her mother she'd just missed her, but that would mean a confrontation down the line.

"I'll take it," she said.

"Hold, please," said the operator.

There was a pause while the line was connected, and then she heard her mother's voice. "Nora, is that you?"

She pressed two fingers to her right temple. "Hello, Mother."

"Good, you are there."

"I almost wasn't. It's nearly five, and I'll be out of work in a few minutes."

"What does it matter the time? You never take my calls anyway," said her mother.

Nora winced because that wasn't an entirely unfair point. "Well, now you have me on the line. What can I do to help you?" she asked, lifting a hand to Maddie in goodbye as the other woman slipped out the door.

"Can't a mother just call her daughter? Do I need a reason?" her mother asked.

"We've never been the type of family who rings around just for a chat."

"Well, yes." Her mother paused. "I just wanted to see how you are."

The way her mother hesitated gave her pause. Caroline Walcott was nothing if not certain. About everything.

"Why do you ask?"

"No reason," said her mother quickly.

"Mother, why did you call me?" Nora asked slowly as the melodic tones of the Walcotts' Hanover Terrace doorbell sounded on the other end of the phone.

"That will be Rosamunde Kilkern now," said her mother. "She's come for drinks. Says she's worried sick about Robert. You remember Robert. He danced a fox-trot with you at Deborah Clifford's debut. He's a lieutenant in the navy now."

"Mother—"

"I'll tell Rosamunde to tell Robert to give you a ring when he's next on leave. Goodbye, darling," trilled her mother before disconnecting.

Nora pulled the phone back from her ear to stare at the receiver.

"Miss Walcott."

She glanced over her shoulder to see Sir Gerald filling the doorway of his office. She set the phone down carefully.

"If you are finished taking that personal call, would you care to join me?" he asked, nodding toward his desk before retreating inside.

Her hands clenched into fists once, twice, and then she collected her paper and pencil to join him.

"Close the door," said Sir Gerald. She did and took the seat in front of his desk.

"Miss Walcott, it has come to my attention that there is a very grave matter about which we must speak," said Sir Gerald.

"I can assure you, Sir Gerald, that I will be the soul of discretion."

"I'm afraid the time for your assurances has passed." He folded his hands on the table. "I find myself concerned about your current living situation."

"My living situation?" She knew that her choice to live in her own house rather than continuing under her mother's roof was unusual— eccentric, some would even say. Yet it was 1940, not 1840.

"You have taken in a houseguest, I believe, who some might consider inappropriate," Sir Gerald clarified.

"I actually have two houseguests at the moment, sir, and I can assure you that both are the most respectable women anyone could choose to live with."

"I'm speaking of your German friend. She is not an appropriate house-mate for a woman working at the Home Office."

The meaning behind his words crashed down on her. "Surely you can't be suggesting that my living with Marie is a problem for my job."

"She is German," said Sir Gerald.

"So is Marlene Dietrich, but the United States didn't seem to take issue with her becoming a citizen," she argued.

"That is America, a country that is not at war with Germany. It is different. You must see how this looks. A German woman with a category B classification attached to her name living with a woman who is the secretary to a high-ranking official in the Home Office."

"I won't turn her away, if that's what you want. Marie has nowhere else to go."

That drew another patronizing little smile. "Even if you did rectify this situation, it wouldn't make a difference at this point in time. This office must be beyond reproach. I'm afraid I have no choice but to let you go."

The entire world tilted on its axis. "You're sacking me?"

"I'm afraid there's no helping it. If what you've done were to get around this building—"

"I've done nothing wrong."

"And yet, even the slightest whiff of scandal could compromise all of the good work we're doing here."

The work I'm *doing here.* But even though the truth was bursting to get out, her rage rendered her speechless. Hot tears pricked the bridge of her nose, and she dug her fingers into crossed arms to keep from spilling them.

Still, she had to *try* to make him see that what he was doing was a mistake. Unfair. Cruel.

"Sir Gerald, you knew my father's reputation. He would have believed in the work we are doing in this war through and through, but he also believed in doing what was right. Sheltering my friend is the only thing I could do, because it is right."

"Your loyalty might be commendable at any other time, Miss Walcott, but that doesn't change the fact that this woman is German. She could be a sympathizer or—worse—a spy. We simply cannot take the risk."

Enough. She had heard enough. Her boss was wrong. Marie's nationality didn't change a thing, even if he couldn't see it.

She stood, but before she could turn to leave, a thought struck her. "How did you know that Marie is living at my home?"

Sir Gerald was visibly taken aback by the question. "I've looked at her tribunal file."

The same bloody file Nora had tried to grab the other day. She could kick herself for not going back and trying again because now it was too late.

But then she paused. "Marie was not living with me when the tribunal happened."

"Miss Walcott," he said, his tone warning.

Still, she had nothing to lose and so she pushed him again. "Marie has the same classification as many others. She shouldn't be punished for this, and neither should I."

"You don't know what is in her file," he said.

"Of course I do. I was at her hearing," she argued.

He put up a hand. "I'm not going to argue with you, but I will caution you. War brings things up—secrets that people don't want anyone else to know, even their closest friends. Are you willing to risk your job for loyalty to someone you may not know as well as you think?"

For a moment, she hesitated. But she *did* know Marie. They were best friends. They knew everything about each other.

"How did you know to pull Marie's file in the first place?" she asked. "I'm sure I've never mentioned her to you."

Sir Gerald's mouth opened and closed, making him look absurdly like a flounder. Finally, he said, "I received a phone call informing me of your arrangement with Miss Bohn."

"Who called you?" she asked.

"If you must know, it was your mother. Mrs. Walcott asked that I not tell you directly if I could possibly help it, but I suppose you have a right to know who brought this to my attention," he said.

Of course. His closed door this afternoon made sense now. Her mother must have rung earlier, and then Sir Gerald sent Maddie downstairs to the Records Department to pull Marie's file.

"Thank you," she said curtly.

"You won't tell your mother that I mentioned this to you, will you?" asked Sir Gerald. "My wife sometimes plays bridge with her crowd, and I shall never hear the end of it if she's cut. Lydia is an avid bridge player."

The man had just fired her for standing up for her friend, and the only thing he could think of was his wife's bridge game? Nora snorted in disgust. "Goodbye, Sir Gerald."

She walked straight out, letting Sir Gerald's door bang shut behind her. Joseph, who was standing by her desk holding a stack of files, looked up.

"What's wrong?" he asked immediately.

"I've been dismissed," she said, angrily whipping her coat off the rack and tugging it on. In her haste, her arm got tangled in a sleeve.

"Wait, slow down." He dropped the files on her—well, former—desk and helped straighten the coat so she could slide both arms in.

"Thank you," she muttered.

"Now, what do you mean you've been dismissed?"

It all came out. Marie, her tribunal, the judgment, her mother's phone call, and the dismissal. Joseph sat listening to all of it, nodding once or twice, but never stopping her.

"I don't suppose you understand," she said at the end.

He crossed his arms. "Why wouldn't I?"

"All of our arguments about internment—"

"That doesn't mean that I can't be sympathetic to what your friend is going through. That doesn't mean that I don't care. Nora, you must know I care." The way he said it, with a hint of longing hidden between the words, gave her pause. But this wasn't what she wanted. She wanted to do something that mattered: a career, a path that let her choose in a way that her mother's expectations for her would never allow. Joseph was a good man, even if they fundamentally disagreed on certain things, but he wasn't what she needed. Not now.

"You could look for me," she blurted out.

"What?"

"Sir Gerald has Marie's file. If you found it, you could see what's written there. Maybe there is something we could use in an appeal, to get Marie's classification lifted."

"How am I supposed to find this file? It's probably on his desk," said Joseph. "And besides, that won't help you with your job."

She stared at him. "That's not the point. I'm not the one who needs help."

"Your friend will be fine. Category B women aren't being sent away," he said.

"Yes, but for how long? If this war takes a turn, how long until women are caught up? Even those who are category B? When do we lock up every German in the country because we think somehow that will make us safer?"

He sighed. "I don't know."

"And you still think mass internment is the best way to win this war?" she asked.

"Not to win the war, no, but to keep us from losing it," he said.

"I believe you think you're doing the right thing, Joseph, but I hope that one day you'll understand how wrong you are."

Without another word, she walked out the door. She had a call to pay.

The heavy black lacquered door to the Walcott family home creaked open, and Mrs. Phillips, the Walcotts' long-serving housekeeper, peered out. "Miss Nora," said the older woman in surprise. "What a sight you are for sore eyes."

"Is my mother at home, Mrs. Phillips?" she asked, her voice barely masking her anger. All the way to the house, she'd clenched her fist so hard she'd checked twice to see if she'd drawn blood.

"She's just having tea with Mrs. Kilkern in the drawing room."

"Thank you," said Nora, maneuvering around the housekeeper.

"Miss Nora! Don't you want to take off your things?"

Without casting a look back, she said, "I won't be staying long."

She could hear Mrs. Phillips scuttling behind her, trying to keep up as she tore through the short corridor that led to the formal drawing room. Not bothering to knock, she yanked open the door and stopped, hands planted firmly on her hips, as her mother and Mrs. Kilkern looked up from their tea.

"Nora, it's lovely to see you," said her mother brightly, sounding more enthusiastic about her presence than she had the last three times they'd shared dinner, all of which ended in shouting and tears.

"Why did you do it?" She gritted the question out through clenched teeth.

"I'm sorry?" asked her mother.

"When you telephoned me this afternoon, you must've known what he was going to do."

"Nora." Her mother laughed nervously. "What's gotten into you?"

Mrs. Kilkern's eyes swept between Nora and her mother and back again. "It's all the same with career girls. They're so forceful. One taste of work, and they lose all sense of decorum."

Nora stuck out her pointer finger as she slowly began to advance on Mrs. Kilkern. "If I were you, I'd not stick my nose into matters I didn't understand."

"Nora, Mrs. Kilkern is my guest!" her mother protested as Mrs. Kilkern reared back in shock.

"Tell me why you tattled to Sir Gerald about Marie," she demanded.

Her mother's back straightened, and her face became serene. "I telephoned him because it was necessary. I cannot stand by and let you compromise your reputation by letting that girl live in your house. The government decided she's dangerous."

"She has a B classification. She hasn't been interned, she hasn't been locked away. She's been charged with *nothing*—no wrongdoing. Do you understand that?" asked Nora.

By now Mrs. Kilkern was openly staring, no doubt absorbing every last word to relay back to her society friends when Caroline Walcott was not there to defend herself.

"Marie Bohn is German," said Nora's mother. "Think of the things you expose yourself to by continuing to associate with her."

"She's one of my dearest friends! She attended Papa's funeral!" Nora's vision was full scarlet at the edges.

Her mother sniffed. "I did what's best for you, just as any mother would. I know you enjoyed playing at work—"

"I don't play at working!"

"Nora Elizabeth Walcott, you will not use that tone when you speak to me," her mother snapped. "I told your father that he was allowing you far too much freedom when you were a child, but he insisted that you would grow out of all of this."

It was incredible how, no matter how long they spent apart, her mother knew just how to hurt her. The suggestion that her father had thought her independence—a trait he'd praised—was merely a phase cut straight to her heart.

"There is a war on. You should be doing things that matter, like charitable work for the war effort," her mother continued.

She straightened. "You want me to do war work, do you?"

"Well, yes. Of course, I do," said her mother, a little taken aback.

Turning to Mrs. Kilkern, Nora said, "I want you to listen carefully and remember this so you can tell all the awful women you two call friends. You tell them that Mrs. Walcott deliberately sabotaged her daughter's job working in the Home Office in a department that is doing its very best to keep people safe when the Germans begin to bomb us. All of the air raid shelters, air raid warnings, and air raid wardens who will help protect you when it starts? My mother thought they were less important than proving a point."

Mrs. Kilkern slowly began to nod, still shocked but with a tiny glint in her eye at the prime gossip she was witnessing.

"Mother, if you ever intervene in my life again, you will not see me again," she said.

"Nora . . ." But her mother's voice faded as she walked out of the room.

Nora put her head down and breezed by Mrs. Phillips.

As soon as she was out of the house, she turned right and began to walk. It was a long way to Chelsea, but she didn't care. The walk would do her good. She had no doubts that she'd done the right thing in offering Marie a home. Even so, she couldn't deny the pain of losing her job. She hadn't always loved it, and she'd certainly begun to buck up against the boundaries, but it was still her job. She'd felt as though she was making a difference.

What she needed was to find a way to contribute to the war effort without becoming the debutante automaton her mother wanted her to be.

She kept walking, mulling over the dilemma as her feet began to ache. And still she walked on, even though she knew that shoe leather for repairs would likely soon become scarcer than it already was.

And then she saw it. Painted high on impeccably polished glass: Women's Royal Navy Service. The WRNS. A poster hung in the window showing a woman sharply saluting in a beautifully tailored navy uniform. Join the Wrens—and Free a Man for the Fleet! shouted the bold letters below the figure.

Without another moment's hesitation, Nora abruptly changed course for the door and walked in. A woman with sandy hair looked up from a large ledger. "We're closing soon, miss."

"I won't take much of your time," she said. "You see, I'd like to become a Wren."

twenty-five

INVASION! GERMAN TROOPS CROSS
INTO FRANCE, LOW COUNTIES
Chamberlain Resigns, King Asks Churchill
to Form Government

—*New Wandsworth Star*, May 11, 1940

Nora knew she had to tell her friends that she'd joined up. The woman at the recruitment office had taken her measurements and details and told her that the WRNS would be in touch shortly with instructions on where to report for her basic training. Until then, it was a waiting game.

Still, every time she sat down to tell her friends, Nora froze. Being a Wren meant that she could be posted anywhere the navy needed the women of its auxiliary branch. She wouldn't be able to reassure Marie as the fighting on the Continent grew more intense and the German troops pushed farther across Europe. She wouldn't be able to comfort Hazel in the moments when Hazel questioned whether she'd made the right decision. She would be so far away.

She'd been leaving the house every day, holing up at the Harlan or spending long hours reading newspapers and books at a little tea-room on Piccadilly where the owner did her best to hide the oddly chemical taste of margarine in the finger sandwiches. But every time she returned home and fended off questions about how her day at the Home Office had been, she wanted to curl up into a ball and sob. And so, that evening, she'd suggested dinner at the Harlan—her treat, especially since it was still weeks before their regular Friday evening.

"Mr. Symthson said that he thought with the right training I might be able to show some of the properties he is representing," Marie was saying as she set down her knife and fork on her dinner plate. "After the war, of course. He's positive he can keep the estate agent's office going for at least another year."

"Hmmm?" Nora hummed.

Hazel, who was sitting across from her, applied a swift kick to Nora's shin. "I think that's fantastic news. Isn't it, Nora?" asked Hazel.

Nora winced, rubbing the spot where shoe had connected with flesh. "If you've snagged my stockings . . ."

"Are you paying attention at all?" Hazel asked.

Nora sent Marie an apologetic look. "I'm sorry, I was miles away."

"You haven't seemed like yourself for days. Is something the matter?" Marie asked.

Her tongue stuck to the dry roof of her mouth, but she forced herself to say the words she'd been dreading.

"I have some news, and I've been waiting to tell you both until the time was right. You know that I've been frustrated for some time at the Air Raids Precautions Department," she said.

"Sir Gerald is an ass," said Hazel.

That made her smile a little. "Well, the thing is . . . you see, I've decided to join the Wrens."

"What? Why?" Marie asked.

"Does it seem so strange that I'd want to do my bit?" Nora tried to laugh.

"But you've always said you were doing your bit in the Home Office," said Hazel.

"You talk about it all the time. You love the work your department does, even if you are frustrated," said Marie.

"I was dismissed from my position in Air Raid Precautions," said Nora.

"Was it because of me?" Marie asked.

Nora wished that she could take back this entire conversation, but how could she avoid it?

"My mother called Sir Gerald after she found out that you were living with me. Sir Gerald looked into your file, and found out that you had a category B classification. He told me that it just wasn't acceptable for Home Office employees to have Germans living in their homes," she said.

Marie covered her face with her hands. "Nora, I'm so sorry."

"No," she said fiercely. "Don't be sorry. You are more important to me than that job. And being a Wren will be exciting."

"You're sure this is what you want?" Hazel asked.

"Yes." She had almost convinced herself of it.

"When do you leave for basic training?" Hazel asked.

Nora swallowed. "I don't know. I'll get a letter. It could be anytime. I don't know where I'll eventually be posted or when I'll be granted leave, but I'll be coming here as soon as I can. London is my home." *You are both my home.*

"I suppose we won't have many more dinners like this," said Marie with a weak smile. "We haven't missed a Harlan dinner in seven years."

Looking between the girls, Nora felt a lump rise in her throat. This was going to be harder than she'd expected. Saying goodbye and not knowing when she would see her friends again felt impossible.

"I'll expect regular letters from you both from the moment I step onto the train for basic training. I want to know everything that's going on at the agency. I want to hear the moment that Dennison fellow shows up again," she said.

"Hopefully he's found better things to do than bother matchmakers," said Hazel. "Did you know, I've actually thought about volunteering as an ambulance driver, although I don't know if I'd be any good at it."

"You drove Nathaniel's car," Marie pointed out.

"Yes, but not much since the war," Hazel said.

"If I thought they would take me, I would join in a heartbeat, but we all know that will never happen," said Marie.

Pierre, one of the few men still working at the Harlan since he was French and not required to enlist, approached their table with a silver platter and a folded note on it. "Miss Walcott."

"Thank you, Pierre." Nora waited until he was halfway across the dining room before opening the note. The moment she saw what was written inside, she bolted up from her seat.

"What's wrong?" Hazel asked.

But she was already speeding out of the dining room as fast as she could in high heels on a deep-plush carpet.

"Nora, slow down," Marie called out behind her.

Halfway down the stairs to the lobby, Nora stumbled on her heels but saved herself with the banister. When she pulled herself back up again, she locked eyes with Joseph, who waited below.

"Did you mean it?" she asked, raising the note aloft.

He took the steps two at a time, his suitcase whacking against his leg with each stride, until he stood just before her. "I wouldn't lie, not to you, not about this."

"This way. Come on, girls." Nora grabbed him by the arm and hustled him up the rest of the stairs. She bustled them all into one of the smallest of the club's drawing rooms. As soon as Hazel and Marie slipped inside behind her, she shut the door and whirled around.

"I want to see it," she demanded.

Joseph fought a smile. "It's good to see you, too." He glanced at Hazel and Marie. "I'm Joseph Fowler, Nora's friend from the Home Office."

"Hazel Carey." Nora watched her friend stick out her hand and give

Joseph a quick assessment, knowing that the matchmaker would have him sized up in a matter of seconds.

"It's a pleasure." He turned to Marie. "Then you must be Marie Bohn."

Marie was a little slower to shake his hand. Nora had noticed that her friend seemed to be more cautious with strangers since the headlines had become more urgent, and it broke Nora's heart.

"Enough with the introductions," she said, holding out the note Pierre had delivered. "Does this mean what I think it does?"

He gave a tight nod. She dropped the note onto the table, and her friends leaned down to read it.

I have what you were looking for.

—J

Joseph set his briefcase down, unsnapped the clasps, and pulled out a thick manila file folder.

"Nora, what's going on?" Hazel asked.

"A few weeks ago, when I was still at the Home Office. It's been bothering me for months that we don't know why you were given your classification, Marie, and I thought maybe I could find out," she said.

"How?" Marie asked.

"Joseph told me that records were being held in the basement of the Home Office's building for overflow because the main storage facilities couldn't take on the volume of paperwork a war creates."

"What sort of records?" Hazel asked.

"Tribunal records," said Joseph with a glint in his eye.

"You looked at my tribunal record?" Marie asked.

Nora glanced at Joseph. "We tried to, but it was harder than we thought it would be."

"The woman who runs the department is—"

"Terrifying," Nora finished for him. "And if we'd been caught with files we weren't authorized to have, we would've been in very serious trouble."

"But now you have my file?" asked Marie.

Joseph nodded.

Marie sat down heavily on one of the sofas. "Tell me what it says."

Nora watched him crouch down to Marie's level, speaking directly to her in a soft voice. "British intelligence has reports that your father is manufacturing parts for the German military. His brother, your uncle, is a high-ranking official in the Nazi government at Munich."

"I don't understand," Marie whispered.

"There's more, I'm afraid. The reason that the Foreign Office was able to make that connection was your cousin," Joseph said.

"Henrik?"

"It might be best if you were to read it yourself," said Joseph, holding the file out.

With a shaking hand, Marie took the file and spread its contents out on her lap. Nora and Hazel both rounded the sofa upon which she sat and began to read the first page, a dossier of sorts, over Marie's shoulder.

```
Female Enemy Alien—Exemption from Internment—Alien
   Resident
Surname: Bohn
Forename: Marie
Date and place of birth: June 8, 1916, Munich, Germany
Nationality: German
```

Nora's gaze jumped down the page, where it listed Marie's most recent occupation as of the time of her hearing ("Secretary") and a series of mundane notes from the tribunal panel that offered little insight into their way of thinking. It also assigned Marie to category B and noted that Marie did not desire to be repatriated.

But that wasn't all. Attached behind the tribunal notes was a sheaf of papers. When Marie peeled back the first page to reveal the next, she saw bold type at the top: Supplemental Investigation Findings.

"Why would they want a supplemental investigation of me?" Marie murmured.

Nora leaned a little closer.

Certain irregularities have appeared in the investigation into Miss MARIE BOHN, who currently resides
at 22 Cranley Mews and is lately of 5 Taviton Street,
London. Although an initial investigation found nothing to indicate that Miss Bohn, a German national of
the Aryan race, poses a threat to Britain's security,
recent revelations of her connection to a deputy of
the Nazi Party in Munich has cast doubt on her claims
to be wholly without threat during this time.

Miss Bohn's father, HERMAN BOHN, is the owner of a
factory on the outskirts of Munich that specializes
in the production of automotive parts. His brother,
PIETER BOHN, has risen up through the ranks of the
local Nazi Party and now serves as adviser to the Gau-
leiter, Adolf Wagner, in the Munich-Obergavern Gau. In
his role as governor of this state, Wagner has direct
communication with Hitler's cabinet. It appears that
Henrik Bohn has not only fully aligned himself with
the Nazi Party through deals struck by Pieter Bohn,
but he has facilitated the correspondence between
Pieter Bohn and a known sympathizer to the German
cause living in Britain. (A translation of an intercepted letter is included in exhibit A.)

"A letter?" Nora asked.

Marie began flipping through the pages until she landed on a piece of paper marked with Exhibit A in slanting handwriting in the top right corner. It was a transcription of a translation of the letter, typed up from the original.

Dear Uncle Pieter,

I hope that I do not offend you by addressing you in such a familiar manner. Although we are not related by blood, the bond of marriage is strong enough that I can hope that you will believe the earnestness of my appeal.

I have been in contact with your brother because I am desperate to do all that I can to help the fatherland's cause. Although I have lived in England since I was a child, I have never felt any love for this country. It is a land that is impossible to love, filled with people corrupted and blind to everything that has gone on around them. I am determined to do all that you need of me here to help the fatherland in any way I can. There is a group of us, small but passionate, who await your orders.

The rest of the letter was brief, filled with effusive thanks and praise for the führer. Nora's eyes skimmed over it until they reached the bottom, where they stopped, arrested by what must have been a signature on the original letter. Clear letters spelled out the name Henrik Müller.

"Oh, Henrik, you fool," Nora murmured.

Marie said nothing as she flipped back to the investigation notes.

At this time, this office has not been able to determine that the group of sympathizers mentioned by HENRIK MÜLLER in his letter to Pieter Bohn has been successful—or is indeed active—in the gathering and transition of sensitive information to Germany. However, the decision was made to allow Müller to continue to live under a category C classification in the hope that he may reveal more of his compatriots and their plans.

Additionally, there has been no evidence of a reply being sent from Pieter Bohn to his nephew by marriage, however, it is the opinion of this office that

```
the possibility such a connection was made through
secretive means cannot be ruled out. It is the recom-
mendation of this office that a restriction and close
monitoring be placed upon Marie Bohn, as she is the
link between Henrik Müller and Pieter Bohn.
```

Nora let out a long, slow breath. Henrik was the reason that Marie was now living with restrictions on her movements. It was a miracle Marie and the Müllers hadn't been arrested and thrown into an internment camp—or worse, for Henrik especially. He was a sympathizer, and Britain had just woken up to the fact that soon only the choppy waters of the English Channel would stand between Hitler and Dover.

"My father wrote to Henrik," whispered Marie.

Nora laid a hand on her friend's shoulder because, for all that Henrik's sympathizing could mean for Marie, she knew it had always been Marie's mother who wrote those dry, routine letters of obligation. Never her father, who had shown little interest in his daughter, save for the day when Marie had told her parents that she didn't intend to return to Germany after leaving Ethelbrook. Marie had told them she'd been shaking as she placed the long-distance call and sat there, listening to her father lecture her about duty and investment and worth. Never once had Marie's father asked her to come home because he missed her. Never once had he acted like a *father*.

"This is completely unfair," Nora said. "Henrik doesn't even have a B classification."

At her words, Marie staggered to her feet. She looked around wildly, then dropped back down into her seat as though her knees had given out. Her hands went to her head, fingers gripping her hair at the roots, hiding her face.

"Stupid, stupid boy. Stupid, careless boy!" Marie flipped her head up, her eyes blazing. "What did my aunt and uncle's files say?"

"I couldn't risk it. It was hard enough to take yours," said Joseph.

"I need to tell them," said Marie, scrambling to her feet again.

Nora's hand shot out to stop her friend. "You can't."

"Why not?" Marie demanded.

"They're her family," Hazel said.

"You know why not," said Nora.

"They might be in danger," Marie said, sadness hollowing her face.

"Nora, be reasonable," Hazel tried.

"If you tell them, they might try to do something to help Henrik. They might tip someone off that they know he's being watched," said Nora.

"You don't know that!" Marie insisted.

"I do," she said.

"What am I supposed to do, then?" Marie exploded. "They're my only real family! I haven't seen my parents in seven years. I thought I could cope with that, even though I never stopped hoping that they might show me some sign that they care, but now I find out they lied to me. They lied to me in their letters and told me that they didn't have anything to do with the party. I knew they didn't love me, but I didn't think they'd lied to me."

"They're not your only real family," said Nora quietly.

Marie stopped and stared at Nora. "What?"

"Your aunt and uncle. They aren't your only real family."

Hazel nodded. "We are, too."

Marie crumpled back down to the sofa. Nora watched as Hazel eased herself onto the sofa to put a cautious, gentle hand on Marie's back and fold Marie into Hazel's shoulder.

"They're all so selfish," came the muffled sobs. "They don't care about us—any of us. And Henrik. Tante Matilda and Onkel Albrecht could be sent away for this, or worse. What he's doing is treason."

"Shhh." Hazel rubbed their friend's back as she would a child. "It's going to be all right."

"How can you say that?" Marie gasped.

"Because Nora and I would never let anything happen to you."

"But we don't know anything about the investigation into Henrik. The police could come tomorrow and arrest all of us," said Marie through her tears.

Nora ached to say something like, "That will never happen," or, "We won't let them take you," but none of them could make that sort of promise. Instead, she said, "We are not out of options yet. There may be something we can do."

"I should go to Canada," said Marie as her sobs slowed to shudders.

"Marie's passport arrived at the matchmaking agency yesterday. It looks as good as real," said Hazel.

Nora slid her gaze to Joseph, who had been standing quietly in the corner of the room, his hands folded behind his back.

"I can't hear a thing all the way over here," he said.

Nora mouthed *thank you* to him.

"Let's not hear any more talk about Canada," said Nora, coming to sit on the other side of Marie. "It hasn't come to that yet. Don't be silly."

"This doesn't feel silly to me. It feels as though I need to be prepared for the possibility that I could be interned, or worse," said Marie.

Nora bit her lip. She didn't want to lose her friend, but she'd never be able to forgive herself if her selfishness led to Marie's imprisonment. Besides, she might not even be in London much longer herself.

"Just take a moment to think about all of this. There must be something we can do to help your cause," said Hazel.

"Yes, Hazel's right. And no one can know that you took Marie's file, Joseph," Nora said.

"I'll put the file back in place as soon as I can. No one will even know it left the building," he said.

"Good," she said, as though it was the end of the matter, but she had a sinking feeling that this was only the beginning.

twenty-six

"Germany claimed a victory in Sedan yesterday with the capture of bridges across the Meuse River, continuing the Wehrmacht's rapid advance across Europe and into France."

—9 a.m. radio bulletin, May 16, 1940

N ora couldn't help but feel like she was in limbo. It had taken years of subtle cajoling and two unextraordinary Seasons—both of which ended without the engagement her mother so hoped for—to convince her father she should be allowed to find a job. She'd been thrilled to join the working masses, taking the Tube, picking up a newspaper, saving her shillings to buy a packet of sandwiches for lunch. Even when the novelty wore off, she found she liked working. She was *good* at it.

But Nora no longer had a job. Instead, she was going to be a Wren—if the WRNS would ever call her up. Until then, she was to be Hazel's assistant, because Hazel had told her in no uncertain terms that she was driving them all crazy with her fidgeting and moping around the house. If Nora was so bored, Hazel said, Nora could come to work with her. That following Monday, Nora had begun her temporary stint at the matchmaking agency.

Hazel proved to be a good boss, firm but patient. Nora had spent time in the agency's offices before, but never had she truly watched her friend work. Again and again, Hazel would sit down and listen to her clients, helping them sort through what they really wanted in a spouse. She could cut through expectations and obligations and find the heart of a person's desires. She was confidant, friend, and matchmaker all at once.

Four days in, Nora had a new respect for her friend and her skill.

"Do you really think you'll be able to find someone for Mr. Newsom?" Nora asked that Thursday just after midday. They were on a bus rolling down the Kings Road in order to collect Marie for lunch. Hazel had cleared the afternoon of appointments, declaring that she didn't know how much longer Nora would have until she was off to basic training, so they might as well take advantage of Marie's day off and spend as much time together as they could.

"Why wouldn't I?" Hazel asked.

"He's so painfully shy. You could hardly get a word out of him," Nora said, pulling on the cord to call for their stop.

"Some women find that sort of reticence appealing," said Hazel.

The bus doors clattered open, and Nora and Hazel clambered down to the street. "I don't know that I could stand it."

Hazel laughed. "Of course *you* couldn't. You want someone entirely different."

"Do I?" she asked, her brow arched.

"You need someone who can stand up to you and won't let you roll over them in an argument."

"You make me sound as though I'm likely to quarrel with everyone," said Nora.

"No, you're not argumentative. Just confident, and you don't suffer fools."

"And where exactly am I supposed to find this man?" she asked, her shoes slipping a little on the cobblestones of her street. She really needed to take them to the cobbler and have the heels replaced, but it seemed like a waste of time given that she would shortly be wearing navy-issued shoes.

"I think that if you stopped and thought about it for a moment, you'd know the answer to that question," said Hazel.

"No one likes a cryptic matchmaker," said Nora, digging into her purse for her key.

Before she could put the key in the latch, the door swung open.

"Hungry for lunch?" But the question died on Nora's lips as soon as she saw Marie in the darkened hallway. Her friend was chalk white.

She pushed into the house, Hazel close on her heels. "What is it? What's wrong?"

Marie shut the door with a heavy bang and leaned her forehead against the white-painted wood. She could see her friend's shoulders rise and fall with a deep breath. Then Marie turned and said, "Come."

Nora tossed her things down without a thought to where they fell and followed Marie into the front room. Marie's aunt sat on the sofa, the radio playing softly in the background.

"Hello, Mrs. Müller." But she stopped when she saw the older woman's eyes were red rimmed and puffy from crying.

"They've taken them," Mrs. Müller sobbed, burying her face into a crumpled handkerchief.

"Who?" Hazel asked.

"Onkel Albrecht and Henrik," said Marie. "Onkel Albrecht's secretary rang Tante Matilda an hour ago. They were both arrested at the office."

Mrs. Müller raised her head and rattled off a long stream of German.

"She says that his secretary said four police officers came and put Henrik in handcuffs," Marie translated. "They told him he was being arrested under Defense Regulation 18B. Onkel Albrecht tried to stop them, but they put him handcuffs, too. They wouldn't say where they were taking either of them. We don't know whether they are together or not." Marie took a deep breath. "This has to be because of the letter. They must've found whatever they were looking for about the group, and now they don't need to watch Henrik any longer."

"I must find my son and my husband. I need to know that they are unharmed," said Mrs. Müller, switching back to English. A little part of Nora broke at realizing that even in this darkest of moments, the woman who'd welcomed them warmly on school holidays despite Nora's mother's snubs and Hazel's mother's notoriety was taking Nora's poor German into consideration.

"I'm so sorry, Mrs. Müller," said Hazel.

Marie's aunt's head snapped up. "You said something about a letter, Marie. What did you mean?"

Nora stole a glance at Marie. "Did she?" she asked, trying to give her friend at least a few moments to think of how to tell her aunt that her beloved son dabbled in treason.

"You said that they found what they are looking for. Who are they? Why would they be watching my boy?" Mrs. Müller pressed.

"Tante Matilda, I'm so sorry."

Mrs. Müller gripped Marie's forearm. "What are you not telling me?"

"Henrik is a sympathizer. He was trying to do whatever he could to help Germany," said Marie gently. "I think that's why he was arrested."

"But that's absurd. He's no more a Nazi sympathizer than you or I," said Marie's aunt.

Marie just grimaced.

"Henrik left Germany when he was a boy," Mrs. Müller said, a desperation to her denial, as though deep down inside, she knew. "He's lived in this country for years."

"What about the summer you made him return home early from Germany? From the Hitler Youth camp?" said Marie.

"That was so long ago. Every boy has phases when he tries things his parents don't approve of."

"Tante Matilda, think of all of the things Henrik has said. You know he hasn't been happy here for years. He tried to push you and Onkel Albrecht to go back to Germany at the start of the war," said Marie.

"He romanticizes Germany because he only remembers what he knew as a child. He doesn't recall how hard it was then," said Mrs. Müller.

Marie took up her aunt's hand in her own. "Henrik believes the things that Hitler says. That isn't being childish or nostalgic. It's dangerous, and the people he's been surrounding himself with are dangerous.

"Nora's friend in the Home Office found out that Henrik tried to get a letter out of the country to Germany offering support for Hitler. Henrik wrote that he and a group of other men were sympathetic to what is happening in Germany. They want to help."

Mrs. Müller hunched over, pressing her free hand hard against her stomach. "No. This is a misunderstanding. I can't believe it's true."

"Mrs. Müller, the Home Office intercepted a letter. We've all seen it," said Hazel.

Mrs. Müller looked to Marie. "You have seen it?"

Marie nodded.

"Who did he send this letter to?" Mrs. Müller asked.

Nora watched Marie swallow around her emotion. "My father's brother. Onkel Pieter. He is a member of the Nazi Party and a deputy in the local Munich government. Henrik has offered to help. He talked about a group of sympathizers living in London who believe in Hitler's message. The treason is there in plain black ink."

Mrs. Müller's rage broke like a tidal wave. "*Dummkopf.* Reckless, stupid boy! What was he thinking? I've looked the other way as he squandered his school away. His father got him a position, and Albrecht does everything he can to make his life easier, even though Henrik seems to do little to deserve it. We've never said a word while he drinks and spends money without a care. All of that I could've endured, but this—" Mrs. Müller's voice broke. "If he is the reason Albrecht is interned, too, I'll never forgive him."

Marie wrapped her arms around her aunt and sat with her, rocking her gently back and forth. Despite the circumstances, Nora could see how glad Marie was to have the truth laid out. To have her aunt back.

"When you left the house and moved here, was it because of Henrik?" Mrs. Müller asked.

Marie stopped rocking and carefully set her aunt at arm's length. "It was complicated."

"It wasn't Marie's choice," Hazel said.

"Henrik told her to go," Nora added quickly.

"Marie, why didn't you tell me?" Mrs. Müller asked. "I thought you wanted to leave. That you regretted agreeing to stay with us when you could've gone back to your own parents."

"Henrik told me that I couldn't tell you. He threatened me," said Marie quietly.

"But what on earth could he threaten you with? You've done nothing wrong," said Mrs. Müller.

Marie's hands knitted and untangled over and over in her lap until finally she said, "You. He threatened to make you choose between the two of us."

"And you thought we wouldn't fight to keep you with us? Albrecht and I love you."

"He's your *son*. He's your flesh and blood," said Marie.

"And you are, too."

"I'm not your daughter."

Mrs. Müller stiffened. "Albrecht and I have *always* loved you like a daughter. You are precious to us. I thought you knew that, but perhaps we did not tell you enough.

"When my sister wrote to me and told me that she wanted us to send you back home after Ethelbrook, it nearly broke my heart. But then you decided to defy her and stay here, and I couldn't have been prouder. I felt as though you had chosen us."

"I did choose you," said Marie softly.

Nora could see tears shimmering in the corners of Marie's eyes, but still her friend's expression hardly changed. This was the Marie who was capable of pushing the rest of the world out and closing in on herself. Sometimes Nora fancied herself the most independent of them, but what she'd done was child's play compared to Marie. When her mother and father had sent her away like a troublesome pet, Marie had built a new family of her own. She loved fiercely, and she was formidable in her own quiet way. Marie was the strongest of all of them, even if she didn't always realize it.

"I think your parents tried to do the right thing for you. Their intentions were good—you could get an education here—but they don't understand how to be parents. They don't understand that children need to see love. To *feel* it." Mrs. Müller gathered her niece against her side. "But, Marie, I'm glad they sent you. I'm glad you chose to stay here. I couldn't love you more if I tried, and if Henrik would've tried to make me choose, I wouldn't have been able to. I love you both so much it feels sometimes as though my heart is too full to contain it all."

"I love you, too," Marie whispered.

Mrs. Müller kissed Marie on the forehead and looked down at her niece with a sad smile. "And that is why you cannot stay in London. You must leave."

"But I can't. You'll be all alone," said Marie, pushing back to stare at her aunt.

"I've never lived alone," said Mrs. Müller, forcing a smile. "Perhaps I'll like it, like you, Nora."

"I can recommend it highly, although taking in houseguests has a certain charm," Nora said.

"I can't leave you," said Marie more firmly this time.

Mrs. Müller laid a palm softly on her niece's cheek. "You *must*. Things are becoming worse. Germany keeps advancing and everything will become worse for us. They'll be looking for reasons to intern Germans because people will be nervous. Because of Henrik, I cannot imagine that suspicion won't fall on you as well, and that will be all the reason they need to send you away. You cannot risk staying here, although I don't know where you will go," said Mrs. Müller, worrying her lip. "You can't hide your accent and you will have to register no matter where you go."

"—*arrests today of thousands of German men*," a radio bulletin cut in.

Nora lunged for the radio dial to turn up the volume.

"Police say that those men who have received a category B classification are being taken into custody and will be interned. The Home Office decision comes after reports that German troops are now advancing unimpeded through France toward the Channel after capturing bridges across the Meuse River."

Mrs. Müller gripped her niece's hand. "You must leave."

"She's right," Hazel said.

Marie looked to Nora as though she held an answer. Her heart constricted. Marie shouldn't have to run—England was her home—but she couldn't think of any other way to protect her. Not if Marie wanted to remain free until this bloody war was over.

"It's only a matter of time before they decide that women are just as much of a threat as men," said Nora.

"Mrs. Müller, Nora, Marie, and I have spoken about this before. As a precaution, I was able to arrange for Marie to have new papers made," said Hazel.

"Is that legal?" asked Mrs. Müller.

"Not in the least bit," Nora piped up.

The older woman pursed her lips but nodded. "Where will you go, Marie?"

"Canada. All we have to do is arrange for passage on a ship," said Marie.

"That will be my job," said Nora, crossing to her rolltop desk, papers jammed into its little pigeonholes. "I have all the shipping schedules somewhere around here."

"Canada," murmured Mrs. Müller. "It's so far."

"It's closer than Australia," said Marie as Nora nosed around for the schedules.

"The Atlantic is so dangerous with the U-boats," said Mrs. Müller weakly.

Nora's hands stilled.

"It's a risk I have to take," Marie said.

Nora squeezed her eyes shut, sent up a little prayer that Marie's crossing would be a safe one, fixed a smile on her face, and turned to wave the schedules. "Here they are."

"What will you do, Mrs. Müller?" Hazel asked.

"I am category C. I'm safe for now," said the older woman.

"Could you try to arrange a passport for my aunt?" Marie asked, glancing at Hazel.

Hazel opened her mouth, but Nora knew she couldn't make herself say yes.

"With everyone on high alert and arrests being handed down, I think the chances are slim," Hazel finally said.

Mrs. Müller patted her niece on the hand. "I wouldn't go even if you could find a space for me on a ship. If Albrecht is interned here, I'll want to be close by, so I can be there when he returns. It will give me comfort."

Nora could see Marie wanted to argue, but she nodded nonetheless.

"Marie, did you give this address to the police?" asked Mrs. Müller, becoming businesslike.

"Yes," said Marie.

"Then you'll need another place to hide until you can get on a ship," said Mrs. Müller.

"I don't know where I'll go. I won't put anyone else in danger," said Marie.

"I could ask Nathaniel," said Hazel, but she looked doubtful about her estranged husband's reaction to such a request.

An idea popped into Nora's head, so obvious she could've smacked herself on the forehead for not thinking of it earlier.

"Marie, start packing," she said. "I know exactly where you can stay."

twenty-seven

"Nearly ten o'clock," said Nora, looking at her watch.

The three of them had been sitting at the breakfast table, nervously sipping at the same round of sidecars she'd shaken up two hours ago in Marie's honor. None of them really felt like drinking, though. There was too much at stake.

As soon as Mrs. Müller left, the house had exploded into chaos. Hazel had raced around, helping Marie sort through her clothes and pack only what she might need. Nora made a phone call and then paid a visit to her banker, Mr. Voigt, where she withdrew enough money that the usually quiet man's eyebrows knitted together. She'd thought that he might refuse to make the transaction, but instead he slipped out of his office, returning ten minutes later with an envelope full of currency. She'd sweated the entire way back, aware of what was in her handbag, sagging against the door with relief when she returned, the strains of an argument between Hazel and Marie about whether or not to bring the secondhand typewriter Richard had given Marie drifting down the stairs to greet her.

She went out again at five o'clock and bought every evening paper she could find. Splashed across the front pages were the same headlines they'd heard earlier on the radio. The Home Office had succumbed to pressure. All category B men were being arrested. Henrik and his father must have been convenient to lump into this group, the investigation neatly wrapped up with an already scheduled round of arrests.

"Are you nervous?" Hazel asked.

Marie pulled her cardigan closer around her. "Yes, but if I have to hide out somewhere, I trust you two more than anyone else."

"Do you remember when we were girls and we would sneak out to the fields at night?" asked Nora.

"Just because you wanted to do something daring," said Marie.

"It wasn't just me. We all wanted to," she protested.

"It was," said Hazel.

Actually, now that she thought of it, her friends were probably right.

"You always were the brave one, Nora. I think I would've followed you anywhere," said Marie with a smile.

"Me, too. I don't think I even realized how lonely I was until I got to Ethelbrook," said Hazel.

"You didn't have many children around you," said Marie.

"Mum's artist friends were terrible playmates. One tried to use my dolls to explain to me Kant's categorical imperative," said Hazel.

"I couldn't believe that the two of you wanted to be my friends. All the children Mother thought were from suitable families were either so dull I wanted to scream or they looked at me as though I was odd," Nora said.

Her taller-than-ladylike height. Her propensity for saying exactly the wrong thing at the wrong time—usually when an adult was around to witness it. It was as though other children could smell the awkwardness on her and knew to stay well away. She'd hoped it would be better when she went away to school, but it was infinitely worse. Suddenly there was no escaping the other girls.

Marie and Hazel were the first friends she had who didn't make her feel as though she had to twist herself like a pretzel.

A car honked its horn in the street, and all three of them tensed. After a few seconds, Marie gave a laugh. "I keep thinking someone's going to come to the door." Someone like the police.

"Have you telephoned Richard?" Hazel asked.

Marie sighed. "Does it matter?"

"I think so," Hazel said.

Marie looked to Nora, and she nodded. She may never have met this Richard Calloway, but Marie seemed to like him and Hazel trusted him. That was enough for her.

"I've never met a man who makes me feel as though he cares so much about what I have to say. It never was like that with Neil. He only cared about what I thought of his speeches," said Marie.

"You are more talented than he is," said Nora.

Marie tilted her head to one side. "Do you know? I think I am."

"And Richard is a smart man. He can see how wonderful you are, just like Nora and I can," said Hazel.

"If things had been different . . ."

"If there hadn't been a war on," Nora prompted.

"But there is," said Marie.

"Would you like us to tell him anything for you?" Hazel asked softly.

After a moment, Marie said, "Tell him that I hope he finds happiness. I really and truly do hope that for him."

The faint chiming of the carriage clock that sat on the mantelpiece in the front room drifted through the open kitchen door. It was time.

Nora nudged Marie with her shoulder. "Are you ready?"

Marie nodded, and they all went to put on their coats.

They hardly spoke on the bus ride over. It was only when they were a block away from the Harlan that Nora stopped them. They huddled into a little circle, like children playing a game. Except this wasn't a game at all.

"All right, remember, you two stay in the service entrance around the side while I go inside," she instructed. "Pierre said the top floor was under renovation when the war started, and all the builders left to join up. Between that and the lift that's been broken for a month, no one will be trudging up there. He'll let me around behind the bar, and I'll slip down the back stairs and collect you from the service entrance."

"Are you sure this will work?" Marie said.

She could've lied to their friend—it would've eased Marie's mind a bit—but Marie deserved better than that. Instead, Nora looked at her friend square in the eye and said, "What I can promise is that Hazel and I will do everything we can to make sure that you're on a boat to Canada as soon as I can find you passage."

"Thank you both," whispered Marie.

Hazel smiled. "You don't need to thank me. You two are the closest thing I've ever had to sisters."

"You know I feel the same way," said Nora.

Marie gave them each a swift hug, and then nodded. "I'm ready."

Nora rolled her shoulders like a fighter ready for a bout. "Right."

Her heels clipped the pavement with purpose as she pulled away from her friends. She didn't look back at Hazel and Marie. Hidden by the blackout, they would wait down the steps at the side of the Harlan's iron fence near the basement service entrance. For now, it was Nora's turn to perform.

It was late enough that no doorman stood at the doors. Instead, she leaned on the brass buzzer to the right of the door handle and waited for a reedy young woman to let her in.

"Good evening, Miss Walcott," said the woman.

"Evening," said Nora, whipping off her chocolate coat with the rounded collar and revealing the silver lamé evening dress she'd put on just before dinner. "Is Pierre still at the bar?"

"I believe he is," the young woman said, taking the coat.

Thank God for that. "Thank you."

Without another word, she marched herself through the lobby, up the center stairs, and into the bar.

It was mercifully empty except for an ancient woman sitting in front of a half-full glass of sherry, a cigarette nearly burned down in her long ebony holder. Pierre stood behind the bar.

"Miss Walcott, what a pleasure," he said.

"Thank you, Pierre. I was passing by after a concert and realized that I meant to look in earlier. I believe I lost an earring the other day."

"What did it look like?" he asked.

She toyed with the pendant of her necklace as though trying to figure out how to describe the mythic earring. "It's three bands of gold that bend over each other into a knot."

Pierre gamely tilted his head. "Perhaps you would like to look at the box we keep for lost items . . ."

She let her eyes slide over to the old woman in the corner as she nodded. The woman's cigarette holder was propped on a crystal ashtray and its owner appeared to be falling asleep.

How obliging.

"That would be very helpful, Pierre. Thank you," said Nora with a smile.

He hesitated. "I would go fetch it, but I have my duties here."

"If you'll just show me where I can find the box, I'll have a look," she said.

He reared back in horror. "But, Miss Walcott, club members are not allowed in the offices. It's not . . . proper."

Good Lord, Pierre. Proper?

Nora drew herself up to her full, considerable height. "I think you understand that exceptions can occasionally be made, Pierre."

He inclined his head, and she followed him through the door just to the side of the bar. As soon as they were through, Nora began to giggle. Pierre clapped a hand over his mouth but shook his head vigorously as they scuttled along the cramped passageway to what had once been the servants' staircase.

With the door shut behind them, Pierre let his hand fall and cackled out a laugh. Nora's giggles burst through, and they both leaned against the wall, shaking.

"All of that for an octogenarian," she said, wiping her eyes.

"Don't you British say, *If something is worth it, it is done right*?" he sputtered.

"'If something's worth doing, it's worth doing right,'" she corrected.

He pursed his lips and shrugged.

"I'm not sure we're going to win any accolades for that performance, but it's done," she said, pushing her hair back from her face.

"Come," said Pierre. "We will let Miss Bohn and Mrs. Carey in."

"Yes, I expect they're wondering what's taking so long and—"

"Miss Walcott, what are you doing below stairs?"

Nora and Pierre froze like naughty children. Slowly, Nora turned to face Lady Dora, who was standing on the landing above them in a long black satin evening dress, diamonds at her throat and ears.

"Lady Dora," she breathed.

"Pierre, you know that members are not permitted in this area of the club." The Harlan's chairwoman slid a sharp glare at Nora. "And *don't* make the mistake of thinking that being a Founding Few's granddaughter means that the rules do not apply to you."

"It is not Pierre's fault, Lady Dora. I made him—"

"There is no excuse," said the doyenne.

Pierre looked frightened, and Nora's stomach churned with the knowledge that she'd likely cost him his job.

"He was only doing what I asked. To help a friend," she said.

Lady Dora arched a brow.

"My friend Marie—"

"The German girl," said Lady Dora, her tone unreadable.

She sucked in a breath. She was going to have to trust that she could appeal to Lady Dora's decency and hope—pray—that she wasn't making a huge mistake.

"The police are arresting category B enemy aliens," said Nora.

"*Male* category B aliens. Miss Bohn is not a man, is she?" Lady Dora said.

"No." She hesitated. "But we believe she is in danger nonetheless. She could be arrested."

"Arrested?"

"Not for anything she did," Nora added quickly. "Because of something her cousin did. Her uncle and father, too. I can't stand by and let her be punished for their mistakes."

The club chairwoman studied her for a long moment. "I take it that Miss Bohn is somewhere on the club's premises?"

"She's waiting down at the service entrance with Hazel," said Nora.

"Mrs. Carey? Why am I not surprised?" Lady Dora began to descend the stairs.

"Where are you going?" Nora asked.

"To see to your friends. Pierre, I suggest that you return to the bar. I believe you'll find Mrs. Thorborough is in danger of knocking over her glass," Lady Dora threw over her shoulder.

Pierre scrambled back through the door, but not before Nora whispered, "I will fix this." Then she clambered down the narrow stairs behind Lady Dora.

For a woman who was presented to the queen in the last years of the previous century, Lady Dora was remarkably quick. Nora was huffing before she reached the lower ground floor, which was why she wasn't fast enough to throw herself in front of Lady Dora when the chairwoman whipped open the door.

"Good evening, Miss Bohn, Mrs. Carey," said Lady Dora as Nora skidded to a stop behind her.

The faint light spilling out from the club's basement was enough that Nora saw the blood drain out of Marie's face.

"L-Lady Dora," Hazel stammered.

"I don't usually find guests skulking outside of the service entrance. However, Miss Walcott assures me that there is an excellent reason for your presence here," said Lady Dora.

Nora watched Marie swallow and then nod once. "I need a place to stay."

"Most of our guests also prefer to go in through the front door," said Lady Dora.

"I told Lady Dora about your uncle and cousin's arrests," Nora said. If only the chairwoman would see how serious this all was.

"Then you'll know that I have reason to be frightened for my own freedom," said Marie. "I had hoped that I would be able to stay hidden away at the Harlan just until I could secure passage on a ship to Canada."

"And you thought to recruit my bartender into helping you?" asked Lady Dora.

"Pierre didn't mean any harm," said Marie.

Lady Dora fixed them with a long stare until Nora began to feel as though she was back at school, waiting for her palm to be slapped by a disapproving teacher. Finally, Lady Dora stepped out of the doorway. "Well, you had better come inside for a moment before the air raid warden yells at us for breaking the blackout."

The three friends exchanged nervous glances, Marie moving first. Nora took Marie's case as she passed, but Hazel stopped just on the threshold.

"What happened?" Hazel whispered, shifting Marie's typewriter from hand to hand.

"She caught Pierre and me on the stairwell."

"Does she seem willing to help?"

Nora shrugged. They didn't know whether Lady Dora was planning to welcome them into the club or lock them in her office and telephone the police to report them for suspicious behavior.

Nora shuffled ahead to keep up with Lady Dora, who swept her long skirts into one hand, the other draping elegantly on the banister, her rings glinting even in the harsh overhead light.

"Your dress tonight is beautiful, Lady Dora. Was there an event at the club this evening?" she asked.

"No. I was dining at the home of a friend of mine. A Mrs. Boyd," said Lady Dora.

Nora frowned. "Then you decided to come in for a nightcap."

Lady Dora turned her head just enough that Nora could see a bemused glint in her eyes. "Rather than guessing how I came to know that you would be here this evening, perhaps you'd like me to tell you. Our head of housekeeping rang Mrs. Boyd's home just as the gentlemen were having their glass of port. She said that Pierre had asked her to service a room on the top floor and she thought that was very odd, so she decided she'd better check with me first since that floor is off-limits to guests."

Oh, Pierre. But she couldn't blame him. He was acting as he'd been trained, taking a guest's needs into consideration at all times. Besides, all they'd told him was that Marie needed a discreet place to stay for a few days. How could he have known that the fewer people who knew about Marie's stay at the Harlan, the better?

She surged forward after Lady Dora. "Are you going to let Marie stay?"

Lady Dora stopped on the cramped first-floor landing. "Of course Miss Bohn can stay. We're a women's club, not the police. And we understand that sometimes there are things more important than law and order, especially when men's foolishness is to blame."

As they resumed their ascent, Lady Dora continued. "You more than anyone else should know the club's history, Miss Walcott. This club has never been political, but that doesn't mean it hasn't had its moments of dissension. It was staunchly in favor of women's right to vote years before it came to be, and once we even harbored several suffragettes after a riot. It was before my time, but my understanding is that the police searched for them for days, while the ladies took over the top floor and toasted their success with champagne and caviar they had sent up from the kitchen in the dumbwaiter.

"We'll see to it that you're made comfortable, Miss Bohn, even if you won't be able to leave your room very often."

"Thank you. You have no idea what a relief it is to hear that," said Marie.

"What about your head of housekeeping?" Nora asked as they rounded the second-floor landing.

"Janet? She's the daughter of my personal housekeeper. Her loyalty is to me and the Harlan. I will speak to her and make her understand the severity of the consequences if she tells anyone about this temporary arrangement. I will tell the rest of the staff that one of our country members fell ill when she was in town, and the doctor has ordered that she should do nothing but rest in complete silence, so we've installed her on the top floor. I will arrange for Pierre or Wallace to bring your meals," said Lady Dora.

They reached the top floor, red faced and out of breath except for Lady Dora, who serenely dropped her hem and pulled out a long brass key that was tucked into the top of her right glove. She fitted it into a door and let it swing open. Inside was modest but comfortable, with a double bed covered with a clean white spread, an old-fashioned pitcher and bowl on a mahogany washing stand, and a large armoire that loomed on one side of the room. The closed door next to the armoire, Nora assumed, must lead to the en suite bathroom.

"I will leave you to settle in, but if you should need anything, you can ring Pierre's telephone in the bar for the next hour or so. Otherwise, don't hesitate to call down to my office," said Lady Dora. "Think of some books that you wish to read; I'll bring them up from the library tomorrow."

"Thank you," said Marie.

Lady Dora waved a hand. "Think nothing of it. The Harlan takes care of its own."

"I'm not a member," said Marie.

"You're Miss Walcott's friend, and you are in need. That's enough for me," said Lady Dora, turning for the door.

Nora darted out after her through the swinging door, calling out, "Lady Dora, please!"

"Miss Walcott?"

"Thank you. I cannot thank you enough," said Nora.

"Don't thank me, Miss Walcott. But perhaps it's time for you to consider taking your place on the club board."

She blinked. "You think I should run for election?"

"Why not? You're a Founding Few's granddaughter, but more importantly, you appear to live by the principles the Harlan should be guided by. I would imagine the membership would be very proud to have you sitting on the board, and I would be delighted to back your candidacy. Once you no longer have responsibilities to the Wrens, of course."

"How did you know that I had joined the Wrens?" she asked.

Lady Dora tilted her head in thought. "Do you know, I believe I heard it from your mother. She sounded rather proud to have a daughter volunteering for duty."

Nora's jaw fell open. Her *mother*, proud? It seemed impossible, but as she stood ready to enter military service and face unknown danger, she found that she didn't hate the idea.

"I've never thought about the board before," she said slowly, "but perhaps after the war."

"Next week or in ten years' time. Ring me if you're ever on leave and wish to speak about it—even if it's just a welcome distraction. I'll arrange for us to have tea, and you can ask me all of your questions," said Lady Dora before descending the stairs with all the elegance of a woman born to another era.

Cↄ

It was well past midnight when Nora and Hazel stumbled through her front door.

"I'm too worried to sleep but too exhausted to stay awake," moaned Hazel.

Nora bent to collect the post they'd neglected that afternoon. "Go up to bed. I'm just going to lock up and check the blackout."

Hazel nodded and began to pull herself up the stairs, tugging mightily on the banister as she went.

Nora shook her head at her friend's dramatics as she locked the back door. She began sorting through the post as she moved from room to room, shimmying curtains and making sure that no light could spill out onto the street. It probably wasn't necessary to be so vigilant and perform these checks every night, but her days in Air Raid Precautions were a hard habit to break.

The downstairs done, she climbed the stairs and pushed open her bedroom door. It was a simple room, all done up in white and soft gray—

the opposite of the frills and flowers of her childhood bedroom. She'd just reached the last letter as she sat on the bed to toe her shoes off. The address was printed on cheap paper using a typewriter that had a misaligned C.

One shoe clunked to the floor. She ripped open the envelope and pulled out the letter. The other shoe clunked to the floor as she unfolded the single sheet.

> Miss Nora Elizabeth Walcott to report at 0800 hours on June 1, 1940, to RNC Greenwich for training.

Underneath was a brief description of what she would be allowed to bring—no need for much, as the navy would be kitting her out now.

She exhaled with relief at finally knowing—in less than a month's time, she would be a Wren.

twenty-eight

Nearly a week after installing Marie in the Harlan, Nora unhooked her umbrella from the rack in the shared lobby of the Mayfair Matrimonial Agency's building and unbuttoned its clasp. The rain had looked like a light drizzle when Nora had peered out the window of Hazel's third-floor office just a few moments before, but now it fell fast and heavy.

"You were right when you said to bring them," said Hazel, shaking her own umbrella out.

"Let's hope that the bus isn't too crowded. I hate the smell of wet wool coats," she said.

Hazel nodded and pushed open the door, when a man appeared on the front steps and she stopped short. "Mr. Calloway? What are you doing here?"

Nora peered around her friend's shoulder at the man. Water dripped from the brim of his hat as though he'd been waiting for a long time. He wore a sheepish smile. "Hello, Mrs. Carey."

"Come in out of the wet. Please," Hazel said, opening the door wide while Nora reversed into the entryway to let him in.

"Thank you." He shook off some of the rain that had clung to his trench coat.

"Nora, this is Richard Calloway," said Hazel.

So *this* was the famous Richard.

"Nora Walcott," she said, sticking out her hand as he took off his hat.

"I've heard a great deal about you, Miss Walcott," he said.

"And I you. You'd better call me Nora," she said, peering at him wide-eyed and wondering what it was about this man in particular that seemed to have captured Marie. He had a good strong jaw and a piercing blue gaze, but what Nora liked the most about him was the little creases at the corners of his eyes. This was a man who smiled openly and often.

"You're soaked through," said Hazel.

"I've been walking around, trying to convince myself not to come see you," he said.

"Why?" Nora asked.

"Because I'm not sure it's my right to ask what I'm about to ask you," he said.

She stole a glance at Hazel. The day that Nora had purchased Marie passage on a ship, the three of them had quarreled over whether or not it was safe for Marie to telephone Richard after she was installed at the Harlan. Hazel was for it, Nora against, arguing that any contact with the outside world could put Marie at risk. Finally, Marie put her hands up and announced that she would call Richard and explain. Somehow. When Hazel had gently asked what she would say, Marie clammed up and Nora knew not to push her friend any more. Now, looking at Richard's slumped shoulders and the weary lines on either side of his eyes, she wondered if she'd been wrong to argue the side of caution.

"I can't stop thinking about her—worrying about her," he said. "She telephoned and said that she couldn't see me any longer. That it was best this way."

"I'm sorry," said Hazel.

"Do you think—did I do something wrong?" He stared down at the hat between his hands. "It's only that I thought there might be something between us. I haven't felt this way about anyone since my wife died."

His words tugged at her heart. By all accounts, he was a good man, a kind one who felt deeply. Now, to hear him speak of Marie, she could understand a little bit more.

"Sometimes things don't work out between people," Hazel said, laying a hand on his forearm.

"I just want the chance to speak with her one more time. To be sure. I miss talking to her. Would you tell her that, for me?"

Maybe it would be easier to tell him that Marie hadn't felt the same way. That the connection he felt wasn't reciprocated. But Nora knew Hazel didn't lie to her clients and this man, raw and vulnerable standing before her, had been a client before Marie. She knew her friend well enough to know that Hazel would believe she owed him at least some sort of answer—if Marie would allow it.

With a sigh, Hazel said, "I can't make any promises, but if you'll come with us, I might be able to arrange something."

He nodded and opened up the door. Nora tugged the collar of her coat up around her neck, put up her umbrella, and the three of them plunged out into the rain.

C~

Nora breathed a sigh of relief when the young woman at the Harlan's front desk put down the receiver and said that Lady Dora was, in fact, in her office and would be down to see her in five minutes.

They'd left Richard in the booth of a restaurant two streets over. If Marie agreed, they would telephone him and give him the club's address. If not, he was to consider that his answer.

"Miss Walcott, Mrs. Carey, I trust you're well."

Nora looked up and saw Lady Dora approaching from down the corridor just to the right of the desk.

"Might we speak somewhere private?" Nora asked.

"The matter we'd like to speak to you about is rather delicate," Hazel added.

Lady Dora led her back down the corridor to the club chairwoman's office—a room Nora had only been in twice before. It was a serious woman's room with a large Queen Anne desk in the bay window, bookshelves lining two walls, and a sofa and three cream-cushioned chairs under a large painting of a group of distinguished-looking Victorian women—the Founding Few, including Nora's grandmother. A record spun on an old-fashioned gramophone, Haydn if she wasn't mistaken.

"Do make yourself at home," said Lady Dora, gesturing to the sofa and offering them each a cigarette from a gold box on a side table. "Turkish on the right. American on the left, although who knows how long we'll have the luxury of choice. I was just about to order up a drink from the bar if you'd like one as well. Another luxury we may have to do without soon."

"No, thank you," said Nora.

Hazel shook her head as well.

Lady Dora tapped her cigarette on the top of the box, stuck it between her lipsticked lips, and tilted her head to light it. "I take it that you're here about our mutual friend on the top floor. I feel for her in more ways than one. It must be terribly dull being locked up, even here."

"She won't have to stay hidden for too much longer. I've booked her passage on a ship bound for Canada on the twenty-seventh," said Nora. Just days before she had to report to the Wrens, a fact she still hadn't told her friends. It didn't feel right to bring it up and pull attention away from Marie. They only had so much time left together. She wanted to spend as much of their time focused on that as possible.

"It's Marie's departure that we wanted to speak to you about, in a way," said Hazel. "You see, before it became clear that she would not be able to remain in this country, I introduced her to a gentleman."

"In your professional capacity, no doubt," said Lady Dora.

Hazel nodded.

"And I take it he wasn't satisfied with letting her go just like that?" Lady Dora asked. "He wants one more chance to fight for her."

"Well, yes," she said.

"Good. I can't abide a man with no backbone. Or a woman, for that matter. We should all know when to fight for what we want," said Lady Dora.

"What about when we know that the fight is no longer worth it?" Hazel asked quietly.

Lady Dora tapped her cigarette ash. "Well, no one wishes to be foolish."

Nora squeezed Hazel's hand. Hazel had seen a solicitor at the beginning of May, and Nora thought that since then her friend had looked more like herself than she had in ages.

"Does Miss Bohn wish to speak to this gentleman?" asked Lady Dora.

"I don't think we can be sure yet," said Hazel.

"You haven't asked her?" asked Lady Dora.

Nora shook her head. "We wanted to speak to you first. To see if it would be possible to arrange a place for her to see him here."

"Well, she certainly can't speak to him in her bedroom. Skirts might be shorter and career girls are running around London at all hours, but there are some standards the Harlan will always maintain, and one is that no gentlemen are allowed on the upper floors," said Lady Dora.

Nora pressed her lips together to keep from smiling. "We would never dream of suggesting such a thing."

Lady Dora tilted her chin as though examining whether there was any sarcasm in Nora's words, and then asked, "Where is this man?"

"He is at a restaurant nearby, waiting for our telephone call," said Nora.

"Well"—the chairwoman snubbed out her cigarette—"I suppose we should find out how Miss Bohn feels about the matter. I was already planning to ask her to my office for an hour to allow housekeeping to tidy her room. Wallace's wife is coming in especially for it. She's a chambermaid at the Lanesborough, you know, and I think we can trust them both to keep this a secret."

"Thank you, Lady Dora," said Hazel.

The older woman excused herself, leaving them to Haydn. Ten minutes later, a side door hidden in the paneling swung open, and Marie emerged from the servants' stairs.

"Why didn't you come up to the room?" Marie asked, hugging them each in turn. Nora hung on a little longer than usual. Just a few more days and she wouldn't be able to hug her friend for—well, she didn't know for how long.

"We had to speak to Lady Dora first. Marie, we didn't just come here to see you. Richard came to see us at the agency this evening," said Hazel.

Marie sank down onto the sofa. "What did he want?"

"He's worried about you. He wanted to know how you are," said Nora.

"He also wanted to know if he'd done something wrong," said Hazel.

"He didn't do anything wrong," said Marie, her voice little more than a whisper.

"He wants to see you," Hazel said.

Her friend shook her head. "That's not a good idea."

"Do you not trust him?" Nora asked.

Marie's eyes were questioning. "We've known each other for such a short time."

"Longer than it takes some to marry," said Nora.

"You seemed so sure of him," Hazel ventured.

"But are a few dinners and a handful of telephone calls enough to truly know someone?" Marie asked.

No, but it was enough to find something. To connect. To understand. Nora had felt that connection with so few people. Marie and Hazel. Her father. Perhaps Joseph.

"He wants to see you," Hazel repeated.

"I want to see him," said Marie. "If only to offer him an explanation."

"If you're sure," said Nora.

Marie gave a little laugh. "What is there to be sure of? I'm hiding out in a club that isn't even my own, full of staff and members who might find me out at any moment. I have a forged passport in my unmention-ables drawer, and a ticket on a ship that sails on Monday. I could be arrested. You both could be arrested."

"None of us are thinking about that right now," she said.

"But maybe you should be. Maybe that's all any of us should be worried about, because if you're found to be conspiring with a German who has ties to the Nazi Party—"

"Ties that are no fault of your own," Hazel said.

"But they're still there. I can't change them. Not Henrik, nor my parents, nor my father."

"You are not to blame for others' choices," said Nora fiercely.

"Then why do I feel as though I'm the one being punished?" Marie asked.

None of it was fair, so they sat for a moment, a symphony softly filling the silence.

"I'll see him," Marie finally said.

"Tonight?" Hazel asked.

"He's here?"

"Close by. I can tell him to come now if you're ready."

Nora could see Marie worrying the inside of her lip, but her friend nodded.

Nora telephoned Richard at the restaurant and told him they were collecting him. They used the service entrance—at Lady Dora's invitation—rather than going through the front door, so they could use the discreet door to the chairwoman's office. Then the baroness melted away, claiming that she was needed to handle an issue with a member in the dining room.

"Are you ready?" Hazel asked Richard, her hand on the mechanism that worked the door.

He touched his tie. "I am."

"If you're hoping for answers to all of your questions, you may be disappointed," Nora warned.

"I just want to see her."

There it was again—the little warmth she'd felt toward him was growing. Nora nodded and pushed open the door.

Marie rose to her feet as soon as they walked in. "Richard."

A smile broke out over his face. "I didn't think that asking to see you again would require so much subterfuge, but I'm happy regardless."

Nora and Hazel stood half in, half out of the room, as though they both knew they shouldn't be here in this moment of intimacy.

"We'll just leave you two—"

"No!" Marie hugged her arms across her midsection, as though holding herself together. "Please stay. I'm sorry, Richard, but this was a mistake. You shouldn't have come."

"Why not?" He took a step forward. When Marie didn't react, he took another, and then another. Nora saw his hand twitch as though he wanted to reach for her.

"You just shouldn't," said Marie, her voice rising.

"If this is a bad time, I'll come back—"

"I'm leaving!" Marie blurted out.

Richard took a step back. "Leaving?"

"I'm sailing for Canada from Liverpool on Monday."

"Why?" he asked.

"I have to leave London. My cousin and my uncle have been arrested. There are reasons why I might be arrested, too. I don't want to be sent to an internment camp for crimes that I didn't commit," said Marie.

"But if you didn't do anything wrong, why should you worry?" he asked.

Marie fixed him with a hollow stare. "I told you that I had been given category B status."

"I don't understand. Category B women weren't arrested last week."

"But you must see that it's only a matter of time," said Marie.

"You don't know that," he said.

"Neither do you."

"That's why you telephoned and told me that you couldn't see me any longer?" he asked.

"Well, yes," said Marie.

"But none of that changes who you are—who you are to me. You should've—"

"Done what?" Marie asked fiercely. "Rung you and said I might be taken away by the police because I'm German, and it looks as though my family may be a bunch of Nazis? That my cousin is an idiot sympathizer? My uncle's been arrested, and now I have to leave behind the woman who was more of a mother to me than my own mother, and you think you can somehow *fix* this?"

Nora made a move from the doorway, but Richard was faster. Without hesitation, he wrapped his arms around her friend, settled his head into the crook of her neck, and held her. Just held her.

Marie turned her face into his chest. "I feel as though I'm being punished, but I'm a good person."

"I know that. I know that," said Richard, stroking her hair.

"How can you? You barely know me."

"I just know."

Nora pressed her hand to her mouth, trying to keep herself from crying. Next to her, Hazel pulled out a handkerchief.

"I thought if I did everything right, I would be safe," said Marie.

"It's not fair. It's never fair," Richard murmured, dropping a light kiss to the top of Marie's head.

"I wish that there was no war, no internment. I wish we'd just met and that you might come to . . . like me one day."

"Can I tell you a secret?" he asked, leaning back so he could lift Marie's chin with a crooked finger.

"Yes."

"I think I've come to like you already."

Marie squeezed her eyes shut and stepped away. "We should say goodbye."

Richard's entire body seemed to stiffen, but he nodded. "I suppose we should."

Marie gave a shuddering breath as Richard leaned down to kiss her on the cheek. He lingered, just a moment, and Nora watched longing, regret, anger, sorrow break over her friend's face. How might it feel to care that deeply about someone?

"Goodbye, Marie," he said as he stepped back.

"Goodbye."

"Let me see you out," said Nora quietly.

"I'll make my own way," said Richard.

She stepped aside to let him through, but he stopped, his hand on the doorframe. "Perhaps we'll see each other again, Marie. After the war."

Through her tears, Marie couldn't muster anything but a nod of her head.

"Take care of her," said Richard, leaning close as he passed Nora. "I don't want to lose her."

"I will," Nora promised, even though she would be losing Marie herself in just a few days' time.

twenty-nine

ALLIED TROOPS FALL BACK IN FLANDERS
Evacuations Begin on Beaches of Dunkirk
—*London Morning Herald*, May 27, 1940

The docks were mobbed with people bustling around the ship's gang-ways as the five-minute warning blast echoed across the water. Little clusters of families said teary-eyed goodbyes to loved ones while porters pushed great carts of luggage. Above them all, the massive ship towered, a wall of welded steel painted stark black.

"Here we are," said Nora, putting down Marie's suitcase, having insisted on carrying it from the train station. Hazel added the hatbox that contained Marie's two best hats, which Mrs. Müller had dropped off at the agency because she thought her niece might want them in Canada. Marie's hands were still wrapped around the handle of the typewriter case, unwilling to let it go no matter how often Nora offered to take it from her on the journey up to Liverpool.

"Thank you," said Marie. They all stared down at the ticket that crinkled between Marie's fingers. This was the moment when they were supposed to all say goodbye, but how did you start to stay goodbye to one of the most important people in your life?

"I . . ." Marie looked up at each of her friends, her eyes beginning to brim.

"No, don't do that," Nora said quickly. "I'll start crying next, and you know how blotchy I become when I cry."

"I never used to cry. Now I can't seem to help it," said Marie with a laugh.

Nora pulled Marie into a hug. "I can't believe you're leaving."

"I can hardly believe it either," said Marie. "We'll always be."

"Just us three," said Hazel and Nora at the same time.

"I'm so sorry," Hazel said.

"For what?" Marie asked.

"For not being able to do more."

"You must stop thinking like that," said Marie, squeezing her hand. "You helped me more than you will ever know."

"You won't forget us in Canada, will you?" Nora asked.

"How could I? My Ethelbrook Misfits," Marie said.

"Surely we've grown up by now," said Nora. "We also have dinners and cocktails and toasts to Pierre."

And dreams and disappointments. Secrets and confessions.

Marie clasped each of their hands. "I'll never be able to tell you how much I love you."

Over Marie's shoulder, Nora saw a flash of silver. She squinted. Badges. The badges on police constables' helmets. Three of them. And they were making their way right for her friends.

"I think we have a problem," she said, pointing.

～

Hazel craned her neck as a fourth man stepped out from behind the constables. "Is that— Oh no, it's Dennison!"

"What?" Nora grabbed her arm.

Hazel's stomach turned sour. What if he'd followed them to the train station? What if he had been following her this entire time and he knew everything—about picking up Marie's false papers from the drop location her contact had given her, about living with Nora, about the Harlan?

"Marie, if I led him to you—"

"I don't care how he figured out about Marie leaving, we need to make sure that he doesn't stop her from sailing," said Nora as the boat blasted its final warning whistle.

Right. She shoved her guilt aside, snapping into action. "Nora, you get her luggage to a porter. Marie, you come with me, now."

"What are you going to do?" Marie asked, panic rising in her voice.

"I'm going to get you aboard."

"They're getting closer," said Nora, her eyes darting to the men.

Hazel grabbed Marie's wrist, the typewriter jostling against both of them. "This way."

They pushed through the throng, trying to make it to one of the gangways. The crowd was thick, and it was slow going. Hazel glanced over her shoulder. Dennison and his police officers seemed to be gaining on them.

"They're catching us," said Nora, echoing her concerns.

"No. We did not make it all this way only for Marie to be snatched up now. She's getting on that boat, even if we have to tie her to one of the ropes and haul her up there," said Hazel through gritted teeth.

But no matter how she pushed and shouldered their way through the masses of people, the reality was that they were nothing compared to the broad shoulders of the four men barreling down on them. When Marie looked back again, Dennison was just twenty feet away.

"Oh, this is ridiculous," muttered Nora, before whipping around to face Dennison.

"What are you doing?" cried Hazel.

"Dealing with him," said Nora.

"Nora, please. I have to leave now," said Marie as attendants hurried the last stream of passengers onto the gangplank.

But it was too late. Dennison bore down upon them until he was three feet from Nora, who put her hands on her hips and said, "Good morning, Mr. Dennison."

"Out of my way, this is a matter for the Home Office and the police," said Dennison gruffly. "An order has been issued. All category B women are to be arrested, processed, and interned."

"You came all the way up to Liverpool to tell us that?" Hazel asked.

Dennison ignored her and stretched out a hand to Marie. "You're to come with me, Miss Bohn."

Marie pressed back as he tried to advance, but Nora stepped in front of him. "I would stop that if I were you."

"Out of my way, or I'll have you arrested, too," he said.

"On what charges?" Nora challenged.

"Perverting the course of justice. We are carrying out orders issued by the Home Office," said Dennison.

"Timothy Charles Dennison," Nora said, her voice raised. "You're currently having affairs with at least two women in the Aliens Department, despite being married. And who knows how many others there are in the Home Office."

Dennison stopped abruptly. "How do you know that?"

Nora's eyes sparkled, and Hazel could see her friend relishing watching this self-important ass fumble. "It's a wonder that the women you're cavorting with haven't figured you out yet. Does your wife know about them? I'm going to guess no."

Dennison's Adam's apple bobbed as he swallowed. "H-how, how . . . ?"

Nora leaned forward on the balls of her toes. "Secretaries talk. You really should be more careful."

Dennison seemed to relax. "You want to blackmail me. Is that it? And who would believe you?"

"I don't have to blackmail you." Nora grinned. "All it would take is three telephone calls to make your life hell. The first one would be to your wife, who really should know anyway, poor woman. The second and third would be to the two women in your department. Imagine all of the ways they could make your life deeply unpleasant. Oh, and I should ask, do you have a preference which one finds out first? Or perhaps there's another woman you've taken up with recently that I'm missing."

Hazel could see the muscles of Dennison's jaw working over. "They wouldn't believe you," he said.

Nora laughed. "Do you really want to test that theory? And then, of course, there is the undersecretary, who I know would hate for scandal to distract from the important work he's doing in the Aliens Department. It would look very bad indeed if there was an investigation into gross misconduct at a wartime Home Office, especially with so many MPs looking to make an impact, now that Churchill's prime minister."

Dennison swallowed but still pointed at Marie. "She's under investigation."

"For something she didn't do. Don't arrest her for her cousin's sins," said Hazel.

"It's my job," said Dennison.

"That's an excuse you wear like a shield, Mr. Dennison. Marie is no more of a threat to this country than you or I am," she said.

"At the end of this war, do you want to be the sort of man who did his job or the sort of man who showed compassion when it was necessary?" asked Nora.

"Please," said Marie.

The man didn't move.

"The ship is leaving. You can let her walk up that gangway, and you'll never see her again," Hazel said. "No one will notice one woman who wasn't rounded up with the rest."

Dennison's gaze locked on Marie, and Hazel knew. He wasn't going to let Marie go. She could tell from the moment that his eyes narrowed just slightly.

"You'll have to come with me, Miss Bohn," he said.

The moment he said it, Nora gave a strangled cry and fainted dead away, crashing into Dennison and knocking him into an empty luggage cart being pushed by two porters. The metal cage crashed to the dock, knocking the feet out from underneath the police officers—as well as about half a dozen bystanders. Shouts and cries went up as women crowded around Nora. One of the porters jumped at Dennison, who was climbing to his feet, knocking him to the ground again with an angry yell. Hazel and Marie stood frozen, watching in horror, until, through the crowd, Hazel saw a smile twitch Nora's lips.

She whipped around to Marie, pulled her into a hug, and whispered, "Be happy." Then Hazel shoved the hatbox and case into Marie's free hand and pushed her in the direction of the gangway. She watched Marie race up, pausing only for the briefest moment to show her ticket and passport to the man at the entryway to the gangway. He already had the rope in his hand, but at the last moment, he shrugged and let Marie through. Then he pulled the rope over the gate, and as soon as Marie was on deck, the gangway was pulled away.

The ship gave a triumphant whistle, and the giant engines that had been idling roared to life. Slowly but deliberately, the ship began to pull away from the dock.

Hazel search the crowd of people crammed against the railing, waving down to their loved ones on the dock below. Behind her, she heard Nora say, "I'm fine. Just a little dizzy still. My sister is on that ship, you see. I don't know when I'll ever see her again."

Hazel searched and searched, looking from face to face as the massive boat glided away. At last, she saw a head of wheat-blond hair push between the shoulders of two women.

"There she is," she murmured to herself, putting up her hand to wave.

Marie waved back.

"She made it."

She turned to find Nora had joined her. "She did. Last one on the boat. I thought they weren't going to let her on."

"But she made it," said Nora, a grin splitting her face as she waved so hard that Hazel thought her hand might fly off.

"What happened to Dennison?" Hazel asked, looking over her shoulder at the upturned faces.

"He slunk off once he realized that Marie'd gotten away. He's not going to tell his superiors that he let three women outsmart him and three constables when he had an internee within his grasp."

"Do you think he'll be back again?" she asked.

Nora shrugged. "I wouldn't match any agents of foreign governments if I were you."

Hazel snorted and gently nudged her friend. "I'll be sure to take that bit of advice under consideration."

As the ship made for open sea, it became impossible to tell which member of the thinning crowd was Marie.

Hazel dropped her hand to her side. "Everything's changing."

"I should think so. I don't think I'd be able to bear it if it all went on just as it was, only without Marie."

"Things are moving forward with the divorce," she said.

Nora pressed a hand to her forearm. "And I've received my call-up. I'm off to basic training on the first."

"You are?" she asked in surprise. "Where?"

Nora nudged her. "RNS Greenwich. Not so far away. And you know I'll be back whenever I have leave."

But Hazel knew that it might as well have been a world apart. Their lives *were* changing. Marie was off to Canada. Nora was in the Wrens now. And Hazel . . . Well, she was beginning to figure out what she wanted her life to look like when she was the only person she would need to worry about pleasing. Perhaps her mother had been right all along.

"Now." Nora hooked her arm through Hazel's and steered her through the crowd flowing off the docks and toward the train station. "I think it's high time we stop somewhere for a cup of tea. You can tell me all about what you have to do for the divorce, and then make me promise fifteen times that I won't get myself torpedoed at sea."

"I think you're right," she said as they took their first steps together as two.

∾

Marie panted as she pushed in between two women waving handker-chiefs to their loved ones. She dropped her things to the deck and peered down at the crowd. She could already see the shiny black police constables' helmets making their way back toward the main road, but that wasn't what she was looking for.

It took her a moment, but she spotted Nora, towering above all the other women around her, and Hazel in a green coat that suited her shining hair. She waved, a little shy at first, but then, when she saw her friends wave back, with abandon. She didn't know when she would see them again, but both had shaped her in their own ways, making her into the woman she was now.

She would miss them deeply, as though she'd left a part of herself in England. But she was determined to live the life they wanted for her, full and happy. It was the least she could do to show gratitude for their sacrifices. Nora had given up an ambition she'd long harbored to stand by her. Hazel had put herself at risk of arrest to ensure her safety.

So she would live for them. But mostly, Marie would live for herself, sailing fearlessly into the future.

SAMANTHA

Now

thirty

The day of Grandma Marie's memorial could not have been more beautiful, without a cloud in the vast sky that stretched over Lake Ontario. A gentle breeze picked up Samantha's light blond hair, dancing around her face until she pushed it behind her ears. All around her, friends and family gathered, each with a unique memory of the woman who had touched lives for more than one hundred years.

"How are you, sweet pea?" Samantha's mother asked, coming to stand next to her. Her father tucked himself into her other side, his hand a solid comfort on her shoulder.

"I'm glad we're doing this," she said.

"It's what Mum wanted," said her mother. "A beautiful day and not a stitch of black in sight."

She grinned, passing a hand over her cotton sundress covered in an abstract red and white pattern. "I can't believe Mr. Wener has a lemon-yellow suit."

"And a straw boater to match," said her mother. "Mum would have loved this."

"She would've," said her father.

"Does Evan have the speakers and the song cued up?" Samantha asked, glancing around for her cousin, who she found laughing as he corralled his twin three-year-old boys while his wife tried to take their photo at the edge of the water.

"He'll be ready as soon as Jessie gets her photo," said her father. "Are you?"

"I am," she said.

Her parents nodded and walked off to gather the crowd. She tilted her head up to the sky a moment, enjoying the July sun. Her parents were right. It was all exactly what her grandmother would have wanted. Open, free, joyful.

Her only regret was that Nora, the person who'd known Grandma Marie the best all those years ago, couldn't be there. Samantha had sent one of the programs her parents had had printed, and she'd received a long email back from Nora five days later telling her she was touched and virtually demanding that Samantha come back for another visit.

Don't spend too long thinking about another trip either. I'll remind you that I am 103 years old.

Samantha had laughed so hard at the imperious, yet matter-of-fact point that she'd nearly cried.

Now she closed her eyes and took a deep breath. It was time.

Her phone dinged as she dug her notes out of her handbag—bright blue leather to stand out against her bold dress. Marisol had texted:

Good luck!!! U will do her proud!

As she silenced her phone, she froze. Standing on the edge of the crowd of well-wishers was a tall man in a navy jacket, white shirt with the collar undone, and the most unmissable bright pink trousers.

"David," she murmured.

He lifted his hand, and since she couldn't think of anything else to do, she did the same.

But her father stepped into her view. "Are you ready, Samantha?"

Shaking her head to rattle her focus back into place, she glanced down at her notes and stepped in front of the people forming a semicircle around her family.

"Thank you all for joining us to celebrate the life of my grandma Marie," she started. "When she passed away last year at the impressive age of 103, it felt like the kind of loss that you'll never recover from. But then we read her will. I think I can safely say that it came as a surprise to all of us that she'd named me her executor. I mean, there's my mother, the businesswoman who always knows what to do—even if I still can't convince her that texting is the way forward. Or Aunt Matilda, who has had an incredible career as an attorney in Toronto." She smiled at her aunt, who'd left her usual uniform of black boatneck shift dresses behind in favor of lime green. "Or my uncle Charles, who is always there with a smile and a quick joke no matter whether you're family, a friend, or one of the many students who passed through his classroom. But instead she asked me.

"I'll be the first to admit that I was confused. Grandma and I had been close when I was a girl, but like many of us, I'd left home for college and wasn't around as much." She swallowed. "I didn't realize how little I was seeing of her until I'd lost her, and I don't think I'll ever not regret that.

"But Grandma Marie was clever. She found a way to bring us closer even after she passed away. But first she had a couple of things she wanted all of us to do as we remember her. One was that she didn't want a funeral. Instead, she wanted to be cremated and her ashes to be spread on this lake, in this town, that brought her and her beloved husband, my grandfather, together against many odds. And, even more fitting, she wanted you all to wear your best, most colorful outfits. That's why we all look like a flock of parrots right now," she said as friends and family chuckled.

"The other thing my grandmother did was leave me a task. She sent me to London, where she'd lived as a young woman, to return something that had once belonged to a friend of hers. That's where I met Nora, one of her closest friends and just as sharp as Grandma Marie was even at 103. Nora knew things about my grandmother no one else did. She told me wonderful stories about a woman I thought I'd known so well, and she made me realize that we like to keep people in this little box of the time in which we met them. I only knew Grandma as an old woman who drank coffee so strong it could strip paint off the walls and watched at least one Astaire and Rogers movie a week. She always had a moment for me, whether I was bored or scared or just a little lonely. Maybe some of you knew her to be that woman, too—quiet, strong, and generous. But I've learned since her death that my grandmother was so many other things as well.

"Born in Germany and educated in England, she made her home in London with an aunt and uncle who loved her. Her aunt Matilda and uncle Albrecht were the parents she needed when her own parents couldn't or wouldn't give her the sort of love that we all want as children. But equally important were what we would call her 'found family.' Nora Walcott and Hazel Carey were her best friends, confidants, stylists, and teachers. They had a standing date, a dinner at a ladies' club in London every last Friday of the month, for years until the war came and changed everything."

She looked up from her notes at the crowd of people watching her and folded her hands. Thanks to Nora and David, she had the words she'd been looking for. "During the war, my grandmother's friends showed who they really were. She was German, and the British had interned Germans during the First World War. They would do it again, taking away the freedom of thousands of German- and Austrian-born people by locking them up in internment camps. Some of these people were Nazi sympathizers, but most were not. They were innocent, in the wrong place with the wrong nationality at the wrong time. Or their neighbors or business rivals had falsely informed on them.

"But Nora and Hazel weren't going to let that happen to their friend. They did everything they could to keep her in the country and free, and when it became clear that was not going to be possible any longer, they bought her forged papers, smuggled her into hiding, and outran a Home Office agent and three police officers to get her onto a ship bound for Canada.

"My grandmother built herself a new life here. Trenton is where she married my grandfather, had her children, and made a whole new group of friends. And although she left behind a hole in our lives that will never be filled, I find comfort knowing that she's always been loved fiercely by people who are willing to do extraordinary things for their friends.

"Now we're going to scatter her ashes, and it seemed only fitting that we have some music, so we thought we would play one of Grandma's favorites." She nodded to Evan, and "Cheek to Cheek" began to play from the speakers.

Samantha's father, aunt, and uncle stepped forward and carefully unclasped the urn containing her grandmother's ashes at the water's edge. As they released the dust into the wind, she couldn't help smiling. At last, Marie was at peace.

After the scattering, it took about ten minutes for people to file by and pay their respects. She tried to steal a look around for David, but it was impossible with all of the hugs and kind words about her eulogy. She finally gave up, hoping that he would follow the cars leaving the parking lot.

When most of the well-wishers had shuffled by, her uncle Charles clapped his hands together like the grade school teacher he was. "Everyone, we're going to be adjourning to my house for a champagne toast, plenty of music, and a good party with good company, just like Mum would've loved. The address is on the program, or you can just follow me."

Samantha turned to her parents. "I'll follow you guys in a few minutes."

Her mother nodded as her father kissed her on her forehead, and Samantha headed down to the water's edge. She slipped her shoes off and stood with her toes in the grass.

"You figured out your eulogy."

She couldn't stop her smile as she turned and found David just a few feet away. "I did. I had a little help, though."

"We all need a hand from time to time," he said.

"I see you got the memo about the dress code," she said, nodding at his pink trousers.

"Would you believe me if I said I bought them especially for this?"

She laughed. "You don't seem like the pink trouser type. I had no idea you were coming."

"Well, I've been given the responsibility of hand delivering this," he said, pulling a little silk pouch out of his pocket.

She took it from him, undoing the drawstring. When she tipped it into her palm, her grandmother's lapis lazuli necklace tumbled out.

"Gran felt you should have it after all. She said she was happy your grandmother wanted you to return it, because it brought you into her life, but the necklace belongs to you now," he said.

She closed her fingers around the cool pendant, almost unable to speak for the emotion welling up in her throat. "I don't know what to say."

"Would you like me to help you put it on?" he asked.

She nodded. His fingers brushed against her palm, sending a shiver through her. She turned, pulling her hair up. Gently, David threaded the necklace around her neck.

"There," he said, touching the clasp with a single finger.

Samantha dropped her hair and faced him. She drew in a deep breath and asked, "David, did you come just to give me this necklace?"

He rubbed the back of his neck and squinted at her, looking unsure. Finally, he said, "I wanted to pay my respects to your grandmother as well, but those aren't the only reasons I'm here. I understand if this isn't an appropriate time, but I wanted to know if you'd have dinner with me on Wednesday. As a date. A proper date."

Her heart sank. "Oh, David, I want to more than anything, but I go back to Chicago tomorrow morning." She knew it wouldn't work—it couldn't—but she wanted so much to see if it *could*. Even dinner on Wednesday would've been part of an answer, but now she'd never get it.

"I see," he said. "But if you were staying . . . ?"

She stepped forward and hesitantly reached out to touch his wrist, offering what little she could despite knowing it was inadequate. "Our timing is terrible, isn't it?"

But instead of pulling away, he flipped his hand so his fingers slid down hers and laced together. "Oh, it isn't that bad. Not when I made the reservation in Chicago."

She startled to look in his eyes. "Chicago?"

"I've been put on a long-term project, working on overhauling digital marketing for a retail chain headquartered in Chicago." He grinned. "It's a big job. At least six months, and I'll probably need an extension. Or two."

"You're moving to Chicago?" she whispered, barely daring to hope.

"As soon as my visa is sorted out. I have meetings with the client and I'm looking for a flat this week, but I wanted to be sure I was here for your grandmother's remembrance ceremony."

"David . . ."

"Yes?"

She went up on tiptoe and kissed him. It was light, just a brush, but then his hand caught the small of her back. He pulled her to him and they sank into the kiss, lingering in the sunlight as the water lapped just a few feet from them.

When finally she pulled back, she murmured, "I think I can squeeze in dinner on Wednesday night, but first you might have to meet my family. They're expecting me."

He laughed. "Do I call your parents Mr. and Mrs. Morris?"

"Yes for Dad, but he'll immediately insist that you call him Henry because he wants to seem very hip. My mother is still a Calloway, thank you very much, and she'll probably get your entire life story from you in five minutes flat."

"I can't wait to meet them." He grabbed her hand. "Let's go together, then, shall we?"

epilogue

JUNE 12, 1943
Trenton, Ontario

M arie's back always ached by the time she made her way to Mrs. Franklin's boardinghouse, but it was a good sort of ache. A useful one. She'd arrived in Ontario frightened and unsure but determined. She'd been given another chance and her freedom, and she wasn't going to squander those gifts.

She'd found herself a place to live and signed on to work at the local munitions factory in Trenton, doing the dangerous work of handling the explosives that would be loaded onto airplanes and flown to the front. Motivated by the hope that she was contributing to the war effort back at home, she'd learned quickly, absorbing everything on the first go. Last October, she'd been promoted to manager of her own line. It was hard work, but the women she worked with were determined and so was she.

She pushed through the front door of the boardinghouse and hung her coat on the peg that Mrs. Franklin had assigned to her the day she'd arrived. On the sideboard, in her little mail slot made from a spare toast rack, stood a letter addressed to her in Hazel's looping hand. From behind the parlor door came a burst of laughter, but instead of going to join in the joke as she normally would, she plucked up the letter. Tonight she wanted news from home.

She was halfway down the hall when her roommate, Josie, stuck her head out of the parlor. "Elsie and Donna are talking about a game of charades. Will you come play?" When Marie held up the letter, Josie nodded. "Never mind. Come find us later if you want to join in."

"You're sure you won't mind?" she asked, feeling a little guilty turning down her friends who had so swiftly adopted her into their little group.

Josie shook her head. "We'll make Constance play with us."

Marie chuckled. "Good luck with convincing her. I think you frightened her too badly the last time. What was the clue again?"

"The Song of Solomon. And I still say she shouldn't have taken offense. It's from the Bible," said Josie with a wicked grin.

"And yet she nearly ran screaming from the room."

"Well, if you decide you're looking for company, we'll be down here," said Josie.

"Thank you."

Marie retreated up the stairs to her and Josie's room. It was not by any means glamorous. It was only a little larger than her bedroom in her aunt and uncle's house—just enough space for a pair of beds and armoires pushed against opposite walls. Under the window was a little writing desk upon which stood the typewriter Richard had given her. Josie kept a footlocker at the bottom of her bed with a stack of books jumbled on top of it. It was simple, but she and Josie had everything they needed.

Marie sat down on her bed, tore open the letter, and began to read as she untied the cotton handkerchief she used to keep her hair away from the machinery.

Dearest Marie,

I've been sitting here, wondering how to tell you all of the news I've had. I suppose I should start with the most important. In a few short weeks, your uncle should be back at home. The government has been releasing those detained under Regulation 18B in larger and larger numbers now that the worries of invasion are virtually gone. The last I saw Mrs. Müller, she seemed almost like a young bride, unable to contain her impatience as she waits for her husband to return so they'll be together again.

Henrik, of course, will remain jailed. Even your aunt recognizes that there can be no hope for his release when he was caught so openly conspiring against Britain. Nora's friend Joseph still writes to her with updates from the Home Office about the group Henrik associated himself with. Two are still at large, but the rest of them are incarcerated.

If you haven't had a letter from Nora in some time, don't fret. She wrote to me to say that her unit with the WRNS had been reassigned, and she couldn't yet say where she was being deployed. However, I know that as soon as she can make it back to London, she will. She sleeps at home when she's on leave, but she spends almost as much time with your aunt as I do. Mrs. Müller is teaching Nora how to play bridge, although she tells me that Nora forgets most of the lessons because of the long gaps between her visits.

I truly didn't know what to expect when conscription for women was implemented and I found myself an army nurse. However, each day I find the work more and more fulfilling. I am, I've found, tougher than I thought I could be, and I long ago stopped flinching at the things that have become part of my every day.

I know you must be—

A knock sounded at the door. She glanced up. "Who is it?"

"Marie, can you come out here?" Josie's voice was muffled by the oak door.

She sighed. "Josie, I'll come down in a minute."

"Just open the door, Marie," her roommate called.

With a groan, she got to her feet, the letter drifting to her bed as she crossed the room. She reached for the handle, twisted, and pulled the door open, ready to chide Josie for being nosy, when her jaw dropped.

"Richard?"

"Hello, Marie," Richard said, smiling shyly, his uniform cap crushed between his hands.

Josie bounced on her toes, looking more than a little pleased with herself. "Aren't you glad you opened the door? He just showed up on the porch, ringing the bell like any other man."

"What are you doing here?" she asked, ignoring her roommate.

"You look as lovely as the last time I saw you," he said.

There was a clatter on the stairs, and Mrs. Franklin rounded the corner huffing and puffing. "Miss Bohn, you know that I don't allow gentlemen to visit my young ladies—especially not above stairs."

"Mrs. Franklin, this isn't just any gentleman," said Josie.

"He's my Richard," Marie breathed. Because that was what he'd become over all of their months apart.

Mrs. Franklin peered at Richard with open curiosity. "This is him?"

Marie nodded.

"Well, in that case, I think an exception can be made," said Mrs. Franklin, the censure gone from her voice. "But keep the door open."

"Thank you, Mrs. Franklin," said Marie.

The landlady took Josie by the wrist and practically dragged her back down the hall, leaving Marie and Richard alone.

"Would you like to come in?" she asked, her whole body shaking as she gestured behind her.

"I would," he said.

She walked slowly into the room, acutely aware of the 738 days that had passed. So many things had changed, and yet here he was. In her room in Canada. It didn't make sense.

"Would you—?"

But before she could fully turn, he'd crossed the space between them and kissed her.

318

Marie melted into Richard's arms. It was a dream. That must be it. The feeling of his lips against hers was the best sort of shock. The weight of his hands around her shoulders and then her waist, his fingers tightening in the fabric of her blouse. They'd almost kissed before—she'd wanted him to kiss her—but that had been back in London, when they thought they had more time. Now she knew that his kiss was full of longing and need and—somehow—it felt like home.

When finally he inched back, he breathed a sigh of contentment, his eyes closed. "I've been thinking of nothing but that since I found out that my transfer was accepted."

She leaned back from him. "Your transfer?"

He nodded. "I put in for RCAF Trenton to work training airplane engineers as part of the British Commonwealth Air Training Plan. I didn't tell you because I didn't want to say until I was here. The Royal Air Force can change its mind sometimes, and I didn't want you to be disappointed if they did." He hesitated. "Was I presumptuous to have put in that request without consulting you first? Is there—" He cleared his throat. "Is there someone else?"

It took her a moment to realize he was asking about another man. It was all she could do not to burst out laughing. How could there be anyone else when the only man she wanted was standing right here?

"There's no one else, Richard."

"When I saw the shock on your face . . ."

"Because I can't believe you're here. A part of me thought I'd never see you again—even when this bloody war is finished," she said.

He breathed out, resting his forehead against hers so their breath mingled. "I'm sorry."

"For what?" she asked, caressing his cheek, still not entirely convinced he wasn't a manifestation of her imagination.

"I should've said hello rather than grabbing for you the moment you walked through the door. I didn't know—"

"I'm happy you kissed me," she said with a little smile. "Our first kiss."

He grinned and pulled her to him to wrap his arms around her back. "A first kiss after nearly two years of letters."

"I was so nervous when I first wrote to you. I almost didn't put the letter in the post," she admitted.

"I'm glad you did. When you left, I felt sure I'd lost you."

She shook her head. "It was the hardest thing in the world to leave my friends and my aunt and uncle behind. Leaving you only made it hurt more."

"But now I'm here."

"And a very dashing RAF man, too," she said, touching the knot of his tie.

He caught up her hand and kissed the back of it. "The RAF needed engineers. And I knew that if I played my cards right, I might be able to secure a deployment to Canada."

"But you joined up just after I left," she said.

"I know."

She blushed at what lay between his words.

"Now, I have a very important question, and I want you to think carefully about this," he said.

"Yes?"

"Miss Bohn, will you do me the very great honor of joining me for dinner on my first night of leave?" She laughed, and he grinned, adding, "I thought it would be best to carry on where we left off."

She slipped her arms around his neck, tilting her face up to bask in the happiness of having him near. "If you're ready to run the gauntlet that is meeting every single woman in the boardinghouse, then I would love nothing more. Let's go to dinner, Richard."

author's note

When you're raised in Los Angeles, there are certain things you feel you've always known. The best way to conquer the freezing cold Pacific Ocean is to run straight into the waves while screaming bloody murder. The city's famous smog and the smoke from forest fires both hurt to breathe but in different ways. Never take the 405 freeway at rush hour. No one makes a better French dip sandwich than Philippe's on North Alameda.

Growing up, I felt as though I always knew that, during World War II, there had been a Japanese internment camp less than four miles from my house. When President Roosevelt ordered Japanese people interned after the bombing of Pearl Harbor, Santa Anita Park—the horse racing track where Seabiscuit won his last start—was used as an assembly center. As the government scrambled to build camps all across the West Coast and the Southwest, people lived in the horse stables and hastily constructed barracks around the park. Actor George Takei has spoken openly about the humiliation and degradation he felt at being forced to leave his home and move into a stable that still smelled like manure.

But the shame of internment isn't unique to my home state or country. Over the years, I learned that the British government was guilty of the same injustice toward many Germans, Austrians, Italians, and others living in Britain during World War II. A great number of those who were interned were Jewish refugees fleeing the atrocities of Hitler's Germany.

Internment in World War II Britain had its roots in World War I, when the government required all foreign nationals to register at their local police stations under the Aliens Restriction Act. Initially, only a small number of these "enemy aliens" were deemed a threat to national security and interned. However, after the sinking of the RMS *Lusitania* in May 1915, the government succumbed to anti-German pressure and ordered mass internment despite the fact that the vast majority of these people posed no threat to the British people. Many were sent away from their families and lost their homes and livelihoods.

When war broke out again in 1939, many in the government were eager to learn from the mistakes made in World War I. It had been expensive in cost, materials, and men to house, feed, and guard so many innocent people. However, mass internment had a passionate number of early backers, including future prime minister Winston Churchill.

Just as Marie and the Müllers worry and wait through the tribunal hearing process to find out their classification and their fate, so did many other families. As during World War I, only a small number of people given category A classifications were interned to begin with. The first months of the war were relatively quiet with few skirmishes, so much so that the period would come to be called the "Phoney War." But in the spring of 1940, German troops began to march across Europe in the blitzkrieg and countries fell in quick succession. As they neared France, the threat of invasion gripped Britain. Calls for internment increased, and the government began to carry out waves of internment. On May 16, 1940, all category B men were taken away. Category B women were arrested eleven days later. When Italy joined the war and allied with Germany that June, many Italians were interned as well.

With so many people in custody, the British government decided to begin deporting them. More than 7,500 people were sent to Canada and

Australia on ships at the end of June and early July 1940. On July 2, 1940, the SS *Arandora Star* was torpedoed by a U-boat on its way to Canada. About half of the nearly 1,200 German and Italian internees and 374 British offices, soldiers, and crew on board lost their lives.

The sinking of the *Arandora Star* began to turn public sympathy in the internees' favor, and the government started to release people that August. By 1942, fewer than 5,000 people remained interned. Their numbers included Nazi sympathizers, suspected spies, and some prominent members of the British Union of Fascists, many of whom were held on the Isle of Man.

At the beginning of 2019, I finished writing a draft of *The Whispers of War*, put my research aside, and boarded a train to Edinburgh to attend my sister's wedding. Over welcome drinks, I mentioned what I was working on to my cousin Derek. He asked me if I knew that my great-grandmother Grace had taught children English in a Japanese internment camp back in the States. Needless to say, I was stunned to find an unknown familial connection to the very subject I'd just spent months writing about.

After the hubbub of my sister's wedding and book deadlines settled, I began to ask my family for more details about Grace. Through Facebook Messenger, my father's cousin Elizabeth confirmed that yes, Grace had taught at a Japanese internment camp in Poston, Arizona. While we don't know much about her time there, we do know that conditions at the camp were so deplorable that she wrote to Washington, trying to get better treatment for the people who had been sent there against their will.

We are lucky enough to also have a few artifacts of Grace's life from this time. There is a photograph of her with the children in one of her classes, and Elizabeth still has the beautiful hand-carved and painted bird pins Grace was given as a gift by some of the internees.

Writing this book when I did made it impossible not to draw connections between internment in Britain and the US during World War II and the ongoing detention of asylum seekers at the US border today. Innocent people are being held, including children cruelly separated from their families. As a student of history and now an author of historical fiction, I believe it's undeniable that history is cyclical. If we don't acknowledge, examine, and learn from the injustices of the past, we will find ourselves facing them again. Fiction has the unique ability to force us to question what we believe to be true about our own age. My hope is that *The Whispers of War* can contribute in some small way to a greater empathy for those now suffering and move us a little closer to change.

acknowledgments

O ne of the great joys in my life is the many wonderful women I've been lucky enough to call my friends. I especially owe thanks many times over to Alexandra Haughton, Alexis Anne, Lindsay Emory, Laura von Holt, and Mary Chris Escobar, who are each extraordinary writers and women.

To the women of the University Women's Club—the model for the Harlan Women's Club—thank you for welcoming me with open arms as I found my footing in London.

Emily Sylvan Kim, you are with me every step of the way through the good news and the bad. I can't express how much I appreciate everything you do.

Thank you to the two editors who worked tirelessly on this book: Marla Daniels, who shepherded it into the world, and Kate Dresser, who helped me make it even better. And thank you to the wonderful team of people at Gallery Books, including Jen Bergstrom, Aimée Bell, Jen Long, Caroline Pallotta, Christine Masters, Michelle Marchese, Yvonne Taylor, Abby Zidle, Tara Schlesinger, Anabel Jimenez, Lisa Litwack, Meagan Harris, and Molly Gregory.

I owe a great debt to the many historians whose work made it possible to research and write this book. Three sources in particular that were invaluable to me were *"Collar the Lot!": How Britain Interned and Expelled Its Wartime Refugees* by Peter and Leni Gillman, *We Are at War: The Remarkable Diaries of Five Ordinary People in Extraordinary Times* by Simon Garfield, and *Marriages Are Made in Bond Street: True Stories from a 1940s Marriage Bureau* by Penrose Halson. Any errors of fact, intentional or otherwise, are solely my own.

Justine, Mark, Mum, and Dad, I am continually amazed at your enthusiasm for the crazy book ideas rattling around in my head. You more than anyone see what actually goes into writing a book like this, and you love me anyway—a fact that baffles me on a regular basis.

And finally, thank you to all of the readers, bloggers, and bookstagrammers who have welcomed my books onto their shelves. You make all of the hard work worth it.